Peter has been involved with ... fetish scene since the early days, which has provided plenty of background knowledge and inspiration for his work.

A Sweetmeats Book

First published by Sweetmeats Press 2015

2 4 6 8 10 9 7 5 3 1

ISBN 978-1-909181-27-4

Typeset by Sweetmeats Press
Printed and bound in the UK

Sweetmeats Press
27 Old Gloucester Street, London, WC1N 3XX, England, U. K.
www.sweetmeatspress.com

MAID SERVICE

◆◆◆◆

PETER BIRCH

ILLUSTRATED BY GIORGIO VERONA

SWEETMEATS PRESS

PART ONE

◆◆◆◆

Broadfields, Berkshire, England
1968

Chapter One

"Five shillings and I'll let you watch while I give her a good spanking."

Peter Finch was holding Tiffany by the hand as he made the offer and pulled her forward a little, allowing his companions to get a better look at her. Willowy, dark, with her lustrous brown eyes looking out from beneath the fringe of her neatly bobbed hair and her lips painted in the latest Quant pink, she looked better suited to the streets of Chelsea or Knightsbridge than the gloomy old barn, and she had certainly outgrown her school uniform. High, white socks covered her long, coltish legs to above the knee, but still left a great deal of thigh showing beneath the hem of her pleated tartan skirt; while her small, high breasts, braless and impudent, pushed up beneath her blouse.

"Well," she asked after a moment of silence, "who wants to watch me get spanked?"

None of the six young men replied immediately, but glanced among themselves and at Peter, as if surprised that Tiffany had dared to speak up at all. Like Peter himself, all six were dressed in the formal uniform demanded by Broadfields College for senior boys: gowns, frock coats, hats and gloves. The breast pocket of each coat was neatly embroidered with the college arms and a blue chevron to indicate membership of Grove House, one of eight that made up the college. All but one of the boys sat on bales of hay pulled down from the stack that occupied half the barn. Daniel Stewart stood, a little in front of the others, in a pose of casual, languid elegance, his arms folded across his chest, one knee slightly extended, his handsome face amused but also calculating. Only when he'd gauged the reaction of his friends did he speak up.

"Five shillings ... We can probably manage that, but you

have to take her knickers down."

Peter gave a casual shrug.

"Ten shillings, if you want her knickers down."

"Hey!" Tiffany protested. "You said a spanking. You never said anything about having to go bare bottom!"

"I didn't say I'd leave them up," Peter pointed out. "You're a girl, and when girls are spanked their knickers are pulled down, everybody knows that."

Tiffany had put on a sulky face but said nothing, apparently accepting the logic of his argument. Gabriel Howard, a dark, handsome boy with a thoughtful manner, raised a hand then spoke.

"Hang on, Finch, if girls always get their knickers pulled down when they're spanked, then it ought to be five shillings, shouldn't it?"

"Why?" Peter demanded.

"Because," Gabriel insisted, "you said you'd let us watch you spank her for five shillings, and if girls always have their knickers pulled down when they're spanked, then that means you were going to pull her knickers down anyway, so …"

"It's ten shillings," Tiffany interrupted, now pink faced with embarrassment. "If you want me bare bottom it's ten shillings, and that's that."

"You heard what the lady said," Peter agreed. "Take it or leave it."

Hunter Rackman, a lanky redhead with a strong American accent, blew out his breath in a wistful sigh before speaking.

"Back home in Arkansas we give 'em the paddle, and it's always bare bottom. Bent over so they're touching their tennis shoes, panties pulled down so their little bare tushies are all on parade, then smack, smack, smack! I say she gets the paddle."

"We don't have a paddle, Rackman," Daniel pointed out. "Well, boys, what's it to be? Ten shillings to watch Tiffs get a knickers down spanking?"

The stocky, blond Ben Thompson nodded immediately, his eyes bright with excitement and fixed on the bare, pale flesh of Tiffany's thighs where they disappeared under her school skirt. Clive Sumner, small and round, gave a more cautious approval but Gabriel Howard spoke up again.

"Seven and six? I've only got one and eight pence ha'penny."

"For God's sake show some dignity, will you?" a voice spoke from the back, Stephen Richards. "It's only ten shillings. Here we are, Finch, you dirty bastard."

"Good man, Richards," Daniel said, taking the ten shilling note being offered by his friend and passing it on to Peter. "Here we are, Finch, to watch you spank her, knickers down and no cheating. I want to see everything."

There was an immediate chorus of agreement from around him, while Tiffany's blushes had grown hotter still and her gaze had moved down to the toes of her smart black school shoes. Stephen had stood up as he took the money from his pocket and came to join Daniel. Both stood taller than Peter Finch, both carried an easy, aristocratic self-assurance, but neither could quite match his complete confidence as he turned to Tiffany.

"Are you sure you want to be spanked, Tiffs? This is your last chance to back out."

She responded with a barely perceptible nod, still looking at her shoes, and Peter turned back to the others.

"Very well, gentlemen, we have an agreement. Come along, Tiffs, spanking time."

Tiffany glanced up from beneath her fringe, her expression still sulky but also excited. Her mouth was slightly open and her full lower lip trembling for the prospect of what was about to happen to her. But she held her ground, allowing Peter Finch to take her hand and lead her across the barn to where a solitary bale of hay sat in a patch of bright sunlight.

Tiffany made to bend over, but Peter sat down, making himself comfortable on the bale. He removed his hat and gloves before patting his lap as he spoke.

"I'll deal with you the old fashioned way, over my knee. Come on."

She was pouting slightly as he pulled her down across his legs, and cast a nervous glance towards the young men watching, but gave no resistance as her school skirt was turned up to expose full cut, white knickers so taut over her sweetly turned little bottom that they seemed to have been painted onto her flesh. Gabriel was already squeezing his cock through his trousers, while Ben gave a low sigh before speaking out.

"Oh yes, so pretty. Pull 'em down, Finch, pull 'em down! You said you would!"

"All in good time," Richards answered, as Peter began to stroke Tiffany's bottom through the seat of her panties. "A good spanking should never be rushed, especially with a pretty lady on the receiving end. You have a lovely bottom, Tiffany."

She didn't answer, but her breathing had grown short and deep, while the expression on her face was flickering between ever greater consternation and involuntary pleasure as he explored her bottom. He was making a thorough job of it too, stroking and squeezing her flesh, occasionally allowing his fingers to slip down to the gentle furrow where her panties were pulled taut between her cheeks and even the soft plump bulge where the thick white cotton cupped her sex. She'd begun to sob and shake as he teased her slit, but she kept her bottom up and her feet braced apart in fine spanking position, while a damp patch had begun to show over the mouth of her vagina. When Ben spoke again his voice was filled with awe.

"She's wet. That means she likes it!"

Tiffany turned her head, her voice a sob as she spoke.

"No. It just means I can't help it. Now if you want to watch, be quiet."

"Of course she likes it," Gabriel put in, ignoring her instruction. "All girls like to be spanked. That's why they don't get it, not so often."

"Yes they do," Ben said, licking his lips as Peter adjusted Tiffany's knickers to leave a generous slice of teenage bottom cheek curving out from each leg hole.

"Yes they do what?" Gabriel demanded. "Like to be spanked or get it a lot?"

"Both," Ben replied with the air of an expert. "Last Christmas Jenny and Hannah both got it twice, bare bottom, and they were wet, just like Tiffs."

"They get it plenty in Arkansas," Hunter put in. "Hell, I've seen six cheerleaders in a row, skirts up and panties down for a paddling, six of the finest pieces of arse you ever did see, but no finer than Miss Tiffany here."

"She is pretty," Clive added, his voice weak with need.

"The best, but better bare. Go on, Peter, pull down her knickers."

"Yes, I want to see her bare. Pull them down."

"I want to see her fanny"

"I want to see her bottom hole."

"Go easy on her, boys," Daniel advised. "It's heavy enough for her being spanked in front of you lot, without a running commentary. Come on, Peter, get her knickers down and get spanking."

"Never rush a craftsman," Peter answered, but he'd taken hold of the waistband of Tiffany's panties.

The plain white knickers were already pulled up so tight that most of her bottom was spilling out at the sides, with the swell of her pussy displayed to perfection. Only the very rudest details of her slit were hidden from view, and those not for long as the tight white cotton was peeled slowly down over her cheeks. Her breathing had grown deeper and faster still as she was exposed, and her lips broke apart in a gasp as the tight, dun-coloured star of her anus came into view. That gasp was followed by another as her panties were given a final, sudden jerk to tug them out from between her thighs and the full glory of her rear view was revealed.

Not one of the young men spoke, Peter included, all six with their eyes riveted to Tiffany's beautifully formed young bottom and moist, nubile cunt. Clive was gawping like a goldfish, Gabriel nursing a very obvious erection within his trousers, while Ben looked as if he was about to begin to drool. Stephen was standing with his feet braced apart as if ready for sudden, physical action and there was a feral gleam in Hunter's eyes. Even Daniel was struggling to maintain his poise, and for all Peter's attempt at nonchalance as he adjusted Tiffany's legs to pull her panties taut between her knees, his lust showed in his eyes.

"Ripe and ready," he remarked, and he began to spank.

A sob escaped Tiffany's lips as the first, firm smack was laid across her bottom—more emotion than pain—but the second was hard enough to make her squeak, and the third harder still. Her feet began to kick and her sobs and squeals turned to gasps and cries of shock and pain as Peter spanked her, until she was wriggling so badly that he was forced to put an arm around her waist to hold her in position over his knees. All six of the young men watched in fascination, eyes fixed to her bouncing bottom as she squirmed and bucked, her cheeks spreading as she struggled not to make a thoroughly rude view of her squeezing, winking bottom hole and her invitingly wet cunt. Gabriel soon had his cock out, his mouth agape as he watched the spanking, and when Daniel told him to put it away he merely shook his head. Peter saw, and spoke out as he continued to spank.

"Do you see what you're making them do, Tiffs? They're touching themselves because of your bare, bouncing red bum. How does that feel?"

She twisted around at his words, her eyes wide and her pretty mouth parted in shock and disgust as her eyes focussed on

Gabriel's erect cock. But she made no effort to get up, or to stop her punishment. Peter was grinning as he carried on, now spanking with real strength, smack after smack delivered across her cheeky little bottom until she was writhing in his grip and kicking her legs in her half-lowered panties, gasping and squealing in an exhibition as comically cute as it was shamelessly erotic. Ben had soon begun to chuckle, and Daniel allowed himself a short, curt laugh, but their reaction only made the situation worse, sending Tiffany into a full blown tantrum, the tears streaming down her cheeks, her fists thumping on the rough wooden floor and her thighs pumping in her panties. Still Peter spanked, his handsome face twisted into a happy leer as she bawled out her feelings, yet she never said a word nor made any effort to get off his lap or even to protect her bouncing bottom cheeks from the smacks. The youths watched enthralled and clearly had no intention of intervening, until, suddenly, Gabriel came, cum erupting from his cock to splash down on the dirty wooden floor. At that, the spell broke, and Ben was first to speak out.

"You are *gross*, Howard! Come on, Finch, that's enough. You've made her cry."

"That's how she likes it, nice and hard," Peter and answered, but he'd stopped.

Still Tiffany made no effort to get up. She lay sobbing across Peter's lap, her red bottom lifted high, her thighs spread to stretch her lowered panties taut between her knees, no longer concerned by the immodest display of her rear view. Peter began to rub her cheeks and she gave a low, soft moan, as much in despair for her dishevelled state as in pleasure.

"That's some view," Hunter breathed, and he'd freed a long, rosy cock into his hand.

"Look all you like," Peter responded. "No touching, that's all. I'm the only one who gets to touch, but I'll show you something."

His fingers had stolen between Tiffany's cheeks, loitering

briefly on the puckered little hole of her arse before moving to her cunt, at which she gave another low, impassioned moan. He began to torment her, deliberately spreading her lips to display the wet pink flesh, the tight arc of her hymen clearly visible. None of the young men watching seemed to realise the implications of what he was doing, but she knew, gasping and sobbing once more as he made an exhibition of her virgin hole. Nevertheless, she'd soon begun to push up her bottom in unmistakable excitement. Stephen blew out his breath.

"You know how to handle them, I'll give you that."

"Practise," Peter said casually. "Now watch this."

He'd begun to masturbate Tiffany as he spoke, with his thumb pushed to the mouth of her cunt and a finger rubbing in her slit. She'd surrendered herself completely, every last scrap of modesty and of dignity abandoned as she wriggled against his hand. Peter began to spank her again, with sharp, left handed slaps applied in turn to each cheek as he rubbed at her sex, her cries growing ever sharper and more urgent. The muscles of her buttocks and thighs began to squeeze and she'd pushed her hips up higher still, showing herself off like a cat in heat, with her wet cunt flaunted as Peter worked her clitoris. She gave a last, anguished sob and then screamed, a sound as rich in pain as in ecstasy as her muscles locked tighter still and a sudden spurt of fluid erupted over the floor and down Peter's leg.

"Wow!" Gabriel breathed. "I didn't know girls could do that!"

"Of course they can," Peter assured him, "and that, my friends, is the secret every young man needs to know. Girls like it too."

"Sure thing," Hunter grunted and he'd stepped forward, jerking hard at his cock to send a long stream of spunk over Tiffany's hot red bottom, soiling her skirt and panties as well as her skin. "And that's how we finish 'em off where I come from. Spank 'em and spunk 'em, that's the way it's done."

The following day Peter and Tiffany met in a favourite, private place, an old railway cutting in the woods between Broadfields and St. Monica's convent, where Tiffany attended the senior school. They kissed before Peter spoke up as he passed her two half-crown pieces and a shilling.

"The extra is from Hunter Rackman," he explained. "He felt you'd earned it."

"He's a dirty pig!" Tiffany stated with feeling. "He did it all over my bottom!"

"A dirty pig," Peter agreed. "But a rich dirty pig. His father's an air force colonel at Alder Heath."

"I don't care how rich he is, he still shouldn't have done it over my bottom."

"I care, and so should you. Money always comes in handy. Anyway, if you want to be spanked in front of an audience, that sort of thing sometimes happens."

"It was … kind of nice," she admitted shyly, "and now I'll be able to buy some cool shades. But I thought there'd be more of you? How many boys are at Broadfields?"

"Hundreds," Peter answered. "But there are only fifteen of us in my year at Grove House and I only invited the ones I could trust. Hunter's a bit of a hill-billy, but he's sound. You wouldn't want people like Algernon Gardiner, believe me."

"What's wrong with him?"

"He's a sneak, worse than a sneak. If he even found out he'd probably try and blackmail me."

"We have girls like that at St. Monica's. Not many."

"Yeah, so you see, Rackman's alright, just a bit wild."

"Everybody else was very polite," she pointed out. "Except Gabriel Howard, and at least he didn't do it all over me.

It went in my underwear, and on my skirt! What if we hadn't noticed and I'd gone back like that? The penguins would have …"

"Given you another dose of the same," Peter interrupted. "Now *that* I'd pay to watch."

"Beast!" Tiffany replied, but there was laughter in her voice and a moment later she'd settled her head on his shoulder.

They stretched out together among the grass and flowers of the old railway embankment and lay in silence for a while, Tiffany playing with the three coins in her hand. Peter had his arm around her and began to fondle one pert breast in an absent-minded way as he let his thoughts wander back to their first meeting.

He'd been intent on a surreptitious visit to St. Monica's, where he liked to watch from the woods as the girls played hockey or rounders in their long white socks and little gym shorts (which were so skimpy as to be more like knickers in their own right). To get there unobserved he followed the cutting, usually without meeting anybody at all, but he was always cautious. He'd noticed the distinctive white and red of a St. Monica's uniform and, without giving himself away, had climbed up among the trees so that he could get close. As he'd moved carefully forward, he'd been hoping the girl would be misbehaving, perhaps using the warm spring sunshine as an excuse to sun herself, maybe even topless, or, joy of joy, nude. He'd read plenty of books and magazines in which girls were always stripping off at the slightest excuse, and he'd enjoyed a few, minor encounters.

The girl had been fully dressed but still enchanting, with her bobbed black hair, her delicate face and her taut, slender figure, while her tie was undone and her blouse open just far enough to hint at the curve of one small, high breast. She'd been sitting on the edge of an old switchgear box, smoking a Sobranie "Black Russian" cigarette, her legs crossed. Her sweet thighs emerged smooth and alluring from beneath her skirt, and her expression was mellow but faintly sulky. Next to her, unopened, lay a copy of Kerouac's *On the Road*. Recognising a fellow rebel, he had abandoned his plans of spying on her and introduced himself instead. The railway cutting had been their private rendezvous ever since.

"What are you thinking about?" she asked suddenly.

"When we first met," he told her. "How you looked so good. I thought you were the most beautiful girl I'd ever seen."

"I was thinking about the barn," she went on, "and how excited they all got when you spanked me, and what ... what you did to me."

Her nipple had grown hard beneath his fingers, but she seemed oblivious, still turning the three coins in her fingers, and when she spoke again her voice was oddly wistful.

"Does this mean I'm a whore?"

Taken aback, Peter found himself stumbling over his answer, eager to reassure her but not sure what he could say.

"No ... no, of course not. How could you be a whore? Whores ..."

"Take money for sex."

"Yes, but ..."

"I took money for sex," she went on as she stretched and sighed.

Peter had been about to launch into a hastily improvised explanation of why what they'd done didn't make her a whore, but stopped at the sudden change in her attitude and tone of voice. He'd always been happy to take advantage of her odd, contrary attitude to sex, from the first time she'd suggested he smack her backside for turning up late to their rendezvous. But the more time he spent with her the less he understood. She seemed to seek out all the things she should have hated the most: being stripped and being spanked, paying dirty forfeits at cards or dice, being tied up and tormented. In her way she did hate them, but she craved them too and it had been her suggestion to invite some of his friends to watch her be punished, and her suggestion that they should charge for the privilege. She often cried when she came.

"Did you like doing that?" he asked cautiously.

Again she stretched, arching her back to push herself against his hand, and her voice was soft and urgent as she spoke again.

"You made me feel so ashamed of myself, telling them all they could watch while you gave me a spanking and made them pay. They know I like it, and that's worse, worse than if you'd tricked me into going to the barn and held me down while you got my bottom bare in front of them, or if you'd spanked me for kicks while they hid and watched. You let them see how much I like it, and you rubbed me off in front of them and you let that horrible pig Hunter do his business all over my bare backside."

She gave a little purr as she finished and her hand had gone to his zip, easing it down to burrow within and pull out his cock. Peter lay back, his eyes closed in bliss as she began to masturbate him, stroking and tugging at his rapidly stiffening penis and speaking in a low, warm voice completely at odds with what she was saying.

"You're such a beast, such a horrible, horrible pig, spanking my bottom like that, with my knickers pulled down in front of all your awful friends and making them pay to watch, making me a whore. Do you know how I felt when you pulled my knickers down, Peter? Do you know how I felt when you held my fanny open to show them all I've never been with anyone, that I'm a virgin? You do, don't you, you beast … you horrible pig!"

Her voice sounded broken and he realised she'd begun to cry, but she was tugging on his now stiff cock with ever greater urgency, bringing such ecstatic feelings that he had to bite hard down on his lip in order to stop himself cumming in her hand. She moved, suddenly, twisting over and around to get herself into a kneeling position, now with her bottom pushed up under her little red tartan skirt as she continued.

"That's what you like, isn't it? Go on, turn up my skirt and pull down my knickers, you dirty pig. Have a good look. Have a good look at my bare bottom and all the dirty details you like to see. Touch if you want. Spank me if you want. Punish me. Spank me."

Peter didn't need telling twice. He quickly flipped her skirt up onto her back and tugged her panties down to expose her fleshy little bottom to the air. He caught the scent of her sex immediately and saw how wet she was, her hand still pulling at his straining cock.

She'd turned to look at him as he exposed her to the air. "Go on," she urged. "Smack it, smack my bottom, Peter. I like it smacked. I need it smacked. I like it in front of your friends, knickers down with their dirty cocks in their hands while they get their thrills over seeing me bare, seeing me spanked …"

She broke off with a sharp cry as his hand smacked down across her bottom. Her knees were once again spread wide, stretching her white school panties taut between her thighs. The pleats of her skirt made a pelmet for her beautiful bottom, the tight taupe star of her arse bared to the air, her cunt wet and open. He closed his eyes, fighting back the temptation to simply grab her by the hips and thrust his erect cock deep into her, bursting her hymen and taking her virginity. One good push and he'd be inside her, a second and he'd have come, filling her with semen and leaving her disgraced, maybe even pregnant.

"Make me come, Tiffany," he gasped. "Make me come, or I'm going to fuck you, I swear."

"Pig … you filthy, pig," she answered, but she moved closer, her mouth wide and Peter cried out in bliss as he realised she was going to take his cock in her mouth.

It was too much, the thought of her pretty face with his erect penis in her mouth and the view of her bare rear end as he spanked her was more than he could possibly resist, and all the while she never stopped her dedicated stroking of his shaft. He came, full in her face, hot spunk splashing across her cheeks and into her open mouth. But even as she cried out in shock and disgust, she took him deeper into her mouth, accepting the second spurt deep into her throat and swallowing it down. She seemed to be both sobbing and laughing as she did it, tears streaming down her face to mingle with the thick, white cum. Still she continued, swallowing again and again until she'd milked his balls of every last drop.

Only then did she come off his cock, to roll over on the grass, her thighs spread wide in her panties, one hand clutching her skirt to her belly, the other busy with her cunt. She was face down, her body lying at an awkwardly steep angle, but she didn't seem to care, masturbating shamelessly with her mouth wide and the spunk trickling out over the side of her lip, only for her to swallow once more and then begin to babble.

"You did it in my face, you filthy pig … in my face …

in my mouth ... you made me swallow it, you made me swallow your dirty squirt, you ... you, and if I hadn't let you you'd have fucked me!"

She broke off with an anguished sob and her back arched tight as she started to come, a long, hard orgasm while she snatched and clawed at her pulsating cunt, her thighs quivering and her skirt rolled high to display herself even more brazenly, her bottom hole squeezing in time with the powerful contractions of her strong, young muscles. Peter watched, delighted and astonished by her utter lack of inhibition and what seemed a bizarre determination to be as dirty as possible while seemingly hating every moment. She'd even slapped her hand to her face at the last instant, smearing herself with a mess of spunk and tears before jamming her fingers into her mouth to suck on them as she rode her orgasm. As she pulled her fingers free, she favoured him with a weak smile before speaking again.

"That was lovely, thank you ... and thank you for not taking advantage."

"That's alright, I understand," he assured her, despite a rising regret for what he'd denied himself. "I know it's important for you, being Catholic ..."

"Oh it's not that," she interrupted. "I wouldn't mind at all, although I do think you ought to make a little more effort to prove your love to me. You know, do some daring deed to prove your worth before you fuck me, like one of King Arthur's knights."

"There are no dragons in Berkshire," Peter pointed out, "and there's no point in sending me off after the Holy Grail. You know I'd only cheat."

"Not like that," she went on, her voice now wistful. "Something daring, like breaking into St. Monica's and ravishing me in my bed. The trouble is, the penguins inspect us at the end of every term and you've no idea of the fuss there'd be if they found I'd been had."

"Inspect you?" Peter asked, intrigued.

"Oh you know," she answered as she rolled over onto her knees, "a medical inspection, to make sure we're pure. Matron does it, and it's ever so embarrassing. We have to go before bed so we're in just our nighties, with no knickers underneath, and we have to take a towel to put under our bottoms when we lie down on the table."

"In front of each other?" Peter asked as he imagined one nubile young girl after another lying back to have her virgin cunt inspected while her friends looked on.

Tiffany had wriggled herself back into her panties, but abruptly changed her mind, slipping them down her legs and off before she carried on talking, her voice quite casual.

"Oh yes. It's like a production line. One of the sisters sits by the door and we have to lift up our nighties to show we haven't any knickers on. If we have, she pulls them down and gives us a smack or two before making us take them off. Then we go on the table and we have to roll our legs back so Matron can hold our fannies open to see we're still intact. Another sister makes a tick in a book."

"And if you're not intact?" Peter asked, his hand now back on his cock as he watched Tiffany mop up the mess on her face with her panties.

"We get spanked," she said blithely, "right there with our legs rolled back to our ears and a sister holding our ankles. It's a really rude position, but the nuns insist on it. All the girls hate it, especially when Matron does the spanking. She's very rough, and she tells us off while she spanks."

"And after the spanking?" Peter asked, shocked and genuinely sympathetic as he imagined the poor girls with their legs held up and their deflowered cunts exposed as they were smacked and lectured for their depravity.

His guilty feelings didn't stop him playing with his cock, so hard and urgent once more, but also slightly sore. Tiffany carried on, the emotion now creeping gradually back into her voice.

"Then your nightie comes off so you're all nude and you get marched up to the Mother Superior's office, right past all the dorms with your red bottom showing, and everybody knows what's happened, of course. Then you get another spanking in the office, much harder, with this big wooden spanking paddle Mother keeps on the wall behind her desk, a bit like the ones your friend Hunter was talking about when the girls get spanked in America, I suppose. You're done over her desk and you have to stay still or you get extra. When she's finished and you're crying your heart out and feeling so, so sorry for yourself, then you get the cane, six hard strokes on your bare bottom, and if you can't take it they hold you down, and then ... then Mother sticks the fat handle of the paddle into your fanny to remind you of what you've done while you get another six, and you're made to confess and tell everything, who the boy was and how he did you, and ..."

She trailed off, breathless and flushed, seemingly frightened and more than a little upset, but with one corner of her mouth twitching ever so slightly. Peter had been tugging himself furiously, his head burning with images of naked, humiliated girls with their cunts held open for inspection or their bottoms presented for punishment, but he stopped suddenly.

"Hold on, you're making this up, aren't you? You're just joking!"

Tiffany burst out laughing, tossed her soiled panties onto Peter's face, and ran. He gave chase, his erect cock sticking from up his fly as he pursued her along the cutting, threatening spankings and worse in retribution for her teasing. She ran well, laughing as she went, her skirt fluttering up to give him enticing glimpses of her bare bottom. But Peter ran faster, and he'd soon caught her, throwing her to the ground and straddling her body, face down in the long grass, her laughter breaking to a weak sob as he turned up her skirt at the back. With her bottom bare to the world she went limp, surrendered to whatever indignity he chose to subject her too.

"Right you little minx," he told her, "just for that I'm going to spank you and I'm going to get myself off all over your bottom. How does that feel?"

"Do it then, you big pig," she answered. "Take advantage of me, why don't you, like the dirty little boy you are."

As she spoke she'd pushed up her hips, taunting him with the bare cleft of her arse and the tender spot within. Peter gave her a smack, then another, left handed, while he pulled at his cock with his right.

"I will," he told her, now spanking with firm, well placed swats as he masturbated, "but not because I'm a dirty little boy, but because you're a dirty little girl who deserves to be punished, for teasing boys by making up rude stories!"

"It's true!" Tiffany answered between squeals as the spanking continued. "We do get inspected, just ... ow! Just not like that ... ow! A doctor comes, an awful old woman who makes us ... ow! Who makes us take all our clothes off, every stitch ... ow! And she puts us in stirrups so she can see up our fannies ... ow! Peter, not so hard!"

"You're a little liar," he chided, "and you deserve it hard, very hard. You had me believing you too, you looked so sorry for yourself. Now, be a good girl and shut up so I can concentrate on what you need!"

"Pig!" Tiffany told him, but nothing about her upthrust bottom or rudely displayed private parts suggested that she was in any way ready for him to stop.

Peter continued to spank her, and to replay the scene she'd put into his head as his excitement rose. Her bottom was a delight, exquisitely feminine and rosy pink with spanking, just the thing to focus on while he pulled himself off, but it would be the second time within a matter of minutes and it might take just a little longer. Yet there was no rush, with Tiffany submissive and compliant beneath him. Apparently, being happily used for his kicks, was just what she needed to get herself off.

"You're lovely," he told her. "Just perfect … so perfect."

He was still spanking, harder than ever, and she gave no response beyond her sobs and squeals of pain, every single one of which added a little something to his excitement. Yet in his mind's eye she was no longer being spanked by him, nor in the old railway cutting. She was in the convent, held down over the matron's knee with her bare bottom squirming and pink, crying her eyes out as she was spanked with half-a-dozen other girls looking on. Each would be in the same sorry state, her nightie held up and her knickers off, her naked bottom exposed and the neat little slit of her pussy bare at the front. Their faces would be full of misery and consternation for their exposure and the thought of the spankings they had coming, each and every one facing the same humiliating treatment Tiffany now received. Others would have already been done, and sent to stand against the wall with their hands on their heads and their red, smacked bottoms naked as the tears of shame trickled slowly down their faces. But even they would be watching as Tiffany was spanked.

"I want to see you done," he sighed, now stroking himself with such furious speed that the motion of his hand was making her bottom jiggle. "I want to see you done by that mad old hag of a Matron, spanked on your bare bottom—and not just you, Tiffs, all your friends too, one after another, girlie little butts spanked one after another, all of you, knickers off and spanked bare … spanked so hard …"

His voice broke to a grunt as he started to come, his fingers now clawed into the soft flesh of one hot, round cheek, spreading her cleft as his cum came again, soiling her cheeks and her slit, pooling in the little brown dimple between. Guilt and doubt hit him the instant he was past the first exquisite peak, but that didn't stop him finishing off … or from considering just how much his friends would be prepared to pay in order to witness a scene like the one he'd just imagined.

Peter sat at the desk in his dormitory bedsit, his mathematics prep piled neatly to one side, complete and correct, the sheet of paper in front of him covered in scribbles and neatly formed little boxes linked one to another by arrows. For the previous hour, he had been attempting to work out how he could set up a group scene which his friends could be invited to watch, for a price. So far, he didn't feel he'd had much success.

It was practical, although the risks were high. Having the girls paraded for the inspection of their virginity seemed likely to be too complicated, but a punishment spanking was at least feasible. The stumbling block was costs. With the exception of Hunter Rackman and one or two others, none of his friends could be expected to go above ten shillings unless they had plenty of warning and he laid on something really spectacular. Perhaps a dozen could be relied on to keep their mouths shut afterwards, at least until the end of the year when they'd all be leaving and it would no longer matter. It was hard to see how he could achieve an income of much above five pounds, ten at a pinch, which looked healthy until the overheads were taken into consideration.

Tiffany was game, as always, and she was confident that she could persuade at least four of her friends to accept spankings in a good cause, as long as they were paid enough. Therein lay the problem. The girls at St. Monica's came from wealthy, respectable families and were not going to be persuaded to let their knickers down for a few pennies, let alone have their bottoms smacked when they knew boys were watching. It was also essential to have pretty, shapely girls; and pretty, shapely girls tended to be vain and therefore expensive. Tiffany had jokingly suggested the idea to her friend Charlotte, a petite, bouncy blonde with a rounded bottom and breasts like a pair of fat little peaches. Charlotte had giggled, considered the idea for a moment, then come back with a figure of five pounds. Even if four pretty girls could be talked down to a couple of pounds apiece, that still left little or no margin. They'd also need two girls who could pass as junior nuns to do the spanking, while there were sure to be other costs. At best they would come away with a few shillings each, which scarcely seemed worthwhile, however exciting the idea.

Never one to be easily dissuaded, Peter spent a moment trying to convince himself to go ahead with the idea anyway, but his mind kept coming back to Charlotte and her casual (but prohibitive) quote of five pounds. He'd only seen her on the hockey field, with her gloriously formed bouncy bottom bulging out the seat of her bottle green gym knickers as she played, and the thought of seeing her with those same knickers pulled right down to bare her bottom for a spanking was enough to leave his cock so hard it ached. It was no surprise that she set such a high value on herself, yet Tiffany felt she was likely to be the cheapest of the four willing girls.

Tiffany's best friend, Alice Shelley, could be relied upon to join in. With her pale hair and winsome, delicate figure she was sure to be popular, but she was going to expect her fair share. Christine, smaller still but with a poisonous reputation and a stockbroker father, apparently wouldn't do it unless she got more money than anybody else. Yet her perfect, haughty face made the idea of watching her get spanked too good to resist. Then there was Emerald Feldkirch, an American girl who seemed to be made of sun, ripe wheat and all things wholesome but, according to Tiffany, was always the first out of her clothes if things got naughty.

Among the other girls he knew by sight only one really stood out: Ayanna, an Indian girl rumoured to be a princess and blessed with a slender figure, a perfect little bottom on long, coltish legs and hair that fell to her ankles when loose. She was always a favourite on the hockey field, particularly as her gym knickers tended to ride up terribly, leaving her scrumptious, nut brown bottom almost entirely exposed, the fabric pulling taut against her pussy and leaving little to the imagination. But it was her air of grave, subconscious superiority that really appealed. To see her spanked would be bliss, although Tiffany had been adamant that she was unavailable.

The thought was painfully arousing and Peter shut his eyes, trying to banish the images of the five or more beautiful girls undergoing the humiliating spanking regime he and Tiffany had devised. As a fantasy, it would have been powerful. But to know that it was possible actually hurt, and he gritted his teeth and squeezed his eyes closed even harder as he struggled to persuade himself that it was both too expensive and too risky.

"Bugger!" he swore, pushing his chair back from the desk just as the door opened.

"No talking during prep," Ben Thompson informed him, "and definitely no swearing."

"Dry up, Thompson," Peter responded, although his friend was already smiling and obviously didn't mean it. "Just because you're a prefect doesn't mean you can boss me around."

"Yes it does," Ben answered. "But never mind that. When do we get to watch Tiff's again?"

"Soon," Peter promised.

"How about a striptease this time?" Ben went on eagerly. "Nice and slow, right down to the bare."

"That could be arranged," Peter admitted. His friend's near-desperate tone caused such pride and satisfaction to well up inside him that he'd continued speaking without thinking about what he was saying. "How about some of the other Senior St. Monica's girls too?"

"Other girls?" Ben asked in awe. "Stripping? Hey, you're pulling my leg. Tiffs is your girlfriend, but nobody ..."

"Not stripping," Peter admitted, hastily pulling back in the face of Ben's disbelief. "Getting spanked."

"What's the deal with you and spanking?" Ben asked.

"Nothing," Peter lied. "That's just what's happening. Some of the girls are going to be spanked, as a punishment."

"What, and we can watch?" Ben demanded, more awestruck than ever.

"Maybe, if things work out," Peter went on, telling himself that there was no harm in outlining his idea, and that he could always claim the girls had been pardoned if the group spanking proved impossible to organise.

"How?" Ben queried. "I mean, they're not just going to let us into St. Monica's when some girls are getting it, are they?"

"Of course not, but there's going to be a spanking, six girls, and for the right money I might be able to arrange a viewing."

"How?" Ben repeated.

Peter had no idea and tapped the side of his nose to suggest mysterious influences, but the look of disbelief on Ben's face was close to scorn and Peter found himself making the effort to persuade his friend.

"I know it's going to happen, because Tiffs told me so. She's one of the girls getting it, and her friend Alice, you know, with the long blonde hair, and Charlotte Mayfield, and three others, including the Indian princess. They're going to get it all at once, lined up and waiting. Knickers down, bottoms up, pussies out. Spanked over the knee by the nuns, then lined up again, against the wall with their hands on their heads and all red behind."

Ben's mouth had fallen open, but closed abruptly to become a knowing grin.

"Yeah, right! Good one, Finch, but I'm not buying."

"I'm serious," Peter went on. "They got caught smoking and the nuns are out to make an example of them. The only hard bit is getting to watch. If you don't believe me, ask Tiffs."

Doubt still showed in Ben's face, but he gave a thoughtful nod before he spoke again.

"How would we get in?"

"That's my business," Peter replied, once again tapping the side of his nose, "and that's why it's not going to come cheap."

"How much?"

"Two quid."

"That's more than I get for the whole term!"

"Maybe a quid, for you, but it's worth it. You saw Tiffs get it for fun, but she's game. Imagine Alice, looking all shy and sorry for herself as her knickers are taken down, then over some old bitch of a nun's knee with everything showing, her fanny, even her arsehole. And what about Charlotte? I bet she'll howl. And that stuck up bitch Christine Arlington, and there's an American girl too, a real beauty, and the princess. Think of the fury of a spanked princess, with nothing but air between us and her naked little virgin fanny ..."

"Alright, alright, a quid," Ben promised. "I can borrow it from Richards or Hunter, I reckon. When does it happen? And it's got to be safe, Finch, I'm not getting kicked out."

"It'll be safe, if it happens," Peter answered coolly, now thoroughly pleased with himself. "I'll let you know."

Ben withdrew to ring the bell that marked the end of prep, leaving Peter to sit back in his chair with his hands behind his head. Ben's mixture of awe and disbelief made him feel good, and he knew his other friends would react the same way. After spanking Tiffany in front of them, nobody would call his bluff. Yet he also felt deeply frustrated, both for the dirty images crowding his mind and the seeming impossibility of making his scheme a reality. His cock was rock hard in his pants and it would have been the work of a moment to bring himself to orgasm, but masturbation seemed an admission of defeat.

With prep over there was an hour of association time

before he prepared for bed. So he went downstairs, hoping that a game of ping-pong or some interesting television program would distract him. The strategy failed, with the ping-pong table already occupied, while the James Bond film projected in the common room contained enough bikini clad loveliness to ensure that his need grew stronger rather than weaker. By the time the bell rang for the seniors to go upstairs he felt as if he would burst at any instant, yet masturbation still seemed an insipid riposte. His heart was racing as he lay staring up into the darkness, with the college now quiet but for the toll of the chapel bell as it marked out the quarter hours.

Three miles away, St. Monica's lay under the same bright, gibbous moon that made silver rims along the curtains of his bedsit. Tiffany would be in bed, just as he was, perhaps asleep, perhaps awake and thoughtful, perhaps with her nightie pulled up over her breasts and her fingers busy between her legs as she thought of him. She'd as good as offered him her virginity if he had the courage to break in. So perhaps she'd be imagining how it would be to wake to the feel of his body as he climbed in beside her, her shock giving way to excitement and submission as he explored her body, her thighs slowly drifting wide until she was ready to accept him into her virgin heat.

The thought made his cock ache with need and he tried to turn his mind back to the more practical matter of getting Tiffany and her friends spanked. But the thought of Alice opened up a new possibility that Tiffany might not be alone in her bed. He knew that her room was in an upper passage with just four neighbours, all senior girls like herself. One was Alice and, while nothing had been admitted beyond a few sessions of kissing practise, he was fairly sure the two girls had at very least explored each other's bodies. Perhaps they were together now, cuddled into each other's arms, fingers moving over nubile breasts and perky bottoms with as much embarrassment as excitement, their lips coming into play as their arousal increased, mouths put to stiff pink nipples to lick and suck before they finally gave in to their need and went head to toe with their faces between each other's thighs.

Peter gave a hollow groan, his hand already stealing to his cock, only to withdraw. Muttering under his breath, he threw the covers back, walked to the window and jerked the curtains aside. The quad lay pale and still in the moonlight, with the buildings opposite creating a silhouette against a sky ragged with cloud. The confinements of school, which he'd found increasingly hard to bear as he came to maturity, suddenly seemed intolerable, a captivity as irksome as it was ridiculous.

"I'm eighteen years old," he sighed, "and I'm cooped up as if I was in the nursery. The hell with it, they can do what they like to me. I'm going out."

He took just moments to dress, pulling on his darkest clothes before slipping into the corridor and downstairs. It was far from the first time he'd ventured outside after dark, and the route he followed to get clear of the school grounds was familiar. Still, he remained cautious, skulking from shadow to shadow and repeatedly pausing to listen until he had reached the comparative safety of the river path.

There was no doubt in his mind as to where he was going—St. Monica's—but he had little idea what to do once he got there. It was all very well Tiffany encouraging him to break in, but the convent kept their charges under a far tighter rein than Broadfields, despite their claims of providing a progressive education. A high brick wall, punctuated with spiked, wrought iron gates, surrounded the accommodation and teaching buildings, and the wall itself was topped with broken glass. The front gate was not even worth investigating, on the main road and in full view of the buildings of Junior St. Monica's should any of the nuns chance to look out. It was locked at eight o'clock each evening, sealing Tiffany and some three hundred other girls away from temptation.

He'd only gone a few hundred yards when he stopped, telling himself that the trip was far too risky, only to decide that at the very least he had to reach the convent and scout out the lay of the land. Gathering his courage, he thought first of his Uncle Charles, a commando during the war, then of Tiffany, warm and eager in her bed, her cunt wet and ready for his cock. Neither ever had to know of his expedition, but the thought of their scorn and disappointment if he turned back was enough to make him push on.

Following a tiny lane and the familiar railway cutting, Peter reached the bank overlooking the playing fields just as the bells signalled midnight. He felt no less nervous than when he had come to peep at the girls from the woods, with every night-time sound magnified and invested with unseen fears, emotions that grew sharper as he stepped out onto the moonlit playing fields. For all his cultivated rationality, his imagination peopled the shadows with huge, vindictive nuns determined to protect their precious charges, and worse, especially where the chapel pushed out to one side and the pale light showed the angular shapes of gravestones.

The buildings were dark but for a few pallid rectangles, most on the upper floors, which suggested the possibility of catching sight of girls in a state of undress, a thought that gave him fresh courage. There was an athletic pavilion nearby, a low wooden building with its back to the woods, allowing him to keep in shelter for a little longer. As he reached it, he reflected that it would be the perfect place to stage his group spanking, perhaps on a quiet evening when anybody coming across the playing fields would be seen in plenty of time to allow him and his friends to melt unseen into the woods. The back door had even been left open and he peered briefly inside, drawing in the scent of wood polish and girlish exertion, before returning outside to check the voyeuristic possibilities of a line of high, algae encrusted windows at the back. They proved ideal, with the bank allowing him to stand in moderate comfort and look down into the changing area, and he was grinning as he moved on.

With no choice but to cross the open fields, he ducked low and ran, imagining the angry cry of some prowling nun with every step until he had reached the shelter of the wall. Nothing happened, but the wall rose a good two feet above his head and was as well defended as the one at the front; and the single iron gate which offered access to the convent was chained securely shut. Getting in was clearly going to be difficult and dangerous, finding Tiffany would be harder still. Feeling somewhat foolish, he tried to tell himself that the trip had been worthwhile both as a reconnaissance and an act of defiance, but the figure of his Uncle Charles rose up in his mind once more, chiding him for his cowardice and telling him to think out his strategy.

High above him the upper part of the convent was a muddle of roofs, gables and leaded flats. He knew that Tiffany's window looked out over the playing fields from the top floor. He could count eight that might be the one, all dark, two rows of three and a pair, but if she had three neighbours it surely had to be one of the pair. To think of her beyond the window gave him fresh determination. Looking around, there seemed to be two possible ways in. The graveyard wall was low and looked easy to climb. But, while the chapel beyond was sure to have several doors, they seemed likely to be locked. In the opposite direction a long, low building thrust out from the wall—clearly an addition after the convent had first been built. If he could get onto the roof it might be possible to cross the main wall, but a row of windows showed pale with light. He moved closer, keeping to the shadow of the high wall, slow, and slower still as he caught a strange, irregular thumping, then a voice, soft and feminine, singing a psalm. Curiosity overcame his caution and as he reached the first of the windows he peered within.

The building was a laundry, with a double row of tubs and various other more mysterious machines. A nun was working at the tubs, her back turned to Peter as she used a baton of bleached wood to push clothes down into the water. But it wasn't what she was doing that made his eyes grow round and his mouth drop open. She had taken off her habit and wimple, presumably to add them to the wash, leaving her in nothing but her underwear, which was plain and ample, but quite revealing enough to send the blood pumping to his cock, especially as she herself was young and beautiful. Her chest and belly were hidden beneath a full girdle, but it held her heavy breasts high and proud while accentuating the sculpted curves of her waist and hips, with the hem half covering her bottom to leave the seat of her full white panties (and quite a bit of plump young cheek) peeping out beneath. Taut suspender straps led down from her girdle, three at each side, to support thick, tan coloured stockings, each topped by a soft bulge of pale thigh. Better still, the way she was working at the tub kept her bottom nicely presented, with her flesh moving to the gentle rhythm of her work.

Time and again Tiffany had railed against the smug, holier-then-thou attitude of the nuns, especially their assumption of superiority through their vows of chastity. To see one of them stripped down to her underwear was a magnificent outrage, better still when she was so attractive, and it was the work of an instant for Peter to free his mischievous cock. He began to masturbate, an act as deliberately and delightfully insolent as it was impossible to resist, all the while praying that she'd add her girdle and panties to the load in the wash tub, treating him to a view of her bare bottom and full breasts.

It was easy to imagine, her girdle unfastened and slipped off to let her breasts loll forward, round and heavy and bare as they swung to the motion of her work, her nipples large and stiff. Then her panties, pushed down over her glorious bottom and down her fine, shapely legs. She'd have to bend down to take them right off, perhaps far enough to allow him one brief, fleeting glimpse of her rear view in its full glory, with her virgin cunt and the tight dimple of her anus naked to his gaze. Not that she showed the least inclination to strip completely, but it was too late anyway. Peter had cum in his hand.

The laundry room had also begun to get steamy, with condensation on the window making it difficult to see. As he sank down against the wall he was glad to have finished in time, and gladder still when the window directly above him was pushed open. He froze, sure that she would lean out and catch him, with his erect cock still sticking out from his trousers, sticky with cum and revealing the full extent of his abominable transgression. But nothing happened, and presently the gentle, rhythmic thump of the washing baton began once more.

Peter moved into the deeper shadows where the laundry jutted out from the wall. As he cleaned himself up, he told himself that he'd done enough for one night: a successful reconnaissance culminating in an act of spectacular impropriety. Tiffany would be delighted, but she would also want to know why he hadn't continued on his mission. He stayed put, his thoughts moving between a bold, near demented delight in his behaviour and the further possibilities that cool, reasoned caution would make all the more probable. His orgasm had taken the edge off his need, but he knew he'd be ready again after a few minutes in bed with Tiffany, while the open window above offered a tempting route into the convent, and out again once he was done.

The light went off, the nun's gentle singing receded, but the window remained open, and with that Peter decided to act. He was inside in an instant, blinking in the gloom until his eyes grew accustomed to what little moonlight came in at the windows. The scent of freshly washed clothes was strong in the air, at which a new possibility occurred to him. To think was to act, and he had quickly wriggled himself into a habit and wimple, with his face contorted into a manic, daring grin as he peered out from the laundry room. A corridor led away into dimness that could only be part of the main building. He was inside.

As he started along the corridor he lowered his gaze to the ground and laced his fingers together across his midriff, a meek attitude he assumed typical for a nun. Nobody was there to criticise, the lower part of the convent silent and dark but for the faint glow of nightlights at well spaced intervals. The corridor met another, with doors leading off to either side, one open to reveal the shapes of bulky kitchen equipment, another half-closed, only to swing wide too suddenly for Peter to react.

He stood face to face with a girl, the two of them frozen in shock. Her eyes were wide in a face framed by dark, tousled hair, her pretty mouth slightly open and sticky with jam from the little jar she held in one hand. She looked terrified and was evidently waiting for the supposed nun who had caught her at her crime to speak. Peter hesitated, not sure if he should tell her off, order her to visit the Mother Superior in the morning, even punish her then and there. The first choice seemed inadequate, the second unfair, the third irresistible. He raised his chin and spoke in his renowned imitation of Mrs. Malaprop.

"Put down that jam, girl, and lift your nightie."

For one awful moment he thought she was going to scream, before her expression of terror gave way to one of sulky compliance. Half turning, she placed the jam on the floor and lifted her nightie at the back, exposing a small, sweetly rounded bottom, already bare, which she then pushed out petulantly, and inadvertently pertly. She braced herself against the wall and Peter swallowed hard, the blood already pumping to his cock for the sight she was presenting. But he managed to keep his voice level as he spoke again, timing his words to five firm smacks across her pert little cheeks.

"You ... are ... a ... little ... thief ... What are you are?"

"A little thief," she answered miserably.

"Exactly," he finished, applying a final smack to now flushed bottom. "But so long as you replace the jam no more need be said. What is your name?"

"Katie Vale," she answered, now sounding slightly puzzled as she hastily covered her bottom.

"Then run along to bed, Katie Vale," he said, only to realise that she offered the perfect opportunity to find out how to get to Tiffany's room. "I am new here, as you no doubt realise. Tell me the way to Tiffany Lange's room."

"Blue Staircase, top floor," Katie answered quickly, pointed back down the corridor and fled.

She'd left the jam on the floor and Peter quickly appropriated it, his fingers shaking with reaction as he tugged up his habit and pushed the jar into his pocket before making a badly needed adjustment to his cock. His heart was hammering with excitement and arousal, bringing on a sense of invulnerability as he turned back the way he had come. He'd spanked a girl and gotten away with it, and while she'd seemed suspicious he was sure she wouldn't be going to the authorities, an act that would inevitably lead to more of what she'd received in the corridor and probably a great deal harder.

The first staircase he reached was marked by a waist-high stripe, just visible as green against the dull magnolia of the wall. He moved on, to another, narrower stair, this time marked blue, right at the end of the building and presumably below Tiffany's corridor. Climbing swiftly and silently, he passed one floor after another without incident, until at last the staircase opened out onto a landing, beyond which a short corridor showed two doors at either side. Each door bore a neatly written nametag, the first of which was *Lange, T.* He pushed inside without hesitation, into near darkness, form which Tiffany's voice sounded clear and sweet but fraught with alarm.

"Alice? Lottie?"

"No, Peter."

"Peter! You scared me! What're you doing here anyway? How did you get in?"

"Sh!" he urged. "I had to come. I couldn't keep away.

Let me into bed."

Tiffany complied, pulling back the covers to let him slip in beside her. The bed was soft, warm and smelt girlishly sweet, while her flesh felt firm and infinitely desirable where it pressed to his own through their clothes, setting his cock stiff as he cuddled close. His lips found hers and they melted into a long kiss, but as he began to ease her nightie up over the swell of her bottom she pushed him back a little to speak once more.

"We're going to get caught, Peter. This is lovely, but you have to go!"

"Not yet. You promised that if I came you'd … you'd let me."

"Yes, but I was playing. I mean, I'm flattered, and I do want to do it, but I can't!"

"Tiffany! Please, for my sake? You can make some excuse."

"They'd know, they're like that! I … I'll do you in my mouth. You like that. But then you have to go. The penguins come round sometimes. They'll catch us! What have you got on, anyway? Are you wearing a dress?"

"I took a habit and wimple from the laundry. I need you Tiffany, please!?"

"You're dressed as a nun!?"

Her voice was half squeak, half giggle as he eased her nightie up over her hips. Like Katie, she had no panties on underneath, allowing his eager hands straight to bare, nubile flesh, first to stroke and squeeze, then to smack.

"Ow! Peter! You really are a pig, did you know that, and a pervert!"

He'd begun to nuzzle her neck as he explored her bottom, one hand slipping between her cheeks to find her arsehole as he moved the other around to cup the soft bulge of her cunt. She sighed and pulled herself closer, but as his finger began to probe the virgin tightness of her hole she pulled back a little and spoke once more, now breathless.

"No, Peter, you can't, not in my pussy. Let me take you in my mouth."

Peter shook his head as he fumbled up his habit. Tiffany gave a soft, abandoned moan, her back arching to push her cunt against his hand as he continued to fiddle with her, and her voice was full of regret as she spoke again.

"No, you mustn't. I want to, believe me, but I can't, not in my pussy, no …"

She broke off with a cry as his fingers pushed firmly to the tight constriction of her hymen, then pulled suddenly back, speaking fast and urgent even as Peter freed his cock from his fly.

"Not my pussy, Peter, no. If you have to do me, do me up my bottom."

As she spoke she rolled over, pushing out her naked bottom into his lap and against his now exposed penis. He began to rub his length in the warmth of her slit by instinct, despite being shocked and surprised by her dirty offer. After all, he'd fantasized about putting his cock into her beautiful arse almost as often as he'd fantasised about fucking her properly.

"Up your bottom, really?" he asked.

"Yes," she insisted, her voice thick with embarrassment. "It's what girls do if a man gets too randy, we let him do it … in our butts."

"It is?"

"Don't talk about it, Peter, just do it. You're making me feel ashamed of myself."

"Yes, but … but won't I need to get you ready?"

"Yes … maybe, spit on your finger or something, whatever you do with your friends!"

"I don't do anything with my friends!"

It was true, but he was the exception. Many of his friends had experimented with each other, and he knew full well that an arsehole needed to be coaxed open before a cock would go in.

Sucking his finger, he eased it between Tiffany's cheeks to find the tiny bud of her anus, tight but moist and receptive, making him wonder if she'd already surrendered herself to another boy.

"Is this your first time?" he demanded as he eased the tip of his finger into the hot, slippery ring of her bottom hole.

"Yes!" she sobbed. "Of course it is! Well, with a man ..."

"Eh? So what else goes up there?" he demanded as he eased a second finger into her now taut ring.

"I ... I sometimes put the handle of my hairbrush up," Tiffany gasped. "I can't do it in my pussy, can I? Ooh! You're hurting."

"Sorry," Peter answered, extracting his fingers as he imagined how she'd look with a hairbrush sticking out of her bottom hole as she masturbated. "Hang on, I've got some jam."

"Jam?"

"Yes. I got it off a girl called Katie Vale."

"Katie? What were you doing with Katie? She's ..."

"She was raiding the kitchens. I didn't do anything with her. Well, not much. I smacked her bottom and took her jam off her."

"You smacked her bottom!?"

"I had to. She thought I was a nun."

"You didn't have to ..."

Peter had retrieved the jam jar from his pocket as they spoke and her aggrieved answer broke to a gasp as he slathered as much as he'd been able to scoop out with two fingers between the cheeks of her bottom, then another as he pushed a finger deep into her now sticky anus.

"You'll get it everywhere!" she protested, but her bottom was still pushed out and she was tugging up her nightie to bare her breasts.

"Kneel up then," Peter instructed, his finger now pushed as deep into her bottom hole as it would go.

"Filthy pig," Tiffany answered, but she lost no time in

obeying him, throwing back the covers and twisting around to lift her bottom.

Peter's finger had slid from her arse as she moved and he quickly got into position, kneeling behind her with his habit held up and his cock in his hand. She was face down on the bed, the contours of her body just visible now that his eyes had adjusted, her nightie rucked up to show off her breasts, her slender waist flaring to the width of her hips and the tempting roundness of her bottom, her cheeks spread wide to reveal the slick, jam smeared slit between.

"I'm going to do it," he sighed. "I'm going to butt fuck you, Tiffs."

"Do it ... do it there, go on."

He didn't need telling, the swollen head of his cock already pressed to her anus. She groaned as he pushed, half pain, half pleasure as her ring began to open, and again, with a note of something like despair creeping into voice as she spread to take him. He pushed again, his cock slipping in deeper with the warm jam to help, and deeper still, with her anus now gaping to accommodate him, she gasped out her passion and squirmed herself against him. Another firm push and he was all the way in, the full length of his erection jammed up into her straining bottom hole and his balls pressed firmly to her empty, virgin cunt.

She was sobbing and groaning in response. Her fingers clutched at the bed sheets and he thought she might be crying, but she made no effort to stop him, holding her pose as he entered her, his arousal rising swiftly as his cock pulled in an out of the tightness of her anal ring and his eyes feasted on her naked body. He was grateful that he'd eased his need earlier. That alone had stopped him from losing his load all over Tiffany's backside before he'd even got in. But he was already having to take it slow to stop himself from losing his cum again when she began to speak once more, her voice soft, urgent and heavy with shame.

"You've got it up my bottom, you dirty pig, right up my bottom ... and I let you ... and it feels so nice. I must be the most wicked girl there ever was, a harlot, a dirty whore. Spank me, Peter, punish me ... smack my naughty bottom while you use me ... use me and my forbidden hole."

He began to spank her immediately, firm, even smacks applied to her parted cheeks as his cock moved in her anus, slowly at first, then faster, until she was gasping out her feelings, her words too broken for him to understand but growing gradually clearer and ever more urgent.

"... punish me, smack me ... smack me harder, Peter! Spank me like the dirty little whore I am, with a boy's prick up my butt ... deep between my cheeks ... do your thing inside me, right up inside me, right into my naughty arsehole while you spank me!"

Her voice had risen close to a scream, and Peter hastily clapped a hand over her mouth to shut her up even as he did his best to oblige, pumping into her, her straining anal ring taut on the base of his shaft and the rest of his cock rubbing in the hot, slippery canal of her rectum. A few more firm strokes and he'd done it, creaming deep inside her in a second orgasm, far, far better than the first as she shook and whimpered beneath him, lost in ecstasy and shame for her once-virgin arse. Even as he emptied the creamy contents of his balls into her rectum, her hand had slithered down between her legs, snatching and rubbing at her cunt with the tears streaming down her face as she brought herself to a hard climax, her anus contracting in orgasm, milking the last of his cream out of him and into her well fucked bottom.

C h a p t e r   T h r e e

Peter stared from the classroom window towards long familiar scenery; the flat green expanse of the playing fields, the line of trees that marked the river, with the woods and fields of the opposite hillside rising beyond. In the years he'd been at Broadfields he'd looked out in much the same manner from a dozen different windows and innumerable times, staring wistfully into the distance and wishing he was anywhere else but cooped up in the classroom, but now his mind burned with thoughts. He'd done it, riding a wave of crazy over-confidence and stubborn bravado to not only visit St. Monica's, but to break in, evade the nuns, spank a pretty young girl and accept the surrender of his girlfriend's anal virginity. He'd even retained the nun's outfit as a trophy.

The achievement made the Reverend Porter's vindication of the philosophy implicit in St. Paul's letter to the Galatians seem even more trivial and irrelevant than it would normally have done, and yet the Headmaster's pious, self-satisfied manner added a certain something to his sense of triumph. He knew that even his Uncle Charles could not have faulted his courage and determination, while his adventure matched anything he'd read in even the most lurid and uninhibited of magazines. Imagining the furious indignation of the nuns, had they discovered what he'd done, made his success sweeter still. One corner of his mouth twitched up into a faint smile at the thought, only for his reverie to be interrupted by the voice of the Reverend Porter.

"And perhaps Mr. Finch would care to favour us with his own opinion on this matter, unless, that is, he considers the prospect of today's lunch more important than Christian teachings?"

"I have an alternative philosophy," Peter answered. "Do

what thou wilt shall be the whole of the law"."

It took the Headmaster a moment to recognize the quote, so that his smug expression changed first to puzzlement, then to a red faced fury that rendered him speechless for several seconds before he once more found his voice and his customarily sarcastic tone.

"Crowley, I see. I am surprised that even you could have sunk to such depths, Finch. But no, I see that you are merely trying to annoy me, and you have succeeded. So I propose that you spend those hours of the afternoon, normally reserved for cricket, in clearing the river banks of weeds, which should allow you ample time for reflection on philosophy. Howard, you have at least a modicum of intelligence. Perhaps you could explain to me why St. Paul's remarks are so important?"

His attention had already moved on from Peter, who didn't respond in any case, equally happy to be on grounds duty as playing cricket, with the thoughts of the previous night's triumph more than enough to sustain him. By the time Gabriel Howard had completed his explanation, Peter's attention had wandered again, with his gaze fixed firmly out of the window, where it remained until the bell signalled the end of morning lessons. He continued to daydream through lunch and afternoon lessons, and was still smiling in a vague and dreamy fashion as he made his way towards the main gate to report for grounds duty. The afternoon was hot and sultry, so he made a point of volunteering to be one of those who actually went into the river, which not only allowed him to keep cool but gave his thoughts free rein as he worked mechanically, cutting back reeds and nettles on the bank.

Made bold by his success, he'd soon moved on from simply replaying the details of his adventure to considering new ones, including further visits to the convent *and* turning his dream of a group spanking into reality. The pavilion at the end of the grounds was the perfect venue, but the problem of persuading the girls to participate without allowing the costs to grow too large remained. In turn he considered the possibilities of blackmail, physical coercion and tricking the girls into thinking they were taking a genuine punishment, only to reject each as either impractical or unworthy. But as he attacked a particularly obstinate tangle of vegetation he hit on a scheme he was sure would tempt even the shyest or most haughty of girls by appealing to what he identified as typically feminine traits—avarice and vanity.

Tiffany sighed as her bottom hole again began to spread to the pressure of Peter's cock. She knelt in the long, warm grass of the old railway cutting, her red tartan school skirt turned up onto her back and her big white panties pulled far down to leave the cheeky peach of her bottom exposed for entry. She'd also had her blouse pulled open and her bra turned up to display her breasts, while the ring of her anus glistened with the Vaseline she'd thoughtfully applied before leaving the convent for their rendezvous. Peter was in heaven, enjoying every exquisite sensation, from the tightness of her straining musculature and the wet heat of her insides to the cruel joy he'd taken in her half-eager, half-reluctant surrender to the second butt fucking of her young life.

She'd begun to cry as he gradually eased the full length of his erection into her bottom. Soft, broken sobs rich with mixed emotion, and yet there was no mistaking the tone of her low purr of satisfaction as his balls finally met the flesh of her empty cunt. He'd already spanked her, responding to her earlier teasing by turning her across his knee to have her bottom exposed and smacked, gently enough at first but then harder once he'd discovered that, for all her protests about taking his cock in her arse, she'd greased herself in readiness for exactly that. Now he began to spank again, making each round, red cheek bounce and quiver to the slaps as he moved inside her.

Now, spanked and fucked with equal vigour, she began to gasp and whimper, hot tears streaming down her face even as she put a hand back to rub at her pussy. Peter grinned at her reaction, unsure as ever what was going through her head, but enjoying every sigh and every moan almost as much as he enjoyed the sight of her spread and penetrated bottom, or the exquisite sensation of having his erection sheathed in hot girl flesh. All he needed was one final touch to make the situation perfect—the dirty talk he knew would take them both over the edge.

"That's right," he told her. "Rub your little cunt like the dirty whore you are, Tiffany. You can't stop yourself, can you? Your knickers are down and my cock's deep in your backside and what do you do? You play with your cunt. You ought to be ashamed of yourself, but oh no, not you, Tiffany. You grease up your arse, ready and willing, and I bet you put in a finger or two when you did it, didn't you? I bet you did, thinking it was my cock inside you, just the way you are now, with your skirt hitched up and your knickers pulled down, you little disgrace, you cock-tease, you ... oh but I love you so much, Tiffany!"

He couldn't hold back any more. His words merged into grunts as he came again in her arse, finishing off with a series of sudden, powerful thrusts that made her scream and tipped her over the edge. For one perfect moment they were coming together, with his cock jammed into her bottom as deep as it would go, while her anus contracted hard on his shaft over and over again to milk the full contents of his balls into her rectum. She seemed to be in agony as her orgasm tore through her, screaming and sobbing and clutching at herself, only to finish with a long, happy sigh as she finally slumped down into the grass. Her bottom was still pushed high and Peter took a moment to extract his erection, grinning once more at the sight of the cum bubbling from her wet, pink hole as it closed and giving her a final, firm slap before rolling over in the grass.

"That was great!" he sighed. "Give me your knickers, would you? I need to wipe my cock."

"You're a filthy pig, Peter Finch," Tiffany replied, but even as she turned over she was levering her panties down and off.

Peter took the white cotton panties and began to wipe himself clean as Tiffany produced a wad of tissues from somewhere within her dishevelled apparel. For a long moment they were silent, each concentrating on tidying up, until Peter was satisfied with his efforts and had tossed her now soiled panties to one side.

"I think I've worked out how to do the group spanking," he told her.

"That was just a fantasy, wasn't it?" she answered.

"So was spanking you in front of my friends, but we did that."

"Okay, but how? I don't want to get caught, Peter, and you take awful risks, like coming to me the other night."

"It was worth it, every second, and besides, I don't intend to get caught. I take risks, yes, but calculated risks. First of all, we use the pavilion at the end of your sports field, and in the evening. That way we can see anybody coming in plenty of time."

"That ought to work."

"It will work, but the clever part is this. To make sure we get plenty of girls, we make it a competition, with a cash prize."

"A competition for what?" Tiffany laughed. "Getting spanked!?"

"Making the prettiest exhibition," Peter explained. "All the St. Monica's girls are vain, and all of them appreciate the value of money. Furthermore, enough girls are either cruel enough to want to watch each other get it, or like you, they enjoy getting it."

"Not all the girls are …" Tiffany began, then trailed off, her expression of instinctive resentment for his words shifting to a doubtful frown before she carried on. "Okay, it might work, with some of the girls. Alice would join in, and Charlotte, if the prize was big enough. But they're my friends and they have to know that there are boys watching."

"Alright, if that doesn't scare them off, but we need more than three of you. What about Christine Arlington?"

"Not with boys watching, but then I don't care if she knows or not. In fact, I'd like to go through with it and tell her afterwards."

"Wouldn't she tell the penguins?"

"Not when she'd allowed herself to be spanked for kicks! I'd be in worse trouble than she would, but not so much. One thing I can promise, any girl who goes through with it won't tell, not then, not ever."

"That's good to know. How about Emerald Feldkirch?"

"Oh she'd do it, just to show off."

"That's what I like to hear. How about Princess Ayanna?"

"Ha, ha, very funny. She blushes when she gets changed for games."

"Katie Vale? She's pretty, and she seems ready enough to have her bottom smacked."

"Katie?" Tiffany responded doubtfully. "Maybe, I suppose … She'll do as she's told anyway."

"Perfect," Peter stated. "So that's five for sure: you, obviously, Katie, Emerald, Alice and Charlotte, six if we can get Christine. That should keep the boys happy."

He blew his breath out, imagining the six girls with their bottoms on parade as they awaited their spankings. Tiffany gave him a reproving look and a dig in the ribs with her elbow, but she was smiling mischievously.

"So who gets to do the spanking?" she asked.

"That's up to you," he told her. "But we definitely need

two girls, one to pin up the girls' skirts and pull down their knickers, another to do the spanking. And the boys have to believe that they're actually nuns. Can you think of a couple of big, plain girls who'd get a kick out of smacking the pretty one's bottoms?"

Tiffany made a face, but then nodded.

"Rosa Mulligan would do it," she assured him. "She threatened to sit on Christine's face for calling her fatty the other day; and then there's Victoria Trent. She's not so very big, but she's tall, she's Head Girl and she loves to smack our bottoms."

"Is she safe?"

"Oh yes. She's just good at fooling the penguins. They even think she's going to become one of them, but what she really wants is to go into finance like her father."

"Excellent, as long as the other girls can be persuaded to take it from them?"

"Not Christine, I wouldn't think, not from Rosa anyway. The others will be okay."

"Okay, never mind Christine, although I would love to see her get it."

"So who does the judging? I can't, not if I'm being spanked."

"That's true, and we can't lose you. You're too pretty, and besides, I already told my friend Ben you were going to be punished. Charlotte, Alice and Ayanna too. I think I said six girls, actually, so maybe we do need one more."

"You could say Ayanna got let off, or was ill, but what about the judging?"

"Why not Vicky Trent? She can do the skirts and knickers and judge too. She could even pretend to be the one who's putting up the prize."

"That's true. Even Christine might go for it if she thought it was Vicky's idea."

"Even with big Rosa doing the spanking?"

"No, but she might let Rosa get her backside bare if

Vicky was doing the spanking. Christine's always been soppy on Vicky."

Peter shook his head, trying to rid his mind of images of lesbian schoolgirls, then carried on.

"Brilliant, now you just need to talk her into it, and the others. Hang on, what if we let Vicky Trent in on the scheme and make sure she gives you the prize? That way we get our investment back, or most of it anyway. Do you think she'd do that?"

"Yes, but it would probably be best if you talk to her. She'd think I was making it up, or trying to get her in trouble with the penguins."

Tiffany's voice had faltered as she spoke and she was blushing, arousing Peter's curiosity.

"Why's that? Tell me."

"Or what?" Tiffany answered, her face now flushed pink but the challenge in her voice unmistakable.

"Another spanking?" Peter suggested, but Tiffany merely laughed.

"Your knickers stuck up your backside?" he went on, recalling a particularly dirty moment from one of the few blue films he'd seen. "Half way up anyway. I'd leave a little tail hanging out and send you back to St. Monica's like that."

"Pig."

"Tell me about Vicky and I won't do it."

"Do it and I won't tell you about Vicky."

"Okay, your knickers stuck in your mouth, then."

"You wouldn't!"

"I would," Peter replied, reaching for the discarded panties.

"Okay, okay," Tiffany said hastily, her face redder than ever. "I used to be Vicky's toasty girl, but ..."

"What's a toasty girl?"

"You know, a girl who warms up another girl's bed for

her … In other words, someone who … helps her out when she's feeling … dirty. Don't you boys do something like that Broadfields?"

"Not normally, no," Peter answered and quickly changed the subject back to more fruitful ground. "So Vicky used to take you to bed, for what?"

"Oh, you know, she'd make me fiddle with her cunt and kiss her tits."

"Did she spank you?"

"Yes, of course, and if I was really badly behaved she'd sit on my face and make me lick her cunt and … and her other hole."

Peter gave a hollow moan and put his hand to his cock, which had begun to swell again, his eyes shut as he pictured the look of consternation and horror on Tiffany's face as the bigger girl squatted down to have her bottom licked. It was immensely appealing and unspeakably rude at the same time, maybe too rude.

"You're teasing me again, aren't you?" he said.

"No," she assured him. "Vicky was the one who taught me how nice it is to fiddle with myself, and to put things in my bottom. I was her toasty girl for two terms, and of course she used to punish me. That's just the way it is. Usually it would be a spanking, across her knee with my skirt turned up for a few smacks on my knickers before she pulled them down, just the way you like to do me. Sometimes she'd use her hairbrush instead of her hand, but if I'd been really insolent, or if she was in a dirty mood, then she'd put her bum in my face. I used to hate it, and I used to love it too. How dirty is that? Then Christine told her I used to play with Alice, because Christine had a crush on Vicky and wanted to be her toasty girl instead of me. Vicky got jealous and she doesn't really trust me now, but if you speak to her she'll know it's for real."

Tiffany went quiet for a moment, then began to talk

again, her voice now soft and urgent.

"Vicky punished us together, Alice and me, after she found out. She caught us and dragged us into the showers, where she made us kneel side by side, in our clothes but with our skirts up and our knickers pulled down. Then she spanked us, with her hand first, then she rubbed our cunts with toothpaste, and put her fingers up our bottom holes to make it sting and got back to the spanking with a big wooden bath brush. It hurt so much and I cried and cried. Poor Alice wet herself, right into her splayed knickers, but Vicky just laughed. Then she came to stand over me, and she made me watch while she lifted her skirt and pulled her knickers aside. She told me she was going to piddle on me, and then she did it, all over my butt and all over my back and in my hair and in my face. She even made me open my mouth so she could pee in it, and she made me swallow, and ..."

"Now I know you're teasing," Peter broke in. "But I swear that if you don't shut up right now my cock's going back in your bum."

Tiffany laughed and jumped to her feet, sticking her tongue out at him before running away. Peter gave chase, but before he could catch her she'd turned, putting her hands out in a defensive gesture as she spoke.

"No, please, I'm too sore, not now."

"Okay," Peter agreed, privately relieved for the dull ache in his now stiff cock. "Just turn around and stick out your bottom."

Tiffany stuck out her lower lip in a sulky pout but did as she was told, pushing her bottom out so that he could lift her skirt and land a single hard smack across her bare cheeks. She responded with a yelp, then smiled and reached out for his hand as they continued along the cutting.

"We could talk to Vicky now, if you like?" she suggested. "She's playing hockey this afternoon, but we can wait til she's finished, if you've got time?"

"I can make time," Peter answered after an instant to weigh the loss of missing dinner against the gain of watching girls play hockey in their gym knickers and singlets. "I'll stay back in the woods if you can get her after the game."

Tiffany nodded and they walked on, hand in hand, to where the cutting began a long, slow turn that took it past the end of the St. Monica's playing fields. It was familiar ground to Peter, from many a voyeuristic expedition. From the safety of the trees they were soon watching the hockey games— a sight which never failed to send the blood to his cock. The senior girls were on the nearest field, one team in bottle green singlets and white gym knickers, the other with the colours reversed, but each and every one of them with making a fine show of nubile curves beneath the clinging fabric.

Alice and Christine were immediately obvious, playing on the wings, also Emerald, captaining the same team with her full bottom straining against the seat of her white gym knickers. The captain of the other team was a tall girl with an athletic figure and a tumble of tawny blonde curls, perhaps not as overtly feminine as some of the other girls, but with an air of confident superiority that made him long to bring her to heel.

"Vicky Trent?" he asked, pointing out the tall girl.

"Yes," Tiffany answered. "How did you know?"

"She looks as if she'd be Head Girl, that's all," Peter replied. "Do you think we could have her on the receiving end instead? I'd love to see her spanked."

"Vicky?" Tiffany said, shocked. "Never! Nobody would dare."

"I would," Peter replied. "But never mind, let's stick to what's practical. Go and talk to her when the game's over, but try not to be too obvious about it or we might arouse suspicions. It's vital nobody suspects that you gave her the idea for the spanking contest."

"Yes, of course," Tiffany replied. "She'll want to talk to

me anyway, because I was supposed to be playing."

"Won't you get into trouble?"

"I got a note from the under matron, she's a mug."

The game was soon over and Tiffany trotted confidently out from among the trees, leaving Peter to watch as she spoke first to the nun who had been referee for the game, then to Vicky. Emerald's team had won and were gathered together in an excited huddle, but most of the others made straight for the changing rooms and Tiffany had soon managed to get Vicky alone. The tall girl's face looked puzzled as she came towards the woods, but she was nodding and greeted Peter with the same casual confidence she'd shown on the playing field.

"So you're Tiffs' mysterious boyfriend, are you?" she asked, looking him up and down. "Not bad, I suppose. A bit scruffy, maybe, but not bad."

Peter felt himself start to bridle at her remark but he forced a smile and extended his hand.

"Peter Finch, pleased to meet you," he said.

"Vicky Trent," she answered, accepting his hand after no more than an instant of hesitation. "Tiffs tells me you've got a money making scheme on the go?"

"Yes," Peter told her and began to explain his plans.

Vicky listened, first looking surprised and a bit annoyed, but not shocked, and as Peter carried on his initial embarrassment began to fade. She shrugged as he finished, gave Tiffany a searching look, then turned back to him.

"You're a dirty pervert, do you know that?" she demanded. "But yes, I can see it would work, done the right way. Only, you have to let me do the organising and I get half the money."

"One third," Peter pointed out. "There are three of us."

"Half," Vicky insisted. "I'm the one taking the risks. If I get caught that means the cane, six strokes in front of assembly, maybe twelve. You do realise I'm Head Girl?"

"Yes," Peter admitted, "but still …"

"And another thing, I'm not dressing up as a penguin."

"But that's essential," Peter protested. "It's supposed to be a genuine punishment, from the nuns."

"That's not going to work," Vicky retorted. "I can tell the girls it's a competition for cash and they'll take a spanking, and maybe I could explain why I was dressed like a penguin. But if we got caught I'd get two dozen strokes of the cane in assembly, bare bottom, and I'd get expelled."

"That's awkward …" Peter admitted, trailing off as he tried to think of a way around the problem, only for Vicky to carry on talking before he could come up with anything.

"You can explain it's a Head Girl's punishment. They'll believe that, and it will explain why the girls aren't all that reluctant too, because I'm sure all you perverts over at Broadfields think we're in and out of each other's knickers all day long. So I want half the money, and I want to do the spanking as well."

"I thought Rosa …"

"We don't need Rosa."

"I want it done a certain way," Peter persisted, "with one nun to pull the girls' knickers down and another to do the spanking. That way there's plenty to see."

Vicky gave him a look of disgust and shook her head.

"You get to see the spankings, and that's more than enough for a bunch of little perverts like you. But don't worry, it'll be knickers down, and I'll make them do time in the corner, you know, bare bottom to the room and hands on their heads."

"That's great," Peter went on, still obstinate. "But I want the girls' knickers pulled down first, like a sort of pageant line. So they're paraded with their bottoms bare while they're waiting for their spankings, then spanked, then sent to line up against the wall. And I want to see everything, so you're to make sure the girls' legs are open while they're spanked."

"You really are a pervert, aren't you?" Vicky answered.

"I don't piss on girls in the shower," Peter answered, taking a chance that Tiffany's fantasy had been at least partially based on truth.

Vicky went scarlet instantly, casting a furious glance at Tiffany, then spoke to Peter once more.

"Okay, if that's the way you want it, how about having the girls pull each other's knickers down before they go over my lap?"

"Alright," Peter agreed, intrigued. This idea seemed likely to be just as shameful for the girls as his own idea had been, even if the situation seemed to be slipping slightly out of his control. "I'll leave the rest of the details to you, but if any of the girls I mentioned won't do it, you have to find a substitute. A pretty one."

Vicky nodded briefly before rounding on Tiffany.

"You little sneak! Some things are secret, really secret!"

"I … I was only playing!" Tiffany stammered. "You shouldn't have said anything, Peter! Sorry, Vicky, but …"

"You will be," Vicky assured her. "Now come here."

"No, Vicky, please, not in front of Peter, please!" Tiffany babbled, backing hastily away.

"Come. Here." Vicky repeated, her voice firm and commanding. "You know the rules."

"Rules?" Peter asked, intrigued and fascinated by what was about to happen for all his instinct to defend Tiffany.

"What girls do together is supposed to be private," Tiffany said weakly. "Sorry, Vicky, I am really am, but couldn't you do me later?"

"Don't be prissy," Vicky told her. "You know you've got it coming to you, and I bet he's seen plenty already, you little show-off. Now come here!"

Tiffany was red faced and looked ready for tears, finally prompting Peter into action.

"Maybe she doesn't want to be spanked?"

"Who said anything about her being spanked?" Vicky retorted. "She's going to get that anyway, isn't she, when your dirty little scheme comes off."

"What are you going to do?" Peter asked in horrified fascination. "Not ..."

"That's right, I'm going to pee on her," Vicky told him. "What, are you shocked? You seemed to think that girls did this sort of thing all the time? Come here, Tiffs, you know you deserve this."

"You don't have to let her, not if you don't want to," Peter said, but Tiffany shook her head.

"I do deserve it, but not here, please, Vicky! I'll be all sticky and smelly, and what if the penguins catch me trying to get in? What am I supposed to say, that I wet myself, all over?"

"You should have thought of this before you told your boyfriend a secret like that," Vicky answered. "It's not like it's just kissing or playing strip, is it? That was special, Tiffany!"

"I thought you did it to punish her?" Peter put in. "But look ..."

"You stay out of this," Vicky told him. "But no, it wasn't a punishment, it was something between Tiffany and me, something I didn't want getting out to a load of dirty minded boys!"

She looked ready to cry and Peter found himself shrugging uncomfortably, realising that his cock was now a solid, aching bar within his pants, as he responded.

"I'll keep it secret, I promise," he said. "Word of honour."

Vicky gave him a doubtful look, but when she spoke again it was to Tiffany.

"Okay, I'll do it in your mouth and you can swallow, but you're not getting off."

"In her mouth?" Peter asked weakly.

Both girls ignored him, Tiffany shame-faced and shaking as she got slowly down to her knees in the leaf mould, Vicky with her hands on her hips and her nose stuck in the air, although she too was trembling.

"Clothes off," Vicky ordered as Tiffany turned wide, frightened eyes up to her. "Or you can leave them on, but they'll probably get wet. If anything drips down your tits you can mop it up with your knickers."

"I don't have any on," Tiffany answered, quickly lifting the front of her skirt to give a flash of the exposed, downy triangle between her thighs.

"You little minx!" Vicky laughed. "Going to meet your boyfriend with no knickers on under your skirt?"

"I had knickers," Tiffany protested. "I lost them."

"Oh and I can just imagine how!" Vicky answered. "Come on then, out of your clothes."

Peter had given up trying to intervene, feeling painfully excited but somewhat helpless as Tiffany began to strip, removing first her blouse and skirt, then her bra, to leave her in nothing but neat black shoes and long white school socks. Vicky also watched, the expression on her face growing ever more smug as Tiffany shed her clothes, and speaking only when the kneeling girl was fully naked.

"Get behind me," Vicky ordered Peter. "I don't want you seeing anything you shouldn't. Okay, Tiffs, open wide."

Peter obeyed automatically, with no more than a twinge of regret for being denied a glimpse of Vicky's sex. The view was quite pretty anyway, with Vicky's two full cheeks tight in her bottle green gym knickers as she pushed her belly out into Tiffany's face. He swallowed as he ducked down to get a still better view, scarcely able to believe that the two girls could do anything so utterly filthy. If Tiffany felt the same it was difficult to tell, as her eyes were now closed and her pretty mouth opened in meek acceptance of what was about to happen to her. Vicky was no less reticent, stepping out of her gym knickers to expose herself and, in doing so, revealing to Peter the globes of two firm buttocks and a hint of her soft crevice.

For a moment the tableau held in utter silence, broken by a sigh from Vicky and the hiss of her stream as she let go, full in Tiffany's face. Peter could only stare, frozen in amazement as he watched the stream of rich white-gold flood over his girlfriend's chin, into her mouth, and trickle from the sides to wet her neck and breasts, dripping from her erect nipples and running down her belly. Then she'd swallowed, deliberately taking a mouthful of Vicky's effluent down into her belly, a sight at once so compelling and so obscene that his efforts to hold back his own needs evaporated on the instant.

Tugging his cock free, he began to masturbate with furious energy, heedless of what Vicky would think, heedless to the risk of being caught or anything else but the sight of Tiffany, nude and dripping, as she struggled to drink down the hot stream still gushing into her mouth. She couldn't cope, Vicky's liquid now running in twin steams from either side of her mouth despite her best efforts to swallow it down. Quite a bit had splashed into her face, and her breasts were dripping and filthy. A moment more and her hand had gone between her legs, clutching at the wet bulge of her cunt in helpless, shame-filled ecstasy.

Peter realised that the two girls had probably set the whole incident up, but it no longer mattered. His cock felt as if it was about to burst, even as Tiffany swallowed one last mouthful before pushing her face forward to deliberately soil herself, Vicky's stream splashing in her face as she masturbated with ever greater urgency, screaming out her orgasm an instant before burying her face between her friend's thighs and starting to lick. Vicky let out a little grunt of surprise and pleasure, but then turned a nervous glance back towards Peter, her mouth opening in immediate exclamation.

"Why, you little degenerate!"

There was laughter in her words and Peter felt a sudden stab of shame, but he was too close to orgasm to stop. Tiffany saw too, staring with wide, dizzy eyes, her fingers still busy between her legs, her body now rocked forward to push her bottom out as if expecting rear entry. Peter thought about taking her, with his cock jammed into her—no doubt still slippery—back hole, to plug her in front of her friend. But Vicky was turning, now emboldened by her actions, her voice rich with laughter and lust as she spoke.

"Go on, now you. Open your mouth."

Peter tried to stop himself but couldn't. He sank to his knees, his mouth opening wide even as the cum began to squirt from his cock, onto the ground and down his fingers. Vicky let go, squeezing out what was left in her bladder, full into his mouth, and to his horror he found himself drinking it down as shudder after ecstatic shudder ran through his body. Vicky was laughing as he swallowed down her fluid, but when he tried to lick at her sex she pulled back, sending a last trickle down his front as she wagged a finger at him.

"Oh no you don't, you dirty little bastard. That's not for you. That's for a real man, someday. Now turn your back while Tiffs gives me what I need."

He ignored her, slumping down with piddle trickling from his lips as his orgasm slowly faded. She didn't bother to repeat her instruction, instead turning once more to Tiffany, taking her firmly by the hair and pulling her face-first into wet, wanting cunt. Tiffany responded eagerly, playing with her wet tits as she used her tongue on her friend. With that, the last doubt that the girls had decided upon this in advance evaporated from Peter's mind, except perhaps for making him accept Vicky's stream into his mouth. Yet it was impossible to resent even that humiliating detail. Despite all the shame that filled his head, as he watched his girlfriend lick another young woman to ecstasy, he began to understand something about the way Tiffany felt when she surrendered herself to him.

"The punishment is going ahead," Peter stated, "and you can watch, for a price."

"How much?" Ben Thompson demanded.

"Two quid," Peter answered, provoking immediate protests from his audience.

They had gathered in the senior common room of their house, Peter and the same six young men who had watched Tiffany spanked in the barn. To set the meeting up he'd had to wait until the junior boys were safely in bed, and with the remaining seniors at various clubs or upstairs in their bedsits Peter felt reasonably safe, allowing him to make his pitch without worrying about being disturbed.

As coincidence would have it, a handful of the St. Monica's girls had been caught smoking. With their plan now confirmed, Vicky had not hesitated to use the smoking offence as an excuse for the spanking. There would still be a monetary prize, but at least the fraudulent punishment now appeared to have some legitimacy.

"Two quid is cheap," he said. "Think about it, six beautiful girls bare to the air, front and back, and not just posing the way they do in magazines, but getting spanked. Think how they'll kick and wriggle about."

"Two pounds," Stephen Richards said, peeling two green notes from an impressively thick wad. "Come on, lads, it's got to be worth it, and think of the risks Finch is taking."

"We're taking them too," Gabriel Howard pointed out, "and not all of us can spare two quid."

"It's a once in a lifetime opportunity," Peter put in, "and there's no risk, not the way I've set it up. Still, if you haven't got the guts ..."

"I've got the guts and I've got the dough," Hunter Rackman broke in. "But if Emerald Feldkirch ain't in the line-up, I want my money back."

"She'll be there," Peter promised, accepting his money. "The Princess has been let off, unfortunately, but Emerald was the one who bought the cigarettes, so she's sure to get it, probably harder than the others. There's a girl called Katie too, a real little cracker. Believe me, I can guarantee a good show."

"And you're sure it's going to happen in the pavilion?" Clive Sumner demanded. "It seems an odd place for a punishment."

"Weird," Ben Thompson agreed. "Hannah says they usually get it right then and there, or at assembly if it's something really bad."

"Because," Peter replied, now sure of his ground after talking the scenario through with Tiffany and Vicky, "this is an informal punishment. At Monica's, the Head Girl is allowed to give spankings, but in this case she's given all the girls who got caught a choice of getting it from her or being reported to the penguins. They chose to get it from her, and she's going to do them in the pavilion so the nuns don't find out. She likes to spank too, so Tiffs tells me, which is why I'm sure she'll do them bare, and hard."

"Crazy, man," Gabriel said, shaking his head as if in disbelief.

"Girls are often crueller than boys," Peter replied, thinking that in Vicky's case that was definitely true. "So come on, who's in?"

"I'll come," Daniel Stewart stated in his usual, languid manner. "But I'll need to get to the Post Office before I can pay. I'd like to bring Dolamore-Brown as well, if that's alright? He can pay."

"Your word is good enough for me," Peter assured him, "but I don't know about Dolamore-Brown. He's a school prefect, and anyway, I want to keep this in the Grove."

"I'm a school prefect," Daniel pointed out. "He's safe."

Peter took a moment to reflect, weighing the extra two pounds against the added risk of involving somebody not in Grove House, but he had learnt to trust Daniel's judgement and quickly nodded.

"Alright, he's in."

"How about Paxton?" Ben Thompson suggested. "He owes me ten and six-pence, and I can make the rest up."

"Paxton's alright, I suppose," Peter agreed. "But that's it, or we won't all be able to see. So what, Thompson, Sumner? Are you in or out?"

Ben Thompson immediately turned to Stephen Richards, who handed over two more pound notes before his friend could even begin to speak.

"Pay it back before the end of term, that's all," Stephen told him.

"You're a sport, Richards."

"I can do it, I suppose," Clive Sumner admitted.

"Of course you can," Peter responded. "After all, think how you'd feel if you missed out. So that's eight of us?"

"Nine," a voice from the door spoke up. "I'm in."

"You weren't invited, Gardiner," Peter pointed out, addressing the newcomer.

"Get lost, Gardiner," Gabriel added as Hunter got to his feet with the clear intention of taking more direct action against the unpopular boy.

"I heard!" Gardiner squeaked desperately as the tall American took him firmly by the collar and the seat of his trousers. "I heard it all!"

"Oh no you didn't," Ben stated. "Now out!"

"Yes, I did!" Gardiner went on desperately as he was frog-marched back towards the door. "You're going to watch a load of girls from St. Monica's getting whacked on the bare. I've got to see that. Come on, don't be beastly. I've got as much right to watch as you!"

"No you haven't," Peter pointed out. "It's strictly by invitation only, and it costs two quid."

"Hold on," Daniel said, raising a hand as Hunter prepared to eject Gardiner back into the corridor. "He's a sneak. We're going to have to let him come."

"I'm not a sneak. You're the sneak, Stewart!" Gardiner exclaimed.

"Stewart's right," Clive agreed. "We can't trust him."

"Why should you trust me if you're not going to let me come?" Gardiner demanded.

"Oh alright," Peter sighed. "That's two pounds, please, and you're to stay well out of sight."

"I'm not paying," Gardiner answered. "I don't have two pounds."

"Why don't we just throw the little sneak in the river?" Hunter Rackman suggested.

"Because he's a sneak," Daniel pointed out.

"You just wait, Gardiner," Hunter threatened, but he'd let go and Gardiner merely stuck out his tongue in response.

Peter drew in his breath, far from happy with the sudden turn of events and desperately trying to think of a way to get rid of Gardiner. Yet there seemed to be no way out. In all the years he'd know the other young man, not only at Broadfields but at the preparatory school they'd shared, Gardiner had repeatedly used the threat of going to the authorities to get what he wanted. It was no idle threat either, as Peter had discovered to his cost years before.

"Nine of us it is then," he sighed, "and that's it, nobody else."

"I thought I said nobody else?" Peter demanded, eyeing the group of young men in front of him with rising horror.

There were at least twenty, including every single one of the seniors from Grove House and several with bad reputations, including the odious Oliver Tinknell, Gardiner's friend and a bully as well as a sneak. Yet there was nothing to be done, with the group spanking organised for that evening and the money from those he'd agreed to in his pocket. To send anybody away was courting disaster. In any case, he had no way of preventing them from following him to St. Monica's. He made to speak, intent on appealing to their common sense, but the expressions of hopeful lechery on their faces were far from encouraging.

"What are we waiting for?" Porky Jupp demanded. "Where's all the fanny you promised?"

Peter let the question hang before choosing his tone carefully. While Porky was no sneak, he had some very unpleasant ways of making his displeasure known to anybody who annoyed him. Others began to echo Porky's sentiments, and even some of Peter's friends were beginning to look doubtful, so at last he raised his hands and spoke.

"Be cool, boys. These things can't be rushed. First off, this is not a free show. I need your money, two quid each."

There was instant rebellion, some declaring the price too high, others refusing to pay at all, but those who'd already put their money down finally came to his rescue, forcing the remainder to pay up or at least give their word of honour to do so later. Peter was pretty sure they wouldn't but, with over thirty pounds in his pocket, the money was the least of his worries.

"Next up," he declared, "we have to get to St. Monica's, so follow me and be quiet."

He set off, keeping a good pace in the hope of losing at least some of his eager followers while frantically trying to work out how to allow twenty excited boys to watch the spanking without giving themselves away. The idea had been to peer in through the windows at the back but, while nine quiet, well-disciplined voyeurs might get away with it, the pack that followed him along the river bank and into the woods was anything but quiet and had all the discipline of a drunken seaside outing.

The spanking was due to start at six and he'd called for people to gather behind the science labs immediately after tea. That would leave enough time for the group to make their way to St. Monica's and get into the concealment of the woods before Vicky led her little troop of girls out from the convent. As it was, he had reached the edge of the playing fields with half-an-hour to spare and, by five minutes to the hour, eighteen of his troop had joined him. The others seemed to have gotten lost or given up, including several of those who would have represented the greatest liabilities, and it was with rising confidence that he peered out from the foliage.

"I told you so," he remarked to Daniel Stewart beside him.

"I never doubted you," Daniel answered, licking his lips in expectation.

It was a long way to the convent wall, but there was no mistaking the quality of the group of girls who'd just come out of the rear gate. All were in uniform of red tartan skirts and crisp white summer blouses, long socks and smart black shoes. Vicky was conspicuous, taller than the rest, Tiffany also, with her dark bobbed hair, bringing Peter an unexpected pang of jealousy and irritation at the thought of some of the people who would shortly be feasting their eyes on his girlfriend's naked rear.

"They look pretty cheerful, for girls who're about to get whacked," Daniel remarked.

"Spankings are pretty regular at St Monica's," Peter assured him with an attempt at bluff confidence. "I imagine they get used to it. Either that or, like Tiffs, they get to like it. Remember, getting it this way means they don't get it from the nuns."

"The nuns do them in front of assembly, sometimes," Ben Thompson sighed, his voice full of longing.

"Just as long as there's plenty of fanny on show, right?" Porky Jupp remarked.

"All you could possibly want," Peter assured him. "Now get back, or they'll see us."

They retreated a little way into the wood, Daniel and Hunter having to pull Porky Jupp back by force to stop him giving himself away as the girls approached. Peter's gaze remained fixed, and he found himself growing ever more excited as the girls drew near, no less delighted then his friends by the thought of so much nubile flesh put unwittingly on display. Even Porky went quiet, his mouth slightly open as he took in the display of bare thighs and jutting impudent breasts beneath white cotton blouses. From such a beautiful procession, it was utterly impossible to decide which of the girls was the most desirable.

Tiffany herself was a strong contender for the most beautiful, and for all their intimacy the thought of seeing her stripped by Vicky helped to set his heart racing. Charlotte came next in line, as bouncy and full of life as ever, as if thoroughly looking forward to what was supposed to be a punishment, somewhat to Peter's disappointment. Alice's pretty, elfin beauty and nervous manner inspired mixed emotions: sympathy and pity for the thought of such a frail, sensitive waif having to submit to the pain and indignity of a bare bottom spanking; combined with a powerful lust for exactly the same reason. Christine was more delicate still. But even if he hadn't known her reputation, the cool arrogance with which she carried herself made him yearn to see her panties pulled from her pert little cheeks before being smacked up to a glowing pink. Emerald came next, as golden and beautiful as ever, but with her face set in a haughty scowl at the thought of what was coming to her. Last was Katie, the smallest of all and the most nervous, with her expression alternating between a sulky, rebellious pout and wide-eyed fear. Katie's neat ponytail and studious little glasses making her seem an even more incongruous recipient.

Peter waited until the last of the girls had disappeared behind the pavilion before signalling his companions forward. They came in a scrum, quiet enough but each eager for a good position at the windows, and when Peter peered inside he half expected to find the girls staring at him and his companions in shock and outrage. But his timing had been perfect and Vicky had only just reached the steps. With a last, urgent signal for the others to be quiet, he made himself as comfortable as possible and settled down to watch, praying that the girls would be too caught up with the thought of their approaching spankings to pay much attention to what was going on outside.

Vicky entered the changing area, to stand with her arms folded beneath her breasts. Tiffany followed, with a quick glance to the window, puzzlement, then shock as she made out the silhouettes of the boys and realised how many there were, but Vicky was already barking out orders.

"Line up, faces to the wall, and quickly, or you'll get extra."

The girls obeyed, some looking genuinely sorry for themselves, others playful, and in Charlotte's case openly flirtatious, sticking here tongue out at Vicky and giving her bottom a deliberate wiggle as she got into position. Peter realised that Tiffany must have told her friend what was really going on. Still, if the boys thought there was anything odd about Charlotte's attitude to being punished, none gave any hint of it, all now silent and alert.

"Now," Vicky continued once the girls were safely lined up. "This is how it works. First, you go bare. Take a safety pin and fasten your skirts up, nice and high so that your knickers show. Got that?"

As she finished she offered a handful of safety pins to Tiffany who, after a moment of hesitation, took one and lifted the back of her skirt to reveal a pair of full white cotton panties. As usual, her undergarments were so tight they seemed to have been painted onto the glorious swell of her rear cheeks. The punishment had begun and the blood was already pumping into Peter's cock as he watched his girlfriend give a shy glance over her shoulder before pinning her skirt up to leave the seat of her panties on show.

Charlotte seemed to be in a hurry to get her knickers on display, tugging her skirt up and fastening it in place to expose a cheeky, rounded bottom well packed into green gym knickers with a good deal of girlish flesh bulging out around the sides. Alice was more hesitant, biting her lip, eyes downcast. But she did as she was told, fumbling her skirt up and pinning it into place to expose her tight little bottom, nicely set off in snug fitting white panties. Christine was more confident, her expression still thoroughly self-satisfied as she casually flipped her skirt up over her panties and pinned it into place. Emerald gave the impression that she felt she ought to have been the one doing the spanking, scowling as she complied with Vicky's orders, but making just as fine and just as undignified a display of herself as the others. Only Katie made any real fuss, pausing with her skirt held up just far enough to hint at a pair of neat, panty clad cheeks before turning to speak to Vicky.

"This isn't fair, Vicky, I ..."

"Be quiet!" Vicky barked and Peter realised that Katie had been on the verge of giving the game away. "I said silence. Now do as you're told and get your skirt pinned up."

"Oh alright," Katie answered. "But I don't see why you can't just spank us, instead of being such a beast about it. It's embarrassing!"

"That's why she's making us do it, stupid," Christine put in.

"It's half the fun," Charlotte added.

"Be quiet!" Vicky shouted again. "Right, Katie,

Christine, Charlotte, for speaking out of turn you can get it with your knickers in your mouths to shut you up. You other three, get them bare and gag them."

"Not that! That's dirty!" Christine protested.

"Silence!" Vicky snapped. "Alice, do it!"

Alice obeyed with a relish that belied her shyness, and in an instant Christine's panties had been whipped off and stuffed into her mouth. Tiffany and Emerald gave Charlotte and Katie the same ignominious treatment, leaving all three girls scowling furiously over mouths plugged full with their own discarded panties, while each presented a bare, pink bottom to the room and the watching eyes of the boys.

"That's better," Vicky said, her voice now soft and cruel. "But in the interest of fairness, I think all six of you so should get the same treatment. Tiffany first."

Charlotte lost no time in ducking down to divest Tiffany of her panties, exposing her perfect bottom and making her step out of them before bunching them up and forcing them into her friend's mouth with obvious relish. Christine followed suit without having to be asked, her expression as cruel as it could possibly be for a girl with her own panties in her mouth, as she stripped Alice's bottom bare and made her eat her knickers. Katie was less forthright when it came to dispatching Emerald, waiting in hesitation even when Vicky gave her an encouraging nod. But Emerald spoke up.

"Go on then, Katie, let the wicked little bitch have her fun."

"I'll remind you of that remark while you're over my knee," Vicky remarked. "Come on, Katie, take her knickers off and in her mouth they go."

Katie made a face, but quickly ducked down, taking hold of Emerald's panties and rolling them down to expose full, golden cheeks. The American girl bent to allow the tiny garment to be removed from her feet, and the movement gave just a hint of the ample fur that protected her precious little peach. Peter swallowed hard at the sight, while a faint but rhythmic slapping noise from his left suggested that at least one of his companions had been unable to contain himself and begun to masturbate.

Emerald's panties were packed into her mouth and the girls' exposure was complete. Each of the six had her skirt pinned tightly up and her bare bottom showing as all the girls got back into line. Vicky now looked exceptionally pleased with herself and didn't seem to be in any hurry, walking up and down the line of humiliated girls before speaking once more.

"Hands on your heads, feet apart, bottoms out. That's right, good girls, push them right back. That's how the rest of you are to wait while I give you your spankings. So let me see, who's first?"

The girls' new position left them even more exposed and vulnerable than before, their bottoms not only bare but slightly spread. What little dignity they had left was now entirely dependent on the how full their cheeks were. For Emerald and Charlotte the new position made no real difference, but the twin swell of Tiffany's pussy lips now showed clearly between her thighs, while Katie was making an involuntary display of a little pink slit and the smooth lines that led up and into her gorgeous derrière. Christine's situation was worse still, with her petite cheeks parted well enough to present a fine view of her sex, and the rich down that sought to cover it. Alice, more slender still, had no modesty left to her whatsoever, with the rear view of her tight pink cunt fully exposed along with the paler knot of her anus, every fold and crevice of private, feminine flesh open for inspection to the line of ogling young men.

A groan from further down the line suggested that the display of female flesh had become too much for another of Peter's companions. He gave a quick, irritable glance to the side although in truth his own cock felt fit to burst. None of the girls took any notice, too lost in their shame and general predicament to take anything in but their exposed backsides and Vicky's smiling cruelty as she continued her inspection. Katie had begun to sob, while the tears were rolling slowly down Tiffany's face, and even Charlotte seemed less sure of herself than before. Only Emerald and Christine were making any attempt to retain their poise, but it was the American girl who broke first, tugging her now soggy panties from her mouth as she twisted around.

"You said spankings, Vicky, that's all."

Vicky gave a single, cool nod, then spoke again.

"Okay, if you're so keen, Emerald. Get your knickers back in your mouth and let's get you spanked. Over my knee, now!"

She pulled out an old, wooden chair as she spoke and quickly sat down, her knees extended to make a lap. Emerald was looking daggers as she came over, but did her best to make a good display of herself, no doubt mindful of the competition prize. Her feet were braced slightly apart on the floor, her bottom lifted high to create a perfect split peach of girl flesh with her plump, golden furred cunt on display between her thighs and the pale brown pucker of her anus winking sullenly in the evening light, while her full breasts hung heavy in her blouse and her hair created a curtain of gold around her face.

"There we are," Vicky said cheerfully. "Just the position for you, Emerald, over my knee with your bum in the air, ready for spanking. Yes, and how does it feel, Emerald, all bare and ready, knowing I'm going to spank you, to spank your naughty bare bottom in front of all your friends. What did you call me, a 'little bitch'? Well, just for that the girls can watch your spanking. Come on, all of you, take a good look and remember her like this, with her pretty golden cunt all bare and her little butt hole showing."

She'd been stroking Emerald's bottom as she spoke, using both hands and squeezing occasionally to part the full cheeks and make a yet ruder display of the tight little hole between, to which the American girl responded with a muffled sob. Vicky laughed and started to spank, her eyes glittering with cruelty and mischief as Emerald's backside began to bounce and quiver to the slaps. One of the watching men swore, and a quick glance to either side showed Peter that several were masturbating openly while most of the others were squeezing erect cocks through their trousers, and every single one of the young men had his eyes glued to the dirty glass.

Peter's own cock was an aching bar, painfully sensitive and near impossible not to touch, yet he held back, determined to watch all six of the girls take their spankings before he let himself go, but not at all sure if he'd be able to hold off for that long. Emerald's cheeks had begun to rouge nicely and she seemed to be struggling to retain her composure as the spanking continued. Soon she was crying, and she didn't seem to care about making a pretty exhibition of herself, as her face grew puffy and her bouncing bottom grew ever redder.

The five girls with their bottoms on parade were growing ever more apprehensive as the spanking became even more fervent. Emerald had begun to kick her feet up and down and squirm from side to side in an effort to avoid the slaps. She failed miserably, but succeeded in making an ever ruder and more undignified display of herself, with her now juicy cunt on open show and her butt hole squeezing and winking to the pained contractions of her full cheeks. Vicky laughed at the lewd exhibition, taking a firm grip around Emerald's waist and teasing as she spanked.

"What a baby! Imagine crying over a little spanking, a big girl like you? You're a big baby, Emerald. That's what you are, a great big cry baby. So come on, spit out your knickers and tell me what you are and I'll stop. Come on, Emerald, tell us all what a baby you are … come on, you know it's true … come on, admit it!"

Vicky had been putting every ounce of her strength

into the spanking as she spoke, sending Emerald into a kicking, writhing frenzy, with her pretty blonde hair tossing from side to side, her heavy breasts bouncing in her blouse, her thighs pumping frantically up and down and her hips squirming in every direction to show off her bare rear in a display that would have been comic were it not so arousing. Yet she fought against the final indignity, her face showing as much obstinacy as consternation and pain, only to suddenly break, spitting out her soggy panties and babbling her confession.

"Okay, okay, I'm a baby … I'm a big baby, a great big baby!"

The spanking stopped immediately but Vicky kept her grip, with her hand resting lightly across Emerald's bottom cheeks as she spoke again.

"Yes, you are. But just so that there's no doubt at all, tell us what you are again."

"I … I …" Emerald began, her voice thick with shame. "I'm a big baby," she sobbed. "A big cry baby."

"I'm glad you realise that, Emerald," Vicky went on, "and perhaps now that we all know what you are, you'll be a bit less stuck up in the future. Now then, a few more smacks and you're done."

Emerald didn't even have the will to protest, her head hung in defeat and her arse cheeks glowed as Vicky finished off the spanking. Peter even felt a little sorry for the American, especially when she was finally allowed to stand and he saw the expression of misery on her tear stained face as she reached back to rub at her blazing bottom. She'd been well spanked and made to humiliate herself, and Peter began to wonder if Vicky was running the competition in the way they'd discussed, or if she'd found some other way to make the girls submit to their degrading punishment. Despite this minor attack of conscience, his cock remained as hard as ever, while Vicky showed no sympathy as at all, awarding the snivelling Emerald a final swat across the back of her thighs as she spoke up once more.

"Up against the wall, Emerald, and keep that hot red arse bare until I'm finished. Right, that's one little brat put in her place. Who's next?"

The girls looked far from enthusiastic, exchanging worried glances from wide, moist eyes. All except Christine, who had her nose stuck in the air and an expression of haughty contempt on her face. The submissive pose of hands on head and her bare arse on show, due for spanking just like the rest, seemed to have no effect on her ego. Charlotte now looked seriously apprehensive, while Alice was so embarrassed that her face was much the same colour as Emerald's bottom. Katie had begun to snivel, with tears running from her eyes and her nose dribbling, while Tiffany was also crying but with her face working between bitter anguish and a near climatic ecstasy as she waited for Vicky's decision.

"Lottie, maybe?" Vicky said. "You seemed to think it was funny earlier, and you really need spanking, hard and often … but not just yet. Perhaps I should wipe that smug grin off Chrissie's face first? You're not so tough, Christine. But no, it will do you good to wait a bit longer. No, Katie, you're not going to get off just because you're blubbering. You get spanked like the rest, but I'll be kind. Let's get it over and done with. You're next."

Vicky had stood far back against the wall so that all Peter could see was the top of her tawny blonde curls. Her position allowed her a full view of the six bare bottomed girls, but it also left Katie an escape route. A dash for the door and she'd have disappeared into the slowly gathering dusk and, while Vicky could no doubt have outrun her, there would have been a good chance of being seen from the convent. But, to Peter's surprise, Katie stepped meekly out of the line to stand by the spanking chair until Vicky had taken her seat.

"Good girl," Vicky said gently and patted her lap.

Katie went down without protest, draping herself across

the young woman's lap, her sweetly upturned little cheeks lifted for spanking, with the tight pink slit of her cunt readily exposed. Only the slow, lewd winking of her anal star betrayed her apprehension as she was taken around the waist. Vicky's knee came up and Katie's bottom achieved an even more acute angle, with her cheeks spread wide and every wrinkle and crease of her most private apertures exposed to the gaze of the men and the women. Peter felt a flush of guilt even as his hand went to his cock, no longer able to resist his arousal and intoxicated with the anticipation of four no less beautiful girls waiting to be put in the same humiliating position.

"I'm going to be nice to you, Katie," Vicky was saying as Peter freed his cock from his fly. "Because you're being so good, but I still think you need a good spanking, and deep down I'm sure you'll agree."

There was no response, save for the slight trembling of the flesh of Katie's perfect little cheeks. Vicky stroked her bottom, not even attempting to hide the pleasure she took in the smaller girl's body. Peter began to masturbate, his eyes glued to Katie's splayed rear view, and at the same moment the spanking began. Vicky started gently, using just her fingertips to apply quick, sharp pats to Katie's bottom, one cheek at a time. Unlike Emerald, Katie made no attempt at all to hold back, and was soon kicking her feet as the slaps grew firmer. Still, she did her very best to behave as Vicky had told her too, even cramming her panties back into her mouth when they accidentally fell out.

Only when Vicky began to use her whole hand full across Katie's cheeks did the spanking really begin to take effect, with the smaller girl's legs kicking up and down or scissoring wide to display the puffy, pink wetness of her pussy. Vicky merely tightened her grip and spanked harder, easily holding Katie in place despite her ever more frantic struggles. Soon the spanked girl had completely abandoned her efforts to accept her fate. She shook her head and thumped her fists on the bare wooden floor of the pavilion, her thighs pumping desperately and spread wide open without the slightest thought for the vulgar exhibition she was making of herself. When her panties tumbled from her mouth again she left them where they'd fallen and began to howl, letting her feelings out with all the unreasoning fury of a baby in a tantrum. The spanking stopped immediately, and Katie slumped prostrate to the floor, disoriented and whimpering. Vicky's mouth curved up into a small, cruel smile before she spoke.

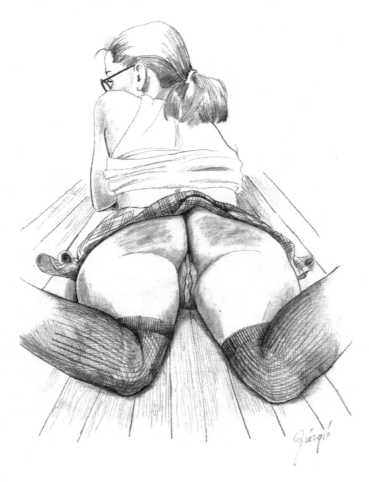

"There we are. I think that's you done, Katie. What a fuss, but then you never pretended to be anything other than what you are. So then …"

She trailed off as Katie got to her feet, red faced and tearful, clutching her hot bottom in pain as she scampered back to her position against the wall. Peter had been on the very edge of orgasm when the spanking stopped and now closed his eyes, willing himself not to come at least until the next girl had been put across Vicky's knee.

"Christine next," Vicky announced. "Come along, over my knee and get that little bare backside in the air."

Christine gave Vicky a look of pure contempt and a defiant toss of her hair as she turned from the wall. She went over Vicky's lap without the slightest hesitation, pushing her bottom up as high as it would go in a gesture of impudent bravado that also served to flaunt her proud and puffy cunt and the tiny rosebud of her arse, as perfect, feminine and virginal as Tiffany herself or anything Peter could have imagined in his most fevered fantasies. With that, he came, unable to control himself as he jerked frantically at his erection with spurt after spurt of cum erupting out against the pavilion wall and down his hand. As he rode out his orgasm, Vicky had begun to spank Christine's perfect bottom, each firm little cheek bouncing as it was slapped and the tight pink eyelet of her arse puckering to the same lewd rhythm.

Peter imagined himself taking over the spanking, with the conceited little beauty held tight over his knee and spanked until she finally broke down and crawled to him to take his cock in her mouth and suck him, her smacked bottom thrust out behind and her blouse open to show off her pert tits. Or waiting until Vicky was done and then thrusting his cock deep into Christine's warm virginity as she was held in place, spanked and deflowered and flooded with cum. Or forcing himself into the pretty pink star of her backside to sodomise her as she was punished, his cock pumping in her rectum as her arse was slapped, before stuffing his engorged penis into her mouth to add a final, filthy detail to her humiliation.

He wasn't the only one to be overcome by Christine Arlington's perfect beauty or her arrogant refusal to give in to the humiliation of taking a spanking. Beside him at the window Hunter Rackman cursed in ecstasy. Further along Gardiner groaned and fell back, clutching at Porky Jupp's jacket as he lost his balance, to tumble onto the grass of the bank, his cock still pumping fluid. Porky swore as cum spattered his leg, swung one massive fist at Gardiner's face even as Tinknell leapt onto his back, and battle commenced.

Inside the pavilion Christine twisted around, her eyes locking directly with Peter's and her mouth instantly coming wide in a scream of furious indignation quickly matched by the other girls as they realised they were being watched. Peter hurled himself backwards, yelling for his companions to get clear even as he stumbled and sat down heavily on the rough grass. Some obeyed but others ignored him, a few of the cruder souls even staying at the window to laugh at the panic stricken girls as they frantically tried to shield their private parts from lecherous, inquisitive eyes.

Screams and shouts were ringing out on every side, with Jupp, Gardiner and Tinknell still fighting on the ground as Daniel and Hunter tried to haul the last of the others away from the windows. Peter had twisted his ankle but forced himself to his feet, taking hold of Porky's collar and struggling to pull him away and break up the fight even as Christine appeared around the side of the pavilion. She hurled herself at him, swearing, spitting and scratching, so that he was forced to defend himself. Vicky arrived, hauling Christine off her feet. Peter staggered back, turned for the trees and ran, only for his ankle to give way and land him face first in the grass. He twisted over, his arms up to defend himself from the furious Christine, but she was being held clear off the ground by Vicky, with her legs kicking out so violently that she was unwittingly giving nearly as fine a display of her bare pussy as she had when she'd been over the knee. She made her feelings clear in no uncertain terms.

"I'm going to kill you, you filthy beast! I'm going to kill you if it's the last thing I do! You … you …"

Her vocabulary appeared to be unequal to the task of expression her emotions, allowing Peter to speak as his sense of guilt got the better of him.

"I'm sorry, but look, let's not get caught, ok?"

"That's exactly what I was thinking," Vicky agreed. "Come on, Chrissie, you said I could spank you and I never said there wouldn't be an audience."

Christine seemed unimpressed by Vicky's logic, still babbling invective and struggling vigorously in her captor's grip even as she was hauled back down the bank. All the boys were now gone, Porky Jupp and Oliver Tinknell still trading punches as they disappeared into the trees. Of the other girls, only Tiffany remained close. Peter went to her quickly, kissed her, bade her goodnight and retreated up the bank, turning as he reached the trees to find her already far across the playing fields. So were Vicky and Christine, close behind the others, including Katie, who still had her skirt pinned up, affording Peter a final view of bobbing girlish butt cheeks before he fled the scene.

"We want girls," Oliver Tinknell announced.

He was not a pleasant sight, tall, bulky running to fat, and with a complexion the colour and texture of suet save for where a gang of angry red pimples had erupted on each cheek. Gardiner stood beside him, smaller but no more prepossessing; with the squat, muscular Vernon Mawby further back by the door to Peter's bedsit. The moment Gardiner's long, ugly and highly unwelcome face had appeared around the door, Peter had realised the visit meant trouble and that it was sure to have something to do with what had become known as the Great St. Monica's Spanking Show.

Even after returning safely to Broadfields, Peter had been convinced that everything would come out, leading to his expulsion. For three days he'd waited for the fateful summons to the Reverend Porter. But it never came and at last he'd begun to relax, increasingly convinced that Tiffany and Vicky had somehow managed to keep what had happened a secret between those involved. The more he thought about it the more sense it made, as the girls had broken the rules by smoking *and* they'd clearly agreed to the spanking. So they'd be in serious disgrace no matter what else happened. The same was true among the boys, those who'd attended now sharing a wonderful secret that could never be divulged to an outsider. Only it now seemed that not everybody was satisfied with what they'd had.

"What do you mean, you want girls?" Peter demanded after a moment to take in Tinknell's question.

"We want girls," Tinknell repeated. "You know, some of the girls from St. Monica's."

"And what am I supposed to do about it?" Peter asked. "You saw Christine Arlington, and you heard what she said! You think I could set you up on a date with her?"

"Not a date," Mawby said, leering. "Just a bit of how-do-you-do."

"Just a bit of how-do-you-do?" Peter echoed. "What do you think I am, some sort of pimp?"

"Well, yeah," Tinknell answered. "You set it all up with Tiffany Lange, didn't you?"

"Who told you that?" Peter asked cautiously.

"Everybody knows that," Gardiner put in. "We're not stupid. Thompson's sister's at St. Monica's and she says the Head Girl's not even allowed to give spankings."

"Don't give us any more bullshit, Finch," Mawby added. "Or else you get thumped."

"Be cool," Peter answered, raising his hands as he tried to decide between risking the drop from his open window or wading in with his fists while yelling for his friends. "Okay, I set it up with Tiffs, but that doesn't mean the other girls will do as I tell them. They didn't even know we were watching, and they weren't exactly happy about it either, where they?"

"That's not our problem," Tinknell answered.

"Come on boys, I'd love to help," Peter lied. "But there's nothing I can do, and anyway, don't you think we ought to lie low for a bit, after what happened?"

"We want girls," Tinknell insisted.

"And if you don't get them for us, you get thumped," Mawby reiterated.

"I want that Katie Vale," Gardiner put in. "She's pretty."

"Lottie Mayfield," Mawby said. "She's got the best tits."

"Alice Shelley," Tinknell finished. "She's like a little doll."

"Jesus wept," Peter despaired. "I can't do that. You must know I can't do that! Okay, Alice and Lottie are close with Tiffs, so maybe, just maybe, they'd be okay about being introduced to my friends, but not you ragtag bunch!"

"What's wrong with us?" Gardiner demanded as he

contemplated the yield of a nasal extraction on one ink stained finger.

"Yeah," Mawby put in. "Girls like men with a bit of beef, like John Wayne. And anyway, you owe us, me most of all. I didn't even get to watch the smackings."

"You got lost in the woods," Peter pointed out. "That's hardly my fault, and I definitely don't owe you, Gardiner, or you, Tinknell."

"Yes you do," Gardiner answered him. "We paid to watch six girls spanked and only three of them got it, two really."

"You didn't pay anything!" Peter retorted.

"That's not the point. You promised we could watch six girls get punishment spankings, proper punishment spanking so they really howled …"

"They did howl!"

"I mean really howl, and we only got to see three, and it was a fix. That means you owe us, and if they're dirty enough to agree to get it bare in front of a load of boys, then they're dirty enough for a little extracurricular."

"Yeah," Mawby agreed.

"Yeah," Tinknell added, "and if we don't get any, you get thumped."

Peter drew in his breath, struggling for an answer, but before he could decide on what to say, two faces appeared in the doorway beyond Mawby—Stephen Richards and Hunter Rackman. Neither measured up to Tinknell or Mawby in sheer bulk, but both were tall and strong, while Hunter's reputation for dirty, vicious fighting was enough to make the largest of opponents think twice. Peter rallied, speaking first to his friends, then to the others.

"It's alright, boys. They were just leaving. Look, you idiots, if you want sex with a girl you have to sweet talk her, seduce her, you know, make her want it too. That or you have to pay for it. I can't do what you're asking, even if I wanted to, so just fuck off."

Tinknell's face had begun to go dark with anger and he'd bunched one massive fist, only to turn away.

"We're not done," he threatened as the three made for the door.

Peter stood at the landing window in the top passage of Grove House, looking out over the woods and fields. Five days had passed since the Great St. Monica's Spanking Show and still nothing had happened. He was growing increasingly restless and desperate to see Tiffany. The two expeditions he'd made to the old railway cutting had proved fruitless, while approaching the playing fields through the woods had been more frustrating still. She'd been there, playing hockey in her white blouse and the barely-there shorts that displayed every contour and lovely bulge to perfection, but there had been too many nuns around for him to dare an approach.

The only news of any kind had come via Ben Thompson's sister when their parents took the two of them out at the weekend, and that was a mixed blessing. It turned out that Thompson's sister was close friends with Katie Vale, who'd told her about the spanking. This meant that the secret was spreading through St. Monica's, but so far had not reached the nuns. Ben had also learned that the spanking hadn't really been a punishment, but Peter had refused to back down, insisting that the show, regardless of its inception, had been well worth the money. His friends had backed him up and the thirty pounds remained carefully hidden in his room, all his, save for what he owed to Tiffany and Vicky Trent. One way or another, he had to get into St. Monica's to see Tiffany, and with the end of term fast approaching it looked as if another nocturnal expedition was the only option.

"Finch?" Daniel Stewart asked as he came up the stairs behind Peter. "What are you doing in Top Corridor?"

"Staring out of the window," Peter stated flatly. "Any

news? Did Porter say anything at the school prefects' meeting?"

"No. He was ragging us about litter. We're safe. Nobody can say anything without giving the game away, girls or boys."

"That's what I keep trying to tell myself, but I've got to see Tiffs."

Daniel was about to reply but went quiet as Gardiner appeared on the stairs, throwing Peter a malicious and oddly triumphant sidelong glance as he passed. Worried for his money, Peter hurried down to his bedsit. There was no sign that his hiding place had been disturbed, but he'd definitely had a visitor and almost certainly Gardiner. On his bed lay the crushed and desiccated corpse of a rat and beside it was a note made of letters cut and pasted from a newspaper—"We get what we want, or Porter gets a letter".

"How are you going to prove it, idiots," Peter muttered to himself, but a sick feeling had begun to well up in his stomach.

Gardiner, Tinknell and Mawby were certainly capable of sending an anonymous letter to the Headmaster, and such an outrageous claim would surely be investigated. Rev. Porter would go to St. Monica's to talk to the Mother Superior, who in turn would talk to the girls. Peter was sure Tiffany could handle interrogation, and most of the others, except perhaps Alice and Katie. But other girls now knew, making it ever more likely that it would all be uncovered. Disaster would follow, and yet what his three schoolmates were asking was impossible. Clearly Tiffany needed to be warned, making a visit all the more urgent.

Evening prep seemed to last forever, and the recreation period longer still, but finally Broadfields had grown dark and quiet, allowing Peter to steal downstairs and out into the moonlit night. Following the familiar route down to the river and up the valley, he twice stopped at unexpected sounds, a prickling sensation on the back of his neck as he stood listening to the night, once thinking he could hear distant laughter. Always he pushed on, chiding himself for night fears and before long he was once more where the woods gave way to St. Monica's playing fields, faced with the challenge of breaking into the convent for a second time.

As before, it took a moment of reflection on his Uncle Charles' heroics before he found the courage to slip on his nun's outfit and make for the convent. Luck seemed to be on his side, at least at first. Nobody was in the laundry, but he'd soon gotten a window open and climbed inside to where the passages and stairways were empty and silent. In just minutes he was at Tiffany's door, but when he pushed it open he found her bed lying empty under pale moonlight streaming in between half open curtains.

His first thought was that she'd merely gone to the bathroom, but a minute passed, and a second with no sound but the occasional creak of a bedspring and, once, a gentle sigh from the room opposite. Peering close, he read the label on the door, *Shelley, A.*, making him wonder if Tiffany was with her friend and, if so, what they might be up to. Half excited, half guilty, he eased the door open, his eyes growing wide as he took in the dimly lit scene within.

On a bed just off to the side were two girls on top of each other, stark naked, their bodies pale in the low light, Charlotte's bouncy bottom spread to Alice's face, both licking eagerly between the other's thighs, their cunts wet with juice and each other's saliva. Neither had noticed the open door, and for a long moment Peter feasted his eyes on the spectacle, watching in ever greater fascination and arousal as Alice's tongue flicked over the folds of Charlotte's cunt, then moved higher. Charlotte giggled as her friend's tongue touched her anus and twisted her head around to chide Alice for being so dirty, then froze as she saw Peter, her mischievous expression switching to guilt and horror.

"Um … I'm not a nun," he ventured, unsure what the polite thing to say would be in the circumstances. "It's me, Peter Finch. Uh … do you know where Tiffs is?"

Alice had seen him too and with that the girls came to life, twisting around and burrowing in under the covers, even their heads concealed as Charlotte answered him, her voice painfully embarrassed.

"She's with Vicky, at the top of the next staircase. Now go away."

"Of course, sorry," Peter replied and withdrew.

His heart was hammering in his chest and his cock was rock hard, while the image of the pretty, delicate Alice with her tongue extended to lick her friend's bottom burnt in his brain. More urgent to get to Tiffany than ever and praying that Vicky's presence wouldn't be a problem, he quickly made his way down one stairway and up the next, eventually reaching a tiny landing with a single door marked *Trent, V. – Head Girl.* He could hear the girls talking within, their voices hushed and excited. Deciding against a tactful knock, he eased the door open, to find Tiffany and Vicky seated side by side on the bed. They still had their nighties on, but their faces were scarcely less horror struck than those of Alice and Charlotte. Tiffany recovered first.

"Peter! I thought you were a penguin!"

"I'm not," he assured her. "Only dressed as one."

"If you ever, ever do that again I am going to kill you," Vicky promised.

"Fair enough," Peter agreed. "Sorry about that, but I had to come and it's the best way to get in. Maybe this will make up for the shock?"

He'd reached in under his habit to extract fifteen one pound notes from his trouser pocket. She accepted them eagerly and hid them away beneath her mattress as Peter bent to kiss Tiffany. Her response was as warm and yielding as ever, to his great relief after what had happened at the pavilion. But when he let his hand stray to the curve of one pert breast, Vicky gave a dismissive cough.

"You can do that later, you dirty little boy. What I want

to know is, how come there were so many of you at the pavilion? We said seven and there must have been ... well, fifteen if you've paid me fairly."

"Eighteen," Peter told her. "Nineteen if you count me. There were some freeloaders. Sorry about that. It all got a bit out of hand, unfortunately. What about at your end? Are we safe?"

"Safe enough," Vicky assured him. "It's got out around the girls a bit, but nobody's going to tell the penguins. How can they prove it anyway? I'd just deny it and they'd be the ones who ended up in trouble."

"Good," Peter sighed. "It was a great show. You were ace. I'm only sorry you didn't get to finish. Oh, and how did the competition work?"

"I changed that," Vicky told him as he and Tiffany cuddled up together on the bed. "I couldn't think of a way to make it a competition without giving the game away, but it was a real spanking."

"I gathered that. The fuss Emerald made! Did you just punish them then? Hannah Thompson said that wasn't allowed."

"It's not, but they know I like to spank, and they are the prettiest girls, so they weren't at all surprised. You see, as Head Girl I get to recommend who ought to be made a prefect, so I said I wouldn't put anybody's name forward unless they took a spanking. That got Emerald and Christine's attention. Plus, it was Emerald who I caught smoking, so she had the most to lose."

"I told Lottie," Tiffany put in, "and she even knew you'd be watching. Then we talked Alice into it too. They really quite like having their bottoms smacked."

"Oh ... fair enough. They told me how to get here, by the way. I walked in on them at rather an embarrassing moment, I'm afraid. And what about Katie?"

"She was smoking with Emerald, so she knew she was in for a spanking."

"But what did you tell them about me and the others?"

"I blamed it on you," Vicky continued casually. "I said Tiffs told you about the spanking and you brought your friends along to watch, but without telling her. They still think it was for real, Christine, Emerald and Katie anyway. It's you they're angry with, and Tiffs. She got it from both of them, over their knees with hairbrushes and a handle up her bum to finish her off, but …"

She stopped at a sound from beyond the door. Tiffany rolled beneath the bed as Peter threw himself behind the curtains to stand stock still against the window as a knock sounded, firm but very gentle. Sure that a nun would have been more assertive and probably spoken too, Peter relaxed a little but stayed where he was as Vicky spoke.

"Who's that? Come in, silly … Ayanna?"

Vicky was clearly surprised by the identity of her visitor, as was Peter. Peering cautiously out from a crack in the drapes, he saw the Indian girl making her way into the room. She was in pyjamas of pale blue silk, loose on her slender figure save where her small, pointed breasts and little round bottom pushed out the fabric, while her hair hung to her ankles in a curtain of midnight black. Her face showed a reserved, haughty expression, but the corner of her mouth twitched oddly, as if in extreme embarrassment and she seemed unable to speak.

"What's the matter?" Vicky asked. "Come out from under the bed will you, Tiffs?"

Tiffany emerged, to swap shy smiles with Ayanna, who now seemed more hesitant than ever. Peter stayed as he was, not daring to move so much as a muscle but with a decent view of the room. Finally Ayanna found her voice.

"I … I want to be a prefect, Vicky."

"You could have come to see me during the day to ask that," Vicky responded.

Ayanna lifted her chin, proud and determined but now shaking visibly as she went on, her voice oddly formal and also defiant, as if she were addressing a mob.

"I understand from Emerald Feldkirch and Christine Arlington that in order for you to put our names forward you feel the need to ... to punish us first ... to spank us ... on our bottoms."

For an instant Vicky merely looked surprised, then amused, but when she replied her voice was cool and even.

"Yes, that's right."

"May I ask why?" Ayanna demanded. "It seems a very undignified test."

"That's the whole point," Vicky continued blithely. "I don't want anybody who's going to get above herself, and the way I see it, anybody who's too stuck up to take a spanking isn't fit to have authority over other girls."

"I already understand this lesson," Ayanna answered. "To rule well, one must understand what it is to be humble."

"Exactly," Vicky agreed. "So if you want me to put your name forward, I want you over my knee. I can't make any exceptions, I'm afraid, not after I've done Emerald and Christine."

Ayanna swallowed hard, then spoke again.

"I do not ask to be made an exception. I would like to be spanked on my bottom."

Vicky's eyebrows lifted in surprise, but she had quickly made a lap, speaking again as she patted one leg.

"Okay then, drop your pjs and we'll soon have you done. But I warn you, it will be a proper spanking."

"I cannot accept that," Ayanna answered. "You may spank me, but only gently, and over the seat of my pyjamas. Tiffany will stand witness."

"Chrissie and Emerald took it bare," Tiffany pointed out, her voice softly seductive. "You should too."

"I am a rani," Ayanna replied, "and the daughter of a maharajah. I should not really be spanked at all, let alone naked."

"You don't have to be naked," Tiffany put in. "Just bare bottom."

"I will still uncover what should not be seen save by my husband," Ayanna insisted. "You must spank me, but on the seat of my pyjamas, as I would be spanked in India."

"Well," Vicky said, "here in England girls are spanked on their bare bottoms. Take it or leave it."

"You may use your hairbrush," Ayanna offered, her nose now lifted high in the air, "to make my spanking more painful, but I do not go naked!"

"Oh yes you do," Vicky answered, and before Ayanna could react, her pyjama bottoms had been whipped down, baring her to Peter's delighted gaze.

Another instant and Ayanna had been turned across Vicky's knee with her little brown bottom stuck high in the air and the lips of her cunt peeping out invitingly between her thighs. The spanking began without further ceremony, Ayanna squealing with indignation as her cheeks bounced and spread, showing off all the soft and secret places she had but a moment before been pledging to a husband, with Tiffany giggling and Vicky chiding all the while.

"Princess you may be, but once you're over my knee with your bottom bare you're no better than any other little brat, are you? You squeal just the same and you kick just the same, and what a surprise, your little pussy's all wet!"

Ayanna had given a gasp of pure, unbridled outrage as Vicky's finger snuck between her thighs to test the state of her cunt. With her secret out, Ayanna lost some of her defiance, now sobbing over Vicky's lap as the spanking continued. Neither was there any doubt of the Indian girl's involuntary response, with the rich, feminine scent of her cunt thick in the air and the slick honey glistening between her legs, so much so that she'd plainly been soaking wet even before she arrived.

Vicky continued to spank, now grinning, while Tiffany began to tease, counting out the smacks as they landed across Ayanna's wriggling cheeks—ten, and twenty, and thirty—with the spanked girl's sobs growing ever more bitter, the syrup from her cunt now so copious that it spattered the tucks of her cheeks and her inner thighs, running from her slit onto Vicky's leg with every swat.

"Admit it, Ayanna," Vicky urged when Tiffany had counted out fifty smacks to Ayanna's flushed bottom. "You like it, don't you? Come on, tell me, then stick your bottom up and let's have some fun."

Still clinging to the last vestiges of her pride despite her blazing bottom and sopping wet cunt, Ayanna said something in a language Peter didn't recognise. Vicky merely laughed and continued to spank, pausing occasionally to rub at Ayanna's cunt or tickle her bottom, until finally the Indian girl broke, lifting her bottom and cocking her thighs wide to offer herself to Vicky.

"That's my girl," Vicky said happily. "There, doesn't that feel nice? Doesn't that feel right, over my knee with your bottom all bare and hot? Now come on, stick it right up high." This time there was no resistance. Ayanna's hips came up, spreading her bottom wide, advertising the opening between her cheeks, her wet cunt wide and puffy between her open thighs. Vicky continued to spank, but more gently now, and with ever more attention to Ayanna's cunt, until at last she spoke to Tiffany.

"You bring her off. I'll do the spanking."

Tiffany complied immediately, extending one knuckle to rub in the wetness of Ayanna's slit as the spanking carried on, firm and even across the little brown buttocks. Peter watched, still frozen and very sure his emergence from behind the curtain would not be welcome, for all that Vicky obviously realised he was watching and seemed to be enjoying making an exhibition of Ayanna's naked rear and helpless arousal.

So was Tiffany, leaning closer to deliberately spread Ayanna's pussy lips wide, showing off the wet, bright pink inside and the taut arc of flesh that sealed her vagina. Vicky gave a sharp tut as she saw Tiffany's crass display of their subject. The sound was half-mocking and half-chiding, but Vicky continued to spank the wriggling girl, until at last their rude treatment had its intended effect and Ayanna came, crying out in ecstasy and squirming her bottom and cunt against her tormentors' hands as they brought her to orgasm.

The moment she was done she collapsed, lying limp over Vicky's knee in a flood of tears, her body now shaking with sobs, although she made no effort to cover herself up, with her bottom still spread and her lowered pyjamas taut between her open thighs. Vicky reached down, to lift Ayanna into her arms, cuddling her close as she slipped one heavy breast from her nightie, offering the engorged nipple to the Indian girl's mouth. Ayanna began to suckle immediately, the tears still streaming down her face but her eyes closed in transcending bliss.

Soundlessly, Vicky made an urgent gesture toward the door, signalling that Tiffany and Peter should leave. He hesitated, sure Ayanna would notice, but her eyes remained closed and she had begun to nuzzle at Vicky's breast as if she was feeding from her mother, an act so intimate he felt too guilty to watch. A few quick steps and he was through the door and on the landing beside Tiffany. She closed the door and took him in her arms, kissing with open passion as her hands fumbled for his cock.

Peter responded, unable to hold back. His cock had been achingly erect since he'd first laid eyes on Alice and Charlotte, and he'd grown harder still as he'd watched Ayanna's spanking, so much so that he was sure he would cum the moment Tiffany touched him. She was no better, fumbling his habit up and wrenching his zip down as she sank to her knees, freeing his cock straight into her mouth. He gasped, his teeth gritted against the ecstasy as she sucked and licked at his erection and at his balls, right on the edge of orgasm and happy to give Tiffany a mouthful of spunk when she suddenly pulled back, babbling at him as she jerked her nightie up over her breasts.

"Do it now, Peter. Take me, fuck me, use me like the little whore you've made me. Take my virginity, Peter, take it now."

He didn't need telling twice, neither willing nor able to hold himself back as he tore her nightie off over her head and jammed her entire body against the wall. She gasped as her thighs came up and open, her arms went around his neck and she was clinging onto him with desperate need as his cock probed for her cunt. He felt her wetness, pushed, felt the tight constriction of her hymen and pushed again, hard.

Tiffany screamed as her hymen breached, a sound of mingled pain and pleasure, despair and delight, emotions far too strong for her to think of their surroundings or the need for silence. Peter didn't care either, already coming as he thrust into her, slamming her body against the wall over and over again as his cock sank deep into her cunt with her fluids running down over his balls, then spunk too as he emptied himself into her. She screamed a second time, in animal reaction to what he'd done inside her, pushed to orgasm by the sheer power of her fucking before their mouths crushed together in a long, fierce kiss that broke only when his cock finally slipped from her freshly deflowered cunt.

They still held onto each other, lost in emotion for what they'd done but slowly coming down. The moonlight shining in at the landing window fell full on Tiffany's face, which was flushed with pleasure and a devotion he'd never seen before. He kissed her again and whispered three soft words, and as she replied in kind she'd begun to cry. Peter tried to find words, wondering if she was pregnant as his mind began to clear and wanting to tell her everything would be alright. But before he could decide what to say a voice called out from somewhere downstairs, female, harsh and pre-emptory, demanding to know what was going on.

"You have to get back!" he hissed, but the nun's heavy tread was already on the stairs. "The roof, use the roof!"

Tiffany was already scrabbling at the window catch, but even as it slid wide the light came on, illuminating a bulky figure at the top of the stairs.

"Sister?" the nun asked as she caught sight of Peter's habit, from behind as he bundled Tiffany out of the window. "What's going on? What's …"

She'd put a hand on Peter's shoulder, spinning him around to reveal his face and also his erection, still sticking up from the folds of his habit. Her mouth widened, forming a scream even as Peter lashed out blindly, his hands flailing, shoving, sending her staggering back against Vicky's door, which burst open, revealing Vicky, stark naked, helping an equally naked Ayanna out of her own window.

Peter didn't wait to admire the view, leaping over the legs of the prostrate nun and hurling himself down the stairs. Two more nuns were coming down the corridor, but he burst past them and down the next flight of stairs, and another, heedless of the shouts and screams behind him. The basement corridor was empty, the laundry also, and he barely broke stride as he crashed through the laundry room door to find himself faced with three nuns in nothing but their underwear.

Yet the window was open and he was through it in an instant, running across the playing fields as fast as he could go with screams and yells of fury and accusation ringing in his ears. Yet he knew he was clear and probably free, too fast to catch and too sure of the way back through the woods for anybody to follow. It seemed likely that Tiffany had escaped too. He knew she would never betray him, and Vicky had nothing to gain by doing so.

There would be trouble though, enquiries at the school, followed by the inevitable accusations. But that was pure routine, something he'd been through half a dozen times in his school career. Porter would call an emergency assembly, at which he would state that they already knew who had perpetrated the outrage at St. Monica's but would give the culprit a chance to come forward and confess his guilt of his own accord. Peter laughed at the simple ruse, which had first been tried on him at the tender age of eight. When suddenly he was brought up sharp, his heart seeming to jump into his mouth at the sound of a voice from the trees directly in front of him.

"What's so funny?"

"Jesus, Gardiner, don't do that!" Peter exclaimed. "What are you doing here anyway?"

"Waiting for you," Gardiner answered, stepping out onto the moonlight. "You're going to get me my girl, Katie Vale."

"Now is really not the time," Peter answered, gesturing back to the convent, which was a blaze of light, while advancing figures were visible on the playing fields. "In fact we need to go, fast."

"What's happening?" Gardiner demanded.

"I got caught, nearly," Peter answered, off guard and with his adrenalin running high. "They couldn't have seen me, not properly. But I had to push a nun over to stop my girlfriend getting caught, and ..."

"Oh yeah?" Gardiner interrupted in his nastiest voice. "So what's going to happen if I tell them it was you?"

"You wouldn't do that, not even you?" Peter demanded, stunned.

"Oh yeah?" Gardiner went on. "Maybe I wouldn't, not if I had thirty quid in my pocket and Katie Vale's juicy little titties in my hands."

"I haven't got thirty quid!" Peter answered. "Not anymore, and I keep telling you, I can't make any of the girls do anything they don't want to. Katie's hardly going to want her tits groped by an ugly troll like you, is she? Now ..."

"That'll cost you another fiver," Gardiner sneered. "And if Katie won't go for it, you'll just have to hold her down for me while I get those little titties out, and lift up that dirty little skirt she wears, and pull down her panties ..."

His voice broke off as Peter's fist connected with his nose.

◆ ◆ ◆ ◆

"Finch?" Daniel Stewart said as he poked his head around the bedsit door. "I'm afraid I have to take to you to the Reverend Porter."

"I've been expecting it," Peter sighed, rising to his feet. "Lead on Mcduff."

"Sorry," Daniel told him.

"Don't be," Peter answered. "Gardiner would have snitched on me anyway, in the end."

"I'll get even for you, Finch," Hunter Rackman promised as Peter started down the corridor between twin lines of his friends. "He's dead meat."

"I broke his nose," Peter answered. "Let it be, and if he tries to drop the rest of you in it, just deny everything. You can count on the girls."

"How about you, Finch?" Clive Sumner asked, his face a mask of worry. "You won't tell, will you, not even if they cane you? Promise me! I'll lose my place at Oxford!"

"Please," Peter interrupted, holding up a hand. "I know what's about to happen, but I am still a gentleman."

Clive extended a hand, which Peter shook, then others, until at last he had reached the top of the stairs. His friends were left behind, save for Daniel, who kept pace as they left Grove House and crossed to the Rectory. With one last wry smile from Daniel, Peter was ushered inside, to where the Reverend Porter sat behind the great mahogany desk set against one wall of his study. On the desk lay a scattering of papers; a fine, large fountain pen; a small statue of Michelangelo's David designed as a paperweight; and a thin, brown cane.

"Here I am," Peter stated. "Shall we dispense with the preliminaries? I take it I'm expelled?"

"No," the Reverend Porter. "We will not dispense with the preliminaries. Peter Finch, you are an intelligent boy, and yet in my thirty-eight years in the teaching profession I have never, never come across anybody with such utter disregard for ... for everything that matters in life. You care nothing for man, nor even for God, you lack even the most basic respect or morality, you ..."

"Broke Gardiner's nose for threatening to touch up a girl," Peter interrupted. "I'd say that showed fairly good moral judgement."

"A somewhat ironic piece of gallantry, considering your own behaviour, don't you think?" Porter demanded.

"Not at all," Peter insisted. "What I did was with the full consent of my girlfriend, while his intentions were pretty unspeakable."

"Algernon Gardiner tells a rather different story," the Headmaster replied. "A story which the evidence tends to support. You were caught fighting with him on the St. Monica's playing fields. He says he followed you in order to be sure you were visiting a girl there, which is a very serious breach of school rules, and which he intended to lay before the proper authorities in the morning. This says nothing of what happened in St. Monica's itself, which I understand is a matter for the police."

Peter merely shrugged.

"Moreover," the Headmaster went on, "as if further proof were needed of your delinquency, you arranged for six girls from St. Monica's convent to be spanked! Not only spanked, but spanked for the enjoyment of you and your perverted friends."

"Ah, but did I?" Peter queried, ready for the sally.

"You did," Porter went on. "I know you did and you know you did. I have all the evidence I need, but I am going to give you a chance to confess first."

Peter merely grinned and after a moment the Reverend Porter drew a heavy sigh.

"The truth will come out," he went on, placing a thoughtful finger on the shaft of the cane. "It always does, with a little persuasion."

"I believe a member of the Gestapo once made a similar

observation to my Uncle Charles," Peter remarked. "That didn't work either."

"There is a difference …," Porter began, only to be cut off by Peter.

"Well, yes. The Gestapo officer in question was probably one of those tall, lean Aryan types, rather than are a flatulent old toad who's likely to have a heart attack during the caning if he gets at all worked up."

"Are you threatening me?" the Headmaster demanded, his face starting to colour. "No, I will not be distracted by your nonsense. So, without further ado, I want the names of everybody who was with you the night of the spanking incident, also the name of the girls involved, and the name of the girl you were with when you broke into St. Monica's last night."

"Never," Peter replied.

"Don't play games with me, Finch. Your broke into St. Monica's convent, where you engaged in lewd acts with a girl …"

"Who's of legal age," Peter pointed out.

"How are we to know?" Porter asked with a sudden smile. "How are we to know when you won't tell us who she is?"

"Good question," Peter admitted. "But I still won't tell you."

"Very well, leaving that aside for the time being, do you deny that you assaulted a nun?"

Peter reflected for a moment, then decided that it was pointless to deny the incident.

"She was quite a big nun."

Porter's face began to colour again and his hand closed on the shaft of the cane but Peter raised a finger.

"One moment, if you please. Am I right in thinking that you intend to cane me until I give away my friends, then to expel me formally before handing me over to the police? If so, there's a fault in your logic. Why should I let you cane me if I'm to be expelled and arrested in any case? Really, I would have expected better of a scholar of your standing."

The headmaster had risen to his feet, his face now dark with risen blood, his fingers clenching and unclenching on the handle of the cane. Outside, a police car was drawing up by the curb.

"Cheerio then," Peter remarked as he sauntered from the room.

PART TWO

◆◆◆◆

London, 1989

Chapter One

Peter propped himself up against the bar and took a sip from his glass of brandy as he cast a critical and approving eye over the club. The take at the door had been good, so good that he could seriously consider giving up his job as a cab driver to concentrate on the club and party scene. Now that he was getting more people through the door he could also consider bigger premises, better equipment, hopefully building the reputation of Club S as the number one party night for fetishists in London. With that, and the regular spanking parties, he might eventually be able to give up renting and put a deposit down on a house. Meanwhile, it was a lot of fun.

Directly opposite him, fixed to one of the pillars supporting the premises' basement ceiling, was a tall St. Andrew's cross. On the cross was one of his regular girls, Michelle to her friends, Candy Doll to the rest. Her long, naturally blonde hair, petite frame and fleshy little bottom always made her a firm favourite. She was stark naked, which was fairly normal for her, her wrists secured to the arms of the cross with leather straps, and her legs kept apart by a spreader. Her luscious backside was pushed out to a flogger wielded by his House Domina, Miss Lash, otherwise known as Karen. Fairly slight in build but heightened by six inch heels, Karen was in a PVC catsuit that showed off every contour of her slender body, including a nicely rounded bottom that not even Peter was permitted to touch, let alone spank.

A crowd had collected around the two girls, mainly men but with a fair sprinkling of women, watching in amusement and arousal as Michelle's sweetly outthrust butt cheeks were slowly whipped up to a glowing red. Karen was good, using the heavy, suede-tailed flogger with skill and precision across Michelle's bottom and up between her thighs. The technique made for an

excellent show, with Michelle ensuring that each push of her
rump gave a teasing glimpse of her pretty shaved pussy and the
pink pucker of her arse.

Certainly the audience were fascinated, with one man's
cock already in his girlfriend's hand and another couple kissing as
they watched sidelong. There was more going on elsewhere: one
sweetly plump girl draped over her boyfriend's knee, her rubber

skirt turned up as she was spanked; several men knelt before more dominant women, either licking and kissing at high-heeled shoes and boots or simply grovelling for the sake of it; while in the shadows of one corner an enormously fat man who appeared to be dressed as Friar Tuck was having his cock sucked by a girl who looked for all the world to be less than half the friar's age.

Peter allowed himself a happy but complacent nod, pleased to see his guests enjoying themselves. His tastes had stayed the same since his days at Broadfields, first and foremost for pretty girls with well-turned bottoms, preferably spanked into endorphin-fuelled ecstasy before receiving his cock wherever it would provide them with the most pleasure. Yet with one club and two spanking parties every month, mere voyeurism did little more than whet his appetite, allowing his arousal to build slowly until he could take his satisfaction at leisure toward the end of the evening. He was now ready, and keen to improve his acquaintance with the delectable Michelle.

He glanced at his watch. It was just past 2am, the time at which the bar licence expired. But with a hundred people still having fun in the club it seemed foolish to close down. Outside, the streets of Putney would be quiet, with just a few late revellers heading home, while the music was only faintly audible from the door at the top of the stairs that led down to the basement. The bar manager didn't seem to care in any case, still serving drinks while simultaneously trying to admire Michelle's flayed and splayed rear. Michelle was truly in her element, her peeping pussy wet with excitement, and so very close to orgasm. She gasped and shuddered as the heavy suede thongs smacked up between her thighs to an even, purposeful rhythm.

Again Peter nodded, this time in admiration for Karen's skill with the whip, and as Michelle at last cried out in ecstasy he joined in the applause before stepping forward to give her bottom a couple of firm smacks. She was in the dreamy, satisfied state she always reached after a good whipping, especially if she'd been brought to orgasm, and correspondingly vulnerable. Peter lost no time in taking advantage. Supporting her half limp body as he and Karen unfastened the straps of the St. Andrew's Cross, he let his hands wander freely over her body. She merely purred in response, nestling against his chest and kissing at his neck, even when his finger slipped between her cheeks to tease at the mouth of her anus.

"I'll take it from here, thanks, Karen," he stated.

"Sure, have fun," Karen answered. "You'd better pick up her keys and money."

Peter picked up the small blue purse from behind the cross and Karen returned to the more casual work of whipping and tormenting those men who lacked regular playmates of their own.

"Are you going to spank me, Peter?" Michelle asked, her voice thick with arousal. "Why don't you take me into a quiet corner and spank me?"

She said the final two words with immense relish, and his cock had already began to stiffen in response to her body and the state of abandoned submission into which she'd been whipped. Lifting her, he slung her over his shoulder, making her giggle as one warm, naked buttock nestled against his cheek. The audience parted as he stepped away from the cross, with many an amused or envious glance and one or two slaps across Michelle's backside from those who knew her well enough to take the liberty.

Peter was grinning as he carried her to one of the club's numerous alcoves, his glass of brandy in hand as he used her bottom to push his way through the crowd. Quite a few people had followed, eager to watch whatever he had in mind for her, which made it all the more enjoyable as he settled himself down and turned her across his knee. She gave no resistance at all, passively accepting her fate as her arse was adjusted into spanking position and his hand settled across her hot cheeks. His cock could not help but respond, now fully hard as he anticipated dealing with her soundly before putting her on her knees to suck and slurp as she knelt on the grubby floor with her back arched and her bottom thrust out for the sake of her own humiliation and the enjoyment of the crowd. He'd been threatening to do just that to her for some time … and that time had come. He decided to tease her, to build her up gradually, knowing that his teasing would both test her willingness and elevate her feelings of shame which, like Tiffany, Michelle also seemed to relish.

"This time, Candy Doll," he chided as he began to spank her. "This time you're going to have to say thank you for your spanking in the traditional fashion. Not with a quick peck on the cheek, not with a wiggle of your juicy little arse, but by getting down on your knees and sucking my penis. Is that understood?"

Her sigh of pleasure was all the answer he needed, and as he began spanking she pushed her bottom higher still, making a thoroughly rude display of herself, her wet and ready cunt and the soft pink dimple of her anus flaunted to the audience. Peter was soon ready for her to give thanks in the way he had prescribed. But he made a point of showing off, talking to the dozen or so eager watchers as he continued to spank.

"As you no doubt notice, she's an eager little slut and thoroughly enjoys a good spanking, which makes this the ideal opportunity to demonstrate a few techniques to those among you who may be less familiar with the art of chastising errant females. For instance, using just the tips of my fingers, like so, produces a sharp stinging sensation and is ideal for the first few smacks, to warm her rump before the spanking really begins. Still, as Candy's rump is already hot enough to fry an egg, firm slaps delivered with the open palm are more appropriate, especially when delivered to the juiciest part of her arse, where her cheeks tuck down to either side of her disgracefully wet cunt. Or, should you wish a particularly noisy spanking, perhaps to attract attention to her situation, you simply cup your hand, like so."

He had demonstrated each technique as he talked, while Michelle had kept her bottom high and her thighs wide, deliberately showing herself off. Most of the audience were regulars and merely grinned, familiar with the game. But one, a tall man in black leather, spoke up.

"And how much do you have to pay her to behave like that?"

There was something peculiar about his tone of voice, but Peter was enjoying himself too much to worry and pushed his concern aside as he gave an answer designed far more to amplify Michelle's predicament than to answer the question.

"Pay her? Not a penny, not today. But yes, you can pay to roast her fat little rump, if you're so inclined. Because she's a little whore as well as a slut, isn't that right, Candy?"

"Yes," Michelle sobbed, twisting around to make eye contact with the tall man. "You can spank me … sir … if you like?"

"Now there's an offer that's hard to refuse," Peter went on. "And given that you're a guest at my club I'm even prepared to postpone my blow-job for a while so that you can give this little slut a thrashing. Okay, Candy …"

"I'd rather not," the man broke in.

"Suit yourself," Peter answered and continued to spank Michelle, only a little less enthusiastically, until the man suddenly moved away through the crowd.

The others had no such qualms, pressing close, one man even extending a hand to stroke Michelle's succulent curves and the hot, reddened skin. Peter raised a cautionary finger.

"I don't think you know her, sir. In this case, it's polite to ask first. Well, Candy Doll, may the gentleman touch you?"

Michelle responded with a soft moan that both Peter and the man chose to accept as acquiescence. Peter cocked up one knee to make her more fully available and the man began to stroke her flesh. When all at once he pulled back as a sudden commotion broke out in the main body of the club—voices raised in protest or command, angry shouts, then a single clear instruction.

"This is the police. Remain where you are."

"Fuck that," Peter muttered, drained his brandy and made for the fire escape, towing Michelle behind him.

He'd always been aware of the chance of being raided. He'd paid the owners of the club in cash, never used his real name and he'd also worked out an escape strategy. The fire-escape doors led up to the street and were sure to be guarded. But they also continued up into the building above, where several small firms kept their offices. He'd also made his staff aware of this plan. But Michelle was frightened and far from prepared for a nimble escape. Only a moment ago she'd been in a post-orgasmic haze, coasting in a sub-zone of humility, spanked by numerous hands, and preparing to please her dominant partner. That, and maybe a touch too much champagne throughout the evening, meant that Michelle was more of a dazed doe than a fleet fox. On top of that, she was naked and there was no time to retrieve her clothes. Instead, Peter gave her his jacket, taking a moment to enjoy the way her reddened cheeks peeped out from beneath the hem as he hurried her up the stairs in front of him.

They'd reached the second floor before he heard the fire door slam at the bottom of the stairwell. Cursing, he hurried Michelle on and up, reaching the door to the roof with the sound of heavy boots now pounding up the stairs behind him. He thrust Michelle through the door, expecting her to keep running. To his surprise, she simply sat down on the casing of a skylight. Peter could only sigh. Together, they would never have outrun the policeman who was quickly closing on them. But it was also clear that he had next to no chance of outrunning the cop even without her. Again he cursed, as he stepped behind the door and waited. The sound of boots drew closer and stopped. The policeman reached the doorframe and stared in surprise at the naked Michelle seated before him. Taking advantage of the officer's lapse of concentration, Peter kicked out, slamming the door closed and sending the man behind it back down the stairs.

Guilt and worry hit him immediately. But the furious cursing and threats from behind the door told him that the policeman could not be too badly hurt. With his concern somewhat alleviated, Peter grabbed Michelle and hustled her away. The roof of their building was flat, as was the next, which ended with the corner of the street. Gabled roofs rose beyond, dipping gently towards the river. They made the most the most of the flat terrain, darting behind ventilation ducts and air conditioning units until they were quickly out of sight, the urgency of their flight and the cool night air having revived Michelle considerably.

Now helping each other, they crossed a series of roofs to where the fire escape from the local cinema led down to an alley, and from there they risked a dash to his car. The one-way system left him no choice but to drive past the front of the club, where police vehicles were parked and angled halfway across the street, with people milling around on the pavement and others being hustled into the back of vans.

"Bastards!" he spat. "Why can't they leave us in peace? We weren't hurting anybody."

"They hate sex," Michelle answered. "Especially kinky sex. A lot of people do."

"Only a minority," Peter insisted. "But then again it only takes one arsehole in the wrong place. Did you focus on that guy in the leather, the one who asked how much you charge? He was one of them, I'm sure of it, gathering evidence."

"So what are you going to do?"

"I don't know. Obviously we'll have to find a new venue, and not too close. But maybe we ought to take a break for a while, just in case."

"What about the spanking parties? Please don't cancel,

Peter. I've got my rent to pay, and bills, and …"

"Don't worry, we'll still have the parties."

Michelle didn't answer, but rested her head against the window, the yellow light from the street lamps flickering over her face as they drove. With her pensive expression and one small breast showing in the gap at the front of his jacket she looked pretty and vulnerable, making him feel both protective and angry. His initial guilt for kicking the door shut in the policeman's face had faded. They'd simply been enjoying themselves, a group of consenting adults indulging their private fantasies, harming nobody. From what he'd seen outside the club some of them had even been taken into custody. That number almost certainly included Karen, who never backed down to anybody and was sure to have told the police exactly what she thought.

"Oh my God, my purse!" Michelle exclaimed suddenly.

"It's in the pocket of the jacket you're wearing," Peter answered.

"Thank you," Michelle breathed, then glanced towards him. "Will you stay with me? I'm really shaken up."

"Of course," Peter promised. "I hope Karen's okay."

"So do I. Turn left here."

They'd pulled into the small, red brick complex where Michelle lived, and which Peter had visited only to drop her off after one of his monthly spanking parties. He'd had another girl with him at the time, making it impractical to explore their mutual feelings any further, but now there was no such obstacle. Michelle was shaking as he led her up to the tiny, one-bedroom flat. But she was obviously eager, kissing him as soon as they were through the door. Peter responded, easing her down onto the bed as she shrugged the jacket from her shoulders. He took one small breast in hand, stroking his thumb over her nipple, savouring the sensation as that nipple grew erect at his touch. Their kissing grew more passionate still, and her hand was already fumbling for his zip.

Michelle's legs had soon parted and Peter ached to mount her and fuck her. But she'd no sooner gotten his stiffening cock free of his trousers before she went down to take it in her mouth. He let her do it, watching the expression of bliss on her face, as if the comfort of suckling a warm, welcoming penis allowed all the cares and stress of the last hour to melt away. She was good too, using her tongue to rub on the underside of his shaft in a way that never failed to bring him to a rapid and happy climax, but that wasn't what he had in mind. Pulling her up from his cock, he made to mount her, only to have her wriggle around onto her knees, presenting him with the cleft peach of her bottom, the cheeks still red from her beatings, her cunt wet and inviting.

"Do me this way," she sighed, "the way you like to. Spank me and fuck me and … and stick it in my bottom."

That was a request Peter would happily oblige. Taking his cock in hand, he crawled into position behind her. She'd put her head down, making her arse the highest part of her body, with both openings on shameless offer and in desperate need.

Peter had enjoyed the effect his dirty talk seemed to have on her in the club, and he was more than happy to play that way again. "Cunt first, you little disgrace," he grunted as he eased his cock into her wetness, his face split by a dirty, satisfied grin as he watched it enter. "Ohh, but that is good. You ought to see yourself, with your sweet pink arse up in the air and my cock in your pussy, you dirty little bitch."

He began to fuck her, his cock squelching in the open, sopping hole of her pussy and his balls bouncing on her fingers where she'd begun to masturbate. He spanked her at the same time, slapping her cheeks to make them quiver and wobble.

"What a sight!" he laughed. "What a sight, you fat bottomed little slut! Just imagine, letting a man who's spanked you fuck you. You ought to be ashamed of yourself. But oh no, not you. You stick your butt in the air and beg to be fucked, fucked by a man who's just spanked you, spanked you in front of a roomful of leering perverts! Michelle, you dirty bitch!"

She moaned, rubbing harder at her cunt as he fucked her, and babbling indistinct words that suddenly grew clear.

"… that's right, tell me what I am! A slut, a whore, and please … please … stick it up my backside!"

"Okay," he promised, easing his cock free. "Up your bottom it goes, if you're really that dirty."

Her vagina had stayed open, dribbling its slick down over her busy fingers as she masturbated. His cock came out engorged and slippery, and he lost no time in pressing the straining head to her anus, lubricating her with her own juice as the soft little hole spread to accommodate him. She felt tight and hot inside, although he surmised he was not the first man to have his cock in that place. She accommodated easily and he was soon in deep, holding her cheeks wide to show off the taut pink ring of her stretched bottom hole as it pulled back and forth over his cock.

"How many men have fucked you like this, you little slut?" he demanded. "Go on, tell me. How many cocks have you taken into this fat little peach, Michelle? How many men have you knelt for, with your backside stuck up in the air, begging for a cock deep in your hungry little hole? How many of them have spanked you, Michelle? How many have spanked your juicy little arse before they fucked it … arse fucked you and … cum deep inside you …"

He broke off, no longer able to speak as his orgasm rose up to explode in his head. His cock pulsed and pumped hot streams of cum into her bottom, just as she screamed out his name and he realised that they'd come together.

As he awoke, Peter's senses came together only gradually, at first puzzled as to where he was, then delighted and finally triumphant as he took in the pale blonde hair of the girl asleep beside him on the pillow, followed quickly by concern and a sinking feeling as the full details of the night before came back.

It was nearly noon and he hastily swung his legs out of the bed as the possible consequences of the police raid crowded in for his attention. All they would get was the name he used for his clubs and parties, Peter Smith, unless they somehow managed to get hold of the number plate of his car, which seemed unlikely.

Nevertheless, there were going to be a lot of ruffled feathers that needed to be smoothed, and at the very least he was sure to lose a fair proportion of his paying guests. A minority were involved with the sex trade or simply free agents, but far more held respectable jobs or visited the club without their partner's knowledge. Then there were the ones he'd seen being put into the back of police vans, who were sure to blame him for their plight or at very least expect sympathy and support. Most important of all was Karen. Not only was she a friend, but she knew far more about him than anybody else who'd been there, even Michelle.

He was cursing softly as he left, saying goodbye to Michelle with a kiss on each cheek, including the two somewhat rosy ones sticking out where the cover had pulled free of her lower body. A swallow of coffee, a promise to be back as soon as he could, and he was gone, driving across South London to the Lambeth flat where Karen rented a room from another professional girl, Violet Campbell. As he parked the car he found himself glancing from side to side, but there was no sign of anybody who could be considered even remotely suspicious.

Karen herself answered the door and relief washed over him as he was invited inside. The sound of leathery smacks indicated that Violet was using the dungeon and Karen put a finger to her lips for quiet as Peter stepped inside. He nodded his understanding, then raised his eyebrows in surprise at the sound of an unmistakably feminine squeal of pain from beyond the dungeon door. Karen responded with a grin, but only when they were in the kitchen with the door closed behind them did Peter give her a kiss and finally speak up.

"Is Violet's client a woman?"

"She's training a new girl, very posh, very pretty. We were going to recommend her for the next spanking party."

"New butts are always welcome, and posh and pretty sounds like a winning combination. Anyway, I am very glad to see you. I thought you'd been arrested."

"Not me, no. Only the bar staff and that prat Master Jacobaeus, who kept mouthing off. There were two men who'd been there all along and they tried to claim I was on the staff, but I just denied it and eventually they let me go."

"Trust Jake the Peg not to know when to back down," Peter assented. "One of the men was watching me spank Michelle, just before the raid. He turned down a chance to play with her, but I thought he was just shy. What else do you know?"

"Not a lot. They made everybody sit down in little groups, with one officer standing over us while they took stuff away, all the bar takings and all the equipment, I'm afraid."

"Damn! That'll cost the earth to replace."

"You might be able to get it back, if the prosecution falls through."

"So they're going to prosecute?"

"Yes, for breach of licensing and running a disorderly house."

"Running a disorderly house!"

"Yes. The law goes right back to 1751, apparently, and can be used to prosecute anybody running any sort of event that threatens public morals. Apparently that's us."

"Just us? After all, they run swinging events there too, and a gay cross-dress club."

"I don't know. Maybe they just wanted to shut the venue down and we were unlucky?"

"Maybe, or they thought we were the easiest target."

"Very likely. They expected everybody to slink off out of embarrassment, that's for sure."

"Master Jacobaeus must have come as a bit of a shock then, and a few others, yourself included."

"I decided it was better not to make a fuss. They were out for blood, especially after somebody slammed a door in a constable's face, somebody who was trying to get away over the rooftops."

"I can't imagine who that might have been," Peter responded, trying not to grin. "Michelle and I just slipped quietly away while nobody was looking."

"I thought Michelle was with you. Did you …?"

"Did I sleep with her? Yes."

"I thought you would, in the end. She's your type, isn't she?"

"Yes, and not just because she likes to be spanked. I really like her. She reminds me of my first serious girlfriend, only a lot less mixed up. Anyway, what to do about the club? I'm not sure whether to go ahead next month."

"I think we ought to, but in a different borough, obviously."

"That might not be enough, if the police have really got it in for us. They can pick up a flyer as easily as anyone else."

"At least the spanking parties should be safe."

"I hope so, but we'll have to tighten up the vetting procedure."

"Make them take six-of-the-best before they can come," Karen grinned. "I'll do it."

"I bet you would, but you know what the old-school male spankers are like. Most of them think only girls should get it, so we'd lose three-quarters of them."

"I wasn't suggesting caning the regulars, although I would love to do some of those old bastards in front of the girls they've just spanked. Imagine Mr. Appleby, in his headmaster's outfit, with all the girls giggling at him as …"

"I'd rather not, thank you," Peter interrupted, trying

to rid his mind of the picture she'd conjured up of the elderly, corpulent Appleby being prepared for the cane. "Ah, here's Violet."

The dungeon door had opened and Violet stepped out, slimmer even than Karen and much taller, currently in a shiny ensemble of black rubber; stockings, mini-dress, long gloves and a hood that left only the pale oval of her face showing, while her long black hair had been pulled up through a hole on the top to make a high, lustrous pony-tail. Behind her was another girl, flushed and dishevelled in a half open plaid shirt and a white mini-skirt, her face lit up with a bright, shy smile. She was young, certainly no more than college age, and blessed with a fine, feminine figure than had Peter nodding in immediate appreciation.

"Put the kettle on, sweetie. I'm parched," Violet addressed Karen. "Hi Peter. This is my new pet, Sophie. Sophie, this is Master Peter."

"Delighted," Peter answered. "But you needn't worry about the Master business. I prefer sir, if anything."

"Peter runs the spanking parties I was telling you about," Violet continued. "Show him your bottom."

Sophie blushed and pouted, but quickly turned to lift the back of her skirt, showing off the seat of a pair of brief, lacy white knickers with a good deal of cheeky flesh sticking out to either side. She was very red, and showed several bruises from her beating, although her now deeply embarrassed smile suggested that she'd thoroughly enjoyed the experience.

"With your panties down," Violet instructed, now with a firm edge to her voice.

The hot blush colouring Sophie's face grew hotter still, but she did as she was told, pushing the back of her knickers down to show off her bare bottom and more bruising, along with two neatly laid tramlines where she'd been given the cane.

"Very pretty," Peter remarked, "and you can obviously

take it well."

"She'd be perfect," Violet assured him. "Come on, Sophie, stick it right out. Boys like to see a little bit of everything."

Sophie made a face but once more did as she was told, turning a little and pushing her buttocks right out, her panties now held down around the middle of her thighs. The peachy split of her cunt was beautifully framed by her thighs and succulent cheeks, while the little star between the mounds was made abashedly vulnerable.

"Very nice," Peter said, "and ever so obedient. Yes, you'd be very welcome at the next party, Sophie. I take it Violet has explained what happens?"

"Men get to spank me," Sophie answered, pulling her knickers up at a nod from Violet. "They pay and I get a share of the gate."

"Exactly," Peter answered. "You'll generally take home around two-hundred, but you can make more if you want to do one-to-ones, or photosets, even video ..."

"No, nothing like that," Sophie said quickly. "Just the spankings."

"Sophie's at college," Violet explained, "and aims to be a respectable lawyer one day, so no photos, just plenty of spanking."

"Cameras aren't allowed at the parties," Peter assured Sophie. "But I can guarantee you all the spanking you can handle. You do realise though that you don't get to choose who deals with you? I do vet the guests and we keep things under control, but they expect their money's worth."

"What sort of men do you get?" Sophie asked. She was hesitant but excited, which Peter liked to see. This dichotomy was something that Peter had long come to associate with girls who clearly enjoyed punishment and humiliation, but were still conflicted as to why.

"Businessmen, professionals, all sorts," he explained. "Nearly always middle-aged but with a few older, retired gentlemen. We get a surprisingly high proportion of teachers."

Sophie responded with a nervous nod and it was Violet who carried on.

"She'll be fine. She's just a bit nervous, but she likes a daddy figure to do the spanking and she's okay for girlie shows."

"That's always good," Peter said. "Are you going to come to the next one, Violet? And if so …"

He trailed off, leaving her to state the obvious, that if she attended she would expect to be on the receiving end.

"Yes, I know," she sighed. "I take it too, at the end, once the old bastards have had their fun with the others."

"Good girl," Peter answered. "Karen?"

"Piss off," Karen replied, joking but firm. "I do the door, as usual."

"Colonel Yates offered her three-hundred for a one-to-one," Violet remarked. "I really thought she was going to go for it, and if he wasn't such an old perv, I reckon she …"

"Shut up, Violet, or you're going to get it right now!" Karen interrupted.

"You and whose army?" Violet asked.

Peter was grinning, but took the mug of tea Karen had made and moved out of range. He was used to the girls' playful attempts to dominate each other and had always hoped the situation would escalate beyond threats to some real chastisement. It never did, but Sophie was looking interested if also a little alarmed.

"Ignore them," Peter advised. "Karen hasn't got the guts to go for it in case she loses, and Violet's not really mean enough."

"I've got the guts to take care of her, believe me," Karen laughed. "In fact I think I should, at the end of the next party. A good spanking first, then maybe queen her in front of all those men."

Violet shrugged. "Fine, as long as I can do the same to you."

"I," Karen stated, "am dominant. Pure. Dominant."

"You," Violet replied, "are lucky I believe in consent, or you'd be getting your arse tanned right now, knickers down, in front of Peter and Sophie."

Karen had begun to flush and quickly turned away, making a deliberate performance of checking the temperature of her tea. Violet allowed a smile to play over her lips for an instant, then changed the subject.

"So who have we got, Peter?"

"Michelle, of course," Peter answered. "You two, with Karen on the door, Tia and probably Davina."

"Five girls then, at least for spanking, and how many men?"

"I don't know. There was a lot of interest, but some of those who were at the club might well back out because of the raid. We'll see."

"You should include some wrestling," Sophie suggested. "That would be popular."

"Gentleman spankers are usually very specific about what they like," Peter told her. "But it might work at the club, if I ever manage to get it running again. Are you volunteering?"

"Maybe," Sophie answered. "As long as I can choose who I get to wrestle against. What did you say you were going to do to Violet, Karen? Spank her and queen her? What's queening?"

"When you sit on somebody's face," Karen answered. "Usually for a lick, but sometimes to humiliate them too."

"And you do that?" Sophie asked, her voice soft and rich with curious excitement.

"Not with men," Karen answered. "It's too intimate. With girls, maybe, in the right situation. I like to get my bum in a pretty face."

"Michelle's usually," Violet put in. "It's fun, Sophie, you should try it."

Sophie didn't answer, but her face was even redder than

when she'd been made to show off her arse, and she didn't seem to know where to look.

"Don't mind me," Peter put in. "I'm not saying I wouldn't like to watch, but I'll leave if you prefer."

"Sophie?" Violet asked gently.

Sophie responded with the faintest of nods and Peter felt his cock pulse as she did so. He was so used to the club and parties that even the dirtiest cabarets and the most revealing of spankings provided no more than a gradual arousal. But there was something special about Sophie's manner, innocent yet undeniably dirty at the same time—special *and* familiar.

"Are you a convent girl, Sophie?" he asked.

"Yes, how did you know?"

"Just a guess. So, um ... are you two going to wrestle, or just get straight to the queening?"

"I'd like to wrestle," Sophie offered.

"What if you win?" Karen asked. "Violet's supposed to be your mentor, and you're going to have trouble looking up to her once you've sat on her face."

"She's not going to win," Violet answered, "and besides, I didn't need to stand on my dignity in order to be dominant."

"Suit yourself," Karen answered, "and here's hoping you lose."

Sophie merely shrugged.

"Shall we adjourn to the living room?" Peter suggested, keen to make sure that this unexpected spectacle of female wrestling didn't stall. "I'll move the furniture."

He quickly cleared a space in the centre of the tiny living room, barely large enough for the two girls to wrestle in, let alone with spectators, but none of them seemed to mind. Karen perched herself on the sofa, her expression amused and disdainful as Violet and Sophie came to stand face to face in the clear area, while Peter stayed back in the doorway and appointed himself referee.

"No biting, no scratching, nothing vicious," he advised. "Or you go over my knee. Hair pulling is allowed and you fight to a submission. Best out of three and the winner gets to queen the loser."

"For each submission," Karen added. "That way we're more likely to see Miss Violet there get a faceful of bottom."

"At least I've got the guts to take the risk," Violet said as she and Sophie began to circle warily in the centre of the carpet.

"You love it, you dirty bitch," Karen answered.

Violet ignored the comment, her eyes fixed on Sophie's as she moved slowly sideways, then darted forward to grapple. Sophie went down with a squeak of surprise and was turned on her back in an instant, her arms pinned to her sides and Violet straddling her neck. She seemed shocked and only kicked a little before going limp, which struck Peter as a rather pathetic effort even for a girl who quite liked the idea of having her face sat on. Still, Violet had clearly won the first round.

"Do you submit?" he asked Sophie, who responded with a rueful nod.

"Then stay down," Violet said and relaxed her grip.

Sophie did as she was told, lying passive on the floor, her eyes wide and her mouth a little open. Her lower lip was trembling and she looked frightened as Violet swung her body around, to kneel astride the defeated girl's head. As she knelt, Violet lifted her bottom high, to make sure Sophie got a good view of what was about to settle onto her face. Slowly, she lifted her short rubber skirt to show off her knickers, also in black rubber and so tight across her firm little bottom that it looked as if she'd sat in a puddle of tar. Sophie swallowed and turned her head aside. But instinctively she seemed to know that was not the done thing and, almost in spite of herself, she turned back quickly as Violet began to sink down slowly, stopping with the taut rubber seat of her fetish panties just an inch or so above Violet's face.

"Kiss it," Violet demanded. "Kiss my arse."

Again Sophie swallowed, hesitant, her expression working between defiance and submission. Then she'd done it, puckering her lips to plant a single, firm kiss on the seat of Violet's black rubber knickers.

"Good girl," Violet said, and sat down.

Peter gave his cock a sneaky squeeze as Violet settled her rump onto Sophie's face. He was hard, and getting harder as he watched the beaten girl humiliated. Sophie began to squirm as Violet's rubber clad bottom smothered her face, Sophie's fingers clutching at the carpet, but still she made no real effort to escape, suffering her undignified fate in meek surrender until Peter finally spoke up.

"And that, Sophie, is a queening. Come on, round two."

Violet dismounted and the girls had quickly faced off against each other once more. This time Sophie put more effort into fighting, grappling Violet and struggling valiantly to stop herself from getting pinned down. Although it was quite obvious that she lacked her opponent's strength or skill. Despite her best efforts Sophie was soon on her back again, her face straining as she tried in vain to prevent herself from being pinned to the carpet.

"I submit," she sighed. "You're too strong for me."

"Yes," Violet said happily. "I am, and now for some real fun."

She swung around as before, tugging up her tight skirt and presenting her rubber clad bottom, allowing Sophie to admire the view for a long moment before Violet began to settle down, pushing the taut black rubber moons closer and closer until it was she more than an inch from Sophie's face. But Violet had something more in store.

"This time, Sophie, I will queen you with my naked flesh," Violet warned, her voice cruel and wanton as she begun to wriggle the tight rubber panties down over her bottom.

Sophie responded with a sob, watching in fascinated consternation as her tormentor's bottom came bare, her eyes fixed on the rounded little cheeks, on the deeply cleft slit between, and on the winking eyelet of Violet's anus. But even through worried lips, the tip of Sophie's tongue had emerged, as if she'd already resigned herself to the fact that she would be made to lick in the most intimate place, and in the most intimate way.

"Kiss my arsehole," Violet demanded.

"Dirty bitch," Karen put in, but there was as much passion in her voice as in Violet's.

"I ... I ...," Sophie began, stuttering. "Not your arsehole, Violet ... no ... oh God, I'm going to do it ..."

Her head had come up as her words broke off. Her lips puckered and she'd done it, kissing Violet's anus. As her lips pressed to the tiny, secretive aperture something inside Sophie seemed to snap. Her tongue came out and she'd begun to lick, pushing deep into the hot little circlet. Her wilful tongue, busy and keen, was a cruel irony in contrast to her screwed up face which seemed to portray very real misery and humiliation. Violet couldn't see, but she could feel, crying out in bliss and wriggling her bottom down onto Sophie's face, eager for more as she began to speak.

"Oooh, you lovely little bitch! Go on, right in ..." she gasped. "Lick me, Sophie ... give me a good, long lick. That's a good girl ..."

Sophie didn't need telling, her hands now gripping Violet's thighs, her face smothered between the round little bottom cheeks and her tongue obedient and deep. Violet responded enthusiastically, pressing all of her slick and intimate pleasure points into Sophie's face. Peter moved a little to get a better view, squeezing his cock once more and wondering if he dared take it out. The two girls didn't seem to care, lost in ecstasy and—in Sophie's case—in shame as well. Karen seemed entranced, but suddenly her eyes locked on him.

"Go on, Peter, take it out," she ordered. "Come and sit next to me."

Peter responded, not sure what she intended to do, but desperate for any feminine attention that might arise from this moment. Violet and Sophie took no notice at all as he pulled his erection free of his fly, but his eyes stayed firmly fixed upon them as he sat down beside Karen. She took hold of his cock, masturbating him in a detached, almost contemptuous manner as they watched the show. Sophie's tongue was working in the velvet softness of Violet's anus, licking, then pushing into the hole; kissing, then pushing up once more, seemingly as much for her own deliberate degradation as to give pleasure to another. Violet was no less abandoned, sitting up straight on Sophie's face, queening her in style, her head thrown back in ecstasy, her eyes closed and her mouth wide. For a long moment she gave in to her regal bliss, before suddenly bending forward.

Sophie's panties were pulled off in an instant, baring her pussy to Violet's tongue as Violet deigned to return the pleasure she'd received by settling into a beautiful sixty-nine. Each woman licked at the other, seemingly oblivious to anything else. Karen gave Peter a wicked grin and nodded to where Violet's prettily spread legs showed off her open, juicy cunt and slickened, half open anus—each as ripe and as ready for penetration as the other.

"Go on," Karen urged. "Fuck her ... she'll love it."

"I'm not ...," Peter began doubtfully, but Violet had lifted her head to utter a single, plaintive word from between sticky lips.

"Please ..."

Karen held Peter's cock as he rose, guiding him between Violet's cheeks to rub the bulbous knob in her slit and over her cunt. Sophie gave a curious choking noise, maybe resentment, maybe capitulation, but as Karen pushed Peter's cock to her mouth she took it in, sucking no less eagerly than she'd been licking Violet's cunt a moment before. Peter began to fuck her mouth, pushing deep to make her gag as his balls squashed pleasingly into her face, only for Karen to pull him free once more, putting his cock to the mouth of Violet's cunt as she spoke.

"Go on, fuck her ... fuck the dirty little slut."

Violet gave no objection and Peter pushed his cock in deep, sheathing his full length in hot, wet girl flesh with his balls still rubbing in Sophie's face as she continued to lick at the carnality surrounding her. Karen had begun to laugh, a sound cruel and indifferent as she masturbated Peter in and out of her friend's pussy. He was on the edge of orgasm and pulled back, ready to finish himself off over Violet's upturned rump, but Karen spoke up once more.

"Up her arse, Peter … stick it in her arse," she hissed.

She'd kept her grip on his cock, now pressing it to Violet's anus, which began to spread around his bulbous tip.

"You fucking bitch!" Violet spat, but she made no effort to stop them as Peter began to push, prying the head of his cock into her bottom. "You fucking little bitch, Karen!"

Karen merely laughed, now stroking whatever length of Peter's shaft wasn't buried in her friend's anus, before issuing another sharp instruction.

"Suck his balls, Sophie. Now, in your mouth. Do it, bitch!"

Sophie hesitated, but quickly gave in, opening her mouth to take in Peter's balls as he continued to fuck Violet, while Karen stroked ever faster at what little of his shaft remained exposed. Violet had begun to sob and gasp, still calling Karen a bitch, despite the fact that it was Peter who's cock violated the velvet clutch of her tunnel. Her hand went back and she masturbated as he fucked, her face dipping between Sophie's thighs so that she was licking cunt the same time. Overloaded with lust, and with the tables well and truly turned on her, Violet brought herself to orgasm in a welter of shame and degradation. The feel of her anal canal tightening on his cock was too much for Peter to bear, and he came too, emptying the sticky sap from his heavy balls deep into her rectum and holding himself there until Sophie finally cried out as she too was brought to orgasm, allowing him a final moment of triumphant reflection. For, as the heady haze of orgasm cleared, he realised that for the first time in his life he'd sodomised two girls in one day.

As he reached the centre of Westminster Bridge, Peter paused to gaze reflectively into the grey-green waters of the Thames below. A week had passed since the raid on Club S and the situation had grown increasingly awkward and frustrating. Not daring to contact the venue manager, he wasn't even sure whether or not the prosecution was going ahead, while the irascible Master Jacobaeus was trying to organise a protest march and a picket of the police station where he'd been held. Peter felt it was far more sensible to let things blow over, but Master Jacobaeus had influence and was definitely somebody to keep on side.

Otherwise things were going rather well, which made the problems with the club far easier to cope with. He'd slept with Michelle every night since the first, indulging their fantasies together in a dozen subtle variations of a similar theme, all focussed on her glorious bottom. The spanking party also looked likely to be well attended, although it was never possible to be sure exactly who was going to turn up until the night itself. With public venues temporarily out of bounds, they had decided that the next spanking party would take place that night in Violet's apartment. As the party began at 8:00pm, Peter found himself at a loose end for the afternoon.

Leaning out over the balustrade, he wondered idly what it would be like to fall in and how he would cope if he did, only to pull back at a sudden touch of vertigo. A man was approaching, short, stocky, with thinning blond hair, dressed in a well-tailored suit and a somewhat loud tie, his expression worried, perhaps thinking that Peter was about to jump from the bridge. He seemed familiar somehow.

"Ben Thompson?" Peter queried. "Surely not! It's me,

Finch."

The man paused, his expression shifting to surprise and irritation, then pleasure as recognition finally came.

"Peter Finch! So it is!"

Both paused, embarrassed, grinning at one another but unsure what to say, a silence finally broken by Peter.

"What are you doing here, and dressed for the City? I thought you'd be running the farm?"

"No, no, we sold up years ago. I'm in Whitehall."

"Congratulations. What's become of the old crowd? Do you still keep in touch?"

"Well, you know about Daniel Stewart, obviously, rising star of the House, a fixture in the cabinet and all that. Gabriel Howard's not far behind, although he nearly lost his seat in 'eighty-seven. Clive Sumner is in the Home Office, and not doing badly at all. We meet regularly, at Lorrimer's, which is about the only half-decent club left in James'. Actually, you should join us next time, see all the old faces."

"Would I be welcome?" Peter queried.

"Of course! You were one of us, after all. We'd all love to see you again. How about yourself, what have you been up to?"

"I run clubs," Peter answered, unable to admit to being a cab driver. "Although not the St. James' sort."

"Oh, yes? Lucrative, I imagine, these big rave parties?"

"No, not raves ..."

He paused, torn between discretion and a desperate need to impress the man whose life had been so much more successful than his own. Vanity won the contest in under a second.

"... rather more intimate clubs, if you follow," he continued. "It's a risky business, but a lot of fun. We were raided by the police last week."

"Raided?"

"Yes. It's a risk you run, unfortunately. They took all my equipment, everything."

"Equipment?" Ben queried.

"Oh you know, spanking stools, a pillory, my St. Andrew's Cross, the whole lot."

"Good heavens, you haven't changed, have you! Did you get arrested?"

"No. I take precautions. That's one lesson I did manage to learn at Broadfields. It was a close call though."

"Do you know why they raided you?"

"No, although my guess is there are one or two fairly senior local officers who don't like other people having fun. Of course they'll say they're trying to clean up the area, but that's what it boils down to, prudishness."

"Hard luck all the same. Will you carry on?"

"I don't give in that easily, but I may have to take a break. I only wish I knew who was behind the raid, then at least I could plan accordingly. If it was just a local decision I can probably find a venue in another borough. But if the orders came from higher up I might have to go outside London altogether. Sorry, Ben, I'm thinking aloud."

"Not at all. I have to admit I'm fascinated. Look, I'll have a quiet word with Clive next time I see him at the club. He can find out that sort of thing."

"That's very kind of you, Ben, but you mustn't take risks …"

"Not at all. I'm only too glad to be able to help you out. Besides, I was the big mouth who let it slip to that awful boy Gardiner that Head Girls at St. Monica's weren't really allowed to dish out punishment spankings."

"Ah, yes, I'd quite forgotten that, and I suppose it might have made a difference. Thank you. Do you know what became of Gardiner, by the way?"

"Yes. He went into MI5 and managed to get himself involved in one of these complicated spy capers, probably as a double agent, if rumour is to be believed. The Russians shot him, eventually."

"Sensible chaps, the Russians. In fact, that calls for a shot or two of a decent vodka. Can I tempt you?"

"Yes," Ben agreed. "Why not?"

A brief walk found them seated in the cellar bar of a quiet pub, double measures of Stolichnaya in hand as they returned to their reminiscences.

"How about the others?" Peter asked. "Richards? Rackman? I've lost touch completely, and as you can imagine I don't get invited to the reunions."

"Well, no, I don't suppose you would. Stephen Richards is out in Australia, managing one of the big, opencast mines run by his uncle's company, but then he was always going to do well. Hunter did a spell in the USAF, then went into diplomacy, if you can imagine that."

"Tact was never his strong point, but he'd certainly fly the flag for the States. None of you seem to have done badly."

"No, we're … oh, sorry. I mean to say, I don't suppose it's been easy for you? It was very gentlemanly of you not to give us all away that time, you know."

"It was a question of honour, but it wouldn't have made any real difference. The police had already been called in, so it was out of old Porter's hands. I got six months."

"I heard. Sorry. So, uh … what happened to that juicy little thing who used to like to be spanked? What a peach, eh?"

"If you mean Tiffany Lange, the whole thing came to rather a sorry end."

"Oh … frightfully sorry. I didn't mean to …"

"Not at all," Peter laughed. "It was probably for the best really. She was lovely, but her family were appalling. I'd have married her, happily, but they took her out of St. Monica's and hustled her off to some distant cousins in Ireland. That was the last I heard of her for ages, and I only knew that much because her friend Charlotte managed to get a letter out to me."

"Bad show, old chap" Ben commiserated.

"It didn't do a lot to cheer me up while I was inside, that's for sure. When I got out I managed to contact Lottie again."

"The bouncy little blonde. I remember her."

"That's Lottie. She told me Tiffany had married a man named O'Neil, an engineer of some sort I think, and was living in Dublin. I felt it best not to get involved, but I kept in touch with Lottie for a few years, until she got married in turn and decided I was too disreputable to keep as a friend, or more likely the new husband did. By then Tiffany had a daughter, Rhiannon, but that's all I know."

"I don't suppose it's much consolation," Ben replied, "but you gave us some cherished memories, especially the Great St. Monica's Spanking Show. It's good to look back, now we're all so bloody respectable. You seem to have made quite a decent life for yourself, an exciting one anyway."

"It could be worse," Peter admitted, "and no offence, but I'd hate to be in your shoes, never mind Daniel's or Gabriel's. Okay, they may be running the county in a few years, but to be under constant public scrutiny. I couldn't stand it."

"They've made their sacrifices, true," Ben admitted. "But that's life. Nostrovia!"

Both men swallowed their vodka and Ben went to the bar to fetch refills. Peter's mood had begun to mellow with the vodka and the nostalgic conversation, which Ben picked up again as soon as he'd sat down.

"That was an extraordinary show you put on for us that night," he stated, shaking his head and smiling. "Six beautiful girls, all in a line. I've never seen anything like it since."

"You must have been to cabarets, strip bars perhaps?" Peter asked.

"Very seldom," Ben replied. "Besides, it's not the same. I remember a place in Paris, with a chorus line of real beauties, twenty-four in all, dressed in the sweetest little military uniforms

PART TWO 137

you ever saw; short skirts, little tight tops. It was a fine show,
don't get me wrong. They even took off each other's knickers,
like the St. Monica's girls were made to do, and for the finalé
the whole line bent over and flipped their skirts up; twenty-four
bare bottoms all in a row, on parade, and twenty-four pretty little
pussies as an added bonus."

"Impressive," Peter admitted. "But these French places
have the budget."

"No doubt they do, but it still wasn't a patch on the St.
Monica's show. I don't know why, but it wasn't."

"I know why. It was safe. There was no thrill, no sense of
the forbidden, no sense of conquest."

Ben nodded sagely and Peter carried on.

"One of my greatest regrets is that we didn't get to see all
six girls dealt with, thanks to that idiot Gardiner, and Jupp, and
Tinknell. What a bunch of clowns!"

"They went into the army, both Tinknell and Jupp, I
think."

"Then the army has my deepest sympathy. Think what
we missed. That little brat Christine Arlington didn't even get it
properly. Once she'd been dealt with it would have been Tiffany's
turn, then Lottie, and last of all Alice. I know she would've been
left until last because she was the most embarrassed out of all the
girls, and Vicky Trent was a sadistic bitch—still is presumably."

"We saw plenty though, all six bare bums and three in
detail."

"Yes, but we missed out on the spankings."

"What is it with you and spanking!" Ben laughed.

"I seem to remember you enjoying the show I put on
with Tiffany," Peter answered.

"Oh yes, it was a glorious view. But I'd have been happy
just to see her strip, and the others. Wouldn't it have been easier
to arrange a game of strip poker, or that game where you spin a
bottle around and the loser gets a forfeit?"

"Probably not," Peter explained. "The thing you have to remember about spanking, especially with Catholic girls, is that it's a punishment. If they agree to a spanking they can tell themselves it's something they deserve for bad behaviour, atonement for their sins if you like. They don't have to admit that it turns them on, not even to themselves."

"My wife's a bit like that," Ben said after a moment to digest Peter's statement. "She always has to have an excuse, being a little tipsy usually. She can never just do it because she likes it. She'd never let me spank her though, not in a million years."

"That's a shame," Peter replied, "and her loss as much as yours. I think every woman should be able to enjoy a good spanking from time to time. Now Tiffany, at least she knew what she liked, but she was still thoroughly ashamed of herself. Christine Arlington couldn't really handle it at all, despite the fact that she was dripping like a tap, which is why she was so furious, or part of the reason in any case. We'd discovered her shameful secret, you see."

"She was a sight to be seen, no mistake!" Ben exclaimed.

"Wasn't she just! I do wish Vicky Trent had finished her off properly, the way she did Emerald, spanking her until she broke down, or not. Perhaps she'd have got turned on, the way the Princess Ayanna did ..."

Ben's eyes grew wide. "You saw the Princess Ayanna spanked!?"

"By Vicky Trent, on the fateful night. The princess needed to have her excuse too, but she ended up letting Tiffs masturbate her while she got it from Vicky. Now *that* was fine."

"I'll say!"

"You see, different girls react differently to spankings, but it always brings out the emotion in them, and that's what I like. Now Katie Vale just let herself go, an absolutely natural, uninhibited reaction to punishment. While my favourite playmate at present, Michelle, likes it to be as sexual possible. But yes, I regret that all six girls didn't get their spankings, especially Charlotte and Alice. I did catch them together in a sixty-nine, though, the night I got caught. But, for me, it's not the same without a good hearty spanking."

"You really are obsessed!"

"I admit it, freely. You should come to tonight's club, you know. There'll be five girls, every bit as beautiful as the St. Monica's girls, if rather less innocent. Michelle's an absolute poppet, small and blonde and full of life, with a bottom like a ripe peach. Or if you like 'em tall and slim there's Violet, who prefers to dish it out but usually gives in before the end of the night. And we've got Tia. She's Jamaican and a lot of fun, gorgeous too, if you like plenty of curves. Spanking her is quite a challenge. And there's Davina, who's half-Japanese and like a beautiful porcelain doll. And there's a new girl, Sophie, who seems very promising."

"You do live life to the full, I'll give you that! I couldn't possible come though, I …"

"You wouldn't be out of place. We have plenty of professional men, teachers mostly for some reason, but a couple of lawyers, a senior cardiologist, even a colonel, although he's retired."

"I was going to say that there's a bit of a fuss on at the department and I'll need to work late. In fact, I ought to get back soon."

"Suit yourself, but here's a card in case you change your mind."

"Elephant Book Club?" Ben queried, taking the card.

"Discretion is our watchword," Peter informed him, "and the Elephant and Castle is the nearest station. Do come, as my guest, no charge, and remember, you don't just get to watch, you get to spank too."

Ben's face was now a rich red, much to Peter's amusement, but he had tucked the card firmly into the inside pocket of his jacket.

"So yes, I'm obsessed," Peter continued. "But I can think of worse things to be obsessed with, and looking back I wouldn't change a thing, except possibly punching that idiot Gardiner on the nose. Prison was worth it though, just for Tiffany."

"So what got you started?" Ben asked.

"I think it was always there, deep down," Peter told him. "Do you remember when Rackman managed to sneak that porn mag in? Even then I thought it was a bit tame, and I'd seen a lot stronger. But there was one picture, one perfect picture, not even a photo, just a cartoon, of a pretty secretary laid across her boss' lap, just at the point of having her knickers pulled down for a spanking, with her face full of consternation for what was happening to her. It felt as if I'd been wired into the mains."

Ben gave a nervous laugh and swallowed the rest of his vodka. Peter followed suit, his mind now drifting back to past glories; Charlotte and Alice tangled together as they licked between each other's thighs, Vicky Trent with the beautiful Ayanna's bottom splayed across her knees, the three spanked girls in the pavilion with three more waiting their turn, but most desirable and most melancholy of all, Tiffany.

Peter relaxed back into his chair, feeling he had earned a rest after his initial efforts to get the spanking party going and a tour of the flat to make sure everybody was having fun and there were no unexpected difficulties. With the five girls and twenty-two men, every single room was in use. Karen was playing hostess, keeping drinks and nibbles replenished for those men not currently involved in any spanking. She was also looking after the money. In the dungeon, Violet was entertaining some of the more conventional spectators with a slow, sensuous striptease, although she was booked to give Sophie a one-on-one, girl-on-girl spanking at nine o'clock. Michelle was in one of the bedrooms, over one man's knee with her school skirt turned up and her big white panties tied off around her ankles to keep her legs still while he spanked her. From the doorway, a gleeful queue watched and waited their turn. The other bedroom was occupied by Tia, also in school uniform and also bare bottomed, but bent over the bed while Mr. Appleby showed off his caning technique by using her ample, dark skinned buttocks to mark out the pattern of a five bar gate in welts of an even darker hue. Even the bathroom was occupied, with three men watching while a fourth put Davina through her paces in an especially rude position, squatting naked over the toilet with her bottom thrust out as she was beaten with the bath brush.

Peter had seen it all as he went round the flat, but as he sipped at his cold beer only one spanking remained visible to him. Colonel Yates, the oldest and most hidebound of all his guests, had Sophie over his knee, as she kicked and wriggled her way through just the sort of old-fashioned, bare bottom spanking the retired army officer felt all girls should receive on a regular basis. She'd had her underwear down from the start, affording Peter an excellent view of her plump, furry cunt and the bouncing cheeks of her bottom. She looked utterly desirable, and Peter could feel his desire beginning to rise right up into his cock. So enraptured was he in Sophie's tortured euphoria that he cursed quietly when the doorbell rang and drew his attention away. Peter set down his beer and made for the door.

"Who do think that is?" Karen asked, plainly worried. "I thought everybody was in?"

"There might be one more," Peter told her. "An old friend of mine, although I didn't actually expect him to turn up. That or the police."

They exchanged anxious smiles as Peter went for the door, half expecting the officious tones of a police officer as he pressed the intercom button. Instead, he was immensely relieved to hear Ben Thompson's voice. A moment more and they were shaking hands, with Peter grinning broadly and Ben trying to look past him and into the kitchen, where Sophie now had one leg clamped beneath the Colonel's knee to control her spasms and keep her thighs spread apart. And the spanking continued, her beautiful cunt on full show.

"Come in, come in," Peter urged, trying to close the door. "I'm so glad you made it. This is Miss Lash, or Karen if you prefer, who looks after the business end of things, and the occasional naughty boy, if you get my meaning. Mr. Jones, Mr. Keats, Colonel Yates, and Sophie, to whom I'll introduce you properly once she's had her bottom dealt with. Beer, or Scotch?"

"A Scotch, please," Ben answered weakly, his eyes fixed to Sophie's naked, bouncing bottom as the Colonel continued with the spanking even as he gave Ben a curt greeting.

Sophie herself was plainly beyond caring, dangling over the Colonel's knee, her face much the same colour as her bottom, dizzy with spanking and dizzy with arousal. As the new girl, she'd been the one to go over Peter's knee as an introduction to the parties and her fresh beauty and shy but enthusiastic manner had made her an instant success. The Colonel was the fifth man to spank her and Peter had been obliged to order that no implements were to be used on her bottom until everybody had enjoyed a session with her by hand.

"Is it always like this?" Ben asked as he accepted a glass of whisky from Karen.

"More or less," Peter told him. "We're quite busy tonight, which is a pleasant surprise after the raid."

Ben gave a slow nod, his eyes still glued to Sophie's rear.

"I'll show you around," Peter offered, "and then perhaps you'd like to take a turn with Sophie?"

"Um ... I'd be delighted," Ben answered. "If that's alright? How does it work? I mean, uh ... what are we allowed to do?"

"The girls are here to be spanked," Peter explained as he eased the dungeon door open to reveal Violet dancing in nothing but stockings and high heels. "Although they have the right to refuse if they really don't want to, generally when they need a break. Anything harder, the cane or paddle and so forth, that has to be negotiated separately and generally only happens later on, otherwise the girls are out of action too soon."

"And other things?"

"We have a simple rule. You're entitled to ask for whatever suits your fancy, but the girls are entitled to refuse and you're expected to accept their decision with good grace. We're not a swinging club though, so don't expect a mass orgy. But the girls are generally happy to provide a little manual relief at the end of the evening for those who need it, and rather more for favourites. I'll show you the dungeon properly when it's less crowded, but come upstairs for now."

"She's very beautiful, the girl who was dancing naked," Ben asked as they started up the stairs. "Who is she?"

"Violet," Peter explained. "Or more usually, Miss Violet. She's Karen's flatmate." The two men reached the landing and rounded the corner into a bedroom. "Ben, this is my friend Candy Doll. Candy, meet Ben."

Michelle managed a gurgling noise in response, then looked up from her recumbent position, brushing the hair away from her face to reveal a puff of white cotton protruding from between her lips where her panties had been stuffed into her mouth. Peter nodded affably to the man who was spanking Michelle and moved on, Ben lingering for a moment to get a better look before he spoke again.

"Do you remember how Vicky Trent made the girls put their own underwear in their mouths? I suppose it was really to humiliate them."

"Of course," Peter agreed. "Although she did genuinely want to shut them up too. Humiliation is an essential ingredient of spanking, for many girls anyway. There are a hundred and one little tricks, like this one, for instance, although I grant you it's not to everybody's taste."

They had reached the bathroom door, and they watched as Davina was beaten, now with her head held over the lavatory bowl and her long dark hair twisted in one man's fist as another applied the bath brush to her bruised bottom. She'd obviously had her head flushed down the toilet once already, with what little hair wasn't caught in the man's fist dripping wet and her pretty, delicate face glistening with water.

"He's bog-washed her!" Ben exclaimed in shock. "He's bog-washed her, but she looks like she's enjoying it!"

"That's the beautiful thing about her," Peter explained as Davina's head was dunked into the toilet bowl and flushed once more. "When it comes to kink, Davina starts where we leave off."

Davina came up spluttering and dripping clear water, her eyes closed but her mouth wide in ecstasy even as the beating continued.

"It's a nuisance though," Peter remarked as he turned away. "After that she'll need a good, hard whipping and they'll probably make her come, but she'll be no good at all for the rest of the evening. I keep telling them to leave the heavy stuff for later." Peter continued on to the other bedroom. "Now here we have Mr. Appleby, who is an expert with the cane, and Tia, who can take several dozen strokes without making a fuss."

As before, Ben had lingered to gape at the scene in the bathroom, but quickly joined Peter. Tia was over the bed as before, her legs braced apart, her bottom lifted to the cane, skirt up and panties down, her flesh now decorated with a dozen rich purple welts, while her blouse had been pulled open and her bra lifted to let her heavy, dark breasts swing free. For all her exposure and the state of her bottom she was plainly enjoying herself, poised and proud, but also playful, turning to greet Peter and Ben with a broad grin.

"Keep your head down, Tia," Mr. Appleby commanded. "Did I say you could move?"

"No, sir. Sorry, sir," Tia responded, her tone pure insolence despite her contrite words.

"You will learn respect, girl," Mr. Appleby responded and brought the cane down across her bottom one more time.

Tia winced as the long, thin rod cut across the soft, fleshy cheeks of her ample derrière. Her legs bent at the knee for an instant and the only sound she made was a low moan, more pleasure than pain.

"You think you're tough, don't you?" Mr. Appleby demanded.

"Yes," Tia answered, just as the cane cut down again, catching her by surprise and striking not across her bottom but her thighs. "Ahh, you bastard! Ow! Ow! Ow! Ow! Ow! Peter, tell him not to cane my thighs!"

"Do go a little easy," Peter instructed. "It's not even nine o'clock yet."

"Sorry," Appleby responded. "But somebody has to take the starch out of the little minx, and most are a damn sight too soft on her, aren't they Tia?"

"No," Tia answered. "They're nice, unlike you, you mean pig! Six more, sir, and I'll find myself a nice, kind gentleman who'll rub in a bit of cream."

She was looking directly at Ben as she spoke, her huge brown eyes peeping out from beneath half lowered lids. He immediately began to blush and she smiled and winked, only to gasp as the cane bit in across her ample globes one more time, a stroke so hard that she was left jumping up and down on her toes for a moment before she could recover herself.

"Maybe that will teach you to flirt with other people while I'm punishing you?" Mr. Appleby demanded. "Come on, stick it out, five more."

Tia stuck her tongue out at him, a piece of insolence that

made his already plum coloured complexion grow darker still. She'd also stuck out her bottom though, and turned her body fractionally further toward Peter and Ben, allowing them an unobstructed view of her plump, dark pussy lips, split to reveal the wet, pink mouth of her vagina. Appleby's cane cut down across her cheeks one more time, making her cheeks and breasts jiggle but drawing only a faint gasp from her lips.

Ben showed no inclination to move on, and they watched together as Tia was given her last four strokes. She was obviously aroused, the syrup running freely from her cunt, and keen to make an exhibition of herself. She repeatedly looked round as if for their approval, all the while making sure that her backside was well presented to the cane. By the end she was fully on show, her feet planted wide apart, her upper body pressed down on the bed to lift her backside and make a swooping swan's neck of her back, her cunt as vulnerable as her anus, both openings squeezing slowly in response the pain of her caning.

"All yours," Appleby told Peter, apparently content with his work. "Did you say Violet was going to spank that fresh little piece Sophie?"

"At nine," Peter told him. "Why don't you get to know Tia Better, Ben? I think she'd like that."

Tia had stood, but the sudden motion combined with the high of her spanking made her dizzy. She paused, resting for a moment on a low dresser, and also taking the time to step out of the little white panties that had settled unceremoniously around her ankles. She reached back to delicate analyse her hurt flesh, but she made no effort to cover herself. Her bottom was criss-crossed with welts, but she gave no more than a slight pout as she craned around to inspect herself, and even that seemed more for Mr. Appleby's benefit than any real distress. One of the men who'd watched her beaten suggested a spanking, but she shook her head and Ben whispered to Peter.

"Do you think she'd really like some cream rubbed into

her bottom?"

"Just ask," Peter replied, and continued, speaking openly to Tia as Ben went the colour of a beetroot.

"My friend would like to make you better with a little

cream on your bottom, if that's alright?"

Tia gave Ben a single, warm glance, pursed her full lips to blow a kiss and then crawled forward onto the bed, tucking several pillows beneath her hips as she lay down. Her bare bottom was raised and exposed, her tiny school skirt still hitched up high.

"I think that's a yes," Peter told Ben. "There's cream in that jar, next to the bowl of condoms."

Ben swallowed and nodded, still hesitant, but Tia had turned to beckon him, the invitation in her eyes unmistakable.

"Don't be shy," she said. "I need my cream, and old Appleby won't do it, nor these two perverts. They just want to spank me and hurt me, but you …"

As she trailed off she lifted her bottom, showing off the wet pink mouth of her pussy once more. Ben gave another hard swallow and moved towards the bedside table where the jar of cream stood ready.

"Let's go downstairs and watch Sophie's spanking," Peter suggested to the others. "She's very shy, and it's her first time from another girl."

It was a blatant lie, as he already knew that Sophie had been having her bottom smacked by her friends for some time. But the idea obviously appealed to the men, and Ben was clearly very shy about playing with Tia in front of an audience. With the others on their way downstairs, Peter threw Ben the key to the bedroom door and pulled it shut.

Sophie's spanking had already begun, somewhat earlier than scheduled, and it was certainly popular, so much so that Peter found the only reasonable vantage point to be halfway up the stairs, where he could just about look into the living room over the heads of the audience. Violet had made the classic choice, seating herself on a plain, straight backed chair in the middle of the room with Sophie across her knee, skirt up and panties down, her bottom already flushed red as she was told what she was going to get. It was a fine sight, but nothing he hadn't already seen, and when the tall, bulky Mr. Cooper moved slightly to completely obscure the view, Peter gave up on his attempts to watch. Climbing back up the stairs he found Michelle seated on the bed, ruefully contemplating the soggy panties she'd been gagged with during her spanking.

"I don't mind them being so dirty with us," she complained as she saw Peter. "But now I have to go home without any panties!"

"Which you'll thoroughly enjoy," he answered her, "and you know perfectly well you could borrow some from Karen or Violet."

"They'd be a bit tight," Michelle pointed out, "but then you like girls in tight panties, don't you?"

"Especially you," Peter told her as he sat down on the bed. "But as these are already off, and very soggy …"

"What are you going to do?" Michelle asked as he took the panties from her hand and turned her deftly across his knee.

Peter ignored her and began to stroke her bottom with the scrap of damp white cotton in his hand. She'd taken at least four spankings over the previous two hours. She was very red … and very aroused, her cunt wet and open, and she'd allowed her thighs to drift wide without hesitation. After a while he began to spank her, just gently, and to tease, pinching her fleshy little cheeks and her nipples, tickling her clit and her arsehole, easing his fingers inside her cunt and making her suck them, until she'd begun to moan and push her hips upward in desperation.

"Patience," he chided. "I know you're a slut and I know you need fucking, or perhaps a cock in your arse, but I'm not ready yet."

"Let me suck you hard then," she offered, and would have wriggled off his lap had he not quickly tightened his grip.

"In a moment," he promised, "but you're to do it kneeling, with your bottom stuck out so that everybody who comes past can see everything, and …"

As he trailed off he had pressed her panties to the mouth of her cunt, pushing them up into the open, slippery hole. She gasped in reaction as she realised what he was doing and called him a bastard, but he took no notice, cramming the panties deep in her pussy until only a scrap of material remained free, peeping from her plugged vagina so that nobody who saw could possibly fail to realise what had been done to her.

"Now you get down on your knees," he told her, "and remember, keep that fat little arse of yours pushed right out."

Michelle scrambled down to obey, casting Peter a single, curious look on the way, something close to worship and yet deeply cut with shame. Peter merely grinned, thoroughly familiar and bemused in equal measure with the emotional complexities of submissive girls. With Michelle on her knees, he unzipped himself and fed his cock into her mouth, allowing her to suck on him in the position he'd ordained, with her bare bottom pushed out towards the open door, red cheeks flaunted, anus stretched wide and vagina gaping wider still, with the scrap of white panty cotton jutting from her, obvious to anybody who passed that she'd had her sex stuffed with her own underwear.

"Good girl," Peter said as he began to stroke her hair. "That's right, nice and slow. There's no rush, and you know where my cock's going once you've got me nice and hard, don't you? Yes, sweetie, it's going right up your fat little bottom, with your panties still in your cunt, perhaps even with an audience. How would that be, darling? How would you like to be sodomised in front of an audience?"

Michelle was looking up, wide blue eyes full of devotion and strangely innocent, considering that she had a mouthful of penis and was sucking with all the skill of a practised whore. She nodded and Peter grinned, hoping that one or two of the men would have come back upstairs in time to watch him butt fuck Michelle. He always enjoyed showing off, especially to an audience who were wishing they were in his place, and while

Michelle gave hand jobs and sucked the occasional cock willingly enough, she never gave herself to the guests for full sex. The only difficulty was holding off long enough for Violet to finish with Sophie, a performance they'd agreed would end with a queening.

He did his best, but Michelle was too good a cock sucker and her body too alluring, especially in her dishevelled schoolgirl outfit. Far sooner than he'd have liked, he was pulsing with pre-orgasmic augury, at which point she began to masturbate him as she licked his balls, a sensation so strong it had him clutching the coverlets and fighting back the urge to simply unload in her face and all over her pretty blonde hair. Finally he gave in.

"Stop it, you little slut!" he gasped, begging as much as ordering. "Right, get on the bed, arse up, now!"

Michelle was giggling as she obeyed, crawling quickly up onto the bed, reaching eagerly for the tub of soothing cream, one of which stood in every room. She got onto all fours with her knees spread wide as she reached back to lubricate herself. Peter got onto the bed behind her, nursing his erection as he watched her ease one creamy finger into her arsehole, and then a second. The meaty slaps and pained cries from downstairs suggested that Sophie was still getting her bottom smacked, and with something quite hard, but he no longer cared. As Michelle withdrew her fingers from the chute of her arse she was left gaping and slippery, a warm and welcoming embrace for his cock. He lost no time, mounting her and easing the full length of his erection into her bottom until his balls touched the flimsy material protruding from her cunt.

"That's good," he praised, as he began to sodomise her. "I can feel your panties, Michelle, tickling my balls. Yes, that's okay, you have my permission to masturbate while I arse-fuck you."

She was doing it anyway, clearly even closer to orgasm than he was, rubbing urgently at her cunt as he moved inside her.

"That's my girl," he sighed. "That's my dirty little bitch,

rubbing your sweet pussy with my cock deep inside your arse. How filthy can you get? How filthy, Michelle, with your panties stuffed into your cunt and my cock in your arse, and after so many spankings. What was it? Four men, five men? They spanked you, Michelle, with your knickers pulled down, in front of other people, and now you've got your panties in your pussy and my cock ..."

She screamed, her entire body jerking with violent contractions as she came, her anus squeezing tight on his cock. He was already on the brink and he began to drive himself in and out of her as hard and fast as he could, making her scream out over and over again. He drove into her harder still, even after she'd slumped down onto the bed, her orgasm complete, as his own orgasm welled up inside him and spilled out, filling her rectum with hot cum before he pulled free to finish himself off over the bulge of white cotton peeping from her pulsing cunt.

Chapter Three

Lorrimer's Club in St. James' was exactly the sort of environment in which Peter had expected to spend much of his life, until his disgrace and imprisonment had set him on a different course. It resembled his father's old college at Oxford, and to a lesser extent the original parts of Broadfields' College, built of buff coloured stone and dark wood, marble and brass, furnished in dark velvet and leather, heavy with antiquity and careless privilege. Old paintings decorated the walls, showing scenes of imperial grandeur and triumph, while the beadles moved with a stately deliberation and wore uniforms cut in a style well over a hundred years out of date. He had even been there before, treated to lunch by his Uncle Charles on a trip up to London as a child, and very little had changed. Standing in the lobby he felt not so much out of place as resentful.

Ben Thompson clearly felt himself very much at home, acknowledging the beadle who had announced Peter's arrival with a casual nod and extending a hand in greeting as he spoke.

"Ah, there you are, Peter. Good to see you again. We've taken a private room, more discreet. Come upstairs. Oh, and I'd be grateful if you didn't mention the other night, not in too much detail anyway."

"What did you tell them?" Peter asked, amused.

"That you invited me to a spanking party," Ben told him, "and that I came to take a look around."

A broad marble staircase led up from the lobby to a balcony from which corridors led away to either side. Peter walked slowly, looking at the paintings and illustrations that cluttered the high walls while Ben kept up a stream of inconsequential conversation until they reached the end, where a tall window looked out over Waterloo Gardens. A door stood open to one side and Peter caught the sound of voices, taking him back across the years and bringing a sudden, unexpected stab of near painful nostalgia, but he was grinning broadly as he entered.

A table had been laid for dinner, with an array of china, silver and glass centred on an arrangement of lilies. To either side sat his old friends, Daniel Stewart, Gabriel Howard and Clive Sumner, while two seats remained vacant. All were dressed in conventional black tie of considerably finer cut than Peter's own efforts, although the instant touch of chagrin he felt for his relative poverty declined as he noticed that Clive was wearing a pre-tied bow tie, while Gabriel's shirt showed the hint of a stain on one cuff.

He hadn't been at all sure how he'd be received by the others and he found himself grinning nervously as he took his seat, but the initial exchanges of conversation quickly allowed him to relax and even regain a little of the cool confidence he'd enjoyed when they were together at Broadfields. Gabriel and Clive even seemed a little in awe of him, as did Ben, while even Daniel made every effort to put him at his ease. A mild sensation of not really belonging remained, even once they had finished off a round of oysters washed down with Chablis, but it was exclusion not of an outsider or inferior, but of somebody who has set themselves apart by deeds beyond the reach of others. They were also somewhat reticent when it came to discussing his lifestyle. Eventually, after the waiters had served out cuts of rare beef and placed a magnum of claret on the table, Gabriel spoke up.

"Ben tells me you invited him to some scandalous party?"

"Yes, it was my monthly spanking party," Peter admitted with mingled pride and embarrassment. "They're great fun. You should all come."

"Not I," Daniel laughed. "Can you imagine the scandal! But that's not your regular thing, is it? You're a club promoter," Ben said, "and you got raided a while back?"

"Yes," Peter admitted, glancing towards Clive, who nodded and spoke up.

"I managed to look into that, informally of course. The raid was organised by an Inspector Lennox. He's eager for promotion and has a bee in his bonnet about vice, particularly closing down anywhere that's prepared to host sex clubs of any kind. He's also keen to identify those he considers the key players and, as he puts it, get them off the streets and into jail where they belong."

"Something tells me you might just prove to be one of those key players, Peter," Ben put in.

"I fear so," Peter admitted. "Although I can't understand why. What harm was I doing to anybody?"

"None," Clive responded. "But vice is an easy target, popular with the tabloids, full of prurient interest and relatively safe. Also, Lennox isn't just doing his job. He's a committed Christian and genuinely believes that he has a moral duty ..."

"... to stop people having fun," Gabriel broke in. "The world seems to be full of people like him, blast them."

"Thank you," Peter told Clive. "That's very valuable information."

"There's more," Clive went on. "I've done the best I can, at least without arousing suspicion. I have no direct influence on policy, but I am in a position to influence the allocation of resources, who gets to sit on senior disciplinary committees, that sort of thing. Your raid cost close on half-a-million pounds to carry out, or will do once the matter is complete. The chances of a successful prosecution are not that high, and certainly don't justify the resources, so I've been able to make sure no further action can be taken along those lines without approval at a much higher level. That's a black mark against Lennox's promotion prospects, so I think you can reasonably assume that he won't be putting a great deal of effort into finding out who you are. Nevertheless, I'd advise you to lie low for a while, or more sensibly, give up the idea completely. Surely you can make a living as a club promoter without going outside the law?"

"Possibly," Peter admitted. "But I hate to back down. How about if I promise to keep a low profile as long as I'm left alone, would that work?"

"In the 'seventies, perhaps," Clive told him. "Not nowadays, and certainly not with Lennox."

"Stand up to the grubby little bastard," Gabriel advised. "What have you got to lose?"

"I could do without another spell in jail, thank you," Peter replied. "Glorious defiance is all very well, but I prefer life with money in my pocket and a woman in my bed. Oh well, at least it looks as if the spanking parties are safe. Thank you, Clive."

"I have to say, I envy you your lifestyle," Gabriel admitted. "I can't sneeze without getting my story in the papers."

"You do project rather a flamboyant image," Daniel answered him. "But I don't suppose even you could get away with being caught at a spanking party."

"So how do they work, these parties of yours?" Clive asked, clearly intrigued.

"It's simple," Peter explained. "Men pay to attend, a couple of hundred pounds usually, with the guarantee of getting to spank at least three or four pretty girls."

"That's all, just spanking?" Gabriel queried.

"That's all I guarantee," Peter told him. "But if the mood's right, who knows?"

"I'd love to come to one," Gabriel sighed. "But I simply couldn't afford to take the risk. You're safely anonymous, Ben, and will be no matter how high you rise, because you're effectively faceless, at least as far as the great unwashed are concerned. You too, Clive. Who cares if a Whitehall mandarin gets caught with his pants down? Not the public, and therefore not the papers."

"The head of his department," Ben pointed out. "The

public may not care, but he'll still be dismissed."

"But why should he get caught?" Gabriel went on, "unless he does something spectacularly stupid. Nobody's going to recognise him, and that's where the problem lies. Even as a junior MP, or somebody just starting to climb the greasy pole of politics, you can't afford to take risks. Oh, it's fine at the time, when you're only really known within your own constituency and the girls are young and pretty and getting plenty of work. But what happens twenty years down the line? You're in the cabinet and on TV every now and again, while she's lost her looks and has nothing to lose by scooping in a few grand from some godforsaken scandal rag."

He was answered with nods and murmurs of agreement as they got on with their meal. The beef was excellent, some of the best Peter had ever tasted, while the wine was of a quality and age he'd last sampled after a daring midnight raid on the cellar of the Masters' Common Room at Broadfields. There was plenty to go around as well, putting him in a mellow mood despite the situation with the club, and making him more inclined to be creative than to wallow in self-pity. Gabriel's comments in particular intrigued him, making him wonder if it might not be possible to organise a superior and more lucrative version of the spanking club, where guests could be sure of their safety from public exposure.

"What you say is true, Gabriel," he admitted after a while, "at least with ordinary girls. But how about girls who've got something to lose themselves, university students with no money but good career prospects, for example? They're no more prim and proper than the rest, when it comes right down to it. They just can't afford to show their true feelings, any more than the men who'd like to be with them can show theirs."

"Perhaps, yes," Gabriel answered him. "But how would you get in touch with a girl like that? You can't just stroll into King's or Magdalen and start asking pretty female students if they'd like to take a spanking."

"No. They have to come to you, or to me, rather. How do you think I recruit the girls for my spanking parties?"

"I have no idea. Presumably you just ask around among the local floozies?"

"Not at all. I only take on girls who are genuinely into spanking, and I test them first."

"I bet you do!"

"I'm being serious," Peter insisted. "The last thing I want is a girl who doesn't like it. Then there's going to be all sorts of trouble. That's where my club comes in, or did, but there are other clubs too. I keep my eyes open, wait until I find a suitable candidate and ask if she'd like to earn some money for what she enjoys anyway. Most refuse, but some accept, and I put them through their paces before they come to a party. It would be harder, but not impossible, to find the sort of girl who'd guarantee discretion. In fact, I think I can honestly say that I already have one, and where there's one, more will follow."

Daniel hadn't spoken for a while, sipping thoughtfully at his wine as he listened to the others, but when he did it was with a clear, decisive voice that drew immediate attention.

"This is how to do it, purely as a theoretical exercise you understand. You, Peter, set up a small cleaning company, let's call it Grove House Maids. The company employs safe girls— and only safe girls. You charge sufficiently high fees to put off casual enquiries, but not so high as to cause suspicion. You then have a club, equally exclusively and equally discreet, members of which can hire girls as necessary. Grove House Maids then bills the club's members at the cleaning rate, which represents Peter's commission, and the girls are paid directly, in cash."

"You're right," Gabriel agreed. "If some obvious hooker turns up at your place, you're going to get spotted in no time. But send a maid around, and who's to know what she gets up to?"

"Nobody takes any notice of the hired help," Ben agreed.

"That might actually work," Peter admitted. "As long as everybody involved has more to lose by breaking their silence than by keeping it. Although the club would have to be a fair size for the operation to be financially viable, and we'd have to vet new members and new girls very carefully."

"Other old Grove House members would be acceptable," Clive put in. "Stephen Richards, when he's in the country, Hunter Rackman."

"Other Broadfields old boys for that matter," Daniel added. "James Dolamore-Brown, for instance. He's a barrister nowadays, Peter, and very high powered, a man you might want to know."

"It would be beautiful," Gabriel went on. "A poem of delectable depravity, right under the noses of all the prudes and nosey-parkers. Who knows, I might even marry one of the poppets."

"You already have a wife," Ben pointed out, "and so do the rest of us, Clive excepted, and Peter, of course."

"Marrying Marcia was a matter of political expediency," Gabriel went on. "Her father is the chairman of my local constituency party. She's as cold as an Eskimo's arse. So yes, I'd be up for the occasional visit from a Grove House girl, at the London flat, naturally, but it would have to be for more than a little spanking."

"What you buy is her time," Peter explained. "What happens between you is entirely the private decision of two consenting adults, and if you happen to give her a generous tip, that's your business."

"That argument would never stand up in court," Clive stated.

"It would never get to court, that's the whole idea," Gabriel replied, "and there is also the matter of keeping it civilised, as long as a good time is guaranteed."

"To precisely the same extent as the money is," Peter told

him. "Otherwise you just get your flat cleaned. And whatever you tell your wives, that's up to you."

"I was faithful to Laura for sixteen years," Ben stated. "Until I discovered that she'd been having regular sex with our jobbing gardener, and I always thought he was just a lazy bastard! I got my revenge by going to bed with her sister. Since then, we've tended to ignore each other's peccadilloes and just get on with life. We even have sex occasionally."

"Celia keeps me happy," Daniel put in, "and until she fails in her duties I intend to keep up with mine. Besides, I have an image to cultivate."

"I've never seen the point of monogamy," Peter went on. "It was all very well for our ancestors, I dare say, without any contraception or social security to speak of. The family unit was what allowed society to function, but nowadays? It's no more than a petty and ridiculous anachronism, like marriage, and religion, and God, all ideas that should have been consigned to the dustbin of history years ago. But we cling to such incongruities out of insecurity, because we can't face the universe as it really is."

"You're an atheist then?" Clive asked.

"An atheist and a nihilist," Peter said. "I believe that the only really valid thing in life is happiness, preferably expressed as sexual pleasure."

The return of a waiter with a second magnum of claret interrupted the conversation, which then turned to more neutral topics, with ever more reminiscences from their school days as the wine continued to flow. By the time he'd taken his share of Sauternes with the dessert, and Port with the cheese, Peter was feeling more than a little drunk and was dominating the conversation, as he had usually done at Broadfields. He also felt distinctly pleased with himself. For all their success, it was clear that he had lived a considerably more interesting and varied life than any of his friends, especially when it came to sex.

Peter awoke to a slight headache and the touch of Michelle's lips to his morning erection. He kept his eyes closed, letting his thoughts drift as she took him in her mouth, secure in the knowledge that she would suck until he came and swallow dutifully when the moment arrived. Lunch at Lorrimer's had stretched well into the afternoon, with brandy after the Port and whisky after the brandy, his friends seemingly determined to introduce him to the club's entire range of malts. By the time he left he'd been having some difficulty keeping his balance and had been very glad indeed to find Michelle still at his apartment where he'd left her that morning. She'd looked after him perfectly, uncomplaining as she made coffee, sucked him to erection and allowed him to butt fuck her over the sofa before he finally fell asleep, only to wake to the scent of cooking as she made them dinner.

"You are such a good girl," he sighed as he began to stroke her hair, something she always appreciated when she had his cock in her mouth.

Her response was to take him deep, deliberately making herself gag on his penis, something else she seemed to particularly enjoy. It was also highly effective, and forced him to concentrate on the pleasure she was giving him. Taking his balls and the base of his shaft in hand, he pushed her head down, making her choke once more before relaxing his grip. She gave an encouraging wriggle and sucked harder still, repeatedly taking him down into her throat until at last he could hold back no more.

"Okay then, if that's what you want, you little slut," he told her as he began to fuck her throat, deliberately making her splutter and glug as he jammed his cock as deep as it would go into her gullet.

His orgasm rose up in moments, a sensation far too good for him even to think about going easy on her, her now pained gulping and choking noises only adding to his pleasure as he fucked her mouth. Another moment and he'd come, emptying the contents of his balls down into her throat. She did her best to swallow but failed miserably, ejecting most of his load and a good deal of spittle from her nose and mouth, all over his balls and belly, and also his hand.

"Messy girl," he chided as she finally came up, gasping for air with her face a mask of cum, drool and tears. "Mop it up."

"Sorry, sir," she answered, quickly peeling off her panties to clean up the mess, before scampering into the bathroom with her bare bottom bobbing behind her.

He sat up in bed, still not fully awake and wishing he'd had slightly less whisky the day before, although it didn't seem to have affected his sex drive. His memory was also clear, especially of the ideas for an erotic maid service, which the five of them had worked out in ever growing and more lascivious detail as the afternoon drew on. Most of that had been wishful thinking, such as their ideas for the girls' uniforms. Most all of the designs put forward had served solely to show the girls off nicely—covering those parts of the body usually left bare and leaving bare those parts usually covered. Yet the basic idea was good, and he had left Lorrimer's determined to make it a reality.

That still seemed feasible, barring a few compromises he considered unavoidable. The way Daniel and the others had set it out, Grove House Maids and the men's club would be entirely clandestine, a secret reserved for those—both the men and the maids—who had far more to lose by giving it away than by keeping it. With the possible exception of Sophie, that didn't include any of those girls who currently came to his spanking parties, but that was not an insurmountable difficulty. He could continue to run the normal parties, after all, which might also be a way to find new Grove House girls.

Some, like Tia and Davina, would have to be kept firmly in the dark. Both were strong minded, independent and above all self-serving, happy to have their bottoms smacked on a regular basis and great fun to play with, but definitely not reliable in the long term. Violet was safer, determined to make her own way in the world and already well on her way to paying off the mortgage on her flat after starting with absolutely nothing. Yet, as Gabriel had pointed out, it was impossible to predict what might happen twenty or thirty years down the line. Karen was, if anything, safer still, level headed and quite capable of making her way in life with her qualifications in accountancy, also the ideal person to run the books for the company. Then there was Michelle, who was now running a bath at the same time as she made coffee and got breakfast underway, with never a hint of complaint. He was already more than half in love with her, and as his partner she would be safe. Again, things might change, but there was no reason for her to know everything. In fact, the whole thing would work much better if there were tiers of secrecy, from the basic level of the spanking parties to the very apex, at which only he himself would know the full truth.

He continued to think as he munched his way through the bacon and eggs provided by Michelle, his plans rapidly coming together in his head. By the time he'd mopped up the last morsel of egg with toast, he was eager to proceed and quite pleased with himself. As he took his plate out to the kitchen, he didn't realise he was singing to himself, until Michelle's voice sounded from the bathroom, asking if a confused tomcat had somehow managed to get in. When he came in she was lying back with her ears submerged, so he took hold of her ankles, tipped her up and applied a few hard smacks to her exposed bottom and cunt lips while she struggled to bring her face above the water, with bubbles blowing from both her nose and mouth.

"I'll have you know I nearly made the choir while I was at school," he told her when he'd finally let go and allowed her to surface. "My choice of song was dictated by my plan of action for this morning. I'm off to see Master Jacobaeus, aka Jake the

Peg."

"Ooh, can I come?"

"Yes, if you're prepared to put up with his eccentric behaviour."

"I'll put my collar on."

She was quickly out of the bath, allowing Peter to shower, dry himself off and dress. It was a fairly warm day, but he took his leather longcoat and boots, black jeans and a black shirt, keen to adopt the image he knew would be expected of him. Michelle was still getting ready and he used the time to make a phone call, moving his plan one step forward so smoothly that he was rubbing his hands in satisfaction when Michelle finally emerged from the bedroom. She was also in black, a mini-dress that showed off her figure to perfection, shiny heels and a studded leather dog collar with a clip at the front where a lead could be attached.

"No underwear, I take it?" he asked. "Master Jacobaeus does not approve of them."

In answer she lifted the front of her dress, exposed the neat triangle of her sex, freshly shaved and moisturised.

"You look like the most expensive girl in a Gothic brothel," he smiled. "If there is such a thing."

"And all you need is a pair of shades and you'd look like a pimp," she told him.

"I'll pick some up on the way," he promised, "and a dog chain, if we pass a pet shop."

"One day he's going to realise that you're only humouring him," she answered.

Peter merely shrugged and they made their way downstairs and out to the car. A short drive brought them to the somewhat decayed Victorian townhouse occupied by Master Jacobaeus. Peter had managed to get hold of a chain, which he clipped to Michelle's collar before putting on his dark glasses and ringing the doorbell. It was answered by a plump, brown haired girl with enormous eyes and nothing on but scarlet lingerie, including a corset that left her more-than-ample breasts riding high and round in perfectly fitted cups of silk and steel wire. She immediately curtsied, which proved too much for her outfit, both plump breasts popping free,

"Very pretty," Peter remarked as he stepped inside. "Hello, Red."

"Slave Red," a voice spoke from the gloom of the passage and a man stepped forward, tall, angular, with a great mass of white hair caught up in a long pony-tail and a hawk-like face. "Kneel, you little bitch. What have I told you about showing respect to visiting masters?"

He cuffed the girl as she quickly got to her knees, where she remained with her head hung and her eyes downcast, her heavy breasts still naked.

"Master Peter," the man said, extending a great, bony hand. "I have been expecting this visit."

"Master Jacobaeus," Peter answered, accepting the handshake. "Yes, it has become necessary."

"Very necessary," Master Jacobaeus agreed. "Come upstairs."

"I brought you a little present," Peter went on, handing over the other end of Michelle's chain. "Although I'd appreciate it if you could return her in more or less the condition she is now. Without any tattoos on her cunt, for example."

"That was a misunderstanding," Master Jacobaeus answered. "I respect your property, and the rite of exchange of gifts. Slave Red, you are Master Peter's for as long as he stays."

"Thank you," Peter answered, reaching down to tickle the kneeling girl under the chin. "But business before pleasure, I think, at least today."

"Yes," Master Jacobaeus agreed. "You two, bring us drinks, then go and amuse yourselves in the dungeon."

Both girls hurried to comply, leaving Peter to follow Master Jacobaeus upstairs to a living room furnished with black leather and steel, while the walls were decorated with prints of girls in various states of anguish. In due course, Red and Michelle reappeared for a moment, and Peter made himself comfortable with a cold beer as Master Jacobaeus opened the conversation.

"You're not going to back down, are you? We have to fight this."

"I spent six months in jail once," Peter answered, "and it is not an experience I intend to repeat. But no, I don't intend to back down, I just don't believe in open confrontation."

"It's the only way," Master Jacobaeus insisted. "We have to show them we are not ashamed of who we are. We have to make them accept our right to express our sexuality, just as the gay movement ..."

"Absolutely," Peter cut in before Master Jacobaeus could launch into one of his favourite rants. "But in this particular case I suggest something a little more subtle. When you were arrested, did you come across an Inspector Lennox? I think he was the one with a round head and a nasty little moustache."

"I met Lennox, yes."

"Do you see him accepting our right to express our sexuality?"

"No, but ..."

"Precisely. He's a Christian, of the worst sort, the sort who can't stand to see anybody else having fun, especially naughty fun."

Master Jacobaeus put his fingers to the gunmetal pentacle at his neck and Peter decided to rub the point home a little more.

"An interfering, prudish busybody who sees it as his duty to make other people behave according to his ghastly, grey moral code. It doesn't matter how good our arguments are, or how much of a nuisance we make of ourselves. He won't back down."

"We still have to try. This is going to be a long, slow battle."

"No doubt, but for the moment I just want to keep my

club going. Lennox intends to close down every single sex club in London and to see the people who run them jailed."

"That's more or less what he said to me."

"Do you still want to run your clubs?"

"Yes, and I'm prepared to go to prison, if that's what it takes. We need publicity, and that's the best way to get it, with an innocent man up for trial on unjust charges."

"Then you're a better man than I am, Jake. How would you like to front Club S?"

"How do you mean?"

"I mean your name goes on the flyer and you arrange the evening, although you can leave the admin to me, or rather, to Karen. If there's trouble, you take the fall, and next month the club runs as usual, only with a different front man, and so on. My priority is to keep the club going, a new venue in a different borough every time, which we run the same way as they run illegal raves, with the details only released at the last minute."

"The police can still find us, and it's a lot easier to close down a club with a couple of hundred people inside than stop a rave where there's two thousand people in a field."

"I know all that. The aim is to force the police to use their resources. So, are you in?"

Master Jacobaeus reached out one massive hand, grinning. Peter took it and shook, then carried on.

"You'll like the venue too. St. Botolph's, Limehouse."

"A church?"

"Not exactly. The building has been sold off, awaiting redevelopment into luxury apartments, but it looks like a church. There's even a crypt."

"And I get a free hand with organising?"

"Yes. That's another issue, of course. They took all my equipment, and while we could probably manage with stuff from Violet's dungeon and elsewhere, I'd rather not have anything else confiscated. The crypt has pillars, even some fastening points that could be adapted for rope and chains. It makes the perfect dungeon. Upstairs isn't quite so good, but all the religious paraphernalia can be put to good use with a little imagination. The altar's still in place, and the font. In fact, why not hold one of your rituals as the cabaret? That'll piss Lennox off if he's got people inside."

"He'll be pissed off alright, but we have to have furniture. Leave it to me."

"Thank you. I knew I could rely on you. Shall we join the ladies ... well, sluts ..."

"Slaves," Master Jacobaeus said emphatically.

Noises could be heard from the dungeon even as they went downstairs, feminine squeals and cries of mixed delight and pain. The entire basement had been converted into one large, open room supported by solid pillars with a cast iron spiral staircase leading down from the ground floor. Everything was either red, black, silver or mirrored, creating what Peter considered a somewhat garish effect. The one discordant note in the chromatic scale came from a litter of turquoise blue underwear on the floor beside a great leather padded wheel. A girl had been fixed to the wheel, naked and upside down, her ash-blonde hair brushing the floor. In front of her stood Michelle, holding a single-tailed whip of plaited leather, and Red, who had a black ostrich feather, which she used to tickle the helpless girl between her thighs.

"Very inventive," Peter remarked as the bound girl began to babble.

"Please, Master, make them stop! I'm going to wet myself, I swear ... and anyway, it's my turn!"

"If you wet yourself, Slave Blue, you'll be mopping it up," Master Jacobaeus replied casually. "In fact ... turn her the right way up, girls."

Red hurried to obey as Michelle stood to one side.

"Something cool and refreshing," Master Jacobaeus

seemed to muse to himself. "Yes, strawberry I think ... Red!" he called, "mix a pitcher of strawberry cordial. Nice and sweet, just the way Blue likes it."

As they waited, Master Jacobaeus kissed and fondled Blue, his touch oscillating from loving to lewd and back again.

Red returned quickly with the pitcher, and Master Jacobaeus tipped the spout to the bound girl's lips. She drank, swallowing down the cool, sweet liquid as best she could despite the growing look of consternation on her face. Peter sat down, watching as Blue was made to drink half of all the liquid in the pitcher, then more, with her expression of self-pity growing ever stronger, until at last she began to beg.

"No more, please, Master. I can't take it ... I ..."

"Shut up," Master Jacobaeus instructed, cutting her off. "Stop whining and do as you're told, or maybe I'll give you to Master Peter instead of Red. You do know what he likes to do to girls, don't you? He likes to spank them and sodomise them, treatment that might just help to teach you manners."

"Sorry, Master," Blue answered, throwing a nervous glance towards Peter.

Peter found himself smiling as the girl was made to drink the remainder of the pitcher, leaving her belly visibly distended and her eyes wide and pleading. He'd seen her before, at various clubs, always on a chain held by Master Jacobaeus and always in blue, but he'd never had a chance to play with her or seen anything done to her. Red had been around longer and he'd twice had the opportunity to spank her, but nothing more, although her figure tempted possibilities only really practical in relative privacy. Signalling her, her patted his lap.

She came to sit down, smiling as she settled her full, fleshy bottom onto his knee. Peter immediately slipped her breasts free of her corset, supporting each for a moment so that he could marvel at their delectable weight, then stroking his thumb across her nipples to bring them erect. Master Jacobaeus had turned away from Blue, grinning as he spoke.

"I take it you prefer Red then?"

"Both have their charms," Peter replied. "But if Blue's going to be made to wet herself, it seems sensible to have something to play with while I watch."

Master Jacobaeus nodded and turned back to the wheel, quickly adjusting it so that Blue was once more upside down before turning his attention back to Michelle.

"You, Candy Doll, are holding a whip. Hardly appropriate, don't you think, for a slave? Give it to me and stick out your bottom."

Michelle quickly obeyed, looking both nervous and excited as she passed him the whip before lifting her dress and offering her bottom out to Master Jacobaeus.

"I see you have her well trained," he remarked to Peter and lashed the whip out to catch Michelle across her outthrust cheeks, hard enough to leave her wide-eyed and gasping. Peter silently praised her for keeping her dress high, rather than pulling it down in defence of her wounded flesh.

"Strip off, darling," Peter advised. "It will make it easier for him."

Michelle hastened to obey, peeling her dress off over her head and kicking her shoes aside to leave her stark naked save for her collar. Master Jacobaeus waited until she was ready before handing her the ostrich feather Red had been using before.

"This is how it works," he began. "You tickle her. I whip you. When she wets herself, the whipping stops. If you must give up, you will go in her place. Got that?"

"Yes, Master," Michelle answered, and gave a sharp, pig-like squeal as the whip cracked across her thighs.

"You belong to Master Peter. I am Master Jacobaeus. Do not forget that."

"No, Master Jacobaeus. Sorry, Master Jacobaeus."

Peter was smiling as he watched, amused and aroused

both by Master Jacobaeus and the state of confusion he'd gotten Michelle into. He'd also been fondling Red's breasts all the while, enjoying their sheer size as much as her low moans of appreciation. Both her nipples now stuck out proudly, as big and as firm as a pair of raspberries, also much the same shape. He took one between his teeth, biting gently as he watched the game that had begun at the wheel.

Michelle had adopted a purposefully vulnerable pose, with her feet set wide apart and her bottom pushed out to the whip as she used the feather on Blue's thighs and belly, midriff and breasts. Master Jacobaeus, meanwhile, deployed the whip with both skill and accuracy, flicking, cutting, stroking, to mark her pale flesh with neatly placed welts, both long and short. She couldn't help but react, gasping and treading up and down on her feet as the pain rose. While her attempts to tickle Blue grew ever more desperate, until Peter was sure she would cry for mercy and end up strapped to the wheel herself.

Blue had been squirming and giggling since the first touch of the ostrich feather to the sensitive skin between her thighs, but she didn't seem to be getting any worse, while Michelle squeaks and pained little hops had been getting ever more urgent, until she'd begun to tremble and could barely use the feather. Peter had even started to feel sorry for her, until she suddenly sank to both knees, discarded the feather, and dug her wriggling fingers into the flesh of Blue's torso to tickle far more forcefully, with instantaneous results. Blue screamed, jerked, and a great gush erupted from her cunt, high in the air, to splash down on her own body and all over Michelle just as the whip cracked one more time.

Michelle's mouth fell open as she cried out in pain, just in time to receive Blue's gush, full force and then some, into her face and in her hair, over her breasts and down her belly, before she finally managed to jerk back. Peter was laughing so hard he could barely keep his seat, Red too, while Michelle was trying not to giggle even as she stood up, utterly drenched. Blue seemed too far gone to notice, gasping out her emotion as liquid continued to burble from her and run down her body, soiling her belly and breasts and neck, to drip from her hair and form a rapidly expanding puddle on the concrete floor. Master Jacobaeus had reacted fast, stepping away the instant Blue gave in. But he hadn't quite reacted fast enough, leaving his immaculate black boots spotted with drops from the edge of the splash zone. Folding his arms across his chest, he pointed to his feet.

"Clean them, Candy Doll."

Michelle made a face and glanced towards Peter, but she

quickly got down on all fours in front of the big man. Extending her tongue, she began to lick the speckles of liquid from his boots, dabbing up each spot separately. He responded by trailing the whip over her already welted bottom and applying the occasional little flick, until finally she looked up, questioning but apparently not daring to speak.

"That will do," he said and nodded to Blue. "Get her down, clean her up, and yourself, then get back here."

"I'll start, if I may?" Peter stated, already easing Red to the floor.

"Be my guest," Master Jacobaeus responded.

"Are you going to do it up my bottom?" Red asked.

"Not today," Peter told her. "I have better uses for you. Or, to be more exact, you have better uses. Which isn't to say you don't have a beautiful bottom, but even I can't resist the charms of your breasts."

She giggled and held them up, making an inviting furrow of her cleavage as Peter released his cock.

"In your mouth first," he instructed, "and no playing with your pussy until I'm done with you."

"Yes, Master Peter," Red answered, and her mouth closed obediently around his penis.

He sat back, watching her as she sucked, her huge eyes turned up to his as though watching for his approval, her breasts in her hands as she played with her nipples. She was in the same position Michelle favoured after a spanking, with her knees apart and her arse pushed out to improve the view for him and for anybody else who happened to see, and—he also knew—to make herself feel more vulnerable. Her position was very pleasing, making him wish he'd spanked her first. His cock was already growing hard in her mouth and the urge to fuck her breasts was as strong as ever, but he couldn't possibly deny himself the opportunity to abuse her succulent bottom.

"Up," he ordered. "Over my knee."

She made a face but quickly crawled into position, presenting her backside. He lost no time, peeling the little red panties off her ample cheeks and setting about them with sharp, stinging slaps. She'd soon began to kick and wriggle, rubbing herself on his erection, which kept him nicely stiff as he spanked her, stopping only when Michelle and Blue came back into the room. Both were still stark naked save for towels wrapped around their wet hair like turbans, creating a curious effect as they went down on their knees in front of Master Jacobaeus. Peter let a hand slip between Red's thighs, absently fiddling with her cunt and arsehole as he watched, wondering if Master Jacobaeus really warranted the nickname Karen had given him of Jake the Peg.

Peter did not need to wonder for much longer, as the two girls reached into Master Jacobaeus' leather trousers. The man's cock was a monstrous, rubbery thing with a shaft as thick as a girl's wrist and a fat, fleshy foreskin. Michelle swallowed as she saw what she was going to have to suck and perhaps take in her cunt or even in her arse. But she did not let her apprehension get the better of her, and she'd quickly taken him into her mouth, sucking gamely as Blue licked as his equally monstrous balls. He had been waiting for them, seated with his legs spread wide, the whip still in his hand. As they worked on him, he began to use the whip once more, flicking casually at their bottoms and backs.

Peter turned back to Red, happy to let Master Jacobaeus enjoy his girlfriend as long as the favour was being returned. He'd now given her full cheeks a nice pink flush, while the gooey state of her cunt left no doubt that this act had aroused her as much as it had him. With his cock in urgent need of attention, he eased her to the floor once more, took her by the hair, and fucked her mouth for only a moment before settling his erection between her breasts. She crawled a little closer, holding up the plump pillows of flesh and squeezing them close around his shaft so that the bulb of his cock bobbed up and down between as he fucked her silken cleavage.

Her flesh felt warm and soft, and the view of her huge breasts wrapped around his erection was pure delight, but he wasn't getting the friction her needed to come. She seemed to sense his problem and reacted quickly, moving her head down with her lips pursed, so that every thrust pushed the tip of his cock into her tight little mouth, as if he was penetrating a small but well lubricated anus again and again.

"That's good," he sighed. "So tight ... tight like your little arsehole ... so good to fuck, and your tits ... so big ... so ... fucking ... big!"

The orgasm came suddenly, welling up inside him to explode in his head just as his jism exploded in her mouth, then into her face as she pulled suddenly back. Still he came, all over her breasts to make a hot, slippery tube of her cleavage as his pulses subsided, and again her mouth was on him, taking him deep to swallow as much as she could of his final flow. He sat back, leaving her face and chest smeared with cum as she rocked back on her heels, her cunt spread wide as she began to play with herself, deliberately showing off.

Peter watched, enjoying the state she was in and her uninhibited excitement as she masturbated with one hand and used to other to rub his cum over her face and breasts, deliberately soiling herself. Keen to help, he reached out to take her by the hair, forcing her down and cramming his still stiff member back into her mouth. She sucked even more eagerly than before, her bottom trembling with the motion of her fingers as she rubbed at her clit, faster and faster still until at last she came with her mouth full of cock. He kept his fist twisted tight in her hair until she'd finished, before finally releasing her to clean up in the bathroom.

Across the room, Michelle was being put through her paces with a vengeance. Mounted up on Master Jacobaeus' lap, the mouth of her cunt was plainly visible, straining wide around his monstrous shaft, with her thighs and bottom spread wide in

Blue's face. He was fucking her slowly, allowing Blue to run her tongue all the way up his penis, right from his balls to Michelle's anus, over and over again, pausing only to kiss at her Master's great, bulbous sack or to probe her playmate's arsehole. She was masturbating as she licked and she came first, with her Master's balls in her mouth and Michelle's bottom slapping in her face as she hit one convulsive peak and then a second, only to return to licking as if nothing had happened.

For a moment the scene continued as before, until Master Jacobaeus suddenly began to thrust hard into Michelle. She cried out, throwing her head back and locking her arms around his neck as she bounced on his monstrous cock. Cum exploded from her straining hole, splashing Blue's face and running down over his balls as Michelle began a desperate squirming motion on his cock, rubbing herself on him without thought for anything but her own pleasure until she too joined them in orgasm.

"Not bad," Peter said. "Not bad at all. What do you think?"

"A bit over the top, maybe," Michelle replied, looking at the flyer he'd given her.

"Over the top is good," Peter stated. "Over the top is what we need."

The flyer advertised Club S, but in place of the usual images of leather clad dominas or pretty girls in dishevelled uniforms, there appeared to be a scene from hell. It focussed on a giant pentagram with a naked girl strapped to it, and she was being whipped to ecstasy by capering devils with improbably large cocks. In the background was a burning cross rising amid the ruins of a cathedral, and various figures having sex. Above it all, looking down as if in approval of his creation, was the face of Master Jacobaeus, complete with horns and lit orange and demonic as if by the flames below.

"Admittedly, we might lose a few of our regulars," Peter went on. "But then we might equally well pick up some of the more Gothic crowd, the more militant sort of pagans, a few Satanists perhaps."

"You're hoping we get raided, aren't you?" Michelle asked.

"Yes, and so is Jake," Peter admitted. "But that's only part of my little scheme. Right, I need to get to work. I have a lot to do, and I suppose I really ought to try and make some money."

He left the flat to start on what had become routine over the years, using his cab to visit the places he needed to go for the club and parties, while earning money at the same time. Having to take fares to the destination of their choosing was always a bit of a problem, but he'd long ago managed to work out routes between the stations, the major hotels and other popular spots in such a way that he could generally get everything done that was needed.

Distributing the flyers was his first priority, with several calls in Soho and the more Bohemian parts of Camden and Westminster, before a lucky call to drive to Moorgate allowed him to cover the City. By mid-afternoon the job was done and he turned his light off in order to make his way to the long, grey student dormitories where Sophie had her room. He noted the name on the door "Sophie Fitzroy" before knocking. She was in, and he was soon sipping coffee in the single armchair provided by the college while she sat cross-legged on the bed. Peter talked of this and that for a while before coming to the point.

"I have a one-to-one proposal for you, if you'd like to take it up?"

"Maybe," she replied cautiously. "What happens?"

"It's simple. You visit a gentleman of my acquaintance, somebody I know and trust. He spanks you, along with anything else that seems appropriate at the time, and I give you two hundred pounds."

"What's he like?"

"Small, dapper, very civilised, my age. He was at school with me, as it happens."

"He sounds like just the man to spank me. But, I mean … I've never done one-to-ones."

"There's absolutely nothing to worry about. I'll drive you over and pick you up if you like? His flat's just off the Horseferry Road, in Westminster."

"That would be kind, thanks. When did you have in mind?"

"No time like the present, really. He's a civil servant, so we can probably predict his movements fairly accurately."

"Is he expecting me *now*?" she asked, surprised.

"You're a present, in return for a favour."

Sophie had begun to smile.

"I rather like that idea," she said after a pause. "Being given away as a present to a man who likes to spank. That way …"

"It's like it isn't your choice," he answered for her. "There's nothing like letting go of your responsibility when it comes to sex, especially kinky sex. Still, perhaps you'd like a warm up?" Peter smiled and patted his lap.

"In a moment," Sophie agreed, before getting up and going to her wardrobe. "What would he like me to wear, do you think?"

"Violet says you have a school uniform?" Peter answered. "That would be sure to appeal to him, especially if it includes a red tartan skirt. The girls at our neighbouring convent used to wear red tartan and it left a lasting impression on me, so probably on Clive too. And that reminds me. When you arrive you're to say you're from Grove House Maids, got that?"

"Grove House Maids, yes. How about a maid's uniform then? I don't have one, but …"

She was clearly angling for a treat and Peter nodded, more than happy to make what he was sure would be a good investment.

"I'll buy you one, French style, perhaps, with a little pleated skirt and lots of petticoats underneath. I saw one in Soho this morning that would do very nicely—real satin, not the cheap nylon stuff. Okay, have a shower, or whatever you were going to do, then come over my knee for a bit, and we'll go shopping before we visit Clive."

Sophie nodded and began to undress, ever so slightly shy as she stripped out of her jeans and shirt, underwear and bra, but clearly aware of Peter's presence and that he was enjoying the view. She stayed fully nude as she dug a towel out from her chest of drawers, leaving her bent over for a moment so that he had a fine view of the split fig of her cunt and the crevice of her bottom. His cock had begun to stiffen in response, and stayed that way as she slipped on a robe and went to shower. He grew harder still when she re-emerged wearing only the towel, and he watched her dry off before applying moisturiser and scent.

"How should I make-up?" she asked when she'd finally finished with her hair-dryer.

"No more than a touch," he advised. "You want to look like a naughty schoolgirl, or a saucy maid as the case may be, but not an out and out hooker. Never use too much make-up unless you're in fetish gear or something else really outrageous, otherwise it just makes you look cheap. First though, come on, over my knee. I've waited long enough."

Sophie's mouth moved into the briefest of pouts before she responded, coming to him and laying herself down across his lap with her hands and feet braced on the floor and her bottom raised high. Peter was smiling as he turned up her towel to bare her arse, and he took the opportunity to explore her bottom for a while before laying on the smacks. She didn't seem to mind, lying passive over his lap even as he lewdly parted her cheeks. The spanking made her wriggle and gasp a little, but she made no complaint. Indeed, she just seemed to accept it as something that happened … and it just so happened to leave her cunt wet and the air full of the scent of excited girl.

Peter's reaction had been much the same, a stiff cock and the need to come before doing anything else. Sophie seemed compliant rather than eager, perhaps enjoying the feeling of being obliged to accept the spanking rather than having to ask for it. So when he'd finished her off with a last few firm swats and helped her down from his lap, he simply unzipped his fly and pulled free his burgeoning erection as he spoke.

"Actually, if you wouldn't mind sucking me off?"

Sophie made a face but got to her knees, accepting his cock in her mouth. Peter sat back, watching her suck. The sight of a pretty girl with a mouthful of cock was always appealing, but

Sophie's reaction was very different to Michelle's. Shy, slightly unsure of herself, her expression suggested that it was something she was doing because she had to, and not really enjoying at all. That didn't stop her doing her best, or milking him into her open mouth when he finally came. But there was no mistaking the disgust on her face as the cum splashed across her cheeks and nose as well as filling her mouth to leave a sticky white pool on her tongue.

"Swallow it," Peter ordered, half expecting her to refuse.

Her response was a weak nod, then a gulp, with her face screwed up in utter revulsion as she took his semen down into her belly. Peter began to apologise, wondering if he'd pushed her too far. But Sophie's face broke suddenly into a wide, beaming grin.

"Thank you!" she said brightly. "That was so … so humiliating."

"I'll take that as a compliment," Peter answered. "Now, once you've wiped your face, dressed and done your make-up, we're off to Soho for the prettiest, kinkiest maid's uniform money can buy. Then to Clive for another spanking.

"Do I have to suck his cock?" Sophie asked, her voice as full of resentment as it had been with happiness a moment before.

"Yes," Peter answered, sure it was what she wanted to hear. "You have to suck his cock, and take it in your face, just like you did with me, and swallow."

She answered with a soft sigh, impossible to interpret, and as she began to rummage in her chest of drawers Peter shook his head and made a quite remark under his breath.

"Catholic girls!"

◆ ◆ ◆ ◆

"Presumably that won't be their normal uniform?" Clive

queried as he sat back in one of the leather armchairs provided by the smoking room at Lorrimer's Club. "It's very attractive, but a bit of a give-away, even with a coat over the top. When she turned up at the door, I thought she was naked underneath."

"I'll choose something more demure once we get going," Peter promised, before taking a pull on the fine Cuban cigar Clive had ordered for him.

"Are we definitely going ahead then?" Ben asked eagerly.

"There are still a few details to work out," Peter assured him. "But yes, we are."

"Might I make a booking?" Ben went on.

"Certainly," Peter answered and reached into his top pocket for the slim black notebook he'd purchased in order to keep his private records. "Once Grove House Maids is registered as a company and fully up and running, you'll be able to call up whenever you please. But for the moment, just leave everything to me."

"I'd like to make a booking myself, as it goes," Gabriel put in. "Just as soon as you have the uniforms sorted out."

"I'll make that a priority then," Peter promised and took another pull on his cigar, followed by a swallow of gin and tonic.

Sophie's visit to Clive had been a great success. She had charmed him from the start, introducing herself with a curtsey and taking her coat off to reveal her uniform, then shyly confessing that she'd been sent for a spanking. Clive had risen to the occasion, turning her across his knee and pulling her knickers down for a happy few minutes that had grown happier still once she had her bottom warmed. She had sucked his cock, tugged him off in her face and swallowed what went in her mouth, exactly as promised. Or so Peter believed, as only one summation of the visit had been forthcoming. Sophie had been more than happy to confess her sins to him, while Clive had shown a very gentlemanly reticence. He'd been unable to keep it entirely to himself, though, and had told Ben and Gabriel before inviting them to join Peter and himself at Lorrimer's. Peter was now basking in their admiration and enjoying the experience immensely, just as he had done at Broadfields when making a display of Tiffany or organising the Great St. Monica's Spanking Show.

"We ought to put Peter up for membership here," Ben suggested after a while.

"Wouldn't my little stay at Her Majesty's pleasure be a problem?" Peter asked, trying not to betray his sudden surge of euphoria at the suggestion.

"Not at all," Gabriel assured him. "We have embezzlers, fraudsters of various sorts, a perjurer or two, mainly to do with finance or politics rather than aggravated assault or whatever it was. But all that was a long time ago. You'll get in."

"Thank you," Peter asked. "I'm very gratified."

"They let grammar school boys in nowadays," Gabriel joked. "So why not the occasional convict? So how many of these scrumptious little poppets do you have on your books? Reliable ones, that is."

"A reasonable number," Peter lied. "The recruiting is going well, but these things can't be rushed."

"Absolutely," Gabriel agreed, "and remember, we're relying on you not to foul it up, myself especially."

"Discretion is my watchword," he assured them, just as an idea hit him as to how to get around the fact that he had only one really safe girl at the moment. "Which is why I'm not going to launch the company properly until the wretched Inspector Lennox is out of the way. Any news, Clive? Did he kick when he heard that he couldn't have all the resources he wanted?"

"Not too violently," Clive replied. "Or I'd have heard, and I haven't. I suspect he's decided to put promotion ahead of personal considerations, for the time being at least. So, while he won't be actively looking for you, it would be foolhardy to run one of your clubs."

"That's more or less what I'd expected," Peter answered. "Thank you. So yes, I can take bookings, but only from the three of you. Sorry, could you excuse me a moment?"

While he'd been speaking a man had walked past the door of the smoking room. He was tall, white haired, elderly but still brisk and with a distinctly military bearing, a man Peter was sure he recognised. There was no sign of him on reaching the lobby, so Peter turned to the beadle behind the desk, thinking back to his first visit so many years before as he spoke.

"Is Charles Finch still a member?" he asked as the beadle looked up.

"The Brigadier? Certainly, sir. He came in this very minute. He'll be in the dining room, I would imagine."

"Thank you," Peter answered.

He was full of doubt as he made for the dining room door. Since his expulsion from Broadfields and subsequent imprisonment he barely spoken to any of his family, all of whom had chosen to put the worst possible construction on his actions. Even before that he had earned his father's disapproval by refusing to go into the army and his mother's when she had discovered his hoards of pornographic magazines and photosets—the majority of which were dedicated to spanking. He had always assumed that his Uncle Charles shared his father's views, but up until that point they had always gotten on well and more than twenty years had now passed since his disgrace.

"Uncle Charles?" he asked as he approached, painfully aware of the sudden catch in his voice.

His uncle turned, his face registering surprise, with recognition dawning only slowly, but when he began to speak it came in a rush.

"Good Heavens, Peter, the black sheep himself! No, don't take offence. I'm very pleased to see you, but what are you doing here? Are you a member?"

"I'm being put up for membership," Peter answered,

now fighting to hold back tears as the old man extended a hand in greeting. "I was lunching with some friends and I saw you pass the door. I had no idea ..."

"That I was still alive," his uncle filled in for him. "Well I am, and I aim to be for a few years yet. Sit down, tell me what you've been up to all these years, or do you need to get back to your friends?"

"I'll join you if I may," Peter answered. "My friends will be coming through in a moment and I'm sure they'll understand."

He sat down, nearly overwhelmed by a sense of gratitude stronger even than when he had met Ben Thompson on Westminster Bridge. So strong was this unexpected response that he was obliged to use the menu to hide his face until he could recover. His uncle seemed genuinely pleased to see him and tactfully avoided any mention of Peter's disgrace as they began to talk, getting on so well that when the others came in they simply joined the same table. Only then did mention of Broadfields become inevitable.

"They take girls nowadays, you know," Charles remarked. "A good thing too, if you ask me."

"My daughters are down for Grove House," Ben replied. "We put their names down as soon as the rules were changed. Daniel's Clementine was one of the first year's intake ... no, the second or third, I think."

"I put both the boys down as soon as they were born," Gabriel supplied. "You have to, or there's a fair chance they won't get in. Mark you, it's all about money these days, and by the time they're through university I don't suppose having been to a decent school will mean all that much anymore.

"Look at Robertson," Charles put in. "Started as a private, and a servant before that, ended up as Chief of the Imperial General Staff. Mark you, when he was about you couldn't get into Broadfields unless you were the son of a gentlemen. It's in the statutes, or it was at the time."

The conversation continued with lunch, growing gradually more nostalgic and gradually more indulgent, until it seemed as if the only really worthwhile thing to be doing on Saturday at lunchtime was sitting in a British gentleman's club eating lunch with old friends, ideally from the same school. Never once did the conversation exclude Peter and, although his sense of detachment remained, the desire to see Broadfields again grew stronger with every rose-tinted reminiscence and with every glass of wine. By the time they had retired to the smoking room for brandy and more of the Cuban cigars, his mind was made up.

Looking down on the rooftops of Broadfields, Peter's feelings of nostalgia had reached the level of physical pain. Little had changed, save for a cluster of new buildings in the valley, but Grove House looked exactly as it had when he'd stared back from the window of the police car twenty-one years before. He could see the window of his bedsit, and above it the grey lead on the roof where he'd climbed up to carve his name below that of his Uncle Charles and others who'd had the courage to climb up from the fifth form dormitory window. The headmaster's house was also visible, although he knew Porter had long since retired. Other landmarks included the river, leading away to the west, although St. Monica's was invisible beyond the low, wooded ridge of the hill, where he could just make out the line of an all too familiar railway cutting.

He had timed his trip with care. The summer term had ended a few days before and not many people were around, allowing him to drive down the hill and in through the main gates to park in the spaces normally occupied by masters' cars. Close up, the place had an unfamiliar, sleepy air. The changes were more evident, with the new buildings raw against the familiar weathered brick and flint. Only the very heart of the place seemed unchanged, with the great ironbound doors standing wide, just as they had when Daniel Stewart escorted him through them on his final walk so many years before. Inside was no different either, although strangely quiet. The doors to the refectory and Grove House were unchanged, while the notice boards beside the masters' common room were the same as ever, down to the notices announcing what had presumably been the last games of term.

Peter stepped closer, smiling at his own foolish feelings as he read the list and remembered how he'd always scanned the names with the hope that his own would not be included, thus allowing him to make a trip to a nearby village for drinks and cigarettes, or to make for St. Monica's to watch the girls at play in their gym knickers. The memory made his smile grow broad and wicked, only for his mouth to come open in surprise as he read down the names on the list for the senior hockey game. Right at the bottom, penned in as if it had been an afterthought, was one name that had haunted his dreams for years—Rhiannon O'Neil.

Bitter disappointment followed close on the heels of his surprise. As a senior girl at Broadfields she couldn't possibly be more than nineteen, which meant she was not his daughter, something he'd long suspected and hoped for. He swore gently under his breath, and was about to take the hockey list as a memento when a voice spoke almost in his ear.

"Can I help you?"

Peter spun around to find a man looking at him. He was young, of middling build and dressed in slightly scruffy tweeds, suggesting that was a master.

"I'm an old boy, Ben Thompson," he replied, deciding it was probably better not to reveal his true identity. "Sorry, I was just having a look around."

"That's fine," the man replied "But you are supposed to make an appointment for a monitor. I'm busy myself, but there are a few senior pupils around, if …"

"I don't suppose Rhiannon O'Neil is here," Peter asked on sudden impulse. "I used to know her mother."

"O'Neil?" the master answered. "Yes, she is as a matter of fact. Her parents are out in Saudi. He's an engineer, I believe."

"Yes, of course," Peter answered. "Although it's been years since I saw either of them."

"One moment," the master said, and disappeared through the doors of Grove House.

Peter stood waiting, his heart hammering in his chest, at once full of expectation and apprehension for his impulsive query, but very glad indeed he'd had the sense to claim to be Ben Thompson. He also felt a lot of guilt, for breaking his promise not to interfere in any way with Tiffany's new life. He kept telling himself he ought to make straight for his car and leave, yet he found himself fixed to the spot until at length the doors of Grove House swung open once more. The master stepped through, followed by a girl a good two inches taller than him, so slim she seemed more gawky than elegant. She had bright, copper coloured hair tied up in a high ponytail and a pale, delicate face marked by a splash of freckles. Still, she was painfully familiar and he found himself gaping like a goldfish. As the master made a brief introduction, her initially mildly irritated expression changed to open exasperation, as though she thought she'd been asked to show the school to some halfwit.

"I must be on my way," the master said and he was gone, leaving Peter desperately searching for something to say as Rhiannon's expression changed once more, to wide-eyed astonishment.

"Peter Finch!" she exclaimed. "You're Peter Finch!"

"Don't scream!" he begged. "Please don't scream!"

"I'm not going to scream," she told him, now with laughter in her voice, which also carried a soft Irish lilt. "Why do you think I would scream?"

"I, uh … no reason," he managed. "You recognise me, obviously, but …"

"Mum keeps your photo in her diary," Rhiannon answered. "The picture from the newspaper, outside the court."

"Ah, yes, that one," Peter said. "I …"

"She's always talking about you," Rhiannon went on. "Especially if she's had a drink, or been arguing with Dad. But what are you doing here?"

"I came to look around," he told her, "and I saw your name on the notice board. Sorry, I couldn't resist the chance of meeting you."

"I'd better show you around then," she offered. "As that's what I'm supposed to be doing, Peter Finch."

There was a glitter in her eyes as she beckoned him to follow her, making him wonder exactly how much she knew. While the knowledge that Tiffany still kept his picture had him on the verge of tears. Indeed, so strong was his emotion that he barely noticed the sweet rotation of Rhiannon's neat little rump beneath her skirt as she led him up the stairs, nor the impressive length of her pale, slender legs. Her own reaction to their meeting was very different—happy, excited chatter and bright-eyed smiles that occasionally gave way to a curious, almost calculating look. She was like Tiffany in many ways, vivacious, mercurial, openly rebellious in her attitudes, and even if she lacked her mother's easy poise she was full of confidence.

"That's about it, really," she was saying as they finished their brief tour of Grove House. "The same old dump, I expect?"

Peter had been walking in a daze, taking in every detail, changed and unchanged, and simply nodded.

"Why don't you take me to lunch then?" she asked, as bold and easy as if he'd been a favourite uncle.

"With pleasure," Peter answered, fascinated as much as disconcerted by the quality of her attention. "Is your housemaster or somebody around? We probably ought to ask if it's alright, or at least tell somebody."

"Term's over," she answered. "I've left, really, or I would have done if I'd been able to get an earlier flight. Who cares, anyway? I make my own choices."

"I'm sure you do," he answered, reflecting that as an adult she could do as she pleased. "Okay, how about the Oak at Yattendon?"

"We never go there. It's always full of teachers. You've got a car, haven't you? Why not drive up to Goring? There's a lovely place, right on the river, where we'll be safe."

"Safe?" Peter queried.

"Oh, you know what they're like," she went on. "Always in a fuss over nothing. I … I'm supposed to be gated. But I don't see how I can be, when term's finished and I'm leaving."

"That's true," Peter said, somewhat doubtfully. "What were you gated for?"

Rhiannon gave him an arch look and her cream pale skin took on a touch of colour as she replied.

"I expect you know what a toasty girl is?"

"Yes," Peter answered, fascinated, despite his best efforts to appear otherwise.

"I made mine wash her mouth out with soap," Rhiannon went on blithely. "For calling me a bitch. She didn't mind, really, but Miss Laindon came in while I was doing it, and of course Clemmie couldn't tell the truth. So I got gated."

"Clemmie?" Peter asked. "Not Clementine Stewart?"

"How did you know?" Rhiannon demanded. "Oh yes, you and her dad must have been here at the same time. I should have taken a leaf out of your book, really, shouldn't I? I should have taken her out to the old railway cutting and given her a good spanking."

Peter didn't answer, rendered speechless not only for what she had said, but for the immense relish she'd put into the final word. She threw him another of her odd, sidelong looks and then carried on as they left the main buildings.

"Oh, I know all about you, Peter Finch. It's all in Mum's diaries."

"I didn't know she kept a diary," Peter managed.

"Well she did, and it's hot stuff, as I'm sure you can well imagine! Of course she doesn't know I've read it, and Dad would freak out completely if he knew. Come on, quick, in case somebody sees us."

She took Peter's hand, towing him behind as she ran for the short line of cars parked just inside the main gate. He was already having visions of a fresh visit to the local police station and quickly drew ahead, helping her into his car and driving away as fast as he felt he decently could. Only when they were clear of the college buildings did he begin to relax, while she was obviously enjoying herself immensely, glancing back over her shoulder as they accelerated.

"I suppose you'll have to bring me back," she said, half-regretfully. "But I so wish that was my last ever view of the place. And just think, abducted by the terrible Peter Finch!"

"But I haven't abducted you, have I?" Peter pointed out. "And what do you mean 'the terrible Peter Finch'? Anyway, don't you like Broadfields?"

"That's three questions all at once," she said, her voice switching to a playful and faintly admonitory tone. "Now let me see … No, of course you haven't abducted me, but it's nice to think that you might have," she laughed. "Kidnapped and carried off over your shoulder to a life of depraved sex in your secret lair! And yes, you do have quite a reputation, didn't you know? Nobody else in the whole history of Broadfields ever got expelled for assaulting a nun, let alone for a night of dirty passion in St. Monica's convent with eight different girls."

"Eight?" Peter queried. "I didn't …"

"Don't spoil the story," she interrupted. "I know it was just Mum, and you watched Vicky Trent spank some stuck up

Indian girl. But the rumours are much juicier. Now you've made me lose my train of thought … Do I like Broadfields? I used to. I used to think it was the most wonderful place in the world, but as I got older I came to resent all the rules, all the restrictions. I mean, here I am, a grown woman, and I still have to sneak away as if I was just a kid."

"I felt exactly the same," Peter told her. "So did your mother, but she was at St. Monica's which was far worse. It was supposed to be progressive, just because they allowed make-up and that sort of thing, but they had endless rules and regulations, mainly designed to stop them having any real fun, especially sex. But then they had to do sports in just their knickers! Well, and tops of course, but you know what I mean."

"That's nuns for you," Rhiannon explained. "It's all about original sin, you see. So girls are assumed to be dirty little bitches until they prove otherwise, while dignity is supposed to be a privilege, hence the gym knickers. Anyway, it's not as bad as Saudi Arabia. I even have to cover my hair. I hate it there."

"Religion," Peter answered. "The bane of humanity. So you want to go to the Duck at Goring?"

"Yes, please, if that's not too cheeky?"

"The Duck is fine. My parent's used to take me there."

Rhiannon was silent for a long time, her expression oddly sulky. Then she spoke up again with sudden determination.

"You're not supposed to say 'the Duck is fine', Peter Finch. You're supposed to say the Duck is far too expensive and that I'm an impudent little brat for suggesting it. An impudent little brat who needs to be spanked."

"Jesus!" Peter exhaled slowly.

Rhiannon giggled.

"Would you like to spank me? I bet you would."

Peter swallowed hard as the blood rushed to his face, a reaction that drew a peal of delighted laughter from Rhiannon.

"Oh you would!" she laughed. "I knew you would! Come

on, I'll take you up into the woods and give you a little show of my bottom. Then maybe you can spank me for being so naughty. Won't that be fun?"

Peter had been forced to slow down to avoid the risk of an accident and still found himself lost for an answer, his head full of guilt and desire, contradictory voices screaming at him. To spank Tiffany's daughter seemed an impossible outrage, let alone when he had just taken her out of school, still in her uniform and without permission. Yet he had spanked more than one nineteen year old at the club without thinking twice. She was lovely too, with her endless legs, glorious hair, pixie face and infinitely spankable perfectly rounded little bottom. Even her slightly awkward physical manner added to his desire, while her impertinent attitude would have had any other spankable girl across his knee with her knickers down in moments.

"I'm not a child," she went on after he'd failed to reply, her tone now sulky.

"I know," he answered, at last finding his voice. "You're a very beautiful young woman ..."

"So spank me."

"... and Tiffany's daughter."

"What about it? I know how you like to spank girls, Peter Finch. Come on, do me. I've got little blue panties on. I bet you'd like to pull them down, nice and slow, while you hold me down across your knee. Think how I'd be, all bare and wriggly with my panties right down and my bottom ..."

"You deserve it, that's for sure," Peter broke in, "and you're going to get it, if it's the last thing I do, which it probably will be, at least this side of jail."

"So make it good."

"I intend to," he answered, pulling the cab to the side of the road.

"Here?" she asked, throwing a slightly worried glance to either side, where open fields bordered the road.

"I ought to," Peter answered her. "I ought to do you over the car with your knickers pulled down so that all the passing motorists can get a good look while you're punished. Unfortunately, some busybody would be sure to interfere, especially as you're in school uniform. But don't you know where we are?"

"No," she answered, now openly nervous as she climbed out of the car.

"I'll show you," he told her, and took her by the hand.

He pushed through a field gate and up between rows of corn towards where a straggling hedge followed the line of the ridge. She came after, willing but ever more nervous, a reaction that reminded him strongly of Tiffany as he'd once led her up the very same hill, and to the same fate. Only in her case there'd been an audience of his friends to enjoy her pain and humiliation. Coming out through the hedge, he stopped beside a decaying structure of black wooden planks half collapsed across mouldering hay bales.

"This is the barn where I spanked your mother in front of my friends," he told Rhiannon. "It's a little the worse for wear now, but it's going to have to do."

Rhiannon merely nodded, her impudence vanishing in the face of her playful and exciting fantasy turning into a painful and very immediate reality, while Peter's initial shock and guilt became subdued by desire. Choosing a stack of bales that were sheltered from view, he sat down as he spoke once more.

"I think you promised me a little show. Front and back, please."

"Yes, of course."

She sounded eager, perhaps grateful to postpone her spanking for a little. But her fingers shook as she took hold of the hem of her pleated blue school skirt, lifting it gingerly to expose the triangle of blue cotton that covered her sex. Her panties had pulled up a little, hugging and accentuating her slit, while her mound was abundant with dark ginger hair, making a bulge in the fabric and spilling out at the sides to create an unkempt, rather rude look that Peter found immensely appealing.

"Sorry," she said quietly, misreading his look. "I'm a bit of a ragamuffin."

"You're beautiful," he told her, "and natural. Now slide your knickers down, just a little, not off."

Rhiannon hesitated only an instant before tucking her skirt up and rolling her panties down to the tops of her thighs, exposing her full bush of hair and the very top of her little slit.

"Now the back," Peter ordered, struggling to keep his voice cool and even. "Show me your bottom, but pull your knickers up first."

"So you can watch me pull them down? That's really dirty," she said, more softly now.

"That's the only way to be. So, a little panty play, then bare. But pull them up again before you bend over my knee."

She had turned her back as he spoke. She watched him over her shoulder, her eyes wide and a little uncertain, although she had pushed out her bottom a little and was holding the little blue panties taut across her cheeks to make the best of her shape. Peter's cock was growing uncomfortably hard and he was forced to make a quick adjustment, at which she gave a nervous, half smile before pulling her knickers tighter across her bottom and a little way up into her crevice.

"Like this?" she asked.

"Perfect," he told her, "and now right up. Let your cheeks spill out to the sides."

Rhiannon obeyed, giggling as her confidence began to return. She'd leant forward and pushed out her bottom, her panties tugged high to leave both small, pale cheeks on full show. She had set her feet a little apart, allowing him to see the swell of her cunt bulging in the cotton that lewdly outlined her dampening slit.

"I have a nice bottom, don't you think?" she asked.

"Very pretty," he told her. "Now bend forward a bit more. Slowly … that's my girl."

She had responded almost instantly, still looking back as she bent down to take hold of her ankles, her hair a glorious cascade of copper, glossy in the sunlight, her back lithe and tensile, displaying her nearly nude bottom to perfection. The little blue panties had pulled so tightly to her that little curls of hair stuck out to either side of the feeble barrier. Again Peter adjusted his cock, now fully erect, and she spoke up.

"Shall I pull my knickers down?"

"Show off a little more," he told her. "Tease me."

Again she giggled. Standing straight, she gave her bottom a wiggle before adjusting her panties to cover her cheeks once more. Her fingers went to her skirt, releasing the hem before rolling the waistband up on itself to turn an appealing but reasonably demure school skirt into a mini so short that the turn of her panties was left peeping out beneath the hem. She'd been looking back all the while, gauging his interest, her eyes flicking between his face and the very obvious bulge in his trousers.

"That's right," he told her. "You've got me hard. Do you want to see?"

Rhiannon gave a single, nervous nod, half-turning as Peter eased down his fly to pull free his straining cock and imprisoned balls. She watched, fascinated, her mouth a little open with the very tip of her tongue just showing, her big green eyes glued to his erection as he began to masturbate.

"Continue," he told her. "I'm sure you've had a man masturbate over the sight of your pretty panties before?"

She shook her head.

"You have. Take my word for it," he told her. "Maybe not in front of you. But boys are pervs. With your long legs and your little skirt rolled up, every other guy who sees you will be tugging on his cock over the thought of how you look in your underwear. Do you go around with your skirt rolled up like that?"

"No," Rhiannon answered. "I'm a good girl. I never let boys see my knickers, or dirty old men, and I'd never bend over in a short skirt, not like this. I'd be scared they might catch me, and spank me, and fuck me."

As she spoke she'd bent down again, as if to pick something off the ground, allowing the full spread of her panties to bloom over her bottom, before taking hold of the hem of her skirt and lifting it high.

"Is that an offer?" he managed, now pulling fast at his cock. "I'm going to spank you, count on it. But ..."

"I'm not a virgin," she interrupted, "and I'm not made of china. You can fuck me, Peter Finch. Shall I take my knickers down now?"

"Yes ... it's time they came down," Peter said. "All the way down. I ... I want to see your cunt, Rhiannon."

Her face went pink at his words, but she quickly tucked her skirt up once more and pushed her thumbs into the waistband of her panties, her eyes locked to his. As she began to push, he struggled not to come then and there, his cock achingly hard and only a few final strokes away from orgasm. The swell of her cheeks blossomed over the elastic, then the upper part of her slit. And finally, nothing of her modesty remained concealed as she pushed the little panties lower, and lower still. The tiny, pink-white star of her arsehole as mesmerising as her sweetly turned, ginger furred little cunt. With her final exposure, Peter could barely restrain himself. He gave in to his need, tugging frantically at his erection, like a man driven mad by forbidden lust. He was going to come and there was nothing he could do to stop himself. But with Rhiannon's beautiful bare bottom pushed out almost in his face, and her wet pink hole tantalisingly on offer, he had no intention of expending himself over his own hand.

"Come here, you dirty little brat!" he gasped. "I'm going to fuck you ... fuck you right now ... and you can get your spanking while I'm in you."

Rhiannon squealed in surprise as he snatched at her, catching her skirt. But she giggled as he pulled her to him, and her half-serious protests morphed into a cry of shock and pleasure as he sat her down on his erection. His full length had settled inside her in one smooth motion, and he'd quickly tipped her forward, spreading the handfuls of her little bottom cheeks with his thumbs as she scrabbled for purchase on another of the old hay bales. He could see his cock, thick and dark in her wet pink hole, with her vagina stretched taut and his shaft slippery with her juice.

Sudden guilt hit him as he realised she'd lied. She'd been a virgin, but she wasn't anymore, her pretty cunt well and truly fucked, with his cock in her to the hilt and her arse cheeks spread wide to show her off. He couldn't stop anyway, his ecstasy already rising towards orgasm, his eyes locked on the junction of his cock and her cunt, and on the pale star of her arse. She was gasping and sobbing out every sensation, every emotion, as she was fucked. She clung desperately to the hay bale to stop herself from going face first into a half-dried puddle of mud, but Peter could think only of his promise to spank her before he came.

His hand cracked down across one upturned cheek, then the other, even as she squealed in reaction to the first strike. With that, it was all too much. As he whipped his cock free at the last possible moment, he aimed another hard slap at her bottom, only to miss as she slipped from his lap, to land in the mud with a cry of shock and disgust. His cum erupted from him, and as she twisted around frantically a second spurt caught her full in the face, laying a thick stream of sticky white across one eye, down her cheek and into her open mouth.

"You …," she managed, only for her words to break to a peculiar gulping noise as Peter filled her mouth with his cock, milking the last of his cum down her throat despite her muffled protests.

He was about to pull free, guilt already welling up inside him for being so rough with her, when suddenly she began to suck, as eager and wanton as any girl he'd known. The force of her suction was not dimmed by her sobs as the tears streamed down her cheeks even as she deliberately swallowed down what he'd done in her mouth.

"Now you can masturbate," he told her. "Go on. I'll keep my cock in your mouth until you come. Do it, Rhiannon!"

A wet, choking noise escaped her throat, but she'd widened her legs and her fingers were already working in the wet slit between, the slender fingers of her other hand stroking at his balls, her mouth pursed around his shaft. Her eyes were closed, her tearstained face full of as much shame as ecstasy while the motion of her fingers on her cunt grew ever more urgent, until at last her body locked tight in orgasm.

"Dear, dear Rhiannon," Peter sighed. "Like mother, like daughter."

Peter and Rhiannon took their time over lunch, ordering the Duck's three course set menu and washing it down with a bottle of cold Rhenish wine as they sat by the Thames. She'd been a little annoyed at first, pointing out in no uncertain terms that when she'd suggested a spanking and a fuck she hadn't bargained on being dropped in a mud puddle, nor on getting a face full of cum. Furthermore, she had no spare clothes. Peter had offered to return her to Broadfields but the idea was clearly impractical, given the state she was in. So, he'd offered to treat her to some new clothes, and she'd accepted his offer. They'd driven into Goring, where Peter had purchased a green summer dress, which she'd changed into in the car before making herself properly decent in the ladies' room at the Duck. She'd been much happier when she'd emerged, skipping down the long grassy slope to the table he'd chosen beside the river and giving him a twirl to make her new dress rise, showing off her legs and perhaps rather more of her panties than she'd intended, to the ill-disguised shock of two elderly ladies nearby.

Peter had been ready to make a full apology for his behaviour, but she no longer seemed to care, chatting happily of this and that and teasing him for his lack of self-control. In return, he threatened to spank her then and there, in front of the three dozen or so people also enjoying lunch in the garden and anybody who happened to be crossing the bridge. She dared him to do it and he found himself forced to back down, but from that point there had been no doubt that it was going to happen. With lunch finished, they enjoyed a leisurely coffee while watching the river before returning to the car.

Instead of turning south towards Broadfields, Peter drove up onto the downs, stopping at the end of a track where they could look out over the Vale of White Horse through air so clear that the spires of Oxford were visible in the distance. Peter had been there just once before, on a summer Sunday the year before his expulsion. As he'd hoped, it had barely changed at all. The lonely beech hanger where he'd relieved his frustration over a copy of Mayfair magazine was as he remembered it, with a screen of hawthorn to shield the interior from prying eyes and ledges of chalk where generations of badgers had dug into the hillside. Rhiannon seemed to have forgotten all about the possibility of being spanked, laughing and showing off in her new dress as she walked, and when Peter took her firmly by the ear and pulled her in among the beeches she gave a squeak of surprise and alarm.

"Ow, that hurts!" she protested. "What are you doing?"

"I'm going to spank you," he told her as he seated himself on a convenient ledge. "Across my knee and bare bottom, for being such a tease. Come on now, over you go. This is what you wanted, isn't it?"

Rhiannon gave a sullen little mewl, her big green eyes moist with apprehension and even a little fear. But she quickly draped herself across his lap as best she could, her feet braced on the ground, her pert bottom lifted into a tempting ball beneath her dress. Peter could feel her trembling, and his own hands were shaking as he stripped her, pulling off the pretty green dress, followed by her shoes and socks, and last of all her panties, to leave her naked in the dappled sunlight.

"It's quite safe," he assured her. "Now come on, get that little rump up higher and we'll get you spanked."

She did as she was told, lifting her hips to let her cheeks spread, exposing her tender anus and the little purse of her cunt. Peter slid a hand between her thighs, cupping the soft, furry swell of her sex and pushing a thumb inside her vagina, only for her to cry out.

"Ow! I'm still sore, Peter."

"Sorry," he told her, "and I'm sorry I took your virginity so roughly …"

"You didn't. Clemmie did me with a hairbrush."

"That doesn't count!" Peter laughed, easing his thumb free. "You need a cock inside you to lose your virginity, Rhiannon, not your toasty girl's hairbrush handle. Does she spank you as well? I'd have thought you'd be the one spanking her?"

"We take turns," she told him as he began to lay gentle pats across her cheeks. "Sometimes one of us feels she needs it, or sometimes we play dice or cards and the loser gets it. Mmm … that's nice. A little harder please."

Peter smiled and began to spank a little harder, just enough to make her cheeks bounce and spread to the smacks. "I take it you do each other bare bottomed?"

"Yes, of course, or completely naked. Clemmie loves to be naked. I'm the one who loves to spank, and be spanked, thanks to you, Peter Finch."

"Always happy to oblige a lady," Peter responded, lifting his knee to tip her up a little as he took her around the waist.

Her feet had come clear of the ground and she'd begun to kick her long, bare legs as the spanking continued. Peter could sense the excitement of her cunt, while his cock had begun to stiffen once more. But he was in no hurry, peppering her bottom with stinging slaps of his fingertips to make her gasp and wriggle in his grip, then slipping a hand between her thighs, this time to rub at her clit instead of penetrating her.

"You're a disgrace, Rhiannon," he told her. "A dirty little brat who badly needs her bottom smacked hard and often. Imagine stripping for your friend and having her spank you for kicks, never mind letting her put her hairbrush handle inside you. What else do you do, Rhiannon? I'm sure you kiss. Do you suck her titties, do you let her suck yours? Do you lick each other's cunts? Tell me!"

"Yes!" Rhiannon sobbed. "You're so dirty! Now harder

… hurt me … punish me, and tell me off."

"I will, because that's what you need, you rude little brat, a good spanking and a lecture. So what else do you do together, Rhiannon? Have you had your tongue in her arse? I bet you have, and I bet she's had hers up yours as well, with your butt in her face as she licks your little hole clean, right inside …"

His words broke as Rhiannon groped back for her cunt, cocking one leg high like a dog about to piddle on a lamppost as she began to clutch and grasp at herself, gasping and crying out to the sting of the smacks, but still babbling words.

"No … not that … I couldn't! It's too dirty … too dirty … But oh I wish she'd make me do it to her … so, so badly!"

She screamed as she finished, her muscles in violent contraction as she went into an orgasm even more powerful than before, with Peter spanking her relentlessly and reminding her of what she'd said.

"You want to lick your friend's arsehole, do you? What a confession. What a confession, Rhiannon! You ought to be ashamed of yourself, wanting Clementine to sit on your face, wanting to push your tongue up into her bottom!"

Rhiannon gave one last cry and went limp, leaving Peter grinning as he lowered her gently to her knees.

"You certainly deserved that," he told her, "and now you're going to say thank you, nicely, the way a spanked girl should."

He'd freed his cock as he spoke and she gave no resistance beyond a mildly petulant glance as he fed it into her mouth. Soon she was sucking earnestly, if a little clumsily, and Peter took pity on her, taking hold of his shaft to masturbate into her mouth. Only when he was close to orgasm did he take a grip on her hair, holding her firmly in place as he finished himself off and making sure she swallowed before letting go.

"Beast," she said, sitting back on her heels. "That was the best spanking, though. Thank you."

"Any time," Peter promised. "I suppose I'd better get you back to school then?"

Rhiannon stood up and stretched in the warm sunlight, naked and beautiful.

"Let's stay here," she said. "Or better still, why don't you take me back home? You can spank me whenever you want, and all the other dirty things you like to do."

"School," Peter insisted. "Come on."

"There's no point," she answered. "It's too late."

"What do you mean it's too late?" he demanded in sudden alarm.

"It's past five o'clock," she told him. "My taxi for the airport was supposed to come at two. My plane left half-an-hour ago."

"I'll say one thing for letting Master Jacobaeus run the club," Karen said. "We don't have to spend half the day setting it up."

"Yes," Peter agreed. "Although I think he might at least have asked you to be club domina."

"I don't think he believes in them," Karen answered. "You know, it's all this crap about men being the naturally dominant sex, even when more than half the men who go to clubs are submissive. You'd think he'd notice."

"Master Jacobaeus only sees what he wants to see," Michelle stated. "But he does have the most enormous cock."

"Very philosophical," Peter said. "Here we are."

They had reached St. Botolph's, a great, squat edifice with a massive portico at the front and a disproportionately small spire stuck on top as if as an afterthought, so that it resembled an ancient temple as much as a church. A corrugated iron fence surrounded it, open at the front where one of the doormen Peter regularly employed stood waiting for guests. Peter parked the cab at what he considered a safe distance and they walked back, drawing curious looks in their longcoats and a couple of wolf whistles for the girls' high heels.

Rhiannon was back at the apartment, sulking because she couldn't come to the party. A terse conversation with her father in Saudi Arabia had ended in Peter taking the phone and telling Mr. O'Neil that Rhiannon was old enough to make her own choices. Still, he'd decided that taking her to a fetish club (a club that was almost certainly going to be raided by the police) was pushing his luck. He'd spanked her afterwards, out of genuine exasperation with her behaviour, but she'd enjoyed it even more than when they'd only been playing, and Michelle's threat of having to take it from a woman too had been greeted with a happy purr. Making her stay in had been the only effective punishment.

All three of them were waived through the fence, to where broad stone steps rose between the great pillars of the church to a pair of high, ornate doors, now open to the summer evening. The interior had been largely cleared of pews, adding to the impression of empty space and drawing the focus to the altar, which was now covered with a black velvet cloth on which a large, golden pentagram had been marked. A second pentagram decorated the floor between the choir stalls. This pentagram was larger still and surrounded by runes and other mystical symbols, all beautifully done in gold, red and black. Peter found himself grinning as he looked around, and he extended a hand as Master Jacobaeus himself appeared from the steps leading to the crypt.

"I know I can always count on you to put on a show," Peter told him. "So what's the program?"

"For the main event, I'm deflowering a new slave," Master Jacobaeus answered, as casually as if he was describing a theatre trip. "Before that there are demos, and wrestling—girl on girl. If you want to sign up, see Blue."

The last remark had been addressed to Karen, who responded with a non-committal nod, but Michelle answered.

"Ooh, yes please! Come on, Karen, sign up with me and you can beat me up and spank me, maybe sit on my face. Let's find Blue."

Karen had opted to wear the slinkiest of catsuits, and Peter enjoyed watching the clearly defined contours of her body as both girls departed and made their way through the crowd. Peter continued to talk to Master Jacobaeus for a while before buying a bottle of lager at the bar. The bar itself had been constructed with beer cases and pews arranged around two huge refrigerators. Master Jacobaeus evidently hadn't bothered with a licence, or anything else official, but he had put a great deal of work into the club. A generator set up in the vestry provided power, with cables snaking across the floor and down the steps to the crypt. Twin gantries had been rigged to support a bank of lights, mostly covered with red or orange gels, while a lanky youth with his naked upper body covered in swirling tattoos had set up an improvised booth in the lectern so that he could look out over the crowd as he controlled the music.

The crypt proved to be even more impressively inappropriate than the main body of the church. It was a broad, pillared vault, with much of the space occupied by tombs, and both floor and walls almost entirely occupied by plaques and engravings to the departed. What open space remained was largely taken up with dungeon equipment, including spanking stools of several different designs, a pillory, a St. Andrew's cross, a curious basket-like device made of webbing and hung from a rusting iron hook in the ceiling, and a massive rack made of black iron and wood. Red lamps and the flickering fire light from two braziers added to the sinister effect and Peter found himself nodding in appreciation as he sipped his beer.

People were beginning to gather, many of his regulars and others who seemed more drawn to the atmosphere than typical practitioners of kinky sex. Goths, ravers and simple voyeurs outnumbered those dressed for sex by at least three to one, with men in the majority, although there was no shortage of nubile female flesh on show. A few had even started already, with a man in nothing but a rubber posing pouch acting as a table and foot rest for a trio of giggling Goth girls, while a well-built woman in a skimpy black rubber outfit was in the pillory being whipped by a man who might or might not have been her husband.

Peter watched for a while, admiring the woman's nicely rounded bottom, but the situation seemed rather too contrived for his tastes, and she was certainly no substitute for Rhiannon, nor Michelle. Returning to the upper floor, he found some of the helpers setting up a wrestling ring in the middle of the floor, while Blue stood to one side with a notebook, organising the schedule. Violet was with her, also Sophie, to Peter's surprise, as he'd advised her not to come. Concerned, he walked quickly over to speak to her.

"Hello Sophie. Aren't you worried about the police?"

"Not really," Sophie answered. "I really want to wrestle, and I don't suppose they'll come until late. I've got no ID on me anyway."

"Your choice," Peter told her. "But whatever happens, don't try and run for it. This place is very easy to surround, with enough men. So who are you against?"

"Red, then one of the other winners. It's a knockout competition."

"You seem very confident. You got your face sat on last time."

"By Violet, and I wasn't really trying."

"Is that so?" Peter asked, intrigued by her tone of voice. "This I have to see."

She smiled, then turned away as Blue approached her, leaving Peter to continue his rounds. The music had begun, a throbbing repetitive beat accompanied by flashing red lights that threw the shadows of the dancers' jerking bodies across the high walls and pillars of the church. Outside, the light was beginning to fade, making what seemed to be Master Jacobaeus' vision of hell more compelling by the instant. Screams from the direction of the stairs drew Peter's attention and he descended to the crypt once more, to find Red strapped naked to the cross while Master Jacobaeus used hot wax on her breasts and belly.

A crowd had gathered to watch and Peter stayed on the stairs so that he could get a proper view of her body. Her full breasts and the plump swell of her stomach were already spattered dark red with wax, while her back was arched in blended pain and ecstasy reflected in the strained expression on her face. She was gasping, her eyes closed, and with each fresh application of wax to her bare skin she would scream and jerk in the leather straps that bound her in place. Master Jacobaeus stood to one side, making sure everybody could get a clear view as he tortured her, slow and calm, betraying no open emotion save for a faint, cruel smile as he moved the thick, blood red candle over her skin. Most of her breasts had been done, each plump white orb thickly coated with wax, save for the area around her nipples, to give the impression of a peep-hole bra with each fleshy little bud standing stiff at the centre of a pale circle. Her shaven cunt had been avoided too, so that the bulge of her sex showed white and nude, save for the glistening pink of her slit.

Master Jacobaeus spoke to her, very softly. She responded with the faintest of nods and her body began to tremble as the candle moved slowly up towards her breasts once more, bringing the hot drips ever closer to her straining nipples. A drop caught one stiff bud. Red screamed, and screamed again at the touch of a second drop, her whole body taut in her bonds, her muscles jerking against the leather, her thighs squeezing tight and parting once more, now wet with sap from her pussy. Again Master Jacobaeus moved the candle, catching her other nipple to set her screaming again, and moving abruptly down to drip wax directly on her outthrust cunt. Red screamed again, louder still, and not once but repeatedly, writhing in her bonds as molten wax splashed her cunt, her head shaking desperately from side to side in her pain, only for her back to arch tight and her mouth to come wide, now in silence as her torture finally brought her to orgasm. Master Jacobaeus stood back, acknowledged the crowd with a complacent nod and began to speak.

"And to answer the earlier question, that is why I call myself Master. It is not a title I take lightly, nor one that should be used by those who have not earned it, as I hope I have made clear?"

Nobody disagreed and he went on.

"We must all learn, but as you have seen there is a great

leap to be made between coming to understand your dominance as a man and achieving the status of Master. So we move on, from fire to water, from wax to another skill which I can use to bring a woman's senses to a peak far beyond what most will ever achieve: the enema. However, poor Slave Red is a trifle exhausted from her experience, and a good Master knows never to abuse his property. So perhaps I could have a volunteer from the audience?"

Nobody answered him outright, but Peter noticed two of his regulars holding an urgent, whispered conversation and the girl had quickly been pushed forward. She was in a leather bikini and high heels, with a collar around her neck and nothing more, while her long, dark hair hid her face as she bowed her head to Master Jacobaeus. Peter knew her as Lily and had seen her bound and whipped on several occasions, but the thought of watching her receive a public enema was irresistible.

Moving behind a row of tombs and climbing on top of one with a conveniently flat lid, he managed to find himself a clear view of the pillory where a fat bulb of red rubber and a length of tubing already hung from one of the hooks in the ceiling. The rest of the crowd moved with Master Jacobaeus, Lily's partner and Lily herself, bringing her to the pillory and quickly fixing her neck and arms into place. An adjustment to the stand forced her upper body down and her hips up, so that her bottom was the highest part of her body, with each cheek stretching out the leather of her bikini bottoms to taut perfection and her cunt outlined in exact detail, a sight so fine that Peter almost found it a shame when she was quickly stripped and her naked rear view put on show.

Her partner moved to the side, leaving Master Jacobaeus to go about his work, as cool and matter-of-fact as ever as he pulled on rubber gloves, applied lubricant and pushed one long finger up inside Lily's bottom. She was already shaking vigorously, and her cunt had begun to glisten, but he took no notice, carefully working her anus with first one finger and then two before reaching for the enema bag and inserting the nozzle into her now expectant hole. He talked as he worked, explaining what he was doing and what Lily would feel with her bottom spread to the audience and her head and hands trapped in the pillory. Peter could well imagine, having inflicted the same humiliating routine on various girls over the years. But it was a sight that never failed to fascinate him, especially when the victim let her emotions go.

Lily looked as if she wasn't going to disappoint. Her head had remained hung in submission as she'd been fixed into place, stripped and penetrated, silent all the while. But once Master Jacobaeus had twisted the spigot that controlled the flow of water into her rectum, she quickly began to respond. First came a low sob as she felt the cool water inside her, a moment of silence, then a faint mewling noise as her belly began to swell and bloat. Before long she was treading up and down on the hard flagstones of the floor, with ever increasing desperation, while the enema bag slowly deflated and her belly grew rounded and fat.

When Master Jacobaeus pulled the nozzle free of her anus Peter was sure the full contents of her rectum would explode back out instantaneously, but she seemed determined to hold off from the final disgrace as long as possible, wriggling her toes and squeezing her bottom cheeks as she gasped out every sensation. The effort was obviously futile and served only to amuse her audience and prolong her ordeal, but still she clung on. Her butthole begun to bulge outward, the flesh pink and glistening, a thin trickle of white fluid escaping from the central hole as she struggled to hold it in. It hadn't been water. It was milk. Somebody noticed and laughed, at which Master Jacobaeus reached out to give Lily a single, resounding smack across her bottom.

She let go, crying out in despair and humiliation as the milk exploded from her body in a high arc to splash down behind her. A second squirt followed, and a third, each accompanied by a cry from Lily, not of pain, but pure emotional anguish for what had been done to her and her utter helplessness to stop the milk now pulsing from the wet pink flower of her arsehole. Master Jacobaeus merely watched, his arms folded across his chest, his face expressionless as Lily let out the rest of her enema, abandoned now to her shame as the milky fluid trickled down over her cunt to puddle on the floor. Only when the flow had reduced to soft, wet bubbles and Lily's head hung in defeat did Master Jacobaeus reach out, using one gloved hand to stimulate her sopping cunt, bringing her quickly to an orgasm every bit as intense as Red's.

The moment she was done the crowd began to clap and cheer, with the exception of a few who stood in the wrong place and been splashed when she let go. But not even they complained. Peter found himself clapping politely, amused and not a little aroused, to the point of wishing that he knew Lily better, as no sooner had she been released then she went down on her knees to her boyfriend, to take his cock in her mouth and suck with frantic urgency. Master Jacobaeus watched with a paternal eye for a while before announcing a demonstration of mummification, a fetish which had never appealed to Peter on the grounds that it seemed counterproductive to conceal a girl's body from view.

He went back upstairs, to find the wrestling in full swing. Michelle was pinned to the mat, panties off, thighs held wide and a fat pink dildo pushed deep into her cunt. The victorious Karen straddled her, rubber-clad bottom pressed full into the defeated girl's face. Blue was acting as referee but seemed in no hurry to bring the bout to an end, waiting as Karen retrieved Michelle's knickers and tossed them into the audience, ensuring that she'd have to go bare under her school skirt for the rest of the evening.

"An easy victory for Miss Lash!" Blue declared. "And so to our third bout of the evening, Slave Red versus ..."

The music had died down for an instant but swelled once more, drowning her voice even as Red stepped into the ring. She was naked, her skin glistening with sweat and spotted with wax, full of nervous energy but clearly in no condition to put up a decent fight. Another girl joined her, Sophie, shrugging off her coat as she stepped over the ropes to reveal skin-tight shorts of blue velvet. Her hair was tied up with a ribbon of the same material, and other than that she was completely nude, with her full, beautiful breasts proudly displayed for all to see.

She looked as if she wanted to lose, as Peter would have expected, but there was really no contest. Red was too small and not nearly strong enough, even without the haze of submission from her waxing. She was pinned in moments, face down on the floor to have her bottom smacked before being rolled over and given a faceful of well filled velvet shorts, with Sophie squirming down onto Red's face to the beat of the music before rising to her feet, victorious.

The next bout was less one-sided, with Violet ending up sweaty and dishevelled before she managed to get the better of a tall black girl Peter didn't recognise. Violet's skin was scratched and her blouse ripped open to leave one breast bare, while her opponent had kept on struggling even after having her lower clothes pulled right off and her cunt splayed to the delighted audience. A pause followed, which allowed Peter to find Michelle among the now dense crowd. He approached her from behind, sliding a hand up her pleated skirt to squeeze one fleshy little cheek. She turned and kissed him, then pointed to where Tia was dancing naked for a man seated in one of the pews—Ben Thompson.

Peter hurried over, dragging Michelle behind him, to be greeted with a wiggle of Tia's bottom and a shy grin from Ben. After placing a perfunctory slap across one bare brown globe, he sat down by his friend, shouting into his ear to warn him of the impending police raid, but Ben merely smiled and leant close to reply.

"Not tonight. Lennox wanted to swamp the place, but

his request for resources was denied. I was looking for you to tell you."

"Thanks!" Peter answered, but he cursed under his breath as he turned away. The dramatic manifesto he and Master Jacobaeus had been concocting would be ineffectual without a police raid. Still, that would not stop him from indulging himself.

Tia was plainly intent on getting both their attention, leaning forward with her heavy breasts in her hands. Peter shrugged off his secondary concerns and sat back to enjoy the show, wondering just how close Ben and Tia had become, and whether she'd let him fuck her glorious cleavage the way he had with Red. She certainly seemed eager to please, displaying her glorious curves with uninhibited delight.

Michelle was equally keen, lifting her skirt to wiggle her bare bottom against his leg as she sat down on his lap before reaching out to take a handful of Tia's rump. Tia responded by pulling Michelle up again and the two girls began to dance together, their hands moving over each other's bodies to a slow, sensuous rhythm that had nothing to do with the pulsing music. Ben was watching pop-eyed and even Peter was giving the girls his full attention as their caresses grew more intimate, while others had begun to turn and stare.

A roar went up from beyond the crowd, audible even above the music, making Peter wonder what was going on in the wrestling ring. But Michelle was now suckling on one long, dark nipple as Tia pretended to breastfeed her, a spectacle he had no intention of missing. His cock was stiffening nicely too, and he glanced towards Ben, wondering if his friend had the nerve to join him in fucking the girls right there with so many people looking on. Ben glanced back, happy but embarrassed and Peter set his plans aside, contenting himself with a surreptitious squeeze of his cock through his trousers as Michelle was pushed down to lick at Tia's cunt.

Another roar went up from the wrestling ring, but Peter's

interest was fixed as he watched his girlfriend taken firmly by the hair and pulled between her friend's thighs. Michelle licked eagerly, her eyes closed in bliss as she suckled, only for Tia to suddenly swing round, pushing out her full, dark bottom. For an instant Michelle hesitated, looking up at her gloating friend with a mixture of accusation and lust, before burying her face between Tia's cheeks. She'd begun to lick, Michelle's pretty, pale face smothered in an abundance of brown flesh, her tongue probing her friend's secretive anus as thirty or forty people looked on.

For Peter it was too much. Freeing his cock, he got down behind Michelle to flip her skirt up over her naked backside, apply a few firm smacks to each well-rounded cheek and drive his erection between, filling her cunt to its depth. She held her position, her face still buried between Tia's cheeks as she was fucked, Peter's cock pumping inside her as she licked her friend's long, deep crevice. Peter circled her waist, rubbing at her cunt as he fucked her, intent on bringing her off while her tongue explored Tia's bottom. Somebody began to clap, then another, matching the rhythm of Peter's thrusts as shudders passed through Michelle's body, faster, and faster still, until she gave a muffled cry. She was so close to orgasm and ready to pull her face free, but Tia wasn't quite finished with her. Caramel coloured fingers twisted into Michelle's fine blonde hair to keep her firmly smothered in plump rump as she was brought to orgasm under Peter's fingers. Michelle pounded her palms on the floor, her orgasm shuddering through her, and all the while desperate to take another breath.

Peter kept up his pace until Michelle had wrung out the last of her orgasm, and still Tia would not release her suffocating grip. Holding off with some difficulty, Peter finally pulled his cock free, jerking himself to climax over Michelle's upturned arse, splashing her cheeks and slit with thick white cum, soiling her skirt and blouse, before whirling her round to sink his still-hard cock deep into her throat. Finally free from the suffocating mounds of mighty flesh, Michelle had time for one desperate gasp of oxygen before her airway was once again halted, this time by Peter's cock. Tia turned and knelt at the same instant, her mouth gaping expectantly. Peter was more than happy to share, feeding her the final pearls of his semen and Michelle's juice before collapsing back to watch as the girls shared a long, sticky kiss with his semen glistening around their mouths as their lips and tongues combined.

While he'd been fucking Michelle, Peter had been vaguely aware of ever wilder and more enthusiastic calls from the direction of the wrestling ring, and as soon as he'd gotten his breath back he climbed onto a pew to see what was happening. Violet was there, her skirt turned up and her panties rolled down around her knees, looking distinctly sorry for herself as she rubbed at one little red arse cheek. She'd obviously been spanked, presumably by Sophie who was now in the ring facing up to Karen.

Both girls were streaked with sweat, their hair in disarray, their eyes wild, oblivious to everything but each other. Their fight had obviously gone far beyond the usual half-playful tussle in which it was obvious who would allow themselves to be beaten. Here, neither was going to back down, nor submit unless she was forced to. That much was obvious, but as they closed, grappled and went down together on the mat it immediately struck Peter that, for all Karen's natural dominance and effortless poise, she was getting a lot more than she'd bargained for. Sophie wasn't giving in, and her size and strength had begun to tell. Karen looked frightened, and there was a sense of desperation as she struggled to break a hold, but she obviously wasn't going to back down.

They closed again, struggling together on the mat, first Karen on top, then Sophie. For a moment they were in deadlock, only for Karen to snatch at Sophie's shorts, tugging them down to bare her backside, perhaps intending to embarrass her and get a telling grip while Sophie tried to cover herself up. The move failed, Sophie seemingly indifferent to having herself on show to the cheering crowd as she took hold of Karen's wrist with both hands and twisted hard. Karen went over, her face set in pain and fury as she was forced onto her front with one arm twisted high into the small of her back. Sophie climbed on, straddling Karen's body and pressing down hard. Karen kicked, scratched and thumped at the canvas in a furious effort to break free, all the while spitting swearwords inaudible above the music. But Sophie merely tightened her grip, freed one hand and began to pull down the zip at the back of the catsuit while Karen struggled in vain.

Karen realised what was about to happen to her and she seemed to go berserk, thrashing in Sophie's grip, her face working between fury and worry as she was gradually exposed. The curve of her back was showing, then the first swell of her bottom. But still she fought, refusing to use the stop word that would have forced Sophie to release her—the same stop word that would also have been an admission of defeat. Still the zip slid lower, around the curve of her buttocks and down between her legs, to show off her full, nude, intimate glory, at which she gave one last, furious jerk, screamed and went limp. Sophie seized on the moment, divesting Karen's temporarily motionless body of her precious catsuit to leave her just as naked as Sophie. With exaggerated indifference, Sophie tossed the catsuit to the side of the ring where it lay crumpled on the floor. It, like Karen herself, having lost all of the sleek elegance it once had. In a final act of defiance, Sophie grabbed two handfuls of Karen's hair and, with a yelp that was more like a battle cry, pulled as hard as she could like some victorious playground bully. Karen let out a wail of infuriated pain and, with that, Sophie began to spank.

Peter couldn't help but grin as he watched Karen's trim little bottom jiggle and bounce to the slaps—treatment she'd dished out so many times and to so many girls but never, ever

received herself. She'd obviously given in too, her face set in sullen resignation as she was given her virgin spanking, all the fight in her gone from the moment her cunt had been displayed. But, while Karen had accepted her fate, others were reacting differently. All around the ring were men she'd dominated before. Each and every one was staring in horror and disbelief to see his Goddess brought low, not merely spanked, but accepting a spanking and a bare bottom beating at that.

Their expressions were so comic that Peter was laughing as he jumped down from the pew, intent on comforting Karen before taking some of the swagger out of Sophie by turning her over his knee in front of the crowd who'd just witnessed her victory. But all at once, before he could get to the ringside, the lights went out. The blackness was sudden and absolute, while the music had cut off equally abruptly, to be replaced by angry or puzzled voices and a single scream as new light flooded the church, blood red and flickering.

Peter turned to see that the tall windows beyond the altar were now lit by what looked like flames from outside. A tall figure was silhouetted black against the light and made monstrous by the great antlers projecting from his head. Master Jacobaeus was standing on the altar, and as the crowd turned to gape he had raised his arms, spreading out his cloak as spotlights came on to splash his naked body with yellow light. Gold and scarlet symbols marked the inside of his cloak, while his monstrous cock stood fully erect from his belly, painted vivid scarlet. In place of the human face Peter had expected to see was the head of a stag, dead eyed and horrid, with the teeth bared in a rictus grin.

More lights came on, white and clear, making a patch on the aisle where a girl stood alone, young and fresh and beautiful, a circlet of oak leaves crowning her blonde hair, her lithe, delicate body pale and naked. Music started once more, a wild, pagan rhythm of drums and flutes, but quiet, allowing the figure on the altar to be heard clearly as he began to chant. The naked girl started forward, her eyes fixed upon the monstrous cock that would shortly be thrust inside her virgin womanhood.

"He's good, I'll give him that," Peter whispered as Michelle cuddled to his side, both of them watching entranced as Master Jacobaeus beckoned the virgin to climb onto the altar.

She climbed the steps and pulled herself up, kneeling in a genuflection of worship, her face level with his monstrous erection. He cried out, inviting the audience to witness as she was deflowered, his arms still raised as she planted a single, delicate kiss on his massive balls. Again the lights changed, a single bright spotlight illuminating the scene as the girl turned, pressing her breasts to the cold, hard stone of the altar, her face looking out to the crowd as she arched her back and offered her sex to Master Jacobaeus. He took her hips, squatting down to press his cock between her thighs, moved a hand to guide himself to the mouth of her virginity, and gave one gentle push. She'd obviously been prepared for the ritual with a soothing lubricant, but still she screamed as she was penetrated, her mouth wide in pain and shock. But as he began to pump inside her, the look changed, first to acquiescence, then to contentment and then to ecstasy.

"Bravo!" Peter said quietly, and as the girl's fucking began in earnest he'd begun to clap along with the rest of the crowd, only to break off at a scream of outrage.

A man burst from the crowd, hurling himself at Master Jacobaeus to send him tumbling backwards from the altar, his cock slurping from the girl's cunt. She screamed and rolled to the side, vanishing among the crowd as the two men rose from behind the altar, trading punches and screaming at each other, Master Jacobaeus grotesque in his cloak and stag's head, the other in rough leathers but instantly recognisable—Inspector Lennox.

"God, or maybe Satan, please let somebody have a camera!" Peter whispered, an instant before the explosion of a flash bulb answered his prayer.

◆ ◆ ◆ ◆

"He's been transferred to traffic. Responsible for coordinating wardens in one of the outer boroughs," Clive remarked, "I forget which. There'll be a full investigation too, and he'll be recommended for psychiatric assessment."

"Thank you," Peter answered, and reached out to clink his brandy glass against his friend's.

They'd assembled at Lorrimer's, to celebrate Peter's election to membership and, incidentally, the downfall of Inspector Lennox.

"Not at all," Clive responded. "I only did what would have been expected of me anyway. And you didn't really need to bribe me, although of course young Sophie was greatly appreciated."

"Think of her as a thank you gift, in advance," Peter told him. "And of course, she only came round to clean, so it wasn't much at all. Not only that, but the best I expected was for you to be able to reprimand Lennox for wasting resources. I knew Master Jacobaeus would annoy him, but had no idea he'd go berserk."

Clive laughed and took a swallow of brandy before he went on.

"I only wish I could have been there to watch."

"It was quite a sight," Ben assured him, "and given the way Lennox was raving about sacrilege and desecration I'd say the psychiatric assessment is fully justified. Not that Master Jacobaeus is much better, but then he's not in public service."

"He should be," Peter remarked. "It would liven things up no end. Perhaps you can appoint him to a church commission or something, Gabriel?"

"Not my department, I'm afraid," Gabriel chuckled. "Now how about a visit from this girl you sent to Clive? She sounds spectacular."

"Everything is in hand," Peter assured him. "I'll put you down for a visit from Sophie this evening, if you like. But Grove House Maids needs to grow slowly. Speaking of which, I need to check that my Uncle Charles was suitably impressed by the service. He had Sophie last night. I'll be back in a few minutes."

He walked from the room they'd booked and downstairs, to where his Uncle Charles was ensconced in his favourite seat in the smoking room. The old soldier greeted him affably, shaking his hand and insisting on ordering double measures of the oldest Cognac Lorrimer's could provide.

"I take it things went well then?" Peter asked as he made himself comfortable in the sage green leather armchair opposite his uncle.

"Couldn't have been better," Charles responded cheerfully. "Three of the sweetest little poppets you could ever imagine, and ..."

"Three?" Peter queried.

"Yes, three," his uncle answered. "There was Sophie— delightfully resilient, and the pretty redhead with the Irish accent ..."

"Rhiannon!?" Peter broke in. "The little cow!"

"... and the sweet little blonde," Charles finished.

"Michelle?" Peter queried. "But she was with me."

"Surely you know who you sent?" Charles queried. "Young girl, slim, very polite, blonde hair down to her backside, loves to go naked, squeals when she's spanked. What was her name now ..."

"That's not Michelle," Peter stated, puzzled.

"... Clemmie, that's it," his uncle finished.

"Clemmie," Peter answered slowly. "As in Clementine Stewart ... Oh God. Well, one thing's for sure, the maid service is going to have to be pretty damn discreet. You've just spanked and played with a Member of the House's daughter!"

PART THREE

◆◆◆◆

The Grove, Hertfordshire, 1997

Chapter One

Rhiannon and Clementine stood against the wall, hands on their heads, the smart green skirts of their maid's uniforms tucked up, panties pulled down to show off bare, red bottoms. Both had been spanked, one after the other, across Peter's knee and were now being made to do corner time while he tried to decide how best to cope with the situation they'd gotten him into, and for which they'd been recently punished.

Unfortunately, just as the he knew there was no real punishment in spanking girls who enjoyed it, he also knew that there was no real choice but to accept the situation. It wasn't all bad in any case, just one more complication to the already labyrinthine condition of Grove House Maids. In general he was doing very well. The idea worked perfectly. More than fifty girls had now been on the books, from those who'd been out only once to the best of his regulars, but not one had ever taken her story to the press or done anything else to compromise the position of the men they'd visited for spankings, for sex, and to satisfy all manner of curious peccadilloes. The tier system in particular worked well, ensuring that all of the girls had more to lose than they could possibly hope to gain, with only the most ambitious going to the men with the highest profiles.

Sophie Fitzroy, technically the first Grove House girl of all, was now a barrister and seemed likely to climb higher still in the legal profession, while others were rising rapidly in their chosen spheres, including politics, diplomacy, the civil and military services, the professions and business. Rather more were wives of politicians, captains of industry, senior civil servants and more, in most cases having met their future husbands while doing maid service. Nevertheless, while recruiting took tact and skill, he'd always been able to keep enough girls on the books to bring in a decent income, allowing him to make Grove House Maids his full time job. The house was another matter, and would have been well beyond his means but for the generosity of his Uncle Charles, who had died a happy man and left everything to Peter, to the astonishment and fury of the rest of the family. The house lay deep in the Chilterns, and was the ideal place for parties and the private meetings so essential to the operation.

Karen and Violet had moved on, and now occupied a smart Pimlico town house, the cellar of which had been converted into a superbly equipped dungeon in which they could entertain their clients, including those who Peter passed on. They in turn sent him men, and the occasional woman, whose pleasure lay in dominance rather than submission. Michelle was now his wife, although their relationship was far from orthodox, with Rhiannon sharing their bed as often as not and both taking their pleasure where and when they pleased. Rhiannon herself was now keeping the books as well as going out to clients, while Clementine had proved extraordinarily adept at recruiting new talent, principally from Oxford, where she was studying for a Master's degree in biochemistry.

The problem was in the very exclusivity that made the organisation safe. Clementine's knack lay in selecting girls she knew were safe, or who could be vouched for in turn. That meant they had to know each other well, and none knew each other better than those who'd been lovers at Broadfields, where the traditions of lesbian sex she and Rhiannon had enjoyed were still going strong. Hence the situation which had led to the two girls taking long and painful trips across Peter's knee before being lined up against the wall with their smacked bottoms still bare as he lectured them.

"She was Felicity's toasty girl," Clementine said plaintively after a while.

"Yes," Peter answered. "I know she was Felicity's toasty girl, but she is also Ben Thompson's daughter. What am

I supposed to say to him if he finds out that I'm sending his precious little princess out for spankings and sex?"

"Tell him not to be a hypocrite," Rhiannon advised. "He has a girl a week!"

"Besides," Clementine put in, "Chloe's old enough to make her own decisions and there's no reason Ben should find out anyway. Dad's never found out about me, has he?"

"No, thank God," Peter answered, "and I suppose you're right. Okay, bring her in, but you can keep your uniforms up. That will help to see if she's for real, with you two parading around bare bottomed."

"We'll trip over our knickers," Rhiannon pointed out.

"And we're supposed to be with Lord Justice Dolamore-Brown at three o'clock," Clementine added. "We'll be late if we don't hurry up."

"Good," Peter replied. "He can give you both another spanking. Now, off with your knickers, if you're worried about falling over, and see her in."

The girls shared a look compounded of embarrassment and resignation, but did as they were told, stepping quickly out of their panties and keeping the skirts of their maid's uniforms tucked up as Rhiannon sat down and Clementine left the room. She was soon back, with a pretty, brown-haired girl of middling height with beautiful, melting eyes and a trim figure—a combination marred somewhat by a slight resemblance to her father. Her face was distinctly pink.

"I'm Chloe Thompson," she told Peter.

"I know," he replied. "I take it you heard what was going on just now?"

"You spanked them both," she said, throwing a glance towards Rhiannon and Clementine, now both sitting bare bottomed on the sofa while their underwear lay on the table in front of Peter.

"Yes, I did," he went on, "and now I'm going to spank

you. You know that, don't you?"

"Felicity explained it all," she said, now with her fingers entwining nervously as she began to fidget. "I need to be spanked to show that I'm genuine."

"Partly that," Peter replied, "and partly because Grove House girls are expected to accept discipline from me as a matter of course. If that doesn't suit you, I'll drive you back to the station and nothing more need be said. Otherwise, come across my knee."

"Bare?" she asked, her voice cracking slightly as she threw another shy glance towards the two girls.

"Bare," Peter confirmed. "Take your jeans down but you can leave your panties up."

"He prefers to take them down himself," Rhiannon put in.

"I'd have thought you'd have learned your lesson, Rhiannon, at least for today?" Peter responded. Rhiannon said nothing more as Peter moved forward to make a lap for Chloe as she fumbled the button of her jeans open. "But yes, Chloe, I'm going to take your underwear down, once I've warmed you up a little bit."

Chloe nodded, now shaking visibly and blushing a rich pink as she pushed her jeans down to reveal firm, well-shaped thighs and a pair of lacy white panties. Peter gave an encouraging smile and she moved forward, to lay herself somewhat clumsily across his lap, her bottom lifted high to show off a silky white lunette bulging with shapely flesh. He took her around the waist and settled his hand across her cheeks, pressing gently before applying the first smack. Chloe responded with a faint sigh and he set to work, peppering her cheeks with sharp slaps of his fingertips to get her warm before removing her flimsy undergarment.

He'd been keeping count over the years and knew that she was the one-hundred and seventy-fifth girl to surrender her bottom to him for spanking, not including the few upon whom he'd used implements but never actually spanked. Each had been a pleasure in her own way, and each slightly different, but he'd learnt to recognise and appreciate certain common traits. Chloe was clearly embarrassed and shy of her own needs, but with the strength to accept them and get what she wanted. That meant it was probably best to be firm with her, telling her what was going to happen and going through with it straight away rather than cajoling or teasing her into surrender, while she clearly wasn't the sort to ask for what she needed.

"Ok, off they come," he announced once he judged her to be warm enough. "Stick it up."

Her hips immediately came up, allowing him to peel her panties down over her bottom and tug them free past his legs and down. A quick adjustment of her feet and her legs were open, her pretty pussy showing between her thighs and her lowered panties stretched taut between her knees as he began to spank once more. She obviously knew how exposed she was, and her gasps and sobs had grown a little more intense, but she made no complaint and kept her legs wide without having to be told.

"An obedient one, I see," he remarked to the others. "That's useful. You'll do well for the sterner gentlemen, Chloe, the sort who believe that girls need regular spankings and ought to be grateful for what they get. Now then, let's get a good look at you."

He'd pulled her cheeks open as he spoke, and she gasped at the sudden, rude exposure but she made no effort to get up, instead lying still with her head hanging down as he inspected the tight pink pucker between her cheeks and the open mouth of her cunt.

"Your excitement is most evident," he told her.

"I … I've been thinking about what was coming," she said, "about how I was going to be spanked."

"Then I'd better not disappoint," Peter answered and set to work once more.

While he always spanked the new girls, he was more diffident about what followed. A very few had made it clear that was all they were willing to submit to and were simply made to do corner time while he masturbated to the sight of their bare red bottoms, or Michelle obliged by taking him in her mouth. Others got to sit on his lap with their panties still down while they tossed him off, or knelt to suck his cock. Some he fucked, and with the boldest or most pliable of all he would treat his cock to their bottoms. Chloe seemed intriguingly compliant, and she was certainly excited, with the juice from her pussy making a wet patch on his knee as her spanking continued. She was also shy, despite the situation she was in, but it was important for her to learn to accept his cock as part of the deal.

"Up," he told her once her bottom had flushed a rich pink all over. "Now, do you know how to say thank you when you've been spanked?"

She'd risen from his lap, a little unsteady and clutching at her panties in embarrassment and confusion, but her eyes turned to him and she nodded.

"Do ... do I have to suck your penis?"

"That will do," he confirmed, "and you can leave your underwear down."

She made a face, but got into position, kneeling between his knees with her arse pushed out. Rhiannon and Clementine were cuddled up together, giggling, as they watched Peter draw down his zip. His cock sprang free and his balls bobbled out behind, as he took Chloe gently by the hair.

"Kiss my balls," he demanded. "Good girl, now put my cock in that pretty mouth. Yes ... that's right, move up and down ... now purse your lips on the head and push down ... Ohh, you are a good girl!"

She'd followed each of his instructions, rather clumsily, with her face full of doubt and not a little consternation, but pleasingly obedient. He glanced at the clock as she continued to suck and reluctantly decided against coming in her face. It was always fun, and especially satisfying to soil a pretty girl's face as she knelt red bottomed at his feet. But she would need to clean up, which meant inevitable delay. Something less messy was in order.

"Make a cunt of your lips," he told her. "That's right, now stay still while I fuck your mouth."

He'd tightened his grip in her hair, holding her head in place as he pushed his now swollen cock in and out between her neatly pursed lips, tugging on his shaft at the same time. The expression on her face changed to resentment and alarm as she realised that he was going to masturbate into her mouth. But that only served to make him all the more excited, as did the delighted giggles from Rhiannon and Clementine as they saw what was being done to their friend.

"That's it, perfect …" he sighed as he felt his orgasm start to well up. "Oh you little darling, you sweet little bitch," he praised, as he savoured the release of his fluid. "Now swallow it, go on, all of it. That's right, down your throat and I'll send you back to college with a bellyful of cum."

She looked almost stuffed, with her cheeks bulging and her eyes popped wide with shock and disgust as he came in her mouth, jamming his cock in and out of her still pursed lips. As the head of his cock pressed into her throat she began to gag, just as he'd hoped, bringing his ecstasy to an exquisite peak before he finished with a long, satisfied groan. He let go and she rocked back on her heels, gasping for breath, her mouth wide to show off the mess of cum and spittle on her tongue and dribbling down over her lips.

"Now do yourself," Clementine said. "He likes his girls to have an orgasm when he's finished abusing them."

Chloe gave no response, her eyes and mouth now shut and her face screwed up in revulsion, fighting to make herself swallow, and then, very deliberately, taking the full load of what

Peter had done in her mouth down into her belly.

"Good girl," Peter told her, surprised but very pleased. "Now why don't you take Clemmie's advice? Don't worry, we've all seen it before."

"Do I have to?" Chloe asked, her voice soft and sullen.

"Do you want to?" Peter retorted. "That's what matters."

Chloe hesitated, glancing towards the girls, her teeth now clamped against her lower lip. Then, she hung her head, shrouding her face with hair to hide her shame as one hand slowly descended to masturbate. Rhiannon giggled and Clementine gave a happy purr as they began to kiss and toy with each other. Peter wagged his finger at them and tapped his watch, but said nothing, allowing Chloe to concentrate on whatever was running through her head as she played with herself, perhaps the thought of what she had just done, or of Felicity, or pure shame.

Whatever it was, she didn't take long, her sobs and gasps quickly rising as her excitement overcame her embarrassment, until she suddenly threw her head back, crying out in wordless ecstasy that quickly broke to a babble as she thanked Peter over and over again for her spanking. He was grinning as he watched, utterly pleased with her reaction, and with himself, but not speaking until she'd finally come down and opened her eyes to throw an embarrassed smile at her friends.

"Welcome to Grove House Maids," Peter addressed her. "I'm sure you'll fit in perfectly. Right, stop it you two, save it for the judge."

The two girls reluctantly pulled apart and got up, Rhiannon to adjust her uniform in the mirror and Clementine to lead Chloe off to the bathroom.

"Shall I put my panties on?" Rhiannon asked.

"Yes," Peter advised, "and with luck you'll be a bit less pink by the time you get to Waddesdon. James likes his girls fresh."

"If you wanted us fresh you shouldn't have spanked us,"

she told him. "Is Chloe coming?"

"No," Peter told her. "Not without a uniform, you know that. I'll drop her back to Oxford on my way to Gabriel's and pick up Michelle at the same time. Right, let's go."

It took another ten minutes before he could get the girls into his car, a dark green Jaguar he'd treated himself to with his uncle's unexpected endowment. Both Rhiannon and Clementine were now in full Grove House Maids uniforms, demure but well cut dresses in a distinctive mid-green and set off with white aprons and lace at the collar to give a formal, deliberately outdated look and yet still show off their figures. The frilly white panties, half-cup bras and suspender belts they wore underneath were anything but demure, but then they didn't show, while it was impossible to tell that they were wearing stockings rather than tights and their heels were sufficiently sensible not to draw comment.

The Grove was at the end of a long, unpaved track that led down into the valley below Ivinghoe Beacon, a spot at once secluded and beautiful, while convenient for both London and Oxford. Sightseers posed a minor problem, particularly in the bluebell season, but he'd taken care to make the trees and shrubs that surrounded the house a very effective barrier. On this occasion, someone had parked their car so that it half blocked the end of the lane, forcing him to let Rhiannon out to make sure there were no oncoming vehicles. So he was muttering curses under his breath as he pulled out and turned north towards Waddesdon, where Lord Justice James Dolamore-Brown lived in genteel and solitary elegance, although rather less genteel than his neighbours might have imagined.

Dolamore-Brown took particular pleasure in booking Clementine, which had always struck Peter as somewhat bad taste, given that she was the daughter of his closest and oldest friend, Daniel Stewart. Not that she seemed to care, happily indulging his favourite kink: watching her have lesbian sex on the bearskin rug in front of his fire, usually with Rhiannon, until he was ready to fuck her while she licked her friend. Dinner would follow, always of the highest standard and served with enviably fine wines, with both girls naked until it was time to leave.

The journey went uneventfully. Although Peter couldn't help reflecting that, as he'd made his way down the road in Waddlesdon, he'd noticed a car parked on the usually quiet street, possibly of the same make and colour as the one he'd had to avoid at the end of the lane. As he picked up speed on the A41 he was telling himself not to be paranoid, but he found himself glancing in his rear view mirror more often than was necessary as he continued towards Oxford. The car didn't follow, or didn't seem to, and he'd quickly put it from his mind as he talked with Chloe, swapping stories of illicit and humorous incidents at Broadfields.

She agreed to be dropped off in St. Giles, which allowed him to find a parking meter and wait for Michelle, who'd spent the day shopping. He couldn't help but smile as he watched her approach, no longer the impudent, rebellious scamp he'd first put over his knee at the old Club S, but a mature, refined woman, whose smart and elegant clothes and regimen of running on the Downs made her perfectly trim and stylish—an effect in no way reduced by the swell of her pregnant belly. He kissed her as she got into the car and put his hand to her bulging tummy as he spoke.

"Did you have a good day? How are you?"

"Tired," she answered. "But okay, except that I'm starting to leak."

"Leak?" Peter asked, puzzled and concerned.

"From my boobs," she explained. "But don't worry, I've bought some pads and a blouse in case I have to change, a bra too. What time are we supposed to be at the Howards?"

"Any time after five," he told her. "But dinner will be at seven, so there's plenty of time."

The late afternoon traffic was already beginning to pick

up, and Peter concentrated on his driving until he was able to pull off the city ring road and turn south towards where Gabriel and Marcia Howard lived by the river in Wallingford. Peter and Michelle were frequent guests, both to dinner and to the garden parties and political functions Gabriel held as the local MP, at which Peter found himself constantly amused by the contrast between his friend's public and private life. Gabriel had done well, now a junior minister in the cabinet and a keen supporter of the government's drive to encourage old fashioned family values, while secretly having kinky sex with as many young women as he could get his hands on, along with a monthly visit to Karen and Violet for what he referred to as personal discipline. Peter chuckled at the thought, but Michelle didn't respond, her face now set in a frown as she examined the front of her blouse, on which two small, wet patches were clearly visible.

"Could you pull over somewhere?" she asked. "I need to change my blouse."

"Couldn't you do it at their house?"

"No! Look at the state I'm in, and you know what Marcia's like. There are going to be other guests too."

Peter shrugged and took what looked like a convenient turning off the main road, which proved to lead to a transport depot, now closed for the day.

"Here?" he asked, pulling to a stop in the shade of a clump of trees.

"It will have to do," Michelle answered, already fumbling with the buttons of her blouse.

Peter watched, intrigued, as she undressed. Her breasts had grown considerably larger over the course of her pregnancy, and changed shape, becoming fuller and somehow more womanly. Despite being a devoted arse enthusiast, he'd always taken a distinct pleasure in girls with large breasts, especially if they got embarrassed about being so well endowed. Michelle could now be included in their number. The faint flush of pink that tinged her face as she hurriedly shrugged off her bra was as arousing as the sight of the smooth, pink curves she revealed. Better still, her nipples were swollen, with white drops beading on the dark skin.

"May I help?" he offered.

"I don't see how you can," Michelle answered, plainly flustered and embarrassed. "Look, it's soaked right through my bra!"

Peter didn't bother to reply, but leant forward to take one swollen teat into his mouth and suck, instantly changing Michelle's shocked gasp to a moan, quickly followed by a giggling rebuke.

"Peter! What are you doing!?"

"Helping you with your milk," he replied, briefly pulling away before taking hold of her other breast and extending his tongue to lap up the tiny white droplets.

"It's not actually milk, it's …" she began, but trailed off with a sigh. "You're getting off on this, aren't you? You're the biggest pervert I've ever met, Peter Finch!"

"I should hope so too," Peter answered, now with one heavy, milk-swollen breast in each hand as he continued to attend to her. "But it's nice, isn't it?"

"Yes," Michelle admitted, closing her eyes. "But do hurry up. Anybody who came past would see."

"They're not very likely too," Peter answered, nuzzling and squeezing at her breasts in the hope of producing more milk, "and besides, why shouldn't a man relieve his wife's boobs?"

"For the same reason a woman shouldn't relieve her boyfriend's cock," Michelle sighed. "Not in public, anyway."

She didn't seem to want to stop him, and Peter ignored her comments, continuing to feed on her breasts as his cock grew rapidly stiffer all the while. The temptation to bring himself off while he suckled from her was considerable, or even to fuck her milky cleavage, but as he began to draw his zip down the clang of the depot gates brought their play to an abrupt end. A man had emerged, looking curiously at the car, then grinning as Michelle frantically tried to cover herself up while calling Peter a variety of names, most of them coupled with "pervert".

He merely laughed and drove off, earning himself a yet more detailed description of his personal faults as Michelle, still topless as they drove through Shillingford, patted her nipple pads into place and struggled into her new bra and blouse as they drove south. Another few miles and they'd reached the Howard's turning, with Michelle still pink faced with embarrassment as they greeted their hosts, although Peter was amused to see how quickly she switched to what he thought of as her respectable mode, chatting happily to Marcia Howard about her plans for the baby.

Gabriel took him through to the conservatory, where he'd been mixing Champagne cocktails for Daniel Stewart and his wife, Celia, along with another, older couple Peter recognised as party stalwarts and supporters of Daniel in particular. Greetings made, Celia continued her conversation, explaining proudly how Clementine had turned down a job offer from a major pharmaceutical company in order to continue her research.

"… but then money was never all that important to her," she was saying. "She didn't ask for an allowance, even in her gap year, although naturally we provide for her."

Peter thought of Clementine, who, if everything had gone to schedule, would probably be sitting naked at James Dolamore-Brown's dining table after being soundly taken from behind as she licked at Rhiannon's cunt. In return, she would receive as much as most women of her age could expect to earn in a week, while she had another four bookings over the next few days.

The crunch of tyres on gravel drew his attention to the window and he saw that another couple had arrived, presumably completing the party. A man got out first, tall, lean with greying hair and an air of natural authority, followed by a woman who seemed as frail and delicate as crystal, while her dress and the collar of diamonds at her neck suggested a level of wealth far beyond that of Peter's connections.

"Is that Stephen Richards?" he asked.

"Yes," Gabriel replied. "Now CEO of the company, and incidentally one of our best donors, gentlemen. His wife's called

Vivienne, American, heiress."

"I didn't even know he was in the country," Peter said, remembering how he'd last seen his old friend, balls deep in Michelle's pussy as they shared her over the back of a sofa. "What a pleasant surprise."

Stephen came inside, grinning happily as Gabriel made the introductions and quickly launched into the topic of the election.

"Are we going to win?"

"No," Gabriel answered. "Frankly, we haven't a snowball's chance in hell. In fact, we'd have been a lot better off if we'd lost last time around."

"As it stands," Daniel agreed, "we're likely to be out of power for two, even three terms."

"By which time you'll be party leader," Stephen went on.

"Hopefully," Gabriel told him. "But that's the difficult part, when to make our move. Daniel's the natural choice and has a lot of support, but he needs to stay in the shadows for now, maybe for quite a while. The thing is …"

Peter had switched off, indifferent to the minutiae of politics, while he and Michelle never bothered to go to the polls on the grounds that their votes cancelled each other out. Vivienne also seemed disinterested, and after a moment admiring her slender figure through her dress, Peter rose to speak to her. The sun had made its way out from behind the clouds, and when Marcia returned she chivvied Peter and Vivienne into the garden, where Stephen quickly managed to draw Peter aside on the pretext of walking down to the riverbank.

"Vivienne is lovely," Peter remarked as they strolled out of hearing range.

"Very lovely," Stephen agreed, "and a lot of fun too, as you may find out if you're very, very lucky. But that's not what I wanted to talk to you about. I need a favour."

"Anything within my power. What's up?"

"You know I'm head of the company now, don't you? Well, I'm on the verge of closing a deal, a deal that's going to leave me in clover and the company the dominant force in our field. To clinch the deal I need to impress certain very important people from a Balkan country we're not particularly friendly with at present, so it's all a bit delicate. They expect to be entertained, and well. It's a prestige thing. That means the best brandies, the best Champagnes, all of which is damned expensive but worth every penny as an investment. Now, they've been hinting that they want girls, and obviously it has to be done discreetly and well. So I need some Grove House maids, at least three."

"Easily done," Peter assured him.

"English maids," Stephen went on. "Tall, blonde, well built, and most importantly, with good accents."

"I think I can guarantee that," Peter replied.

"I'd really like to choose myself. Do you have a book or something?"

"No, that would be far too indiscreet. You know Felicity, that's one, and ..."

"Clementine?" Stephen suggested.

Peter winced and cast a guilty glance to where Daniel and Celia had come out to admire the rose beds. But he nodded.

"Why not? She's perfect. Rhiannon?"

"Too Irish, and she's not blonde."

"Are they that fussy? How about Henrietta Clark?"

"Too short."

"Michelle?"

"Too pregnant."

"That's all the blondes I've got on my books at present, I'm afraid."

"Couldn't you persuade somebody to dye her hair?"

"I suppose so, if that counts. I signed up a new girl today, as it goes, a girl you know, Chloe Thompson."

"Ben's daughter!? You really are beyond the limit, Peter,"

Stephen chuckled. "Okay, she'll do nicely."

Some of the other guests were approaching and Peter quickly changed the topic of conversation. They continued to talk until the light had begun to fade, then went indoors for dinner. Conscious of the drive home, Peter limited himself to a small glass of each of the wines, while despite his best efforts the conversation kept drifting back to politics and the forthcoming election. The food at least was good, while he was seated diagonally from Vivienne Richards in such a way that the light cast interesting outlines through her flimsy dress, sometimes the curve of one small breast, sometimes a pert nipple, adding to the arousal he'd felt since suckling on Michelle in the car. Stephen's hint that Vivienne might be available only made matters worse as, whatever might happen, it clearly wasn't going to be that night. By the time the dinner party broke up he was feeling more frustrated than he had in a long time, while Michelle was smiling, tipsy and unabashedly playful. He'd already begun to plan what he was going to do with her in the car on the way back when Gabriel came over to ask if he'd mind giving an older couple a lift as far as Tring.

By the time they'd dropped off their passengers, Peter had heard enough political conversation to last him a lifetime. While Michelle had been a constant tease as they drove, with her blouse half undone as she chatted with the couple in the back. The temptation to take her somewhere quiet and deal with her in the car was considerable, but it was only a few miles back to the Grove and he decided to make for the comfort of home, ignoring the torment of her teasing.

She'd shrugged her top off as they turned into the lane and her bra quickly followed, leaving her heavy breasts naked in the faint light from the dashboard, the soft curves glossy with milk as she began to rub it over her skin. Peter swore in awe, putting his foot down to send the Jaguar bumping over the rough ground until he could bring it to a halt in front of the house.

Michelle was giggling as she climbed out, topless and bright-eyed with drink and arousal, her carefully contrived air of refinement completely lost.

Peter wasted no time, pushing her down across the front of the car and flipping her skirt up. She was in maid service panties—full, white and frilly—which he'd quickly pulled down to bare her bottom to the night air for a vigorous spanking, the smacks blending with her laughter and the slap of her big, milky breasts on the front of the car. His cock had been half stiff for most of the evening, and he'd quickly liberated it, intending to get himself rock hard in her mouth before fucking her over the car—the lure of their soft bed forgotten in his urgency.

"I have to fuck you," he growled as he twisted her around to push his cock toward her face. "I have to fuck you, just as soon as you've sucked me hard."

Michelle took him in her mouth, sucking eagerly as she massaged her breasts to squeeze out the milk from her nipples, before using it to wet his balls. He began to fuck her mouth, his cock growing with every thrust, until he was hard. She moved closer, holding her breasts up to make a warm, milky slide for his cock, allowing him to fuck in her cleavage, a sensation so sweet he'd quickly abandoned all thoughts of entering her, content to come between her breasts and in her face.

"I've got to come," he sighed. "Right now ..."

"Do it," she gasped. "Do it all over me, cover me in cum while I get off ... right here. Go on, Peter, fuck my boobies ... come on me ... cover my face ..."

He was there, manhandling his cock to empty the contents of his balls all over her milk-slick breasts and in her face before jamming himself deep in her mouth for his final euphoric spurts. She sucked and swallowed, swallowed once more and slumped down against the side of the car, her thighs spread to present her pussy and the great, straining bulge of her pregnant belly, with her boobs sitting fat and round and wet above, streaked with cum, her face too. Her eyes had closed as she began to masturbate, one hand busy between her legs as the other wiped the sticky mixture of jism and milk over her breasts.

Peter waited, grinning, his cock in his hand, watching as her arousal heightened, until the final, perfect moment. As she started to come he let go too, sending an arc of sparkling water all over her belly and breasts, into her open mouth and between her thighs, soaking her skirt and panties, her hair and face, soiling every square inch of her skin with his effluent as her body shook and shivered in a climax that left her lying limp and exhausted in a rapidly spreading puddle on the concrete of the drive. Only then did Peter realise that the front door was open, with Rhiannon standing in the light of the porch in nothing but a tiny, see-through nightie and a pair of fluffy slippers as she struggled to hold back her giggles.

Peter accepted a glass of champagne from the tray offered to him. The waitress was a pretty blonde with a snub nose that gave her a look of permanent impudence: Felicity Chamberlain, ex-pupil at Broadfields College, ex-toasty girl to Clementine Stewart, and currently with Grove House Maids while she worked as an intern in the City. She was one of six employed to serve at an embassy reception and potentially for more intimate services later in the evening.

"Thank you," he said as she bobbed a curtsey so impudent it bordered on sarcastic. "How are we doing?"

"Very well," she answered. "Looks like it's going to be a late night."

"Excellent. I'm sure I can find a way to amuse myself while you ladies do what you do best," he answered and took a sip of champagne as she turned to another guest.

Ignoring the temptation to pinch or pat her sweetly rotating rump as she moved away, he went back to contemplating the other people in the room. Chaperone was not a job he particularly enjoyed, but there were worse things in life than sipping Champagne, eating canapés and making small talk, especially when being at a foreign embassy allowed him to avoid conversation about the election defeat a few days before. Such evenings also tended to end well, at the very least with a quick hand job from one of the girls in his car, and often a great deal more. On one particularly memorable night, a corporate function had proved so heavily overrun with wives that he'd ended up sharing a hotel suite with four of the girls. But this embassy reception seemed unlikely to come up to the same standard. Both Rhiannon and Elspeth Fraser had been booked in advance, for one thing, and it now looked as if Felicity's services were also going to be required. That left Chloe Thompson, now with her newly blonde hair and currently the focus of attention of three swarthy, bearded men at the far side of the room; the tiny, elfin Henrietta Clark; and Clementine Stewart. No less than eight of his clients were also present but unattended, so it seemed likely that the options for his own gratification would be limited. But the money, at least, would be good.

He took another swallow of champagne and glanced at his watch, wondering how long he ought to wait before retiring to his hotel room. As usual, the reception involved a great deal of social-climbing, one-upmanship, carefully judged snubs and other tedious social interactions that didn't concern him, but did mean that it was almost impossible to have an interesting or amusing conversation. And obviously, discussing his own business was out of the question, despite the fact that it was going on in flagrant discretion all around him.

"Peter!" a voice called out, directly behind him and loud enough to startle him.

He turned, to find a man coming towards him, tall, lean, with an air of strength and purpose that suggested the outdoors even in his smart white tuxedo.

"Rackman. Hunter Rackman!" Peter answered, shaking the big man's extended hand after an instant's hesitation before he recognised his old friend. "I didn't expect to see you here."

"Well you should," the American answered. "Lopez wouldn't be president without our backing, count on that."

"Yes, but why are you in London?"

"Promotion, or an easy number to say thanks for Central America. But say, can we have a private word?"

Hunter didn't bother to wait for an answer, but took Peter by the elbow and led him to a clear space where a microphone had been set up for use later in the evening. They were on a low stage, and Peter felt distinctly conspicuous. But Hunter didn't seem to care, continuing in a low, conspiratorial voice.

"Look, I've been speaking to Ben, and I understand you're up to your old tricks and then some. Now my Emerald's back at home …"

"Emerald?" Peter queried. "You married Emerald Feldkirch?"

"After that night? I'd have married her if I had to kill for it. So yeah, I married Emerald, and she's given me three fine sons and the most beautiful little girl you ever did see. But Emmie's back home, if you get my meaning."

"Which means that you're alone and might need the services of a maid?" Peter answered.

"Exactly that," Hunter said with a wink. "But not any old maid. The best. The girls in the green outfits are yours, yes?"

"Yes," Peter admitted. "The tall red-head is Tiffany's daughter, Rhiannon, by the way, but she's booked. So's the other red-head, Elspeth. But I'm guessing you prefer blondes, which is just as well."

"Who's the cutie with the pug nose?"

"Felicity. I think she's booked too. The tiny one is Henrietta …"

"Jesus, Pete, she'd barely come up to my dick. How about the tall girl with the tits at ten and two?"

"Clementine, yes, she's lovely, but I ought to warn you that she's Daniel Stewart's daughter."

"She's old Dan's daughter? You don't say! Now I've *gotta* fuck her."

Peter stifled a sigh. He'd tried to avoid pairing the daughters of old school chums with other school chums. And yet, he couldn't deny the perverse twinge that overrode his reluctance. "I'll introduce you," he said at last.

Hunter was already striding across the floor and Peter hurried to catch up. Introductions were made and Clementine smiled and bobbed, a reaction as cool as it was charming, instantaneously putting a feral look in Hunter's eyes. Peter left them to it, glancing around the room to locate Chloe, who was pouring champagne for Clive Sumner. Her overtly flirtatious manner suggested she too was taken; and Henrietta wasn't visible.

On a sudden impulse he made for the kitchens. As he'd hoped, Henrietta was fetching more of the canapés she'd been handing out, with a full tray on the table in front of her as she put the finishing touches to the arrangement. He went straight to her, twisting her around to press his lips to hers, a kiss she returned after a moment of hesitation. Of all the girls, she was the one who most enjoyed rough treatment, preferring her spankings and sex sudden and unannounced as long as she was in the mood. The passion of her kiss made it clear that she was most certainly in the mood, and Peter wasted no time in talk.

As she pressed her body to his, he took a firm grip on her waist and twisted her round once more to face the table. He popped her tits free from her bodice, taking one in each hand as he rubbed his crotch against her bottom. She rubbed back, purring in anticipation for the hard bulge of his cock as it bumped between her tiny butt cheeks, encouraging him still more. Peter's mischievous streak got the better of him and, with a single shove, he planted Henrietta's tits and face firmly in the canapés, her squeak of alarm and surprise muffled by a mushroom vol-au-vent. Two swift tugs and her uniform skirt was up around her waist and her frilly panties were down to her thighs. A quick adjustment of his fly and his cock was free in his hand, not fully stiff, but stiff enough to push into the wet, accommodating aperture of her vagina and then deep inside her.

She'd pulled herself up onto her elbows as he began to fuck her, his fingers locked around her hips as he jammed himself in and out with short, hard thrusts, his belly smacking on her naked bottom with each and every one. He pushed her down again, rubbing her face in the mess on the tray and ignoring her protests, before scooping up a handful of dainties to smear them over her chest, soiling her breasts. More went into her mouth and hair, rendering her both speechless and completely unfit for polite company, an effect enhanced as he pulled his cock free to jerk himself off over her bare bottom and into her panties, across the back of her dress and lastly in her face as he pulled her around one last time. Her mouth was already full of food, with bits of pastry, mushroom sauce and lumpfish roe spilling out around her lips. Peter was too far gone to let this dissuade him, and he crammed his cock into her over-full mouth, sending food squirting from the sides as it was displaced by his girth and he finished his orgasm in her throat.

"Right," he told her as he finally pulled back. "You're mine for the evening, Henrietta, as I hardly think you're in a fit state to serve the ambassador's guests. Out the back way with you, and don't worry about the cash. I'll see you get your share."

"You are a complete bastard, Peter!" she managed, spitting out the mess from her mouth. "You didn't even spank me first!"

"I'll make up for it at the hotel," he promised her. "Now run along. The others are all booked up and we've got until at least two or three in the morning."

"Clemmie's going to spend the night with Mr. Rackman," Rhiannon announced, bouncing down on the bed. "You know about Elspeth, Chloe wants you to pick her up from Clive's flat and Flick's still at the embassy."

"Doing what?" Peter asked as he pulled himself upright in the bed.

He'd been asleep, and his head still felt as if it was full of cobwebs, while even Rhiannon's noisy arrival hadn't been enough to wake Henrietta, who lay beside him, nude, the covers twisted around her body with her well smacked bottom sticking out from among them. She'd been given her promised spanking, followed by a second, more leisurely fuck, but by the time they'd both come he'd been too exhausted to stay awake.

Rhiannon hadn't answered him, her eyes closed and her hands on her chest, gently stroking her breasts through her uniform. Peter recognised the symptoms: a girl who'd been thoroughly fucked and probably put through her paces in a number of other ways, but hadn't had a chance to achieve orgasm. It was by no means uncommon with the Grove House girls. Most of the clients took the attitude that—as it was their money—their pleasure was what counted. So Peter had become something of an expert at masturbating sleepy but turned-on girls to climax. Now was not the time.

"Doing what?" he repeated.

"Getting fucked, I imagine," Rhiannon replied. "Three of the embassy staff took her upstairs, and …"

"Staff?" Peter cut her off. "Not Grove House members?"

Rhiannon merely bit her lip softly.

"This is not a freelance operation. This whole thing works because we are exclusive and discreet." Peter fought to keep from raising his voice. After all, Felicity's indiscretion was not Rhiannon's fault, and he had no right to be annoyed with her.

But Rhiannon seemed not to notice. Her thoughts were elsewhere.

"Peter … get me off," she said softly.

"Later," Peter promised her, glancing at the clock radio beside the bed. "It's nearly four o'clock in the morning. Wake up, Henrietta."

He'd applied a firm smack to her bottom as he spoke, but she merely groaned and twisted herself tighter into the sheets. Peter hauled himself out of bed and padded across to the bathroom, where he splashed water on his face. His eyes were red and he looked drawn. He was wondering how much longer he could keep up a lifestyle that allowed so little sleep, when a commotion from the bedroom pulled his thoughts back to the present.

Rhiannon had unrolled Henrietta from the bedcovers and, after what had sounded like a brief but spirited struggle, sat directly upon her face. Rhiannon's eyes were now closed in bliss as she sat bolt upright in the middle of the bed, playing with her breasts as she squatted over Henrietta. Rhiannon's panties were around her knees, and her uniform skirt was splayed out like a flower, while Henrietta licked and lapped at her cunt and bottom from beneath. Peter merely shook his head, used to the girls' behaviour, but he watched from the corner of his eye as he dressed, while Rhiannon took the orgasm she'd needed so badly before going down on Henrietta to return the favour.

His cock had begun to stir as he watched, but he was concerned for Felicity and already late for Elspeth. So he put his needs aside, doing his best to hurry the girls along and get them all out of the hotel and across the street to where the green Grove House Maids minibus was parked. As he was climbing in Felicity appeared, her long blonde hair loose and disarrayed, her shoes in one hand a champagne bottle in the other, her uniform dishevelled.

"Just get in," Peter told her as she began what was clearly a well-rehearsed apology. "You know perfectly well it's club members only. I'll deal with you later."

She made a face at him but climbed into the back of the minibus, taking a swallow of wine from the bottle before passing it to Rhiannon. Peter was trying to look stern as he started the engine, but he felt only mild exasperation for her behaviour and was looking forward to the opportunities it presented. Felicity was usually well behaved, and resentful about spankings, preferring to dish them out than take them. But she would accept a just punishment if she broke the rules, which she clearly had.

Chloe was at Clive Sumner's place in Westminster and

had soon been collected, while Elspeth was staying the night with her client. With Chloe safely in the minibus he allowed himself a sigh of relief. The opportunity to provide maids for the reception had been too good to turn down, with Clive making a generous block booking in his position as a senior official at the Foreign Office, to which he had moved some years before. Clive had assured him that neither Daniel nor Ben would be at the function, while both Clementine and Chloe had been keen to attend, but he was very pleased indeed to be away without incident. Daniel knew about Grove House Maids but he had never made use of the service, preferring to avoid all risk of scandal. Although Ben was a regular client.

As Peter drove, he reflected on the odd behaviour of his friends, which Rhiannon had called hypocritical. There was no doubt at all in his mind that Ben would be furious to discover that Chloe was a Grove House Maid, and yet he himself was especially keen on Clementine, and generally liked to watch her strip, then have her go down on her knees to suck his cock hard before she was taken from behind. Peter had always assumed that this was because Daniel had been very much the leader of their group while they were at Broadfields—not to mention a school prefect—so that using his daughter for sex became a way to offset feelings of inferiority. Gabriel also enjoyed Clementine, and Hunter Rackman had lost no time in booking her, which fitted the pattern, if less well. But Clive and Ben had always been very much equals and Chloe was now being given much the same treatment as Clementine.

He continued to ponder the question as he drove east with the four girls drinking champagne and laughing together in the back of the minibus, but the only postulate that seemed to fit was that his friends shared a highly perverse sense of humour. Unfortunately it was also a dangerous one, and he decided to impose new rules to reduce the risk of disaster, which served to remind him of Felicity's breach of agreed conduct. She was the first to be dropped off, at the apartment on the edge of Docklands which she shared with two other girls, both innocent of her lucrative sideline. That meant she had to be dealt with in the van. Not easy in the middle of London, but he knew the perfect place.

A slight adjustment to the route allowed him to park behind what had once been St. Botolph's Church. It was now a block of exclusive apartments, but it looked much the same and the alley behind it was no more busy that it had been on the memorable night nearly eight years before. He was smiling as he drew the van to a halt, thoroughly happy with his life despite his tiredness and looking forward to the prospect of dishing out one more spanking.

"Why have we stopped?" Felicity asked, although the tone of her voice suggested that she knew the answer perfectly well.

"Three of the embassy staff, I believe it was?" Peter queried. "I don't imagine they were members of the club, either?"

"They paid," Felicity countered, now openly alarmed. "Quite well, too. One of them was the ambassador!"

"I don't care if he was an emperor," Peter replied. "You know the rules."

"Oh come on!" Felicity urged. "Not now, and not … not in front of Chloe!"

Peter ignored her, but climbed into the back, seating himself in the seat he invariably used for spankings, where he had plenty of leg room while the girls' backsides remained nicely on show to other passengers.

"A spanking now, or the cane later," he told her, "and either way, it's going to have to be in front of Chloe."

"Why?" Felicity demanded. "That's not fair!"

Rhiannon giggled at her friend's petulant tone, earning herself a smack on the leg.

"Don't laugh at me," Felicity told her. "Or the next time

you get it I'll make sure he uses a hairbrush!"

"Ooh, good idea!" Rhiannon laughed, digging in her bag to pull out a long handled, wooden hairbrush. "Go on, Peter, spank her!"

"Bitch!" Felicity snapped. "Look, Peter, I ..."

"A spanking now," Peter interrupted. "Or the cane later."

"Oh all right," Felicity answered, pouting badly as she lay herself down across Peter's legs. "You can spank me, but not with her hairbrush."

Peter said nothing, but took a firm grip around her waist, fixing her in place before he turned her uniform skirt up onto her back and pulled down her panties. The other girls quickly gathered around to watch—Rhiannon and Henrietta bright-eyed and giggling, Chloe shocked but still fascinated to see the girl whose knee she'd been over so often get a dose of her own medicine. Felicity stayed silent, sulky but compliant, until Peter took the hairbrush from Rhiannon.

"Hey, no!" she squeaked. "That's not fair, come on ..."

"This is discipline, hence the hairbrush," Peter stated and brought it down with a firm smack across Felicity's bottom.

"Bitch!" Felicity repeated, twisting around to stick her tongue out at Rhiannon. "I'll get you for this, and you needn't think you're going to get a show out of me."

Peter didn't comment, but began to spank harder and faster, vigorous smacks delivered full on the tuck of Felicity's fleshy little cheeks in rapid succession, instantly robbing her of any chance of coping with the pain. She withstood it for a few seconds, grunting through gritted teeth as she struggled to retain her dignity before giving in. First she began to wriggle and toss her hair, then to squirm and kick her legs. Finally, she surrendered completely, letting go of her emotions in a fine spanking tantrum with her fists thumping on the floor of the minibus and her thighs pumping to make a thoroughly rude show of her most private places. Peter continued to spank until he was sure the other girls had all had a good look, then stopped. Felicity jumped up, open mouthed with shock and clutching her hot bottom as she jumped up and down in a futile effort to dull the pain, which only served to inspire more giggling from the other three. Rhiannon retrieved her hairbrush while Peter, now grinning broadly and more pleased with himself than ever, pulled down his zip.

"Not that too!" Felicity protested as he exposed himself.

"Go on, Flick," Henrietta mocked. "Be a good girl and say thank you nicely."

Felicity turned a furious scowl toward Henrietta, but she got onto the seat beside Peter, kneeling with her bottom lifted high as she took his cock into her mouth. He began to stroke her cheeks as she sucked, enjoying the heat of her skin and the faint trembling of her body. A finger snuck between her thighs to reveal that she was every bit as wet as he'd expected, while the other girls gathered close, Henrietta and Chloe with their arms around each other, Rhiannon cupping Peter's balls and gently masturbating him into Felicity's mouth.

It took him a few minutes to get fully hard, his balls still drained after fucking Henrietta, by which time Felicity had begun to stick her bottom up higher still, making the pout of her pussy and the pucker of her arse available to his fingers. He took full advantage, easing open her vagina, as Rhiannon smiled conspiratorially and pulled a tube of lubricant from her bag. Peter grinned, watching as Rhiannon drizzled the fluid between the crests of Felicity's well-reddened bottom, and still more between her cheeks, directly onto her anus. Felicity gave a muffled sob as she felt the cool fluid on her skin, but she began to suck harder on Peter's erection as Rhiannon massaged her flesh and Peter continued to finger her.

Chloe had soon joined in too, taking over with the lube while Rhiannon and Henrietta began to kiss. Peter began to wonder just how far he could take it, with Felicity's head now bobbing urgently up and down on his straining cock. They'd fucked twice before, and she'd already had three men that evening. But her luscious bottom had been on full display during her spanking and Peter was quite sure she had not been entered there. Easing his fingers from her vagina, he began to tease between her arse cheeks, rubbing lube over the little textured crevice of her anus as he spoke.

"Maybe, Felicity, what you really need is a nice, big cock in your arse?"

Her sucking immediately grew more urgent, maybe in a desperate effort to make him come in her mouth before she was sodomised, maybe in anticipation of exactly that. Peter chose to assume that she would let him, easing one finger up into the tight little hole he'd been lubricating. She gave another heartfelt sob and suddenly she'd come up off his cock, only to start to rub it all over her face and lick at his balls.

"Up the back it is," he told her, fingering her anus for just a moment longer. When she didn't protest he pulled her around.

She let him guide her, her bottom pushed out into his lap, pale and round and beautiful in the dim light, in full view of the other three girls. Grinning more broadly than ever, Peter pressed his cock to her anus, watching as the slippery little ring began to open, taking him gradually inside. Rhiannon took hold of his cock, steering it up into Felicity's back way until she was sitting firmly on his lap, now upright, her thighs spread wide, his balls pressed to her equally slippery vagina. He took her by the waist, bouncing her on his cock as she gasped and panted her way through the lewd act, when suddenly Chloe scrambled over the seats, got down on her knees and buried her face in Felicity's cunt. She was licking at Peter's balls as well, pushing him closer to orgasm, but he held off, eager to feel Felicity's anus tighten on his shaft when she came, which seemed likely to be at any instant. Already her muscles had begun to contract, and she was begging Chloe to lick harder and squirming her bottom into Peter's lap, her voice thick with ecstasy, then breaking to a scream as she hit her orgasm.

Peter began to pump hard into her rectum, eager to fill her with cum as she came, with the glorious sensation of her anal ring tightening over and around his cock. She screamed out again, her body locked in orgasm, her belly pushed out into Chloe's face—too far. His cock slipped from her bottom just as he started to come. Cum splashed into Chloe's face, but she'd taken hold, and to Peter's astonishment fed his cock into her mouth, drawn fresh from her girlfriend's arse, to suck and swallow, choking as she received the rest of his spume down her throat, keeping him deep in her mouth until at last he was spent.

Chloe had made herself come with busy fingers, in a perfect trio of orgasm, while Henrietta was already pulling down Rhiannon's uniform to get at her breasts. Leaving the girls to play together, Peter climbed down from the van to check that no one had seen, and to draw the cool, pre-dawn air into his lungs. The eastern sky was already getting light, but the streets were quiet, save for a car that pulled away from a space directly opposite the entrance to the short blind alley where he'd parked. It had been small and dark coloured, much like the one he'd seen near the Grove and at Waddesdon. The driver had been in a hurry. He walked quickly to the end of the alley, but the car was already gone.

"You're getting paranoid, Peter," Stephen Richards laughed as he sat back in his armchair at the Grove. "The world's full of little blue cars."

"I find it pays to be cautious," Peter replied. "So, if you don't mind, I'll go on ahead while you keep an eye on the end of the lane, then follow five minutes later. We can meet up again at the golf club and run through the same procedure when we come back with your clients."

"If you insist," Stephen answered. "But you make it sound like something out of a James Bond film, except that I'm sure no self-respecting movie spy would be caught dead driving a Ford Fiesta."

"It was a Mini Metro, I think," Peter told him, "and it's probably nothing, but I'm sure you'll agree that this afternoon's entertainment is best kept private?"

"Absolutely," Stephen agreed. "Ah, there you are, girls. They're going to love you!"

Clementine, Felicity and Chloe had come downstairs, shepherded by Michelle, while Rhiannon could be heard laughing from the bedroom. All three of the younger girls were in identical outfits, and all three looked somewhat sheepish, Clementine most of all.

"I feel silly," she announced, lifting the hem of her Union Flag minidress.

"Blame the Spice Girls," Peter answered, trying not to laugh.

"Geri Halliwell didn't have to wear frilly knickers under her dress," Clementine pointed out, "and they didn't show either, not like this. I mean, look!"

Even from the front, a puff of frills had been visible below the hem of her dress. But as she turned to show off the back, Peter gave up trying not to grin. The dress was tight at the waist and flared to a pleated skirt that was not only far too short to cover Clementine's bottom properly, but pushed up and out by a great froth of lace that nevertheless did very little to conceal the contours of her cheeks. The upper part of her dress was scarcely more decent, with the material tight over her breasts to make it very obvious indeed that she had no bra underneath, while Union Flag stockings, little white pumps on her feet and a bright red ribbon in her hair all combined to make her look both rude and ridiculous. Felicity was no better, identically dressed but for a blue hair ribbon, although the sulky scowl on her face didn't really suit the image. Chloe was more stoical, and merely looked embarrassed, although her fuller bottom made the effect of comic smut even more exaggerated.

"You look lovely," Peter said. "Well, sexy, in a Benny Hill sort of way."

"I'm sorry, really," Stephen added, chuckling. "But that's what they wanted, and the client is king."

"The client is a pervert," Felicity put in.

"But a rich pervert," Peter pointed out, "and rich perverts tend to get their way. Come on girls, cheer up. Smile, wiggle your bottoms, and remember, plenty of deference. But don't overdo it. Too much and they'll think you're making fun of them. They may be perverts, but they're not stupid."

"We know what to do," Clementine assured him.

"You don't expect us to come to the golf club like this, do you?" Chloe asked.

"Of course not," Peter assured her. "Michelle and Rhiannon can drive up with us to keep them happy, and you're to be ready with cold beers when we get back, along with anything else they want, and that means anything."

"We know," Felicity answered him.

"Excellent," Peter said, rising from the sofa, "and do you remember what I said about the wrestling?"

"Yes," Clementine confirmed. "We're to make it look as if we really hate each other."

"Think humiliation," Felicity added.

"That's right," Peter said, "and above all, make it look real. Ok, let's go. Five minutes behind me please, Stephen."

They followed the plan but nothing untoward happened, leaving Peter feeling slightly foolish but very relieved as they pulled up in front of the golf club where Stephen had installed his clients for the weekend. There were six of them, all dressed more or less alike, in sober, well cut suits with plain ties and highly polished shoes. All were as fastidious in their manners as in their dress, but there the similarities ended. One, Mr. Drach, was plainly the senior man, older than the others, with a brisk, business-like manner and a hard edge. His accountant and lawyer, Zoran Zoranov and Miroslav Petrović, were short and tall respectively, but united by a cruel humour. Two others, both large, silent men with dark glasses and carefully trimmed beards, hadn't been introduced by name but appeared to be security. The last, introduced simply as Kralj, had no obvious function and seemed cold and humourless, while even his polite manners somehow came across as sinister.

The three who seemed to be the actual businessmen were at least easy to get on with, and as they talked over glasses of gin and tonic Peter began to relax. They seemed to have an almost infantile delight in their desire to have British girls thoroughly humiliated, in which he could see at least a reflection of his own sexual preferences. Nevertheless, they were extremely courteous to both Rhiannon and Michelle, but made no effort to conceal their lust, as if the women had been created purely for their sexual entertainment. It was an attitude very much in accordance with some of the girls' darker fantasies, if very different from the way they handled men in day-to-day life. By the time they were ready to leave, Peter was thoroughly looking forward to the afternoon's entertainment.

Nothing out of the ordinary happened on the way back to the Grove, allowing Peter to expand on the scenario he and Stephen had set up to make the entertainment exciting for their guests. He was already on first name terms with Zoran and Miroslav, who were seated to either side of Michelle in the back of the Jaguar. Kralj rode in the front, maintaining a slightly unnerving silence while the others listened to Peter's descriptions of Clementine and Felicity.

"... natural blondes too, as you will see. In fact, they're so alike they could be sisters. But they were rivals at school and they absolutely hate each other, so you can be sure of a good fight. Not only that, but the winner gets a nice bonus to take home, as well as being allowed to do as she likes to the loser, who then gets six of the cane to finish her off."

"You know how to handle a girl!" Zoran laughed.

"Stick and carrot, we call it," Peter explained. "An expression that comes from an old fashioned way to make a donkey move along, with a carrot dangled in front of his nose and a stick to beat him with. Only in this case the donkey is a girl, the carrot is money and the stick is … well, a stick."

Both Zoran and Miroslav laughed, and even Kralj's stony expression seemed to flicker towards a smile for an instant as Peter turned into the lane. Chloe was waiting at the door, looking pleasingly shy and embarrassed in her over-the-top outfit with her breasts lifted up high and bare in two demi-cup froths of lace. She also looked distinctly submissive, with a silver tray fastened to her wrists by slender chains. The same chains also led to tiny clips made in the shape of dragon's heads, each with its teeth clamped onto one stiff nipple. On the tray was a bottle of Champagne and several full glasses.

"Champagne, Gentlemen?" she offered, bobbing a curtsey as Peter and the others climbed from the car.

"Pol Roger, Winston Churchill's personal favourite," Peter explained as they took their glasses. "Which is why the cuvée is named after him, the 'eighty-five in this case, and made using grapes exclusively from Grand Cru vineyards."

Both Zoran and Milosevic were plainly more interested in inspecting the now blushing Chloe's firmly clamped tits, while Kralj was looking at the open, empty fields and hedges as he spoke into his mobile phone.

"We're quite secure, I assure you," Peter told him, although he found himself glancing nervously at the line of trees along the road and at a distant row of walkers on Ivinghoe Beacon. "You'd need an extraordinarily powerful lens to see that

Chloe's dress is anything more than a cheeky costume, while all the action will be around the back, where we're screened in all directions. Do come in."

Kralj responded with a single, crisp nod and followed through to the garden, leaving Chloe to greet Stephen and the remaining guests as their car drew up. Clementine and Felicity stood on the lawn, glowering at each other from either side of a pool of thick, greyish mud.

"This is our clay pit," Peter announced, indicating the depression he'd hollowed out in the middle of the lawn. "Just the thing for girls to wrestle in, I'm sure you'll agree?"

He'd chosen the position well, making sure that the house and trees blocked the view in every direction, with the peak of the hill barely visible between the tall trunks. Considerable trouble had also gone into the design. First he had marked out a circle ten feet wide, then dug a shallow bowl from the chalky soil. A pond liner had ensured that the bottom was smooth and the water wouldn't drain away too quickly, while a local quarry had allowed him to collect a quantity of chalky slurry. All of his efforts had resulted in a very natural-looking pit of notably disgusting clay.

Stephen and the remaining three guests had joined them, sipping Champagne and passing remarks in a language completely lost on Peter. But the crude jokes made at the girls' expense, and speculation as to what could be done with each of them, barely needed translation. Mr. Drach was the first to touch, walking over to Felicity to push one breast up and out her of her bodice. He gave the nipple a firm tweak and set it erect, before treating the other to the same. Felicity managed a giggle in response, while there was nothing false about her blushes. But Mr. Drach seemed concerned only with her body, merely passing a remark in his own language as he began to fondle her breasts.

"Hands on your head, Felicity," Peter ordered, "and you, Clementine. Show the gentlemen some respect."

Both girls complied, Felicity struggling to maintain her composure, Clementine cool and serene even as her breasts were popped out in turn and her nipples tweaked to erection. Chloe had joined them, and she was similarly perused, Zoran holding up her skirt to show off the seat of her frilly knickers and allowing Miroslav to take a leisurely fondle of her bottom. Kralj and the two big, quiet men had disappeared in among the trees, presumably to make sure they were unobserved, and Peter took the opportunity to speak with Stephen.

"Well, they seem to like the girls."

"I should hope so too," Stephen answered. "I just hope the girls like them enough to put on a good show."

"We should be okay," Peter assured him. "That's one of the many good things about ex-toasty girls. They're used to humiliation. In fact, they'll probably be disappointed if they don't get a good spanking, especially Clemmie."

"I'm not sure our friends are into spanking as such," Stephen replied as they watched Chloe's frilly knickers pulled down. "Or at least, not in the English style. Mainly they just seem to like girls they can interfere with."

Peter nodded. Mr. Drach now had Felicity's breasts fully out of her dress, one cupped in either hand as he sucked and licked at her nipples. She stood bolt upright, her hands on top of her head and her eyes closed, her emotions betrayed by the faint trembling of her lower lip. Zoran had gone to Clementine, one hand down the front of her knickers. Despite his sober demeanour, she seemed to savour his touch as her mouth grew slack and her calm expression gave way to reluctant pleasure as she was molested. Miroslav had stayed with Chloe, her knickers now around her ankles, as he squeezed and licked at her bottom while she struggled not to giggle through her scarlet blushes.

Mr. Drach gave an order, laughing but also stern. All three girls had quickly been divested of their knickers, leaving them bare both front and back as they hurried indoors to fetch more refreshments and the men came over to compliment Stephen and Peter on the arrangements. Kralj returned with the two bodyguards to make a brief report in his own language before taking a glass of champagne from Chloe as she re-emerged. Rhiannon appeared, carrying seats for the wrestling, only to be caught by Zoran and Miroslav, molested and stripped nude as she scampered back for more chairs. Peter said nothing, and when she came out again she was quickly seated on one of the chairs as Zoran's cock was fed into her mouth. Mr. Drach also unzipped, guiding Felicity's hand to his cock, while Clementine was put on her knees to suck Miroslav erect. None of the others took any notice and Peter decided to follow their example, expounding upon the beauty of the Chilterns to Mr. Drach and Miroslav even as the girls worked on their cocks.

With a grunt from Zoran, Rhiannon received a faceful of jism, with creamy ribbons hanging from her nose and chin as well as a long white streak down one cheek and more still in her mouth. Miroslav promptly excused himself to Peter and ducked down to turn Clementine onto her knees, easing his cock into her cunt with no more self-consciousness than if he'd been fastening a cufflink. Mr. Drach guided Felicity down to where she took his cock in her mouth, with Peter now amused but a little shocked as he continued the conversation.

"I must say, you use the girls very casually, Mr. Drach."

"That is what they're here for, no?" Mr Drach responded as Peter watched Zoran wipe his cum into Rhiannon's face with his still hard cock.

"That's true enough," Peter answered, now talking to the sound of the squelching noise of Miroslav's cock in Clementine's cunt. "Would you like to um … finish off before the wrestling?"

"I am so sorry," Mr. Drach replied. "We are being rude. The girls must get ready for the fight, of course. Miroslav, fuck the other one, the red head. You can stop now, little one."

"You'd better get changed," Peter told Felicity as she

came off Mr. Drach's cock. "You too, Clemmie."

Clementine was still on her knees, her cunt agape from Miroslav's cock, but she nodded and followed Felicity indoors. Chloe was put down in Felicity's place, still with her tray in her hands as she sucked on Mr. Drach's penis, while Miroslav held Rhiannon's legs up to watch his erection slide in and out as he fucked her. Peter watched, along with the others, his own cock now starting to stiffen in response to the abundant show of bare, female flesh. He also could not deny finding a perverse and unexpected pleasure in the casual way the girls were being used so crudely. But he was determined to save himself for later.

Miroslav obviously wasn't, suddenly pushing his trousers down and mounting Rhiannon, to fuck her on her back with her legs up and open, his cock pumping in and out, his balls slapping onto her spread bottom until he'd unloaded deep inside her. Mr. Drach showed more patience, simply enjoying Chloe's mouth until Clementine and Felicity came back out, now ready to wrestle. Both wore bikinis, red for Clementine and blue for Felicity, tied with bows between each girl's breasts and at her hips.

"What are the rules?" Mr. Drach asked.

"They fight in the mud," Peter explained. "The first to be made fully nude is the loser, including the ribbons in their hair. The winner can then do what she likes with the loser, who'll also get six of the cane from me, or you if you prefer, and, I don't know … staked out on the lawn for general use? Whatever takes your fancy, really."

Mr. Drach gave a pleased nod and reached down to cuff Chloe gently across the face as he spoke.

"You'd better get on with serving the drinks, little one. The redhead can suck my penis while I watch."

"Rhiannon," Peter said, gesturing to her.

She'd clearly been included in the entertainment, and Peter found himself glad Michelle had remained in the kitchen. There was something unsettling about the way the men used the girls and, while he could see the appeal, he preferred not to have his heavily pregnant wife involved. Rhiannon at least seemed to accept the situation, crawling across to where Mr. Drach had sat down, and taking his erection in her hand as she began to lick at his balls. The others also took their seats, with Clementine and Felicity already at either side of the clay pit, sizing each other up with convincingly hateful glares.

Peter waited until Chloe had served out fresh drinks, then signalled for the fight to begin. Both girls started forward, cautiously, but in Clementine's case not cautiously enough. Her foot slipped on the sloping bottom of the pit and she went down sideways into the mud, quickly catching herself even as Felicity darted forward, only to slip as well and go down full length in the mess, saving her face by a miracle. A peel of laughter went up from the watchers, the two bodyguards included, followed by cries of encouragement as Clementine threw herself on top of Felicity.

The girls went down, sprawling in the mud, both already filthy and getting rapidly worse as each struggled to get at the other's bikini bows. First Clementine seemed to have the advantage, jerking Felicity's bikini top loose and pulling it free to show off her naked breasts, each slippery with clay save for a pink triangle topped by even pinker nipples. One firm push and she was faced down in the clay again, both tits now filthy all over but her face still unsullied as she gave a furious sideways twist.

Clementine went down, her legs waving in the air as she was unseated. As she twisted over in an attempt to get up, Felicity caught her around the waist. Struggling to rise, Clementine's knees began to slip in the clay without moving her at all, a sight so comic that even the bodyguards were roaring with laughter, and all the more so as Felicity scooped up a massive wad of clay and stuffed it down the back of Clementine's bikini bottoms. A second handful followed, adding to the weight in Clementine's bikini, which now hung down in a heavy, rounded ball, as if she'd had an extremely unfortunate accident.

Zoran passed a remark to Miroslav, in Serbian but easily understandable, raising fresh laughter, which Peter rejoined as Felicity began to spank the helpless Clementine, squashing the soggy clay across her bottom with firm, accurate smacks. Most of the muck squeezed out around the side of Clementine's bikini briefs but, as she gave a gasp of outrage and disgust, Peter realised that some of it must have slithered into her cunt. Felicity laughed, and Clementine used the distraction to snatch at her opponent, catching one of the bows at Felicity's hip.

Already topless, Felicity was forced to defend herself, grabbing at the bow, but too late. Her bikini bottoms had come lose, unfastened at one side, then hauled off as Clementine tightened her grip and threw herself backwards in the same instant, sprawling in the mud with her own bikini briefs halfway down and her muddy cunt displayed. Still, Felicity was now completely in the nude with only her hair ribbon between her and defeat.

The girls rested for a moment, gasping, their bodies slimed with clay except for the occasional patch of sweaty pink, their hair matted and foul, Felicity nude but for decoration, Clementine with her top half on, and her bikini bottoms bagging around her thighs with the weight of the clay within them. If there was anything fake about the fury in their faces Peter couldn't see it, and Felicity screamed as she threw herself at Clementine once more. They went down together, grappling, scratching, pulling hair, Felicity even using her teeth to try and rip off Clementine's bikini top while she clutched at her own hair ribbon in a desperate attempt to defend herself.

It worked, briefly, both of Clementine's tits now bare and pink, with her bikini up around her neck. But she'd snatched a handful of clay and slapped it into Felicity's face, filling her mouth and smearing it over her eyes. Felicity jerked back, scraping at the mess on her face and spitting filth, only to have

a second handful of clay crammed into her mouth, making her eyes pop with shock and disgust. With that, her will to fight seemed to go. Clementine closed in, catching Felicity by the knot of her hair, to hold her head above the puddle of slime for a long moment, allowing the defeated girl to see exactly what was about to happen to her. Then, with a snarl, Clementine pushed her opponent's face into the filthy mess with a heavy squelch, rubbing the whole of her head into the muck before pulling her up once more. Her face was a mask of clay, her open mouth full of filth, her eyes closed, utterly defeated, so that when Clementine let go of her hair she simply slumped back into the mud. With her last ounce of determination, Felicity jerked violently to the side, flailing blindly at Clementine's hair ribbon, which she managed to catch and remove.

Mr. Drach began to clap and the others joined in. All were grinning, laughing and passing remarks as the girls continued to grapple, both now caked in slippery grey clay from head to foot, snatching furiously at each other's bodies, indifferent to the lewd display of breasts, bottoms and cunts they provided to their audience. Clementine's bikini bottoms loosened further and finally fell off, exposing the wad of dirty grey clay packed into the mouth of her cunt and (as she struggled into a crawling position) her arse too. One vicious snatch and her bikini top was gone, but Felicity had already lost. Clementine raised a triumphant fist, opening her fingers to reveal the other girl's hair ribbon. As the unassailable realisation dawned on Felicity, she slumped back into the mud once more, now truly defeated.

Clementine rose from the muck, unsteady on her feet, shaking badly, but triumphant. She was grinning as she showed off the hair ribbon to the cheering audience, with her feet planted to either side of Felicity's body where the defeated girl lay sprawled in the muck. Peter nodded and gave the private signal they'd agreed. Felicity took note and reluctantly assented, staying down in the mud where she lay. Clementine gave a curt order, and Felicity responded by opening her mouth wide and squeezing her eyes shut. Clementine turned her body a little to ensure that she was full on to Mr. Drach, then let go of her bladder, pissing full

and hard into Felicity's face and over her chest, filling her mouth
and soiling her tits anew as bare skin emerged from beneath the
mud. Clementine sank down onto her haunches, scooped up a
handful of mud and crammed it into Felicity's mouth, to leave
the hapless girl coughing and spluttering as she tried to spit it out,
only to have her nose pinched and her jaw pressed shut. Her eyes
popped, her struggles grew desperate, but Clementine refused to
back off and Felicity was finally forced to eat mud, her face set in
furious resentment as she swallowed down the filthy mess in her
mouth. The clapping and cheering had stopped, all but one of
the men staring opened mouthed in shock and pity as well lust,
save for Kralj, who now wore a small, happy smile, and Peter
himself, who was grinning as he got up to hose the girls down.

It took a moment for the spell to break. Rhiannon had
been working on Mr. Drach's cock all the while, half turned so
that she could watch the fight from one eye as she sucked and
licked at his erection. She was now pulled closer and forced to
take him deep as he twisted his hands into her long red hair,
fucking her mouth with short, hard thrusts clearly intended to
take him to orgasm. Kralj gave a nod to the bodyguards and
they quickly had Chloe on her knees. Her tray was taken off her
and the men unzipped, their stout pale cocks and heavy balls
protruding obscenely from their suit trousers as she did her best
to cope with both at the same time, sucking and tugging at them
until they were hard enough to wedge her into a firm spit roast.

Peter was himself undeniably turned on, and Rhiannon's
bare, outthrust bottom made a fine sight, with her cunt deliciously
puffy and wet and ready for entry—and the tight pink star of her
anus a no less tempting a target. He pulled his cock free as he
continued to hose down the girls, and Clementine immediately
crawled close to take him in her mouth. Felicity had rinsed
quickly and scurried indoors to shower, leaving Peter to enjoy
Clementine's lips as he played the hose over her naked body.

To his left, Mr. Drach had come in Rhiannon's mouth,

securing her head to make sure she took every last drop of his seed, as she struggled bravely to keep his full length in her throat. Taking Clementine by the hair, Peter pulled her face between the cheeks of Rhiannon's bottom as Mr. Drach finished. Clementine knew exactly what was expected of her, licking eagerly at Rhiannon's arse as Peter masturbated over the sight. Rhiannon got down, her bottom pushed high as she was prepared for Peter's cock, her anus quickly relaxing and opening beneath Clementine's tongue. Peter moved closer, still holding Clementine by the hair as he pushed his cock deep into her throat, withdrew, and pressed the head to Rhiannon's anus.

Clementine continued to lick, her tongue flicking over Peter's cock and Rhiannon's bottom hole as he pushed himself slowly in. Soon he was deep in Rhiannon, and Clementine nuzzled down between their thighs to lick at Peter's balls and her friend's cunt as he took his pleasure in Rhiannon's arse. Clementine's own thighs were spread too, her fingers plucking at her cunt as she masturbated, even as Zoran arrived to ease his cock into her pussy. Miroslav joined in, settling his semi-stiff cock into Rhiannon's mouth as she was sodomised, the taut and shiny ring of her sphincter now pulling and stretching around Peter's increasingly rapid thrusts.

As he plunged into Rhiannon again and again, Peter was vaguely aware that Stephen and Kralj had gone indoors. He sped up, knowing that Michelle was more than likely to be ready to play, but wary of what the other men might do to her. Clementine opened her mouth wide to take in Peter's balls, sucking hard to make him gasp with ecstasy right on the edge of pain. Rhiannon began to gag on Miroslav's cock as the pumping in her rectum grew faster. A cry of pain rang out from somewhere behind him and Peter began to push faster still, desperate to see what was going on but too close to orgasm to hold back.

He came, ejaculating deep in Rhiannon's rectum before pulling his cock free and sinking it as far down Clementine's throat as it would go, hitting a second peak as he watched her eyes pop wide in shock, and a third just as a fresh cry of pain rang out from behind him. Cursing in surprise, he twisted around, to find no sign at all of Michelle. Although Felicity was in the living room, visible through the French doors as she licked at Stephen's balls and cock while Kralj applied a cane to her naked bottom.

"Just a beating. Thank goodness for that," he sighed, and looked down at Clementine. "Come on, Clemmie, swallow it all down like a good little girl. Your next booking won't be half as much fun."

"I have to confess that this is one situation I didn't foresee," Peter mused. "Hiring the girls out for ordinary functions, such as this one. Still, the client was willing to pay our rates. So I didn't feel it was sensible to turn it down."

"You're still earning money," Gabriel responded. "Just not as much."

"Not nearly as much," Peter told him. "But then again, we do have five or six regulars here anyway, so perhaps it won't be a total loss."

"Ah! So normal service is not completely restricted!" Gabriel chortled. "I'd like to reserve little Chloe, in that case. She gave me a wonderful time the other night."

"She's a wonderful girl. Shy, but very, very dirty."

"Extraordinarily dirty, although I have to say I preferred her with her natural hair colour. She's makes a pretty blonde, but it robs her of something of her innocence, and with that you lose some of the fun of being naughty with her. Or I think so anyway."

"I agree, but we had to dye her hair for some clients of Stephen's."

"Ah, yes, I'd heard something about that. How did it go?"

"He got the contract, and so he should have. Given what those fellows got up to. Not that they were especially perverse, and Clemmie and Flick even managed to shock them. But they were pretty hard on the girls, expecting rough sex without so much as a by-your-leave."

"Going by what Stephen told me about those chaps, it seems the girls should count themselves lucky. So can I have Chloe?"

"Yes. I'll tell her."

"Thank you. The rest of the party will now be a great deal less tedious. I had better circulate. That's the trouble with being an MP, never a moment's peace, and as for these damn charity people, they seem to think I'm made of money."

A cluster of people nearby had obviously been waiting to talk to Gabriel and he went across to greet them with handshakes and smiles, his manner far more effusive than it had been with Peter, but obviously put on. Peter smiled as he turned away, walking down to a small square of rose bushes surrounding a pond, with Koi carp gliding among the water plants. The garden party was a fund raising event for Caring Planet, a charity for which a Grove House client served as honorary chairman. But the booking had come from the secretary, a brassy, forceful woman who knew nothing whatsoever about the truth behind Grove House Maids. The secretary had been at another event and liked the idea of well-spoken British girls serving at her function.

So far he had managed to avoid making a contribution to the charity, which he was fairly sure existed mainly for the purpose of paying its senior people large salaries. He was keen to maintain his donation-free streak, while the carp struck him as much better company than most of the people there. Despite the fishes' habit of repeatedly opening their mouths, they never actually said anything—and that really was a pleasant change. Rhiannon, Felicity, Chloe and Henrietta were all there, wandering among the guests with loaded trays. But the formal garden was far too open to allow him to take one of them into a secluded corner.

The possibilities for later that evening were another matter, as long as all four girls didn't get booked. Still, it would be more than two hours before the event ended. When it did end, he was going to have to drive, but he had decided to risk another glass of wine. As he turned to go back inside, Peter noticed a woman coming towards him in a disturbingly purposeful manner, smiling but without the slightest trace of warmth. She was tiny, perhaps as little as five feet tall, but with even more poise and confidence than most of the other women present, while her simple black dress was perfectly cut and the diamonds in her ears and at her throat showed a restrained perfection that suggested both taste and wealth. There was no doubting her appeal either, at least physically, her figure petite yet elegant, her face beautiful if cold, while her age was hard to judge.

"What a surprise," she said. "If it isn't Peter Finch. Are you on day release?"

"I'm sorry," Peter replied, affronted, "but I have absolutely no idea who you are."

"No?" she queried, her tone cool and light, as if in casual conversation. "I'm surprised. Perhaps if I was the other way up, wearing a school uniform and being spanked?"

Peter had nearly dropped his glass at the final word, uttered with sudden venom. But at her change of tone the years fled and he realised who she was.

"Christine! Christine Arlington!"

"Yes," she answered. "Christine Arlington."

"Well, um … hello," he tried, unsure how best to address woman who'd been doing her best to scratch his eyes out the last time they met. "What a surprise. How have you been?"

"Very well, no thanks to you," she answered. "You, Peter Finch, are the lowest, the …"

"Come, come," he interrupted. "There's no call for abuse. It was just a bit of fun, after all. You know, just messing around."

"A bit of fun?" she retorted. "Messing around!? You arranged to have me spanked!"

"You volunteered to be spanked," Peter corrected her. "In return for a favour from Victoria Trent."

"I volunteered, yes, and I suppose I should have known that mad bitch Vicky Trent would do her best to humiliate me. But I did not volunteer to be punished in front of two dozen leering boys."

"I think there were nineteen of us in the end," Peter broke in, now beginning to enjoy himself as his initial shock died away.

"One would have been too many," she answered, her voice now edged with ice. "Especially if that one had been you, you little pervert."

"I apologise," Peter went on. "I apologise unreservedly. It was very unfair of me. But in my defence you undoubtedly had one of the prettiest bottoms in your year at St. Monica's, small but perfectly formed, as the saying goes. Not only that, but you were a brat, and brats need spanking, as I'm sure you realise?"

"You little bastard!" she spat.

"Oh come on," he chuckled. "With such a pretty bottom and such a vicious personality, how could you possibly expect not to get spanked? Just like gin needs tonic or peaches need cream, as the Americans say. It's just the way things are. There's no point in complaining about it. Besides, as I recall you were—to use a somewhat vulgar turn of phrase—absolutely creaming yourself while you were getting you rump roasted."

Christine had been listening to him wordlessly, her mouth opening and closing, tempting Peter to draw a comparison between her and the carp in the pond beside them. But he changed his mind when he saw the raw fury in her eyes. Surely she was about to hit him, and he stepped back a little to make sure he was out of reach. But Christine had quickly regained control, her voice once more calm as she continued.

"You'll regret that little speech, Peter Finch, every rotten word. I know you're up to something. I'm not entirely sure what it is yet, but I know it involves some pretty high profile people and I'd bet absolutely anything that it's *extremely* shady."

"How do you mean?" Peter asked with a sudden sense of dread. "I'm not 'up to' anything, as you put it. What makes you think I am?"

"You run an agency, don't you?" she said, her voice dripping venom. "An agency that supplies maids, very exclusive maids. Most similar agencies employ the cheapest labour they can, all sorts of people, from all sorts of backgrounds and of all ages. Your maids are all very young, very pretty and very British."

"As you say, we offer an exclusive service," Peter countered.

"Suspiciously exclusive," she went on. "But don't worry, if you're really above board you having nothing to worry about. Otherwise ..."

"Grove House Maids is a legitimate company," he insisted. "You can go over our accounts, if you want to. But anyway, why all the fuss? Wouldn't it be better to let bygones be bygones?"

"No," she answered emphatically. "Besides, even if this was nothing to do with you, I'd still be interested. I didn't tell you what I've been doing all these years, did I? I, Peter Finch, am a journalist."

◆ ◆ ◆ ◆

"We're going to have to draw our horns in a bit," Peter insisted, leaning forward in his chair at Lorrimer's. He'd called an emergency meeting of the key players who'd been instrumental in developing the business.

"No," Stephen answered. "That would be playing into her hands. You don't think she tipped you off to make life easier for you, surely?"

"She lost her temper," Peter pointed out. "But then again ..."

"Always assume your opponent is at least as clever as you are," Stephen went on. "Maybe she lost her temper and blurted it out, but maybe she did it on purpose in order to force you to react. She's watching you, and if you change the way Grove House Maids works, let alone shut down completely, that will only confirm her suspicions."

"I agree," Gabriel put in, "and besides, I need girls."

"Surely you can manage without for a while?" Peter queried.

"Not for sex," Gabriel retorted. "Well, obviously for sex, but not personally. I'm not too popular with my local committee just now, with my majority down in the hundreds, so I've been keeping old man Broughton sweet by sending Elspeth round to service him now and again."

"You're not really supposed to do that," Peter told him. "Sir Edmund Broughton is not a club member."

"He thinks she's a friend of my niece's," Gabriel explained. "But never mind that. I need to be able to hire Elspeth, and Stephen's right anyway."

"Well?" Peter asked, looking to Ben Thompson and Clive Sumner.

"Stephen is definitely right," Ben answered, with Clive nodding agreement. "Keep things as they are and perhaps we can get rid of her."

"How?" Peter demanded, alarmed.

"Nothing too drastic," Ben answered him. "But she's a journalist, with a long history of digging up inconvenient facts and catching people in awkward situations. She'll have her share of guilty secrets."

"Or," Gabriel suggested, "we could offer her boss a little light entertainment. He's a randy old goat by all accounts, old Lord Bearslake, with some highly peculiar habits if the rumours are to be believed. Okay, so he supported the other team at the election, but he's one of us at heart and I doubt he wants a party scandal at present."

"I wouldn't count on that," Clive advised. "Loyalty is not exactly his strong point and we're pretty unpopular just now. Think of all the papers he could sell with a nice juicy sex scandal."

"Ah," Gabriel went on, "but if he was a member of our club I'm sure he could be persuaded to keep Christine on a tight leash—literally, with any luck."

"I can't see that working," Peter put in. "Maybe he is a randy old goat, and I wouldn't be surprised if Christine is fucking him. But I can't imagine him putting sex before profit."

"Hang on," Clive queried. "Gabriel, how do you mean 'literally'?"

"Apparently," Gabriel went on, grinning, "he likes to dress girls up as animals, preferably so that he can hunt them down on his estate in Gloucestershire."

"Good grief!" Ben exclaimed. "And what does he do when he catches them?"

"He fucks them, I'm guessing," Gabriel laughed. "I don't think he's a complete maniac."

"More to the point," Clive put in, "how has he managed to get away with something like that for all these years, maniac or not?"

"Much the same way we do, I imagine," Peter replied. "Posh girls, well paid."

"That and a reputation as a litigious bastard," Gabriel told them. "After all, who would believe that the great philanthropist and guardian of the nation's morals, Lord Bearslake, would get up to that sort of thing? I was a bit dubious myself, when I first found out."

"How did you find out?" Peter asked.

"A little bird told me," Gabriel answered. "A very pretty little bird I happened to meet in Oxford after the Caring Planet event."

Gabriel had taken Chloe back to her college to have sex with her, and Peter felt a sharp pang of guilt as he glanced towards Ben. But his friend's face showed only interest as Gabriel continued.

"It was a wonderful moment, and one you'd particularly appreciate, Peter. After I'd um ... finished, I dropped in at the Eagle and Child for a refreshing pint. I was about halfway down the glass when I realised that this girl was looking at me. She was an absolute poppet, little and pretty with a splash of freckles across her nose and a bouncy little pair of tits, and as pink as a raspberry. I thought I was hanging out of my fly at first because, handsome though I am, I don't usually get college girls chasing after me these days, and she was clearly fascinated. Well, the snake was still in his lair, and she was still looking at me, so I introduced myself. Do you know what, she'd spotted that I'd got spanker's hand!"

"Wonderful!" Peter said.

"Who had you been spanking?" Ben asked.

"Clemmie," Gabriel responded without so much as faltering. "Anyway, so there I was, caught red handed, literally. But you know what these girls are like—when there's spanking to be done, they prefer an older man. So I took her over to Port Meadow and gave her the pinkest little bottom you ever did see, then taught her how to say thank you properly. Ophelia, she's called. Naturally I'd thought about signing her up to be a maid, so I took her out to dinner to sound her out, which is when she told me about old Bearslake. He used to run her on his estate, dressed as a vixen fox, with a big fluffy tail on a butt plug wedged in her arse. So there we are, Peter, your problem is solved."

"Very neatly," Peter replied. "Very neatly indeed."

He sat back, thinking deeply as the others continued to talk. An hour later the meeting broke up and they went their separate ways. But Stephen stayed with Peter, talking as they walked up Piccadilly towards Green Park station.

"Am I right in thinking you could do with some assistance for this business with Lord Bearslake?" Stephen asked.

"Very possibly," Peter replied. "I haven't thought

through all the permutations yet, but we're going to have to be very careful."

"You can count on me for support," Stephen assured him. "Financial or otherwise. I need to make a booking too, Clemmie probably. I need somebody tough."

"Why's that?"

"Kralj has taken a liking to English corporal punishment. He wants to beat Vivienne."

"Are you're not going to let him?"

"No. I spank her occasionally, and she quite likes it as long as I'm not too rough. But she couldn't handle six-of-the-best, let alone what Kralj wants to dish out. After the party I made the mistake of telling him about the birch, and you know what a cold, sadistic bastard he is. He didn't even get his cock out with Felicity, did he. But I'm sure he came in his pants while he was beating her. That wasn't enough for him, though, because she got off on it too."

"Isn't that the whole point?"

"Not for him. He wants a girl who's going to hate it, not a masochist. I can't let him have Vivienne, but I need to stay on his good side. That's why I need a substitute, and fast."

"Bastard. Still, that can probably be arranged, but I don't think Clemmie's the right choice. He's seen her in action."

"Perhaps you're right. Who then?"

"Not Flick, obviously, and Chloe couldn't handle it. Maybe Elspeth, unless the girl has to be blonde?"

"That was Drach's personal kink. This is a one to one."

"Okay. Elspeth is due a spanking anyway, for breaking the rules."

"That was mainly Gabriel's fault."

"True, but that's just the way it goes. He gets a light ticking off and she gets spanked, or in this case, birched."

"Are you sure she can handle it? He means to hurt her, and he's not the sort of man who'll stop if she can't handle the pain. In fact, that's exactly what he wants."

"I'll make sure she knows what she's in for," Peter assured him. "But she's tough, and a good little actress. Besides, if it's her or Vivienne …"

Elspeth swung from the tree by her bound wrists, her feet barely in contact with the ground. Her beautiful, pale body was naked and slick with sweat, her mouth hung slack and open, her eyes were unfocussed and her long red hair hung in dishevelled wet rat's tails. Welts from the birch criss-crossed the front of her body, turning the flesh of her breasts, belly and thighs an angry red. But it was her bottom that had received most attention. Her lovely, rounded cheeks glowed red with abuse, squeezing slowly in her pain.

She'd been put through the full birching ritual, first taken deep into the Berkshire woods and ordered to strip as Peter and Kralj watched. Then made to pick birch twigs in the nude. Long before she was finished she'd been in tears, with her fingers shaking as she used the fine red ribbon from her hair to tie off the handle, making the implement she was to be beaten with. Peter had felt more pity than lust, despite knowing that she was putting on an act. But Kralj had been delighted, his thin mouth twitching with pleasure for every step of her degradation and finally breaking into a skull like grin as she was strung up by her wrists from an overhead branch, so high that her toes scarcely brushed the forest floor beneath her.

He'd taken his time with her, using the big, bushy birch to tease her breasts and cunt, touching her as intimately as he pleased, keeping his black leather gloves on even as he penetrated her cunt and anus before making her suck his fingers. When the beating had finally begun he'd shown no mercy at all, laying in

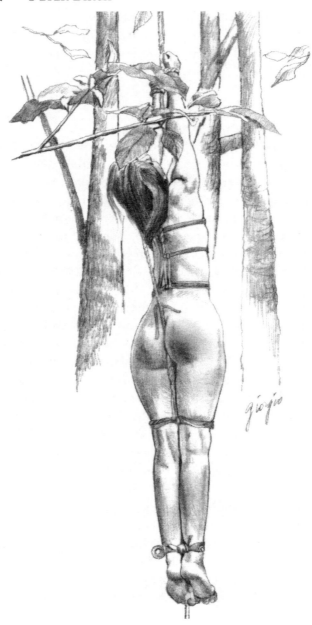

with the birch so hard that she'd bounced and swung from the rope, jerking wildly and trying in vain to turn away from the blows, alternately screaming and begging for mercy—no longer in pretence—as the supple twigs bit into her flesh over and over again.

Her pain had only served to enhance her tormentor's pleasure and amusement, until he'd finally stood back, leaving her to hang limp and broken on the end of the rope, as he freed his cock. Peter had been told what to do and quickly released the rope from her knees and ankles. From there, he went to where the rope was tied off to another tree, tugging the knot lose. Elspeth collapsed into the leaf mould, unable to stand, too far gone even to try and close her legs, and as her body hit the ground her bladder gave way, an arc of fluid spraying out from her.

Kralj watched, grinning, as Elspeth wet herself, his hand tugging at a long, almost unnaturally pale erection above a pair of rounded little balls that jutted from the opening of his black leather coat. She could do nothing, spread helpless in the dirt with her wrists bound tight above her head and her thighs wide as her gushing stream gradually died away in a series of little spurts that finished with a thin trickle running down between her cheeks. Only when she was fully done did Kralj step closer, to mount her, driving his cock deep into her sopping cunt with a single, hard thrust.

A low, despairing moan escaped her lips as she was entered. Her moan gave way to bitter sobs as her fucking began, Kralj's long cock pumping into her as his balls squeezed against her anus with every thrust. As with the whipping, he took his time, withdrawing after a while to roll her over and fuck her from behind with her bottom held up high to greet the thrusts of his cock; then making her suck him; rubbing his prick over her welted breasts and in the slit of her bottom; then mounting her once more before pulling out to finish himself off over her face and in her open mouth. Even then he wasn't finished. Elspeth lay spread out in the dirt, naked, soiled with sweat and cum, her body a mess of whip marks. Still, even after he'd come he showed no mercy, no sympathy, waiting until his cock had gone limp before casually urinating over her prone body. He then put his cock away and turned to Peter, extending a distinctly sticky hand. Peter shook it anyway, determined not to offend, and Kralj grinned as he spoke, his voice now cheerful and friendly.

"Thank you, that was a pleasure. You English, you have an art with girls. If there is ever any little favour you wish to ask of me in return, you must do so."

With that he left, joining the two burly bodyguards who'd been watching from among the trees to make sure they weren't disturbed while Elspeth was used for his pleasure. Only when he was sure that the three men had gone did Peter step forward to untie Elspeth's wrists as he spoke to her.

"Are you okay?"

"No ..." Elspeth sighed, "I need to come ... and I need to come *now* ..."

Peter smiled and shrugged as he put a hand to her cunt and began to masturbate her.

Ophelia proved to be every bit as appealing as Gabriel had said—small and winsome, strikingly pretty, with a coquettish manner and a round little backside that was ripe and ready for corporal administration. Despite his friend's commendation, Peter had insisted on vetting her properly, with a long session across his knee while Gabriel looked on, before she was put on her knees to fellate them both with her hot red bottom pushed out behind. She'd passed with flying colours and happily agreed to introduce them to Lord Bearslake at his country estate. Bearslake had been doubtful at first, but had finally agreed on the condition that Peter bring down two girls of his own.

In response, he'd taken Rhiannon and Elspeth to Master Jacobaeus, who'd whipped and sodomised both girls before agreeing to loan two of his own, both highly experienced and safe from any risk of scandal. One Peter already knew, Slave Green, or Gemma, who'd surrendered her virginity on the night of the party at St. Botolph's church. The other, Slave White, or Laurel, was new to him, but easy going and friendly. The three of them had been swapping dirty stories as they drove west on the M4, and they were on the best of terms by the time Peter drew the Jaguar to a halt on the carriage sweep of Bearslake Hall.

"That's quite a place," Gemma breathed, looking up at the facade of the great mansion. "He must be loaded."

"Loaded indeed," Laurel agreed.

"Never mind the scenery," Peter instructed. "Strike a pose. Tits out, please."

Both girls were giggling as they quickly pulled up their tops to show off braless breasts, allowing Peter to take a series of pictures with the hall in the background. As he slipped his camera back into the pocket of the scarlet hunting coat he'd bought for the occasion, a man appeared between the high gates to one side of the building and beckoned to them.

"Not out in the front," the man said as Peter and the girls drew close. "Bring the car in here. Discretion is essential."

"Of course," Peter agreed. "I'm Peter Finch. This is Gemma and this is Laurel, and you are?"

"John," the man answered. "I work for Lord Bearslake, as a gamekeeper, so to speak."

"Ah, I see, good. Is Ophelia here too? …"

Even as he spoke, Ophelia was stepping out from one of the old stable buildings behind John. The sight of her left Peter opened mouthed for an instant, while Gemma gave a squeak of delight and excitement. Ophelia was stark naked save for heavy boots, a cleverly designed fox's mask and a huge, bushy, red-brown tail rising behind her and quite clearly plugged into her anus. Her entire body had been painted too, with a fox's red back and flanks, but a paler abdomen and darker limbs, cunningly executed to show off her breasts and belly, making her at once exotic and intensely sexual.

"Are we going to be painted like that?" Laurel asked hopefully.

"No," John answered her. "You two are the hounds. Come in here and I'll show you. The car please, Mr Finch."

Peter went to retrieve the Jag, returning to find John and the girls in a big, open building that looked as if it might once have been a forge, only it was now being used for very different purposes. A table ran the full length of one wall, loaded with tools, leather straps, body paint and more, while the wall above was hung with coils of rope, handcuffs and whips. Opehlia had been put in a collar and was fixed to an iron ring at the far end of the room, while Laurel and Gemma were in mutual ecstasy as they examined the gear, comparing articles to things they owned or they'd used. But Peter's attention was drawn to a set of brushes laid out on a newspaper beside pots of black and white body paint.

"Are they going to be collie dogs?" he asked. "I thought they were used for rounding up sheep?"

"Dalmatians," a deep voice spoke from behind him. "Not strictly authentic, perhaps, but then, I make my own choices."

"Absolutely," Peter agreed, turning.

He'd known Lord Bearslake was a big man from pictures in newspapers and the occasional television appearance, but he'd never realised how big. Not only was the newspaper magnate immensely fat, but he was well over six feet tall, giving an impression of daunting bulk even without his commanding manner and deep, masculine voice. Both Gemma and Laurel had backed away a little at his appearance, and John's voice was positively servile as he spoke.

"We're almost ready, your Lordship. I just need to get the girls painted up."

Lord Bearslake merely grunted in response, then lowered his bulk onto a chair, watching as John began to fuss around the girls. Peter had expected to be offered drinks, or at least some form of hospitality, but Lord Bearslake appeared indifferent to his existence, small, piggy eyes feasting on Laurel and Gemma as they stripped to John's command. Both looked impressive nude, Gemma a little taller, Laurel slimmer, both gloriously feminine. Master Jacobaeus had trained them exquisitely in the art of erotic display so that now it was instinct. They were also full of enthusiasm, perfectly happy to be nude and giggling at John's attentions when he allowed his hands to stray to their breasts and bottoms.

Being painted made them giggle still more, and gasp at the sudden cold as the body paint dried on their skins. Each was painted white first, then given a moment to dry before large black spots were added in an irregular pattern that nevertheless drew the eye to their figures. Unlike Ophelia, they were not given masks, just black running shoes, but by the time John had finished there was no doubt at all that they were intended to resemble Dalmatians. Already they'd begun to get into character, barking and sniffing at each other as Lord Bearslake rose to extract two curious objects from a long box.

"Perfect," he announced. "Very pretty indeed, both of you, now pop these up inside yourselves, my dears; not your front, your back, if you please."

He was holding out what appeared to be Dalmatians' tails, but at least twice the normal length, while the base of each was equipped with a shaft that ended in a thick rubber plug. The girls took them, sharing nervous smiles as they realised how thick the plugs were, but Master Jacobaeus had trained them well. Gemma had quickly found a tub of anal lubricant among the items on the table, and the girls took turns to prepare each other's backsides, making a deliberate show for Lord Bearslake, who became ever more excited.

The tail was designed so that the base ran up between the wearer's bottom cheeks in such a way that it appeared to be growing from the base of her spine, and Peter found himself nodding his approval as Laurel turned to show off how she looked with the tail in place. Gemma took a little longer, her mouth widening slowly as her bottom hole stretched to take the plug. She was waddling a little once she'd got it in, but Lord Bearslake didn't seem to mind, clapping his podgy hands in delight as the two girls presented themselves for his inspection, bottoms pushed out and tails wagging over their bouncy butt cheeks as they gave him a teasing wiggle.

"Very nice, my dears," he drawled. "But I won't touch you yet, as it would be a shame to spoil your paintwork. So, I expect you know the rules? The fox gets five minutes start, then you chase her, run her down and tie her up nice and tight, then leave her to us for fucking."

Both girls nodded and Lord Bearslake finally turned to Peter.

"Well, Finch, I suppose you want your jollies too, as well as the money? Yes, I thought as much. Very well, you can run with the dogs and you should carry the rope. You can fuck the fox too, I suppose, but take her up her backside. I'm not having some pimp's sloppy seconds."

Peter hadn't had a chance to reply, but found himself nodding dumbly, unable to find the right words to cope with Lord Bearslake's arrogance. Given the man's personal tastes, Peter had been expecting to be treated as a fellow enthusiast for kinky sex, or at least with the warily conspiratorial attitude he'd become accustomed to from those of his clients who weren't personal friends. Lord Bearslake evidently didn't care, nodding to John and then glancing at his watch as Ophelia was released from her collar.

She immediately sped away, leaving what would have been an awkward silence but for the happy giggling of the girls as they admired each other's Dalmatian painted bodies. The five minutes seemed to take forever to pass, but Lord Bearslake finally declared that time was up. Both girls dashed out across the stable yard and onto the lawns beyond, Peter following at a slow lope, with John beside him, while Lord Bearslake seemed in no hurry at all, ambling slowly after them. The girls had quickly disappeared into a pine wood on the far side of the lawns, at which John signalled to Peter that they should take different paths.

Peter knew that the entire estate was surrounded by a high brick wall, making it impossible to stray beyond the boundaries, so he was glad to set off alone. Behind him, Lord Bearslake was only just starting across the lawns. While the path that led into the wood among the big pine trees curved sharply, so that the house was quickly lost from view. He could hear the girls calling to each other, with the occasional flash of black and white visible as they ran through the trees. There was no sign at all of Ophelia, but there didn't seem to be a great deal of cover for her to hide in—though surely most of the fun was in being caught …

Sure enough, as he emerged from the pines onto an area of heath he caught sight of her, hiding among a coppice of scrubby birch trees. He called out, yelling to the others that he had a view, and then that the fox had broken cover as Ophelia dashed out from the trees, her tail bobbing behind her as she ran. Gemma appeared, far to his left, then Laurel, the three of them closing in on Ophelia as Peter sped up to turn her away from a patch of dense woodland to his right. His tactic worked, forcing her to double back along the boundary wall in a desperate attempt to evade Gemma. She was too slow, slipping between Gemma and the wall with just yards to spare but not fast enough to get away. Peter watched as the gap narrowed, grinning with the thrill of the chase and imagining Ophelia's adrenaline rush as Gemma drew closer. But it was Laurel who finished the chase, bringing Ophelia down in the rough grass. Laurel had caught up in seconds, pouncing on Ophelia and pretending to bite her neck before helping Gemma to spread her out on the ground, face down, her tail waving with the squirming motions of her bare brown bottom as she fought to get away.

"Well done," Peter panted as he reached the others. "Okay, Gemma, get her hands behind her back. I'm going to tie her up."

Ophelia's arms were quickly forced into the small of her back, allowing Peter to tie her wrists with a tight cinch. Her ankles followed and she was helpless, her squirming now only serving to make her more tempting. There was no sign of either John or Lord Bearslake, to Peter's relief as he freed his cock into his hand. Both Gemma and Laurel were very adept at giving pleasure and immediately moved closer, guiding his hands to their breasts and bottoms as they took hold of his cock and balls. Ophelia twisted around, looking back to watch as the girls brought him to erection, her eyes wide and questioning, her bottom pushed up to show off her tawny brown fox's cunt, painted to enhance the swell of her lips and the pink crease at the centre.

"It's a shame I'm not supposed to fuck you," Peter sighed. She just looked so utterly ravishable. "Maybe I will anyway. Do you mind if I have you before that great tub of lard Bearslake?"

Ophelia shook her head, her eyes never leaving Peter's rapidly growing erection, now in Gemma's hand as Laurel licked his balls. He was already filthy with paint, but didn't care, eager only to enjoy his prize before the other men caught up. Wasting no time, he moved closer to Ophelia as soon as the other girls had him good and hard. Gemma and Laurel moved aside, to help lift Ophelia's hips and to cradle her head as Peter straddled the helpless girl's legs. She gave a little whimper as his cock touched her flesh, and did her best to keep her bottom up as he pulled the fox tail free. The plug came out reluctantly, leaving a slick and gaping black hole. He watched the ring of her arse squeeze slowly shut before he mounted her, his cock pressing to the entrance of her cunt and then deeply up inside her.

She'd begun to pant as they fucked, encouraging Peter to push harder and faster, while the temptation to come inside her and deliberately leave her soiled for Lord Bearslake grew with every thrust. Only the thought of missing out on the sweet peach of her arse made him hold back, and he had withdrawn an instant before it was too late, with his erection rearing up over her paint smeared cheeks as he took a moment to get his breath back.

"Ok," he told her, "now it goes up your backside, Ophelia, and I'm going to come inside you."

He'd deliberately given her a chance to refuse, but the other girls had pulled her face between Gemma's thighs where she'd been made to lick. Ophelia managed little more than a sob, her face wedged into Gemma's sex, her bottom still pushed up and waving high. Peter chuckled as he guided his cock down once more, this time pressed to her arse. She was still relaxed from the plug on the end of her fox's tail, and Peter's cock slid in most accommodatingly, pushed deep into the hot, wet cavity of her rectum with just two firm thrusts, as his balls squashed up to her empty cunt.

Her cheeks had puffed out and her eyes had begun to water as his cock slid in and out, but she'd soon returned to licking Gemma's cunt, encouraging Peter to make the most of her compliance. He took her by the hips, pumping his way towards orgasm as she gasped and shuddered beneath him, her fingers clutching at the rope binding her arms. Gemma came, crying out in ecstasy under Ophelia's tongue; then Peter, his cock jammed in deep, erupting so copiously that the cum squashed out around his shaft to coat Ophelia's stretched anus.

"Maybe that'll teach old Bearslake some manners?" he chuckled when he'd finally withdrawn and the slick concoction from Ophelia's valiant bottom had begun to run down onto her cunt. "If the old bastard ever turns up, that is."

He stood up, watching as Laurel took her turn with Ophelia, pulling the bound girl's head between her thighs and forcing her to lick. Ophelia hardly needed telling, her tongue emerging eagerly and instantly, despite her bonds and her recent exhaustive exploits. Gemma took pity on their compliant captive, cupping her cunt in one hand, dipping a thumb into the open, slippery hole and busying her fingers over the wet, sensitive flesh between her sex lips.

"Dirty bitches," Peter chided as he turned to scan the area.

The heath was empty, but as he looked towards the long, red brick line of the boundary wall he caught a movement. A figure rose up, small, female and holding a camera with an impressively long telephoto lens—Christine Arlington.

Lord Bearslake sat with his fingers laced together over the more than ample bulge of his waistcoat. His face was serene, betraying no more than a hint of malign amusement, the greyish-pink polyp of his mouth pursed as if in thought. Peter sat opposite him, waiting for the other to speak. On the table between them lay Peter's camera, the film pulled out. Christine stood to one side, her own camera still around her neck, the huge lens cradled in one arm. By the door was John, his brawny arms folded across his chest, his eyes fixed on Peter. The girls had been allowed to clean up, using a pump in the stable yard to wash each other down. Finally Lord Bearslake spoke up.

"You're not a particularly intelligent man, Peter Finch, or you wouldn't have fallen for our little trap so easily, but I trust that you do at least have the wit to realise that you have no choice but to co-operate?"

Peter merely shrugged.

"What we want from you," Lord Bearslake went on, "and for which you will be paid a substantial sum, is a complete list of all those involved in your dirty little money making scheme, along with plenty of detail so that we can give the readers something to get their teeth into."

"No," Peter answered.

"Clearly you are duller than I thought," Lord Bearslake continued. "Christine, the photographs, please."

Christine picked up a blue folder from the table at her side, to extract a large print and throw it down in front of Peter as she spoke.

"Your old school friend Hunter Rackman, now a senior diplomat at the US embassy, pictured taking Clementine Stewart up to his apartment at two a.m. on the morning of May the third, this year."

"He was merely looking after the daughter of an old friend while she was in town," Peter told her, "as any gentleman would. There's nothing wrong with that."

"Not usually, no," Christine went on as she tossed a second photograph down on the tables. "But here she is again, leaving the building shortly before noon the following day."

"So, she stayed the night," Peter answered. "What are you trying to imply?"

Christine raised one delicate eyebrow and threw another photograph onto the growing heap. It was very different to the others, clearly taken from a long way away and with an exceptionally powerful lens. It showed the front of the Grove, with Peter and others climbing from the Jaguar. Chloe stood by the door in her Union Flag dress, her bare breasts clearly visible with the chains running from her nipples to the tray.

"You mix with some very peculiar company," Lord Bearslake stated.

"It was a fancy dress party," Peter said casually.

"Involving topless girls with their nipples clamped and some extremely shady Serbian businessmen?" Bearslake chuckled. "Come, come, Finch, you can do better than that. Unless I'm greatly mistaken, and I never am, the girl is Chloe Thompson, daughter of your old friend Ben Thomson, civil servant and also a recipient of your largesse, although presumably not with her. In fact, I don't suppose that he's even aware that you're hiring his daughter out as a prostitute, is he? Any more than Daniel Stewart is aware that you're doing the same with Clementine?"

"I don't know what you're talking about, I've never …," Peter began, then stopped as Christine added another picture to the pile.

It was far from clear, and seemed to have been taken from the very summit of Ivinghoe Beacon, looking down through the trees into his garden. None of the figures could easily have been identified without detailed knowledge of who'd been there, but it was clearly no ordinary party. Rhiannon's distinctive red hair stuck out as she knelt to suck on Mr. Drach's cock, and while the girls in the clay pit were so filthy and indistinct as to be completely unrecognisable, there was no doubt about what they were doing.

"The lens I was using has a focal length of seven hundred and fifty millimetres," Christine told him as she added another picture to the heap.

"You should have bought a bigger one," Peter said. "You can't see a thing!"

"We can see enough to know what was going on," Lord Bearslake told him, "as I'm sure you realise, but not as much as we'd like, otherwise the whole sordid little escapade would already have come out in my papers. I could publish, but I prefer to get the big scoop, and that's why you are going to help us."

"I think not," Peter replied, not bothering to look up as he scrutinised the added photos, none of which showed anything more than the first. "That's the thing about stick and carrot, Bearslake. You need a donkey, and when it comes to persuading me to do things I don't want to, you'll find I bear a far greater similarity to a mule."

"Aren't they brave before they get the full picture?" Lord Bearslake remarked to Christine, before turning back to Peter. "So, what do we know? We have the daughter of a prospective leader of the opposition sleeping with a U.S. diplomat and ... well, behaving in a thoroughly bizarre fashion with some Serbian businessmen, including the notorious Budimir Kralj? You do know who Budimir Kralj is, don't you?"

"A Serbian businessman?" Peter suggested.

"A Serbian businessman, yes," Lord Bearslake agreed. "Also an ex-army officer with a speciality in shall we say 'intelligence', and shortly to be among the most wanted men in Europe. It will be the biggest scandal since the Profumo Affair, maybe bigger. You, Peter Finch, will be right in the middle of it, and can no doubt be charged with a broad range of offences, certainly enough to ensure that you don't see the outside world again until well into the coming century. Or, you can play ball, give us the information we want and walk away with a cool twenty thousand pounds."

"That's an insultingly low bribe," Peter answered.

"I suspect it will seem quite generous when you're sewing mailbags in Wormwood Scrubs, or wherever they decide to put you." Lord Bearslake went on, "But I'm forgetting, not only are you a hardened jailbird, but you're a man of honour. The story we want is Stewart, along with Gabriel Howard, and I'm afraid poor little Clementine can't really avoid getting caught up in it all. But I imagine you'd like to spare the blushes of your other girls; Chloe Thompson, for instance, and the pair of little tarts you brought along this afternoon? I say two, of course, because as you must have realised by now, the girl you know as Ophelia …"

"… was a honey trap, I know," Peter finished for him. "Chloe Thompson has nothing to do with this. But as for Gemma and Laurel, please feel free to publish, although I suspect the pictures Christine took will prove to be a little strong for a family newspaper."

"What a very feeble bluff," Lord Bearslake went on. "We know how you operate, Finch, courtesy of the fair Ophelia. All your girls have as much to lose as the men they serve, which is why they're safe. I don't know who the two you brought today are, but I'm very sure they wouldn't want their pictures in the paper."

"To the contrary," Peter told him. "They'd be delighted. In fact, if you spent an afternoon going around the phone boxes in the less reputable parts of central London, you'd recognise them. You see, they are a 'pair of little tarts', but they're not from Grove House Maids, which is a perfectly respectable company set up to help students through university. Expose Gemma and

Laurel, please do. It would be excellent publicity for them."

Christine's face showed irritation, but only for a moment.

"You're in those photographs too, Finch," she pointed out.

"I am," Peter admitted. "But I don't suppose there'll be much public interest in little old me, surely not? Aside from that, I believe that anal sex has been legal since around nineteen-ninety-four, and light bondage is okay, and group sex, I think, especially as I was on private land, your land, in fact, Lord Bearslake."

"What do you mean by that?" Lord Bearslake demanded.

"Precisely what I say," Peter went on. "You have photographs, no doubt of excellent quality, that show me and three girls having sex—quite imaginative sex I'd like to think—and the animal get-ups were a wonderful touch, by the way. We're at Bearslake Hall, and you watched as the two girls were done up to look like Dalmatians, and encouraged me to sodomise Ophelia, to say nothing of your attempts at blackmail. Yes, if I had brought Grove House girls, as you expected, you'd be safe. I couldn't ask them to testify and they'd refuse in any case. But I didn't bring Grove House girls, did I? I brought Gemma and Laurel, who'll be only too pleased to testify."

"Nobody would believe them, or you!" Lord Bearslake blustered, although he sounded worried. "A pair of whores and their pimp against a man of my reputation?"

"A pair of whores who can describe your stable yard and grounds in some detail," Peter went on. "You do realise that I knew it was a trap all along, don't you? It was far too great a co-incidence, Ophelia meeting Gabriel in Oxford like that, immediately after the Caring Planet party. You know he's one of my oldest friends, so it can hardly have been difficult to figure out that I was providing girls for him."

"Why did you come to Bearslake then?" Christine demanded.

"To trap you, of course," Peter told her. "You and your

appalling boss. It didn't work quite as well as it might have, admittedly, as I didn't think he'd be able to resist the girls. But then, I imagine he's expecting to get his jollies later, with you, isn't he?"

Her face had turned scarlet and Peter quickly pressed his advantage.

"Look, you impudent little pimp!" Lord Bearslake roared. "Try anything and I'll sue you for every penny you have, and believe me, I'll win."

"Very possibly," Peter admitted. "Which is why I took a few extra precautions. You see, Lord Bearslake, a girl who can be bribed once can be bribed again, which is why I'd have the additional support of Ophelia's testimony, including a recording of you setting up today's little outing. We also know which stores you bought the body paint from and so forth, in cash of course, but I venture to suggest that John here is quite easily recognised. Then there's the fact that while you managed to confiscate my camera, you failed to realise that I am wired for sound, so to speak. So that if things get really unpleasant I have this entire conversation on record, you blackmailing old heap of blubber. Don't worry though, I won't use it, just so long as nothing appears in that grotty little rag you call a paper. Oh, and just in case, perhaps I should also mention the three Serbian gentlemen currently waiting in a car outside your house, with the girls. They are not nice people, as you doubtless know, but then one can't always help the company one keeps. Good day to you, Lord Bearslake, Christine."

He nodded to each and left the room.

"Do you think we're safe?" Michelle asked.

"Yes," Peter told her. "At least from Bearslake. He's

notoriously cautious with his own skin and he has far too much to lose. Remember, it's only a story to him anyway. It's Christine I'm worried about. With her it's personal. Hopefully she values her job more than getting here revenge on me."

"I'm sure she does," Michelle said.

"I still wish we'd got something on her," Peter said, flopping down in his favourite armchair. "But we've yet to turn anything up, aside from letting old Bearslake hump her, which may be a trifle grotesque but it's hardly a crime. Now pour me a drink and then get your mouth around my cock. I'm still shaking."

"You poor thing," Michelle answered, making for the kitchen. "I'd have been terrified."

"I was," Peter admitted. "He had his gamekeeper with him, not at all the sort I'd care to try and tackle. He was going to go for me as I left, but Bearslake called him off. Now come on, the Serbians got their bjs and I imagine Christine was over Bearslake's knee before we'd reached the end of the drive, but …"

"Patience," Michelle chided gently. "Do you want my dress on, or off?"

"Off," Peter answered, easing down his fly, "and your bra."

"I'll leak!"

"That's half the fun."

"Pervert!"

"You married me."

Michelle came out from the kitchen as Peter pushed his trousers down to expose his cock. She was holding a large brandy balloon, half full, which she handed to him before peeling off her dress and unfastening her bra. As the cups came lose he gave a happy sigh, marvelling at the size and weight of her breasts, while little spots of milk had begun to form on her nipples before she'd even managed to get to her knees.

"Bliss!" he sighed as she wrapped both heavy breasts

around his cock, smearing her milk over his shaft and the skin of his balls. "Christ they're big!"

"I'm glad you appreciate them," Michelle answered. "A lot of men don't find pregnant women attractive."

"Idiots," Peter replied and sighed again as she began to lick her breast milk up from his genitals.

He'd closed his eyes, sipping at his brandy, with his tension slowly draining away under Michelle's skilled and completely uninhibited ministrations. Her heavy bosom wobbled as she moved, to press against his legs, which she'd soon eased wide apart so that she could lick his arsehole while she stroked his now erect cock shaft.

"I've known a lot of very, very bad girls," he said softly as he reached his free hand out to stroke her hair. "But you take the prize."

Michelle responded by wriggling the tip of her tongue deeper in, and Peter tightened his grip in her hair, wondering if he should simply let her take him to orgasm with her mouth, or if it would be safe to slip into her arse with only a few days left until she was expected to give birth. On the whole it seemed better to let her continue. But even as she moved in closer to take his cock in her mouth once more, he heard the sound of car from outside.

"Don't worry, it'll be Rhiannon," he said and Michelle nodded on her mouthful of cock.

"I might have known it!" Rhiannon laughed as she came through the front door. "I take it everything went well then?"

"I'll tell you later," Peter answered her. "But in one word—yes. Now why don't you join in?"

"Love to, but let me put my bags down," Rhiannon answered. "I'll have a drink while I watch you two, then maybe I'll come and stick my bum right in your face, Mr. Finch."

"Yes, please," Peter answered.

He relaxed once more as Rhiannon disappeared into the kitchen, now imagining how it would feel to have her beautifully rounded little bottom in his face while Michelle worked on his cock. She'd come to take particular pleasure in having her anus licked, usually in preparation for anal sex, and she was generally the first to get her bottom into another girl's face when the chance came, often with Michelle.

"Don't make him come yet, you greedy bitch!" she called from the kitchen. "He never licks properly when he's empty."

Michelle responded by sitting back, and Peter let go of her hair as he saw what she was going to do. She'd taken one plump breast in each hand, squeezing them to a gentle, even rhythm to make her milk come. There was now plenty of it, with tiny jets squirting from her nipples as she pressed them between fingers and thumbs, to run together into little white rivulets. Her knees were spread wide, her heavy belly resting between her thighs and her bottom pushed out as she milked herself, smiling all the while, with her eyes fixed to Peter's as he nursed his erection. A few firm jerks and he'd have been able to reach orgasm, perhaps leaning forward to do it all over Michelle's breasts and belly, leaving her to masturbate in a mixture of milk and cum, but he wanted both girls and forced himself to hold off.

Michelle's face had grown loose with pleasure as she continued to play with her milk, which was coming so fast it had begun to run down over the fat, swollen globe of her belly. She put her hands underneath, lifting the weight and catching the longest of the little trickles, then moving slowly up, spreading the pale liquid over her flesh to leave her bulge glossy and slick. Peter began to hammer on his cock, unable to hold back a moment more, and as Michelle saw she caught up her breast's again, lifting one swollen nipple to her mouth to suck at the teat, beading her lips with her own milk before she swallowed it down.

"Here I am!" Rhiannon announced as she bounced out from the kitchen, a drink in her hand and stark naked.

"Feed on Michelle!" Peter gasped. "I can't hold back, but I want to see you feed on Michelle. Go on, darling, cradle her, let her suckle, please!"

Rhiannon giggled and had quickly curled herself into Michelle's lap, held as if she was a baby. Her eyes were full of mischief as she glanced at Peter, but as she took Michelle's nipple into her mouth her expression changed instantly to bliss, her eyes closed, her lips puckered as she suckled. With Michelle's arms curled around her back and beneath her, Rhiannon's position also served to show off her pert bottom, her sweet little cheeks pushed out, with the lips of her cunt emerging from beneath as she fed.

Peter moved quickly forward as he felt himself start to spurt, aiming his cock at Michelle's chest and at Rhiannon's face. Cum splashed out, soiling Michelle's neck and one fat breast, and again, to leave a sticky streamer joining Rhiannon's nose to the teat she was feeding from. Rhiannon's head turned, her lips wet with Michelle's milk as she opened her mouth wide for Peter's cock. He pushed in with a groan, letting her suck and swallow, feeding on his cock just as she'd fed at Michelle's breast, before he finally collapsed back into the chair.

"That was so dirty!" Rhiannon said, a broad smile upon her sodden face.

But she was nowhere near finished. Rhiannon fastened again onto Michelle's nipple, feeding eagerly. Michelle tightened her grip, holding Rhiannon firmly to her breast as she suckled her, with Peter watching in fascination. Rhiannon's hands went between her legs, one to rub at her pussy and the other to tease at the slit of her arse and the tiny hole between, masturbating freely without a care for the show she was making of herself.

Michelle's milk came fast now, and as Rhiannon grew more excited she began to lose control, her mouth wide and slack with tiny rivulets of milk running from the corners to dribble down onto her breasts. Not that she cared, sucking more eagerly still as her fingers stroked at her clitoris, while another of her slippery fingers eased up into her arse. Her muscles began to contract, her back arched and she'd pulled off Michelle's teat as she started to come, milk bubbling from her lips. Michelle gave her breast a sudden, firm squeeze, sending a powerful blast of milk into Rhiannon's open mouth.

Once more Rhiannon pressed herself to Michelle's chest, now coming in a shivering, jerking climax as she sucked on the slippery, milky nipple and rubbed her face into the softness of her friend's breast to deliberately soil herself with milk and semen, her fingers still clutching at her sex and her anus now plugged and twitching around fingers buried deep. Michelle held on, cuddling Rhiannon and stroking her hair, soothing her, and praising her for how far she'd let herself go. At last, it was the younger girl who finally pulled away.

"You're a disgrace!" Peter said happily as Michelle rose ponderously, and began looking for something with which to clean herself off.

Rhiannon simply giggled, and at that moment the doorbell rang.

"That must be Stephen," Peter said. "He's very early."

Rhiannon gave a squeak of alarm and started for the stairs, only to be brought up short as Peter grabbed hold of her wrist. He was grinning as he wagged a finger in her face.

"Oh no you don't, young lady. Go and answer the door to our guest."

"Not like this!" Rhiannon protested.

"Why not?" he asked innocently.

"I'm covered in milk and cum!"

"Okay," Peter offered, "but I'm going to the door, right now."

Rhiannon fled up stairs, her face scarlet with blushes. Peter was laughing as he pulled open the door, making sure that Rhiannon managed to get clear, only to find that the visitor was not Stephen, but Christine, her scowling face streaked with tears, her eyes blazing hatred.

"You got me fired, you bastard!" she raged. "I'm going to see you brought down, Finch. I'm going to see you back in fucking prison if it's the last thing I do, you fucking bastard!"

"Calm down!" Peter urged, stepping hastily back from the door. "You're the one who tried to expose me. What was I supposed to do, just let you get away with it?"

"Why couldn't you work with us?" she demanded. "It would have been so simple, but oh no, you have to play your stupid little games, and ..."

"Oh right," he interrupted, his own temper flaring, "so I'd have betrayed my friends and ended up as a spy for that bloated oaf Bearslake. Never, Christine, not in a million years. I would rather be in prison, seriously."

"With any luck you'll get your wish," she answered, suddenly cold. "I'm going to another paper, with everything I've got, the pictures, everything, and what I know from way back, about how you arranged to have me spanked in front of your filthy friends, the others too. You do know little Katie Vale is married to a high court judge now, don't you? And Ayanna? Do you know how much she's worth? Over a billion! When she finds out ..."

"I didn't do anything to Ayanna!"

"Oh yes? You had her spanked by Vicky fucking Trent and Tiffany, so you could watch, didn't you?"

"No. I ..."

"Bullshit! I know you, Finch, you pervert, and that's what I'm going to tell her anyway, so ..."

"She came in to Vicky's room to ask for a spanking," Peter broke in. "But look, seriously, have some compassion, Christine! My wife's pregnant, Daniel's career will be ruined and he doesn't even know about Clementine, Ben Thompson ..."

"Did you show me any compassion?" she demanded, fresh anger flaring in her eyes.

"Yes!" Peter answered. "I refused to give any names

out, even when I was being threatened with a caning, or to the police. That meant your name, Christine, as well as the others', and besides, you knew what you were letting yourself in for. You volunteered to be spanked, remember, and it's not as if it was even the first time. You were Vicky's toasty girl, for Christ's sake!"

"That was private," Christine answered. "Something very private and very special between Vicky and I, something which a clod like you could never hope to understand."

"You snitched on Tiffany and Alice to make Vicky jealous!" Peter exclaimed. "Face it, Christine, you're no angel. And what about Ophelia? You and Bearslake had her dressed up as a fox, chased around Bearslake Estate and sodomised, not to mention being made to lick two girls out. I bet that wasn't in accord with the paper's code of conduct!"

"She was well paid," Christine assured him, "and anyway, you subverted her!"

"And she thoroughly enjoyed the whole thing," Peter added. "But that's not the point. You're taking the moral high ground when you have no right whatsoever to do so. Can't we talk about this? I'm sorry about the spanking, I really am. I never realised you'd take it so badly, and you're really no better than me anyway, so why ..."

She screamed and flung herself at him, but Peter caught her arms and quickly twisted her around, lifting her clear of the ground with her legs kicking frantically in every direction, just as Stephen's black Mercedes appeared in the mouth of the lane. Peter kept his grip on the still struggling Christine, doing his best to evade her teeth and nails, but suffering several nasty kicks from her heels. She was still spitting curses as the astonished Stephen climbed form the car, along with Vivienne.

"What the hell is going on?" Stephen demanded. "Is that ... Christine?"

"Yes," Peter did his best to explain over the shoulder of the writhing, spluttering woman. "She's been sacked by

Bearslake, so she's more determined to expose us than ever."

"Hell!" Stephen exclaimed. "Look, Christine, calm down and let's talk about this sensibly."

She didn't answer immediately, but her protestations diminished enough for Peter to let her go and take a step back.

"It really would be best to talk," Stephen went on. "Sure, you could sell your story to another paper, and there'll be one hell of a scandal, a lot of careers ruined certainly. Maybe you can even ensure that Peter ends up as the scapegoat. Maybe he'll have to do a few months in jail, but is that really worth it?"

"Yes," Christine answered.

She was still seething, her fists clenched by her sides and her eyes burning cold fury, one shoe had come off and her fine, dark hair was in disarray. Vivienne was trying not to giggle as Stephen carried on.

"Really? You're not under Bearslake's protection any more, you know. You'll get sued, extensively, and then there's the little matter of some of your previous scoops, achieved with the assistance of phone taps on a range of celebrities and politicians who are going to be extremely upset with you when they find out. No, don't bother to deny it. We have some very good contacts indeed: government, police, security services, judiciary, all sorts. So let's all go indoors and sort this out like civilised people, shall we?"

Nothing would take the scowl from her face, but she accepted the invitation and the four of them stood together in the small hallway.

"I was going to tell you that our research had borne fruit," Stephen told Peter. "But that doesn't mean your efforts were wasted this morning. Bearslake might well have managed to wriggle out of it anyway, by blaming his subordinates, including you, of course, Christine. Loyalty is not his strongpoint."

Christine didn't answer, angry and silent as she tried not to let her temper get the better of her once again. Rhiannon joined them, now in an evening dress and asking puzzled questions until Stephen and Peter had managed to get them all seated, save for Christine, who had opted to stand in the doorway of the kitchen, not yet prepared to make herself comfortable among her adversaries.

"What we need here," Stephen stated, accepting a drink from Rhiannon, "is a damage limitation exercise, and on a fairly grand scale. First, Christine."

"Indeed" Christine responded, "What are you going to do to get me on your side?" she asked, still defiant but with a flicker of concern showing in her eyes.

"Nothing melodramatic, I assure you," he said. "In fact, Christine, I'm going to offer you a job with my company. You're an unscrupulous little bitch, and a hard headed one at that, which is just what I need. I can promise you a decent salary."

She didn't answer, obviously taken aback, and Stephen continued.

"Peter, I hate to say this, but I think you're going to have to call it a day. Things are getting out of hand, especially with Chloe Thompson now involved as well as Clementine."

"But … but it's my only source of income!" Peter protested.

Stephen shrugged and reached into the top pocket of his jacket, pulling out a cheque.

"Consider this a consultation fee for my Balkan deal, which is how it will appear in my books. Cash in your investments, maybe even sell up here, and you should be able to manage in modest comfort, I imagine?"

He had dropped the cheque, allowing it to flutter down onto the table. Peter looked at the row of figures, counting the zeros after the initial figure over and over again in the expectation that he was seeing double and half of them would disappear. They stayed the same, but a dozen conflicting emotions were chasing through his head at the same time, regret, relief, inferiority, gratitude and more, leaving him unable to find his voice. Stephen at least had the courtesy to seem a touch embarrassed, taking a quick swallow of brandy before he continued.

"Think it over for a while, if you like, but you know it makes sense."

Peter hesitated a moment, then nodded.

"Excellent!" Stephen went on. "Good man, and of course there's no reason why we shouldn't carry on having fun. In fact, to seal the deal, why don't you give Vivienne a good spanking, if I might perhaps borrow Rhiannon at the same time?"

"Stephen!" Vivienne squeaked.

"Don't be prissy," Stephen told her and made a casual gesture of his hand towards Peter. "I did say that you could expect a spanking this evening."

Vivienne came, pink faced and struggling not to pout, to lay herself across Peter's lap, still with considerable poise despite the indignity of her position. Rhiannon showed no such restraint, climbing quickly into position over Stephen's knee with her bottom raised to make it easier for him to pull her dress up. It had been done in a moment and her panties came down with no more ceremony, leaving her wriggling her bare bottom in encouragement as Stephen laid one large, bony hand across her cheeks. Vivienne had seen and threw her husband a worried glance.

"I don't have to have my ..." she began, but broke off with a little gasp as Peter began to lift her beautiful silk evening dress.

"Yes you do," Peter told her, lifting the dress up to show off a bottom even smaller and tighter than Rhiannon's and covered only by a miniscule pair of lace panties.

"And your panties, I'm afraid," Stephen said as he began to spank Rhiannon.

"No, Stephen, please, they'll all see my ... my pussy," Vivienne babbled, her voice breaking as Peter slowly but firmly turned down the little lace panties to bare her bottom.

"Always such a fuss when it's time for their panties to come down," he remarked. "Do you remember how Tiffany charged double to let you watch her get it in the buff?"

"You'd have thought they'd be proud of their pussies," Stephen replied.

"They are," Peter said, making a final adjustment to Vivienne's undergarment and lifting his leg to make sure that she was suitably and comprehensively displayed from behind. "But they like to make sure we realise they're showing off something precious. Anyway, the really embarrassing thing is if people see their arseholes."

Vivienne gave a gasp of shock and outrage as her tiny cheeks were hauled wide to expose the perfect little star of her arse.

"Not that you should worry, Vivienne," Peter went on. "Not when you have such a pretty one—so tidy and cute."

Christine looked disgusted, but she did not turn away.

"Don't tease Vivienne like that," Michelle put in. "You're making her embarrassed."

"That's half the fun," Peter replied, and he began to spank.

He'd taken a good grip on Vivienne's waist, making sure there was no escape as he applied his hand to her perfect little cheeks. She'd tried to keep her poise, even as her panties were removed, but with the pain of her spanking she'd lost it in moments, squirming and wriggling over his lap, kicking her legs and tossing her beautiful pale hair. Her reaction only encouraged Peter, who spanked all the harder, until her indignant cries and yelps of pain had turned to sobs and a soft, whimpering noise as she began to cry.

"Spanked to tears, perfect," he said, and let go of her waist. "Okay, sweetie, you can get up. But I think you ought to leave that pretty little bottom on show for a while."

"Yes," Stephen agreed, releasing Rhiannon. "Up against the wall, the pair of you, with your dresses held up."

Rhiannon obeyed without hesitation, scampering across to the wall to stand with her red bottom bare to the room. Vivienne followed, snivelling slightly and pausing to take a tissue and wipe her tears before taking her place beside Rhiannon, her dress held up in the same fashion, while her pretty lace panties had fallen down around her ankles.

"Such a pretty sight," Stephen remarked. "I wonder how many girls have been spanked as a consequence of that time you did Tiffany in front of us?"

"Easily over a hundred," Peter assured him. "Nearer two hundred in fact, and that's just the ones I've done myself. In total, I don't know, but I'd like to think that we have played our part in ensuring that spanking remains a regular occurrence for the women of Britain, and elsewhere. Cheers."

They clinked their glasses together and each took a sip. For a long moment there was silence broken only by Vivienne's faint snivelling. Christine had stayed as she was, watching and listening with an unreadable expression, but she finally spoke up.

"Okay, Stephen, I accept, but ..."

She'd turned to Peter.

"I want to see that bastard spanked, just like I was, with the rest of you watching."

"Spanked?" Peter echoed. "Me?"

"Yes, you," she answered him. "Or can't you take it?"

"That seems fair to me," Rhiannon put in before Peter could find an answer.

"Yes," Vivienne added, turning her tear stained face to the room. "Very fair."

"You have to admit," Stephen said, trying not to laugh, "in the circumstances it does seem a reasonable request."

Peter threw a pleading look to Michelle, but she merely shrugged.

EPILOGUE

◆◆◆◆

La Fesse en Rose, Dordogne,
France 2016

Peter lifted his glass to the sun, admiring the golden gleams in the rich, sweet wine Michelle had poured for themselves and their guests. To his side, Ben Thompson lowered himself into a chair, smiling with amusement as he watched the scene beside the brook at the end of Peter's garden, where a blonde girl lay face down on the lawn, her mini skirt lifted and her panties turned down to present her perfectly for the spanking being administered by the somewhat taller blonde sitting astride her back.

"Just like the old days, eh?" Peter remarked.

"Very like the old days," Ben agreed, then turned to Gabriel, who was watching the spanking with equal amusement. "So, did Daniel make it?"

"Yes," Gabriel replied. "Which is why he can't be with us this weekend, unfortunately, but he sends his regards, along with a request, Peter. The day he steps down you're to send him Angelica and Siobhan, together."

"That seems fair," Peter answered, then called to the two girls at the bottom of the garden. "Come on, you too, stop fooling around. You're supposed to be entertaining our guests."

The blonde girl merely stuck out her tongue and continued to spank the red-head's wriggling pink bottom, before the two of them burst out laughing, as Rhiannon emerged from the house with a broad, wooden paddle in one hand. Peter chuckled and took another sip of wine, then spoke again.

"What was it old Porter used to say? 'The wages of sin is death', a statement I had to write out on the blackboard fifty times. Complete nonsense, of course, as I like to think my own life demonstrates. Rhiannon, if you're going paddle Siobhan, make it quick. I hear a car on the lane and it's probably your mother."

Vanessa de Sade
IN THE FORESTS OF THE NIGHT

In the Forests of the Night is a darkly sensual collection of erotic fairy tales. Each story blends the magic and fantasy of the traditional fable with the carnality and lust we've come to expect from Vanessa de Sade! In the timeless tradition of the storybook, each tale is vividly illustrated by Vanity Chase. Beautiful, visceral and devoutly debauched, Vanity's illustrations bring the book to life and explore a much more grown-up side of fantasy. The seven sexy stories within these pages offer up a mind-bending, pulse-quickening twist on a classic genre.

If you think you know how a fairy tale is supposed to end, this book will make you think again! Sexual and cerebral, magical and modern, In the Forests of the Night is the ultimate collection of sexy, adult fables!

Also available from Sweetmeats Press

Kay Jaybee
MAKING HIM WAIT

Maddie Templeton has always been an unconventional artist. Themes of submission and domination pulse through her erotic artwork, and she's happily explored these lustful themes both on and off the canvas.

But, when Theo Hunter enters her life, she is presented with a new challenge. Maddie sets out to test his resolve as she teases, torments and toys with him. However, as Maddie drives Theo to breaking point, she soon becomes unsure whether her own resolve will hold out!

At the same time, Maddie must put on the exhibition of a lifetime. As the hottest gallery in town clamours for her best work, Maddie pushes her models harder and higher until they are physically, sexually and emotionally exhausted. Will Maddie's models continue to submit to her, or will she push them too far? And will she be ready for the exhibition in time?

The only way to find out is to wait and see … and the waiting only makes it sweeter!